WALKS THE FIRE

A NOVEL

Stephanie Grace Whitson

THOMAS NELSON PUBLISHERS
Nashville • Atlanta • London • Vancouver

Published in Nashville, Tennessee, by Thomas Nelson, Inc., Publishers, and distributed in Canada by Word Communications, Ltd., Richmond, British Columbia, and in the United Kingdom by Word (UK), Ltd., Milton Keynes, England.

Unless otherwise noted, Scripture quotations are from The Holy Bible, KING JAMES VERSION.

Scripture quotations noted † are from THE NEW KING JAMES VERSION. Copyright © 1979, 1980, 1982, Thomas Nelson, Inc., Publishers.

Library of Congress Cataloging-in-Publication Data

Whitson, Stephanie Grace.
    Walks the fire : a novel / Stephanie Grace Whitson.
        p.   cm. — (Prairie winds ; bk. 1)
    ISBN 0-7852-7981-4 (pb)
    1. Frontier and pioneer life—West (U.S.)—Fiction. 2. Indians of North America—West (U.S.)—Fiction. 3. Man—woman relationships—West (U.S.)—Fiction. 4. Women pioneers—West (U.S.)—Fiction. I. Title. II. Series: Prairie winds (Nashville, Tenn.) ; bk. 1.
PS3573.H555W34 1995
813'.54—dc20   94-29787
                                              CIP

Printed in the United States of America
1 2 3 4 5 6 7 - 01 00 99 98 97 96 95

For Bob

my leader, my example,
my beloved, my friend

Acknowledgments

My acknowledgments must begin with praise to the Lord. "Now unto him that is able to do exceeding abundantly above all that we ask or think, according to the power that worketh in us, unto him be glory in the church by Christ Jesus throughout all ages, world without end. Amen" (Eph. 3:20–21). This passage describes my life. God has constantly poured out exceeding abundantly above all that I have asked or thought. I pray that in some minute way, the use of his eternal Word in this book will bring honor and glory to him.

In a more earthly vein, I would like to say . . .

Thank you, Mother, for teaching me to love books.

Thank you, Dad, for modeling Titus 1:6–9 and 1 Timothy 3.

Thank you, Bob and Brooke and Zachary and Shannon and Max, for hugs and love and willingness to help.

Thank you, Pastor Gil, for teaching me to cherish and believe the all-sufficient Word of God.

Thank you, Janet, for doing more than your share in our partnership.

Thank you, Kate, for listening to the first few chapters and crying and telling me I had to finish it.

Thank you, Frenchy, for your expert advice.

Thank you, Lonnie, for making the "offer I couldn't refuse."

Prologue

LisBeth stared in disbelief at the patchwork that spilled out of her mother's lap onto the floor. She studied the hands that held it, noticing for the first time how time had worn them. Deep wrinkles accented every swollen knuckle. What had once been a sprinkling of freckles had become dark splotches. "Age spots," Mama called them. The hands that had always gone about their work with deliberate calm now twitched nervously as they clutched the quilt. Finally, LisBeth looked into the eyes of the woman who had borne her.

Jesse was no longer just Mama. With the telling of the quilt she had become a woman who had loved and hurt and kept her faith and grown and triumphed in her own, quiet way.

The silence became too heavy. Jesse broke it. "So, LisBeth, that's how you came to be." As she spoke, Jesse's eyes searched her daughter's face anxiously.

How can I ever marry MacKenzie? LisBeth thought. *Now that I know, how can I ever marry any respectable man?* . . .

Chapter 1

My heart's desire and prayer to God . . . is, that they might be saved.

Romans 10:1

He had seen cholera decimate the ranks of the fur train in Bellevue and had endured the taunts of the rough-hewn mountain men. He had struggled to stay astride his mule when illness made him too weak to mount without help. His pulse had quickened at the sight of a galloping party of Indians closing in upon the train from the west—and then slowed again when they shot their guns into the air to show their friendly intentions.

He had doctored and suffered and hungered and prayed. But none of these things had prepared Marcus Whitman for the sight of an Indian camp boasting 2,000 inhabitants. The village stretched for miles along the Laramie River, just above where the river emptied into the Platte. The meeting of the two rivers was a natural crossroads where fur traders had built Fort Laramie. The fur train was to stop here on its journey to the great rendezvous site on the Green River.

Whitman and his fellow missionary, the Reverend Samuel Parker, had joined the fur train in Bellevue, Nebraska, and would travel with it to their destination in Oregon. They had heard that the Indians in that land wished to know about the white man's God. At the rendezvous they would have opportunity to investigate the veracity of those rumors. Then, they would journey west to carry the gospel, "even to the ends of the earth."

The arrival of the fur train caused a great commotion in

the Lakota village. Children tumbled out of tepees, shrieking greetings and questions. Dogs joined in the tumultuous escort, yapping at the heels of Whitman's cantankerous mule until the beast lashed out in fury. Reaching the fort, Whitman dismounted carefully, thankful for his returning strength.

Hungrily he drank in every detail of the scene before him, filled with compassion for the vast nation of unreached souls. But when whisky kegs were brought out later and drunkenness prevailed, the missionary's compassion was mixed with disgust. As night fell, the Lakota entertained their white visitors with a buffalo dance, leaping high in the firelight, reeling in drunken ecstasy.

As Whitman turned to retreat to the privacy of his own tent, his attention was drawn to one handsome warrior standing at the edge of the firelight. Huge brass rings hung from each of the warrior's ears, and eagle feathers dangled from his thick dark braids. A string of bear claws adorned the muscular neck.

Whitman wondered at the Indian's reluctance to join his friends in their wild celebration. He studied the face. Intelligent dark eyes squinted slightly, studying every movement of the dancers. Resting one hand on the shoulder of a beautiful young squaw at his side, the Indian gestured and whispered. The corners of his well-formed mouth turned up in a half smile. A few wrinkles across the high forehead and at the corners of his eyes made him appear older than the woman. Still, she looked up at him expectantly, clearly enjoying his attentions.

As Whitman watched, the Indian turned sideways and took a step toward his woman. Shadows from the firelight accented his square jaw and cleft chin. Suddenly, the half-smile disappeared. The brave clenched his jaw and jerked his head sideways, looking away from the fire. His hand dropped from the woman's shoulder to his side. He gripped the fringe along the side of one legging.

Then the doctor saw it. The right legging had been slit to the knee, revealing a leg tightly bound with strips of leather from ankle to knee. As Whitman watched and wondered, the Indian moved away from the fire, pressing his lips together and setting his jaw against the pain that shot up the injured leg with every step. He limped into the darkness, and Whitman turned to go, too, wondering about the injured Indian.

Fur traders and natives alike met the dawn with groans and complaints about the effects of the night's celebration. Still, they packed up to continue to the Green River rendezvous, chiding one another for their behavior the night before and shouting anecdotes from last year's rendezvous to encourage one another to travel quickly. Whitman was left with unanswered questions about the injured warrior and his lovely companion.

∿

Twelve days later the fur train and the missionaries arrived at the Green River. The traders set up shelters to show the fabric, ribbon, beads, knives, and axes they had packed so far to trade for skins.

Whitman had been repulsed by the drunken display at Fort Laramie, but the debauchery at the rendezvous left him speechless. Indians, mountain men, and traders drank and feasted and shouted and fought until they passed out. They slept only to begin the cycle again as soon as they awoke.

Late one evening as Whitman sat straining to read by his dying campfire, a young boy beckoned him to follow him across the camp to another fire. There, waiting for the doctor, sat a mountain man and a few other traders. The man did not rise, but drawled gruffly, "Boy here says yer a doctor."

Whitman bowed. "I am a doctor, sir."

Lifting his fringed shirt and turning his back to the campfire, the man said, "See that lump on the shoulder? Been carryin' that near three years now. Blackfoot arrowhead. Hurts like the devil. Think you can dig 'er out?"

The doctor examined the area. "I can remove it, but there is no anesthetic . . . "

The man lifted a flask at his side and took a long draught. "Got my anesthetic right here, doc. Dig 'er out."

Whitman retreated to his tent to get his surgical instruments. Returning to the trader's campfire, he began. The arrowhead was covered with a thick layer of scar tissue, and Whitman apologized as he hacked away at the wound, intent upon success. At last, he pulled the point out. The trader gasped only once. Otherwise he sat immovable while the doctor performed his crude surgery. The operation complete, Whitman stepped away and wiped the sweat from his forehead.

"Yer all right by me, Doc. What can I trade ya fer the chop job?"

"I was glad to be of service, sir," was all the missionary could say. He watched in amazement as the trader donned his shirt, wincing only a little, stood up and turned his head slowly from side to side, then shrugged his shoulders as if nothing had happened.

The trader retreated to his tent and came out again with two beaver pelts, which he handed to Whitman. "Heard ya got a missus'. These'll make her a right nice lap robe . . . tell 'er I'm beholdin' to 'er husband."

It was said gruffly, but sincerity shone in the trader's eyes. With a few brief instructions on keeping the wound clean, Whitman picked up the beaver pelts and returned to his own campfire, ignorant of the fact that his surgical skills were fast being told throughout the camp. He was soon the center of attention, and a long line of patients formed outside his tent to have the doctor treat various wounds and complaints.

It was late before Whitman could retire. As he lay back wearily on his bedroll, his tent flap was pulled back soundlessly. Almost before he could look up, an Indian's imposing form filled the doorway. The brave wore a necklace of bear claws and deerskin leggings. Silently he sat before Whitman and began to unwrap one leg that was tightly bound with strips of leather from ankle to knee. Whitman recognized the Indian from Fort Laramie.

He moved to help unwrap the leg, but the brave waved him away. Perspiration formed on his forehead. He grunted under his breath and his hands trembled, but he persisted. The skins nearest the leg were crusted with dried blood. At last, he pulled them away, and Whitman drew in a sharp breath as the putrid smell of the wound filled the tent. Gasping with the effort, the Indian straightened the leg out before the doctor and leaned back on his hands, waiting. The dark eyes met Whitman's in a wordless plea.

The doctor saw that infection had set in. He moved quickly to cleanse the wound. His patient gasped, but somehow controlled the urge to cry out.

"With daylight, I can do more," Whitman explained, despairing of the language barrier. He had done all he could by the light of the fire. But words weren't needed to keep the Indian in his tent. With the last ministrations of the doctor, he gave one small agonized cry and passed out.

At dawn Whitman had the Indian carried outside where he began the process of removing dead tissue. The man refused the whiskey offered as an anesthetic, pressing his lips together and turning a stony face away from the flask.

"Tell him I have to break his leg again," Whitman said. The trader who had been summoned to interpret shared the bad news. The Indian looked long into Whitman's face. The missionary's gaze did not waver.

Asking a question, he waited as the trader interpreted. "Why d'ya have to break what has already been broken and healed?"

Whitman explained. "The break hasn't healed correctly. The bone is still jutting out too far, and that has caused the swelling and infection. I must break it, set it correctly, and then stitch the skin together so it will heal properly."

The interpreter repeated the information to the Indian, who interrupted with a question. "He wants to know if what you do will make him able to walk straight again. Says he walks like a wounded buffalo now." The trader turned abruptly to Whitman and offered his own comment. "This here feller's name is Rides the Wind. I seen 'im at the last rendezvous. He's a dancin' fool when he's in shape. Got his wife by dancin' to impress her. He ain't too quick to have you breakin' that leg again unless it'll help him dance again."

The trader winked at the doctor. "Even the redskins like to impress the ladies, Doc."

Whitman cleared his throat and moistened his dry lips before responding. "Rides the Wind," he said, looking directly at the warrior. "I am Dr. Marcus Whitman. I have come to this land to tell your people of the God who created us all. I tell you by that One that I do not know if you will dance again. But I do know that if I do not do this, you will lose this leg. You may die."

Whitman's honest gaze never left the eyes of the Indian as he spoke. His voice was gentle, filled with compassion.

The trader interpreted, and when he had finished there was a long silence. Rides the Wind pondered the doctor's advice. He looked away for a moment and then back again at Whitman and gravely nodded his assent.

Several Lakota men were summoned to hold the warrior down while Whitman grasped the injured leg and twisted it. The sickening sound of the bone snapping caused a murmur to rise from the crowd of men. Rides the Wind bit the stick he gripped between his teeth in two and fainted. Whitman welcomed the chance to thoroughly clean away infected tissue and stitch up the leg.

One of the traders contributed the clean cloth that Whitman used to bind the leg. He worked quickly and efficiently, and when consciousness returned, Rides the Wind saw that his leg, which hurt worse than it ever had, was bound in clean cloth between two straight tree branches. He was carried away to his tepee where his wife and the tribal medicine man took over his care.

On the day Whitman began packing to leave for the west, the trader who had served as interpreter called on him, summoning him to Rides the Wind's tepee. Stooping low the doctor went inside where Rides the Wind lay on his buffalo robe. He was alone in the tepee, and as the doctor settled onto another buffalo robe, the Indian looked steadily into his face and said slowly, "You have medicine."

Whitman stared, dumbfounded, as the English words were pronounced.

The trader grinned. "He's been comin' to the rendezvous a long time, Doc. He understands more'n he lets on. Too smart fer his own good, prob'ly. Fer some reason, he's decided it's all right to let you know he can talk a little of the white man's talk."

Whitman smiled warmly and turned to Rides the Wind. "Yes, I have medicine."

The Indian pointed to his leg. "Make strong."

"It will take much time, but it will be strong again. However, I fear you will always walk with a limp." The Indian frowned and turned to the trader, who interpreted what Rides the Wind could not decipher.

Impatient with the primitive speech, Rides the Wind returned to his own language, speaking rapidly. Finally, the trader raised his hands to interrupt the long speech.

"Well, Doc," he began. "It seems you've made quite an impression on this Injun. He's sayin' you've got good medicine. He wants you to make sure his leg heals right. Says he'll travel with you 'til yer sure it'll be okay."

Whitman interrupted, "But he can't ride."

Understanding, Rides the Wind interjected angrily. The Trader grinned and shook his head. "He says even with a broken leg, he can outride a white man any day. He rode here from Fort Laramie."

Whitman turned to look at the warrior and saw the challenge in his dark eyes. The Indian reached out to grasp Whitman's arm. His huge hand completely encircled the doctor's thin forearm as he said, "I ride. You talk." Then, Rides the Wind again spoke rapidly to the trader and motioned for him to translate.

"He wants you to take care of his leg, Doc." As Rides the Wind talked on, the trader stopped and shoved his hat back on this head. "Well, I'll be . . ."

"What is it?" Whitman urged.

"He says he wants to learn more white man's talk. And he wants t' hear more about that God you talked about the night you set his leg. The one you said created all things."

The trader smiled broadly at Whitman. "Looks like you got yerself a prospective convert, Doc." His voice dripped with sarcasm. "Just make sure he don't scalp ya' when he finds out that *your* God says he's supposed to love the Pawnee that butchered his ma and pa last winter."

Whitman rose to the challenge. "It is my God who died for even his enemies, sir."

The trader was unimpressed. "Save it, Doc. I ain't buyin'. Anyhow, this Injun says he's goin' along. So you can practice your sermons on him." The trader abruptly left Whitman alone with Rides the Wind.

With a prayer for wisdom, Whitman spoke slowly. "You come. I will care for your leg." Rides the Wind nodded his agreement. Whitman added, "I will talk of God." Again, the Indian agreed. As Rides the Wind struggled to rise, Whitman reached out to help him, but the Lakota brave shook his head and pushed the doctor away. With great effort he managed to stand, bearing all his weight on his uninjured left leg.

As Whitman watched, he reached up for the knife and arrow sheath that hung from a nearby pole. Strapping them on, he grabbed a recently cut stick that leaned against the pole. Using it as a cane, Rides the Wind hobbled to the entrance of the tepee. Motioning for Whitman to precede him, he bent awkwardly and lunged outside, nearly falling and gasping with the effort to stand straight. His wife approached. Rides the Wind spoke rapidly to her, and she obediently trotted away to fulfill his demands.

"Go. I come," was all he said to Whitman. The missionary started toward his own campfire to pack, looking back over his shoulder to see Rides the Wind re-enter his tepee.

When the fur train pulled out of camp later that morning, Whitman's mule was followed by an Indian pony carrying a wounded Sioux hunter.

Rides the Wind stayed with the train until his broken leg was completely healed. The fur train had long since entered territory inhabited by enemies of the Sioux. Rides the Wind seemed unconcerned. With fierce determination he learned to speak the "white man's talk." With equal determination, he listened and questioned as Whitman talked night after night of the God who had sent him to the Indians.

When at last they parted, Whitman placed a Bible in the hands of the warrior.

"This book tells of God, Rides the Wind. I give it to you in friendship." It was an odd gift, Whitman knew. Rides the Wind couldn't read. Still, the missionary felt impressed to give it.

Rides the Wind took the bear claw necklace from around his own neck and handed it to the missionary. He held the Bible to his chest and watched as Whitman rode away. When at last the missionary was lost from view, Rides the Wind wrapped the book carefully in deerskin.

Upon his return to his band, he stored "the book about the God who created all things" in his parfleche. Often, he unwrapped it, turning the gilt-edged pages carefully, staring at the strange designs on each page, wishing he could know their meaning.

His leg had healed, but it remained crooked. Rides the Wind could no longer dance about the fire. His lovely wife insisted that it didn't matter. But Rides the Wind saw into her soul, and the fire that had burned there for him grew dim.

When Dancing Waters dared to mock the strange things he told her he had heard from the missionary, Rides the Wind reacted in uncharacteristic anger and demanded that she show more respect. Often, he pondered the images Whitman had shared—a man and a woman in a beautiful place . . . the eating of forbidden fruit. . . a God-man dying on a kind of tree . . . that same man living again. He longed for someone to come and tell him the mystery of the missionary's gift, but he did not speak of it.

From hundreds of miles away, a faithful missionary prayed, *Somehow, Lord, send someone—so that Rides the Wind will one day know you.*

Chapter 2

Pride goeth before destruction,
and an haughty spirit before a fall.
Proverbs 16:18

Jesse King stood at the counter of the general store in Independence, Missouri, preparing to order provisions for the trek west. She waited patiently behind a tall, slim woman in the long line. The woman's thick dark hair was piled high atop her head. A huge yellow bonnet hung about her shoulders, and it shook as the woman energetically barked out her order. She examined every item carefully and then directed a young boy to deliver her things to the wagon parked just ahead of the King rig outside the door of the store.

Jesse held back until the woman finished. Turning briskly, the woman bumped into Jesse and exclaimed, "Goodness me, I'm sorry! Oh, I didn't waken that darling baby, I hope! My name's Lavinia Wood. Are you on the trail too?" The words tumbled out as Jesse adjusted her sleeping child to extract her own list from her pocket. Jesse replied, "No, no—that is, you didn't bother Jacob, here. He can sleep through thunder and lightning, thank the Lord." As she uncrumpled her carefully written list, she answered the rest of Lavinia's questions, "Yes, we are going west—I'm Jesse King."

"King," Lavinia repeated. "That your rig outside? Fine horses . . ." When Jesse nodded yes she added, "Well, them's our yoke of oxen and our wagon just ahead of you. Maybe we can see one another on the trail . . . unless you've already got another wagon picked to buddy up with?"

Jesse shook her head, "No, we just got into town . . . and Homer's not one for talk. He's been busy helping me write this list of provisions . . ."

The women's attention was drawn outside by the sound of angry voices.

❧

Everyone in Illinois who knew Homer King knew that when he had set his jaw against an idea, no one could change his mind. And Homer had set his jaw.

"I durn near sweat blood buildin' the finest wagon ever to cross the territory in. And I will *not* have those mangy critters hitched to my wagon! Give 'em to somebody else, that's what I say!" He stood in the dusty street and stared up at the trail boss. "Our horses'll do just fine. Why, they won first place last year in the wagon pull back home." Homer swatted the broad rump of Gabe to emphasize his point. The horse patiently nodded, half asleep despite the hubbub around him.

From inside the mercantile, Jesse listened anxiously. Homer's voice had the strained tones she had come to know well. Words shot out in short bursts. Each sentence ended in a low rumble, the words drawn out for emphasis. Jesse did not need to look out to know that his jaw was set, his head tilted to one side. The gray eyes would be partially shut in an intense squint.

Marshall Applegate, however, would not retreat as Jesse always did. His voice came back, strained, but hard and uncompromising. "Mr. King, if your horses bolt, I will not waste the other settlers' valuable time to help you round them up. If they turn up lame you will have to beg passage from another wagon. Now, sir, I have other duties to attend to. Once again, I urge you, this trail is no place for horses.

Buy a team of oxen." The last warning given, Applegate strode away.

Jesse unconsciously hugged her sleeping child tighter and turned back to the counter to order the last of the provisions. Lavinia rushed to change the subject from pulling teams, "Well, now, aren't we going to be on an adventure? When my George asked me what I thought about going to Oregon, I just said right back, 'George Wood, I can't think of a more exciting thing to do!'"

Jesse responded, "Well, Homer's never been a man to talk his plans over with me much. If it were me, I'd have stayed closer to the home place. But after Dr. Whitman spoke at our church, Homer's mind was made up. It was nothing but Oregon after that. He built the wagon, sold off the livestock, and here we are. . . ." The child on her shoulder lifted his head and then snuggled into her shoulder once more. Homesick tears had started to dampen Jesse's eyes, but she forced them back, lifting her chin stubbornly and smiling a tight, prim smile that barely curled up the edges of her mouth. ". . . and little Jacob here will have a chance to make his way in a whole new world. That's worth crossing the plains for—I guess."

Lavinia patted her shoulder as she passed by. "Well, dearie, you just stay close to me, and we'll dance all the way to Oregon!" She bustled out the door, calling over her shoulder to Jesse, "My name's Lavinia, but my friends call me Vinnie. So you just call me Vinnie and let's thank the Lord we made a new friend so soon on the trip!"

Jesse nodded gratefully.

And Homer King set his jaw and left his horses in harness.

Chapter 3

Be anxious for nothing, but in
everything . . . let your requests be
made known to God.

Philippians 4:6†

Jesse and Homer had been in Independence only a few days when Homer began to grumble about what he called unnecessary delays.

"They say we have to wait—the grass is too short to support the stock. If they didn't have to take their whole darned herd along, there'd be plenty of grass!"

He complained bitterly about the organization of the train. "Fifteen platoons of four wagons each . . . as if we were back in the army. And the way they elected the platoon leaders! All bunched up like cattle—the would-be 'captains' in a line, marching off ahead. Then the rest of the fools ran out to get in line behind their choice for captain . . . Hmph! A bunch a grown men lookin' like school boys playing 'crack the whip'!"

"And whose line did *you* choose, Homer?" Jesse's voice was soothing, gentle. "Did George Wood win a place?"

Homer would not calm down. "Choose? *Me?* Huh! Let *them* choose! I ain't no school kid! I'm forty-two years old, and I don't set store by such nonsense. We'll make our own way!"

Marshall Applegate had won neither Homer's respect nor his trust. His insistence that Homer replace Beau and Gabe with oxen was not their last disagreement. When Applegate realized that Homer was determined to keep his horses and was ignoring the elaborate wagon train organization, he came back, insisting that Homer buy feed. Homer resisted, and Applegate lost his temper.

"A man's a fool who won't take the advice of those who have gone before him! I'm telling you for the last time, King, plains grass is too dry for horses to forage much. They'll be pestered by insects and likely get distemper from the waters of the Platte. If you don't haul grain to help 'em out, they'll never make the trip. You'd better take along horseshoes and nails and plenty of clinches, too . . . and if either of 'em gives out, we'll leave you!" Applegate stormed off, determined to stay as far away as possible from this cantankerous emigrant.

Jesse was not oblivious to Applegate's logic. She ventured an opinion. "I heard today that oxen aren't very expensive, Homer—only $50 a head. Couldn't Gabe and Beau just follow along hitched to the wagon?" She added convincingly, "Then they'd be fresh for plowing in Oregon."

"We are *not* buying oxen!" Homer snapped back. "And I'll thank you to remember yer only twenty-one years old and you don't know *nothin'* 'bout *nothin'* outside o' Illinois. Jus' keep your attention on women's work and don't butt into things that don't concern you!" He turned his frustration with Applegate against her, reinspecting everything she had packed for the trip. He complained about the "luxuries" she demanded. "Bread, bacon, and coffee's all a man needs for crossing the plains, woman! Don't know why you gotta' take along dried peaches and apples. There won't be no parties along the way."

"I just thought a peach or an apple pie would taste awful good, Homer," Jesse replied. "And it'll be a reminder of home when we're lonely."

Homer retorted that *he* planned on being too busy to feel lonely and that she'd better get a more realistic idea of life on the trail.

As the time to leave grew near, Homer's temper grew shorter. Jesse avoided him as much as possible and prayed for patience to deal with his uncertain moods. Jacob took the adventure in stride, giggling and babbling about every new sight and sound. The family camped just outside of Independence waiting for the time to leave.

Finally, after a meeting with Dr. Whitman, it was decided they would depart on May 22.

"Finally!" Homer said, "And it's about time too!"

"Finally," Jesse whispered with dread in her heart and a prayer on her lips.

❧

The sun rose, whips cracked, men shouted, and dust flew as the wagon train headed west. Overwhelmed by the great throng of emigrants, Jesse clutched Jacob and leaned back in the wagon seat. They passed a young girl dressed in her Sunday best, tripping lightly through the dust of the road with an open book before her. Jesse wondered if she could really be reading. The girl caught the admiring glances of many a young gentleman, one of whom called out, "Nymph, in thy orisons, be all my sins remembered!"

Jesse blushed at his forwardness and leaned a little closer to Homer than usual.

They were traveling in the great Santa Fe trace. Again and again they passed long trains of merchant wagons loaded with goods headed for Mexico. In a few hours they had crossed the western boundary of the state and entered the territory of the Shawnee Indians. The land was beautiful and fertile, and many of the Shawnee had good farms and comfortable homes. Some even spoke English, but that brought little comfort to Jesse, who viewed the Indians as godless creatures to be feared and avoided at all costs.

Jesse soon gave up the thought of riding to Oregon. The jostling and bumping of the wagon made it impossible. As soon as she had nursed Jacob, Jesse jumped down from the wagon and walked alongside for the morning. By noon, when the wagon train stopped to "rest," she was more tired than she had ever been. Beau and Gabe were unharnessed and led to cool water and fresh grass for the nooning. Homer checked the harness, greased the wagon axles, and sat down to watch Jesse build a fire and cook their lunch. The hour went quickly, and they were soon bumping along the trail again.

Jesse carried Jacob some of the time, but he seemed impervious to the bumping of the wagon and squealed with delight most of the day, peeking at Jesse over the back of the wagon box, pointing at birds and rabbits that popped out from behind bushes or rocks.

They traveled nearly twenty miles that day. At sunset, four platoons circled to form a small corral. The animals were unhitched, and the tongue of each wagon was chained to the rear wheel of its neighbor's wagon. Oxen and horses were allowed to graze until sundown when they were driven inside the corral.

Jesse thought she had been tired at noon, but by nightfall she was close to tears from exhaustion. Homer seemed to be in better spirits. Beau and Gabe had performed beautifully that day, stepping lightly and pulling out ahead of the other wagons. Compared to the plodding oxen, the horses were grace in motion, and many an admiring glance was shot their way. Homer saw them all and his stern countenance softened a bit. By nightfall, he felt that his decision to keep Gabe and Beau was vindicated. Homer spoke pleasantly to Jesse and even accepted George Wood's invitation to pair up with them for the remainder of the trip.

Lavinia took care to make certain that Homer did not see her wink at Jesse when the invitation was proffered and accepted. Jesse smiled back shyly.

At last the evening chores were done. Jesse sank onto the featherbed in the wagon gratefully. Jacob had been asleep for hours. When Jesse tried to awaken him to eat, he nursed half-heartedly for only a few seconds. Jesse feel asleep even as she buttoned the bodice of her dress. Homer kept watch from beneath the wagon, lest his horses be harmed by some belligerent ox.

As the days went by, the land became more barren. Wooded strips still abounded along the creeks and streams, but there was a stillness about the land that filled Jesse with a longing for home. Her dread of the unknown ahead increased. Homer was intent upon Oregon. He seemed to have no regrets for what they had left. Each morning when she awoke, Jesse listened for the familiar honking of her mother's geese or the cheery cry of the cardinal. Here on the prairie there was none of that. The light of dawn brought only stillness broken by the sound of the wagon train and its animals.

Only Jacob filled the vast emptiness around and within her. Jesse walked alone much of the day. She tended to Jacob, prepared Homer's meals, mended his clothes, and fell into an exhausted sleep where she dreamed only of what was behind her. She awoke to be reminded that home was very far away, to walk unfamiliar barren hills, and to long for the deep woods that flanked her father's farm.

Added to the loneliness of the prairie was the terror of Indians. Jesse heard the many tales around the evening's campfires. They had now left the land of the peaceful Shawnee and were in the territory of the Kansaz, who lived in huts made of poles and bark. Somehow they curved the roofs, and Jesse thought their dwellings looked like iron rendering pots turned upside down. She saw with horror that these Indians were almost entirely naked.

"They're thieves," George Wood expounded, adding, "and they love children . . . especially *blond* children." Lavinia hushed him, but after that, whenever the Kansaz came close, Jesse would climb into the stuffy wagon and pull Jacob down beside her.

"Be anxious for nothing," she read, *"but in every thing by prayer and supplication with thanksgiving let your requests be made known unto God. And the peace of God, which passeth all understanding,*

shall keep your hearts and minds through Christ Jesus. "Jesse read and reread the passage by the light of every night's campfire. It comforted her enough that she could sleep. Yet, each new day brought renewed fears.

Jesse was nearly in despair on the day that her friendship with Lavinia Wood was cemented. Lavinia had been too involved with her own brood to think much about Jesse. The wagons had been beside one another, and yet Lavinia had done little to reach out to Jesse other than to shout encouragement to her, occasionally laugh at Jacob, and frequently scowl at Homer.

Finally, Lavinia had organized her family into an efficient platoon. Emily, the oldest, was assigned to baby Esther. "Keep her away from the wagon wheels and snakes, and I'll try not to demand much more," Lavinia ordered.

Amanda, next in line, tended the cow while her mother made lunch. They had brought only one cow along, but by milking her in the morning and hanging the milk pail on the back of the wagon, they had butter for supper.

Amelia and Ophelia were four-year-old twins. They helped gather firewood, aired out bedding, and performed tasks that amazed Jesse as she watched them all from her own fire.

Each day at noon, the Woods had their fire going and lunch eaten before anyone else. By evening, when everyone else on the trail seemed to have become the color of the brown dust that covered everything and everyone on the trail, Lavinia had unending energy. She cleaned and mended and cooked and still had time to laugh and play with her girls.

Jesse wondered at her courage. Homer called her "that interfering, uppity woman." Yet, as Jesse observed Lavinia and George, she could not help admiring them. They seemed to be friends. Jesse wondered what it would be like to be married to your best friend.

Late in the night of the second week, a storm broke. The

sky became dense black and rain fell in torrents all night. Thick darkness was interrupted only by dazzling flashes of lightning. Thunder kept up such a constant roar that even Jacob could not sleep and clung to his mother in terror. Jesse was unable to comfort him. Her own heart beat fast, and she wondered if the animals would break through the makeshift corral. Once, in a lull between thunder, she heard Homer's voice calling to his team, but the wind blew so hard it was impossible to know exactly where he was. Jesse feared that the wagon would topple over.

Early in the morning the ground began to flood with water. Jesse looked out to see that several wagons had, indeed, lost their covers to the wind. The Big Blue, which they were to cross that day, had overrun its banks. It churned and roared, but Homer and the other men were not to be stopped. They felt the urgency of "getting on" and thought they could float their wagons and families across safely.

Applegate was not so certain, "but if someone could get across to tie a rope to that huge cottonwood on the other side, we might be able to rig a ferry."

Two cottonwood trees were felled and lashed together. Cross timbers were added so that wagon wheels could be braced against them. The goods of each wagon were unloaded to be ferried across separately.

Jesse was horrified when Homer announced that he had volunteered to cross the raging current with Beau. "We'll tie a rope to that cottonwood yonder, and then ferry the goods across," he explained. Then he added, "Beau can do it, Jess. He's strong. He can do it."

Jesse knew it would do no good to protest. She wanted to encourage him, but the water inspired such a fear in her that she could not face the thought of Homer in its current. She cried and begged him not to go. He grew angry and strode off.

Lavinia had witnessed their altercation from a respectful distance. As soon as Homer left, she arrived quickly. "Jesse, dear, would you be so kind as to help me unpack our wagon? I just can't seem to get it done fast enough to please George."

Jesse knew that Lavinia was inventing the need for help, but she was grateful for the opportunity to be with others. Ten-year-old Emily swooped down upon Jacob and took him to scout for worms in the mud left by the night's storm.

Jesse helped Lavinia unpack, listened to her rattle on about the wonders of Oregon and the excitement of the journey, and tried to relax. But the tightness in her stomach would not go away. Her hands shook, and finally she became physically ill and bent over double, sobbing.

Lavinia's arms engulfed her in a great, motherly hug. She led Jesse to the opposite side of her own wagon, so their view of the river was blocked. Homer leaped onto Beau's bare back, rope in hand, urging him into the churning waters. Then, Lavinia did the only thing she could do to assuage Jesse's fears. Lavinia prayed.

"Dear Lord," she whispered, just so that Jesse could hear, "help us both. You know that I'm afraid too. I just show it in a different way. But Jesse, here, Jesse needs special grace. Her husband's in the water, and we know you promised to be with us. So please, Lord, keep Homer safe. You know that Jesse needs her husband. Keep him safe, Lord."

Jesse did not hear the specific words, so caught up was she in her own thoughts. But she felt Lavinia's concern in the arms about her. As her attention was turned heavenward, to the One who ruled the raging flood, she was comforted. Her hands shook less and the knot in her stomach relaxed.

Jacob came toddling back, squealing with delight. He held up a very long, very fat worm for Jesse's inspection. She knelt and hugged him, admired the worm, and praised the Lord as she heard voices cry out, "He's across! He's made it!"

Indeed, Homer had made it. As Jesse peeked out from behind the wagon, she saw both Homer and Beau shaking off the waters of the Big Blue.

The wagon train spent three weeks along the banks of the flooded Big Blue. Hours of working with terrified animals, digging wagons out of the mud, trying to keep clothes dry, and putting food into the mouths of all wore everyone's patience thin. Enemies were made, but friendships were also kindled. By the end of the three weeks, Jesse King and Vinnie Wood were fast friends.

Lavinia was brash and courageous. Jesse's shyness softened her and made her more gentle. Jesse was timid and lonely. Lavinia's outgoing personality overcame that, and Jesse began to laugh again. She was even convinced to join in the Woods' Sunday hymn sing. Homer refused to hum a note, but he was secretly proud of his wife's lovely voice, so he went along and held Jacob on his knee while everyone else sang.

Jesse and Lavinia discovered two things in common. They both loved the Lord and they both loved quilting. Every woman on the trip had made quilts for the journey, but Lavinia and Jesse had particularly loved the task. They talked of patterns and their plans for new quilts by the hour.

"I don't know what I was thinking when I packed pieces for this one," Lavinia said one day, showing Jesse a pile of brown calicoes and muslin. "Guess I thought I could piece a bit . . . but, land, the wagon rocks so, and at night we're all so beat . . ."

"I know what you mean," Jesse agreed. "I've got pieces, too—for the Tree of Life, but they're so tiny . . ."

"Jesse King!" Lavinia exclaimed, "now, you told me Homer inspected every inch of that wagon and took out most of what you wanted to bring. Just how did you manage to get your Tree of Life *pieces* along? He'd never approve, my dear!"

Jesse's eyes twinkled and she smiled demurely, "Homer didn't check the flour sack. He just assumed it was completely full . . . of flour."

George Wood and Homer King maintained a respectful distance. Homer was not inclined to grow close to anyone. His reasons for going to Oregon included total independence, and he saw no need to create ties that might at some point incur obligations on his part. If Jesse wanted to have a friend, that was all right with him, as long as it didn't make any demands on him.

When the Kings' and the Woods' turn to ferry across the Big Blue came, God had mercifully quieted the waters. The wagons slid across uneventfully, and Jesse heartily praised God when her feet touched the opposite shore.

After the Big Blue crossing, the land changed quickly. The hills became little more than huge piles of sand. There was rich grass for the livestock, but there was also an abundance of prickly pear cactus. Homer drove carefully, fearing those thorns in the feet of his team.

April and May had been uncomfortably cold. Now the weather moderated and Jesse despaired of ways to keep mosquitoes away from Jacob. In spite of her efforts, he looked like he had measles most of the time. Dust was so thick at times that Jesse had trouble seeing the lead wagon. On windy days, dust was flung against her face and hands. When she could bear the stinging no longer, she took shelter inside the wagon until the bumping and jolting became unbearable. Then she would climb out and carry Jacob for a while, until the dust drove her back in again.

It took only one day to cross the barren land between the Big Blue and the Platte, where they would be turning due west. It was evening, and the panoramic view of the Platte Valley held even the most seasoned travelers in awe. "I saw it for the first time back in '35," Dr. Whitman shared, "but it still amazes me."

The vast, shimmering flatness of the Platte Valley stretched away from them in a wide plain that appeared totally level. "I declare," remarked Homer, "looks like that there water is just floating on top of the land . . . looks like a yeller ribbon stretched acrost the valley."

The river looked wider than the Mississippi, but there was no timber on the banks. It was unlike any river they had ever seen before. Deceptive in its appearance, it proved to be only three or four feet deep, and they crossed it easily. They had to begin collecting "chips" for campfires. Jesse was surprised to learn that dried buffalo dung made a good, hot fire. She prepared her peach pie that evening. Homer seemed to have forgotten his earlier complaints about her "foolishness" and ate three pieces.

The next day, they saw great numbers of game, but Dr. Whitman explained that with the land being so flat, they would have great difficulty approaching anything close enough to shoot. Homer proclaimed those who tried fools and told George Wood, "I think too much of my horses to go chasing after game after they've pulled my wagon all day. They earn their night's rest, and I'll not ask 'em to run like idiots after game we can't catch."

Gooseberries, chokecherries, and serviceberries abounded along the banks of the Platte, and Jesse enjoyed adding them to their otherwise monotonous fare. Lavinia picked greens and showed Jesse how to prepare them so that Jacob would be spared scurvy. The child made a face when the green substance was presented to him, but he willingly swallowed it when "Aunt" Vinnie encouraged him.

The trip became monotonous. Walking miles each day, Jesse tumbled into bed exhausted and woke so sore that she whimpered in pain as she climbed down from the wagon each morning. Lavinia despaired of her hands, which she declared to be "rougher than a hemlock board."

"How will I ever quilt again, Jess?" she wondered aloud. "My hands are so stiff I can barely keep things mended . . . and to think," she sighed, "I used to pride myself on twelve stitches to the inch!"

"We'll have a *real* quilting party again as soon as we get to Oregon!" Jesse said. "Won't it be a joy?"

It was at the end of a particularly hot and dusty day that Lavinia overheard Homer complaining about the sameness of their meals. "Bacon, coffee, and biscuits—that's all we ever eat!" he said, "When I been fightin' broke wagon wheels and tired horses all day, it sure would be nice to have somethin' special to eat once in a while. Now, I gotta oil the harness, and I can't be watchin' little Jacob every minute, either. You call me soon as you got somethin' edible ready."

Lavinia bustled over. "I declare, Jesse, why don't you stand up to that man! If George ever tried that nonsense on me, he'd get cold biscuits and jerky for supper until he came to his senses!"

Jesse smiled at the prospect of Lavinia ever leaving "her George" to such a meal. "It's not so bad, Vinnie. Homer means well. He's just tired. And worried, too, about Gabe and Beau." The team had begun to show the strain of their trek, just as Applegate had predicted. Homer had refused to buy grain in spite of Applegate's advice. Foraging had, indeed, proven difficult. The horses' ribs were beginning to show a bit, and their coats had lost the sheen Homer had taken such pride in. Groom as he would, he could not help noticing that his team was wearing down. He even mentioned the possibility of leaving the cook stove beside the trail.

Lavinia refused to be sympathetic. "Tired?! Man alive! Aren't you tired too?" she sputtered. "Goodness, aren't we *all* tired! I swan, I'm so sore all over I can scarcely move." Then, brightening, she added, "Well, dearie, the girls picked gooseberries today, so we'll have gooseberry slump tonight. And you're invited."

She hurried away to begin supper, adding over her shoulder, "and I suppose you can bring that varmint you call your husband along too. Maybe gooseberries with plenty of sugar will sweeten him up a little!"

Chapter 4

The LORD is my shepherd; I shall
not want.

Psalm 23:1

The next day Jesse and Lavinia walked together
after breakfast. They didn't talk much, sharing
comfortable silence all morning. As noon approached, they
began collecting buffalo chips for the campfire. After nearly
an hour of collecting, the women noticed that two of the
wagons had lumbered to a halt. The dust cleared, and the
women noted with a catch in their throats that it was their
own wagons that had pulled out of line. Then they saw that
the entire train had begun to pull up. A cluster of people
gathered around one wagon. Jesse dropped the pile of chips
she held in her apron and began to run. As she ran, cockle-
burrs shredded the hem of her dress. The wind and dust
burned in her throat, but she ran on until, coming to the
cluster of people, she saw him.

On the ground lay Jacob, one arm thrown up over his
head. By his side knelt Dr. Whitman. Seeing Jesse approach,
he rose immediately and moved to her side.

"Mrs. King, I am so sorry. There was nothing any of us
could do. He is with God now." The grave face of the
missionary was lost in a mist of tears. Jesse looked about
wildly, and her gaze settled upon Homer. Hunched over, his
hat off, his shirt tail flapping, he approached her. His words
were a groan. "My God, Jesse, my God. He woke up and came
to sit by me . . . an' before I knew what happened he fell. I
tried to catch him . . . I tore his little dress trying to hold on

. . . and I had a grip and then. . ." His voice trailed off. " . . . an' then the wagon lurched, an' I lost my hold . . . the wheels . . ." He could not go on, but just stood before her, turning the hat in his hands round and round by its worn brim.

Jesse wanted to cry out, but the sounds caught in her throat. *All these people, all these strangers watching* . . . Her grief was too deep, too great to share with them. She took a breath and lifted her chin. Taking Homer's hand she squeezed it. He dropped his hat and clasped both her hands in his. He held them so hard it hurt.

"The wagon train must move on, Dr. Whitman," Jesse heard herself saying. "How often have I heard you say, 'onward . . . we must move ever onward.' And we started late. Please, instruct these good people to leave us to our grief. We can follow later."

Dr. Whitman placed a hand upon her shoulder. "But, my dear Mrs. King, do you not want us to stay and offer our prayers over the final resting place?"

Jesse croaked an earnest response, "No prayers will bring him back . . . you can all pray for us from the wagons as you move on." Then, lowering her voice a little she pleaded, "Please, Homer . . . make them all go. We can say good-bye to Jacob alone. Homer, all these strangers . . ." Her voice failed her, but the pleading tones settled matters. The wagon train would move on.

People began dispersing in small groups, whispering as they walked away. Only Lavinia remained.

"Jesse, dear," she whispered, "come look at Jacob. He looks just like he's sleeping."

In the eternity it had taken for the crowd to disperse, Jesse and Homer had stood, heads down, waiting. From somewhere Lavinia had produced a clean gown for the baby. Jesse allowed herself to look, and a small cry escaped her throat. Kneeling beside the toddler's lifeless form, she scooped him up in her arms and began to croon softly, rocking the baby. Tears left tracks on her dust-streaked face. Lavinia knelt beside Jesse in the dust with her arms about her friend's bowed shoulders.

Homer left Jesse to her tears, standing by the wagon, waiting for her to finish. Nervously he twirled his hat in his hands. At last, Jesse's grasp on the child loosened.

Lavinia slipped away as Jesse numbly rose, went to Homer's side, and waited for him to speak.

Finally he placed an arm across Jesse's shoulders and repeated, "I had a grip . . . and then . . ."

Jesse interrupted him. "It wasn't your fault, Homer. It could have happened to anyone."

The words seemed to release something within the man. As his body shook with a wave of relief, a sigh escaped. He stepped away from Jesse, straightened his shoulders, and reached into the wagon for a shovel. He almost growled the words, "I may not have kept him safe . . . but I'll make sure the dang coyotes leave him in peace now."

Furiously he began to dig the small grave. Deeper and deeper the spade went into the hard prairie until, exhausted, he sat on the edge of the hole. He looked at Jesse again and found her standing next to the wagon where he had left her. When her eyes met his gaze he looked quickly away and spoke to the distant horizon, "Guess we'd better be done with it."

"Wait a moment—please." Jesse struggled with Jacob's body, but managed to get inside the wagon with the still form in her arms. Homer heard things being moved about inside. It seemed to take a long time, but he could not bear to join her in the wagon. It would be too intimate, somehow, to be cooped up with her now, just when she had lost her child.

Jesse emerged from the wagon, carrying Jacob wrapped in the blue and white baby quilt Homer had not seen since Jacob had begun to toddle about. He did not even realize that she had brought it on the trip.

Jesse tried to wipe the dust from Jacob's face as she handed him over to Homer. He laid the body in the grave, and then hesitated, not knowing quite what to do. "Seems like there ought to be a word said . . ."

Jesse retreated once more into the wagon and returned with her Bible. For once, Homer did not frown at the appearance of the book. In the past he had accused Jesse of shirking her chores in favor of reading the worn book. "Homer, dear," she would say gently, "I can do my work so much better, and be of much more use to you, after I have spent time with the Lord." It was the one area of her life where she seemed bent on having her own way. Homer grudgingly gave in to her "woman's weakness" and let her read the Bible. But today, it seemed right that she should read from the book. He was grateful that she had it and that she would know where to read.

Jesse did know what she wanted to read. Not that it would be of any help to her precious Jacob, but her own aching heart sorely needed the comfort of familiar words. And so she turned to the beloved passage and began to read. *"The LORD is my shepherd; I shall not want."* She read quietly, with dignity, her voice faltering a little when she read the passage, *"Yea, though I walk through the valley of the shadow of death, I will fear no evil"* but otherwise she read steadily. At the close of the psalm she bowed her head. Homer followed suit and listened as Jesse talked to her God.

"Lord," she said softly, "we do not know why you would take our only child, but we know that you love us, and that you will cause it to work for our good. . . . Lord, help us to trust you even now, when our hearts are broken." She wanted to say more, but found that she could not. She did not even whisper, "Amen," but turned and fled to the wagon. She flung herself inside and onto the mattress, where, away from every eye, she could spend her grief.

When Jesse looked out later, she saw that Homer had filled in the little hole and covered it over with many layers of huge rocks. He was sitting by the grave, mopping his forehead. Slowly he straightened up and walked toward the wagon. His once strong gait was slowed to the crabbed shuffling of an old man. It was then that Jesse realized that, in his own way, Homer was suffering too. *Perhaps more,* she thought, *he does not have the comfort of the Lord.*

The sun was setting, and Homer moved about, building a fire. Jesse joined him and cooked supper. They ate in silence and slept fitfully, Jesse in the wagon and Homer stretched out below it, his rifle at his side.

Chapter 5

He causeth it to come, whether for
correction, . . . or for mercy.

Job 37:13

At the first light of dawn, Homer hastened to
harness Gabe and Beau. Gripping the side of
the wagon, he climbed up, grabbed the reins, and clucked
to the horses to "git-up." The lurch of the wagon tore Jesse
from an unnaturally deep sleep. She sat up and stared
blankly at the tiny pile of rocks just beginning to recede from
the shadow of the wagon. As the team lumbered along, the
rocks blended in with the landscape until finally they were
gone, and she could only stare at the spot on the horizon
where they had been. The creaking of the wheels that only
yesterday had seemed a rhythmic song of promise took on
ominous tones.

As her body demanded to feed the child that was gone,
Jesse prayed. *Lord, I don't understand . . . but with your help I
will believe that this is somehow for our good.* Her voice broke as
she whispered aloud, "Oh, but Lord, he was such a . . ." she
sobbed, "*little* boy. . . ."

When they halted for the noon rest, Homer appeared at
the back of the wagon. He didn't speak right away, but
reached out to clasp her clenched fists. The calluses on his
hands were rough, but he stroked her hands gently, tracing
the thin blue veins that coursed just under her skin.

Jesse focused on those hands, then gazed up the powerful
forearms to the plaid shirt, and finally to the bowed head.
Could that be tears moistening the thin eyelashes? The

possibility of Homer feeling such emotion wrenched Jesse's mind away from the little grave.

"I must get the fire started." She said the words, but they held no meaning, for she remained seated, clutching at the strong hands in her lap.

"It's all right, Jesse." Homer almost whispered. Then, clearing his throat he added, "You know I didn't want to leave him there . . ."

Jesse interrupted, "But, Homer, we had no choice." The chasm of grief that had separated them seemed to close.

Jesse stirred, reaching for the flour sack. Homer lifted her down from the wagon. It was a gesture many would take for granted, but Homer King was not a man given to such gestures. Jesse had always found her own way into and out of the wagon. She had been left to make friends on her own in the wagon train and to adapt to life on the trail as best she could. This small show of caring comforted her.

"We'll catch up with them by dark," Homer assured Jesse. "I won't unhitch the team today . . . just give 'em a short rest."

Lunch finished, Homer squinted toward the horizon. "Sounds like there's a storm comin'. Let's be on our way."

The two of them worked quickly, Jesse listening to the low rumble of thunder in the distance. Glancing up she saw a dark cloud on the horizon.

"Oh, my . . ." her voice caught in her throat. She laid her hand on Homer's shoulder, and as he stood up from quenching their camp fire, she pointed in disbelief at the cloud.

The roar of the buffalo stampede reached their ears and instantly Homer flew to the wagon. Jumping up onto the seat he grabbed the reins. Screaming to Gabe to "git-up!" he motioned wildly to Jesse to climb aboard. The desperate tone in his voice and the shaking of the reins communicated danger to the horses. Already restive from the sound of the distant stampede, Gabe and Beau snorted and plunged ahead.

Jesse dropped her shawl on the prairie, grabbed the wagon side, and hauled herself up beside Homer. Her bonnet hung down her back, and as the wagon jolted across the prairie her hair came loose, flowing in a red torrent down her sweat-stained back. Homer shouted, "Get inside—safer" as he urged the horses forward. His eyes searched the terrain for a large rock or a copse of trees—anything that might serve as a shelter against the oncoming river of animals.

Jesse tumbled over the seat into the wagon bed. It was a jumble of barrels and sacks. With every bounce of the wagon, she felt a new pinch from some out-of-place bundle. One glance out the rear of the wagon brought a gasp of dread as she saw the danger approaching.

Homer drove skillfully, but the buffalo came on, gaining steadily. He searched in vain for the shelter to pull up next to. He would have to keep his horses running and hope that the overtaking herd would run with them and not crush the wagon. Beau and Gabe bounded forward, pulling with all their great strength. Lather appeared on the horses' rumps. Foam flew from the bits. Gabe stumbled, then lunged forward in response to Homer's desperate urgings. The earth shook as the buffalo came closer.

Jesse watched, caught in a slow-motion version of reality. Through the dust-filled air she saw Homer's hand raise the whip—the tool he had always refused to use on his beloved team. Her mind registered the picture of that whip poised in the air, silhouetted against the blue sky. Then the whip came down, again and again, across the rumps of the laboring team.

The roar of the buffalo was deafening now. Jesse clutched wildly for something to hold on to inside the lurching wagon. Scrambling toward the back, she peered into the eyes of a huge beast. It stared blankly ahead, nostrils dilated, tongue lolling out of one side of its mouth. They were caught in a rolling sea of thundering hooves and dark brown, shaggy bodies.

The sound of those pounding hooves drowned out Homer's futile urging to his spent team. Gabe and Beau staggered and went down. Jesse instinctively leaped backward, away from the oncoming rush. Her head hit something hard. Darkness and thunder and the sound of splintering wood all melted together into unnatural silence.

Chapter 6

. . . Be not afraid, only believe.

Mark 5:36

Jt was hot. And quiet. So quiet that Jesse could hear the high-pitched whine of a fly as it buzzed about her head. *But no,* she thought, *I hear Gabe and Beau stomping about, too. And* . . . a shadow fell across her face. The lessening of the sun's warmth made her open her eyes. Someone stood over her, but the bright sun from behind made it impossible to see his face. *Homer? No, not Homer. His hair is not quite so long.*

Then, all in a rush, Jesse remembered. The buffalo stampede! She recalled those last terrifying seconds and with that memory came the realization that this man was not Homer. She was looking into the face of a Sioux warrior.

Where is Homer? Jesse lay still, silent in her terror. *Oh, to be saved for this! In the hands of these savages, what will become of me?*

"*Be not afraid,* . . . *for the LORD thy God is with thee whithersoever thou goest.*" The words came again and again: "*Be not afraid* . . . *Be not afraid* . . . *Be not afraid.*"

Jesse offered herself up to her Father's keeping and, without actually forming any conscious words, Jesse prayed.

As her thoughts turned heavenward, the Indian who stood above her reached down to investigate the glint of gold at her neck. Jesse clutched at her mother's cross and chain. The Indian was insistent. He pried her fingers away from the cross but, to Jesse's surprise, did not snatch it from her neck. Instead, he examined it carefully, let go, and stepped away.

Jesse sat up. Every muscle screamed in pain. She was stiff and sore and thirsty. Still, no bones seemed broken. She looked about her at what was left of the wagon. And then, toward the front of the wagon, her eye caught a flash of red flannel waving in the breeze. *Homer?* No, not Homer any longer, yet it had been Homer only a little while ago. Gabe and Beau were there too. Their valiant efforts to outrun the buffalo would be their last pulling contest.

Jesse realized that she was alone and at the mercy of the Indians who stood about, looking through the wreckage as their ponies snatched up mouthfuls of coarse grass. They were a quiet bunch, commenting occasionally on what they found in the wreckage, examining the iron stove with curiosity. The flour and grain and stored foods were scattered about, ground into the dust and useless. Only one wheel of the wagon remained unbroken. The rest were shattered, so that the wagon stood askew, propped up like a newborn colt on its long, spindly legs.

"Be not afraid . . . Be not afraid . . . " The words kept drumming in Jesse's mind as she watched the Indians move about. They ignored her for a long time, and then the one who had seen the cross made his way back to her. She noticed for the first time that he was taller than his companions—or would have been, had it not been for one bad leg. He had apparently broken that leg in the past, and it had mended badly, for now he walked with a lurching gait, his braids shaking with each step. His face was painted red. Three stripes of black paint adorned each cheek; bright yellow rings encircled each eye.

His face was grim as he approached Jesse, and she shrank away from his grasp. But he pulled her to her feet, and as he did so, the soreness in her back and legs made her cry out in pain. She stumbled, tried to stand but could not. The brave grabbed her roughly about the waist and half pulled, half carried her to his snow white pony. He was strong and lifted her up on the bare back effortlessly. Jesse clutched fearfully at the dancing pony's mane and prepared to be led away.

But the Indian brave leaped up behind her. He smelled of war paint and sweat. Jesse's stomach lurched. She took a deep breath, praying, *God, keep me on this pony. Surely I was not meant to die out here, like this—alone—God, help me!*

Jesse tried to look back at the wreckage. She was surprised when the Indian turned his pony to allow her to look back. *How did I survive that?* she wondered in amazement as she surveyed the scene. A flash of white caught her attention, and she saw that her best quilt now lay across the back of one of the other ponies. It was the all-white quilt that she had worked steadily on for months before she and Homer were married. She had quilted it meticulously, stuffing the designs in each large block so that flowers and wreaths stood out from the stippled background. Homer had complained about bringing it, but Jesse had insisted. "No matter where we may live, Homer," she had said respectfully but firmly, "if I can put that quilt on my bedstead on Sunday, I'll feel like I'm keeping a proper home." For once, it had been Jesse who "set her jaw," and Homer who acquiesced.

Now the quilt shimmered in the hot sun. It was dusty, but seemed to have survived the tragedy unscathed. Jesse smiled grimly as she wondered if she would have such good fortune once these savages got her back to their camp—or wherever they were taking her.

"Be not afraid . . . Be not afraid . . . Be not afraid . . ." The words were drummed into her heart in rhythm with the clip-clopping of the pony's trot across the prairie. They seemed to ride for hours, leaving the level plains and ascending the distant bluffs. Jesse's legs ached and her heart lurched each time the pony made a sudden move.

They forded a small creek, and the Indians dismounted to drink. Jesse's captor pulled her down from the pony and pushed her toward the water. She drank deeply, splashing her hot face and rinsing her trembling hands in the clear water. Her eyes searched the distance for signs of a search party. Would they come from the wagon train?

The Indian tugged at her arm and pulled her away from the creek. He gestured, seeming to wave, then pointed to her. His right hand turned palm up as he moved it side to side across his abdomen. Jesse watched dumbly and stood still, afraid to move. The Indian repeated the three motions more forcefully. Then she understood. It was the sign language she had seen Dr. Whitman employ with other Indians along the trail. But the motions held no meaning for her. She shook her head nervously, fearful of the reaction.

The brave showed little reaction except to reach into the pouch at his side and offer her a tough strand of dried meat. Jesse took it obediently and forced herself to bite off a piece. Her stomach refused the offering.

Rinsing her mouth again in the creek, she glanced up fearfully. The Indian lifted her onto his pony again, and they trotted away, this time in the lead of the band of warriors. It was a torturous, day-long ride. Jesse clung to the white mane of the pony, too numb to pray, too tired to be afraid anymore. Finally, the band halted for the night, turned out their ponies to graze, and built a fire. Several prairie chickens that had been shot earlier in the day were roasted. Her captor repeated the gestures of earlier in the day and then offered Jesse a portion. This time she took it eagerly. She sank, exhausted, onto the ground and fell asleep as soon as she had eaten.

Low thunder and a sudden cool breeze awoke her sometime in the night. Hurling itself across the open prairie, a violent storm arrived. The Indians collected their horses and held them fast while lying flat on the prairie, defenseless against the onslaught of torrential rain.

Lightning ripped open the night sky, illuminating the surroundings in a freakish light. Great sheets of water poured upon them, and still the Indians lay flat on the prairie, simply waiting for the storm to pass. The white pony she had been forced to ride stood by his master, nose to the earth, calmly enduring the downpour.

Jesse trembled with fear and crouched low, her head on her knees. Wrapping her arms about her legs she rocked back and forth. She remembered the storms at home in Illinois when, as a girl, she ran indoors and clambered into her parents' rope bed, hiding beneath the pile of comforters until the storm had passed. She had nearly succeeded in imagining herself there when a brilliant flash of lightning struck the earth nearby.

The creek had swollen, and she heard its rushing waters come nearer. Then she felt it pulling at the hem of her water-logged skirt. Another burst of lightning and she screamed aloud. A strong hand pulled her away from the water. A rain-drenched forearm flattened her against the earth. She was pinned to the earth by that arm and lay there, face down, for what seemed like hours.

At last the storm began to abate. It was passing to the east. The arm across her back was lifted, and she pushed away, raising her head to see that the clouds were breaking apart. Stars twinkled in the patches of sky that appeared. At last the moon shone a bright light over the sodden landscape. In the eerie predawn light, the white pony resembled a ghost-horse as it moved about grazing.

As dawn broke, only the swollen creek remained to tell of the violent night. The Indians mounted early, and Jesse was once again forced up onto the dancing white pony. With a jolt she realized that the storm would have washed away all trace of their journey. No search party would be able to find her.

Near evening of the second day's journey, the band of Indians topped a rise, and Jesse saw an encampment of tepees arrayed on the prairie below. The rhythm of her heartbeat matched the pony's swift hoofbeats, and she clutched desperately at its mane, wondering, *What will happen now?*

Everyone in the village came out to meet the returning hunters; children shouted welcomes. As they passed among the east-facing tepees, curious women stared at Jesse. Numb from fatigue and fear, Jesse stared blankly about her. *Soon, it will be over,* she thought. *I will die here, and it will be over.* Death would bring welcome relief from the torture of riding and riding with every muscle agonizing as each stride jarred her weary body.

At last the pony stopped outside a large tepee, and the brave leaped to the ground. He grabbed Jesse roughly, appearing to throw her to the ground. But his strong arm actually broke her fall so that she landed quite gently at the door of his tepee. His voice was angry as he motioned for her to get inside. The village women and children looked on quietly. One squaw whispered something to her companion, and they nodded and smiled to one another. Jesse gathered up her skirts and hurried inside.

The brave limped after her and snatched down the doorflap. Instantly his demeanor changed. Jesse watched as he removed his weapons. He turned to her, and she backed away. He waited until she looked up into his eyes. The tension about his eyes relaxed. *Could it be that he does not plan to kill me after all? But then . . . no, death would be preferred to some things.*

The Indian turned abruptly, muttering to an old woman who squatted by the fire stirring something in a kind of bag hanging on a tripod made of sticks. She cackled a response and the man left, leaving the flap open. Sunlight poured into the tepee, and across its expanse Jesse spotted the reason she had been brought here.

Over the top of a cradle board two dark eyes glistened as they watched the old woman move about. Jesse heard a soft cry that quickly grew to an intense wail, and the old woman shuffled over to the cradle board. Gently she pinched the infant's nostrils and a gasp for breath interrupted the wail. The old woman set to work quickly mashing grain and adding liquid to make a runny gruel. Each time the infant began to wail, she hurried over to repeat the pinching of his tiny nostrils until a gasp for breath would again stop the crying. At last the woman began to dip her fingers into the gruel and then into the infant's mouth. He sucked greedily at her fingers, but soon began to wail again in frustration.

Jesse felt her body respond to the cries and looked down, embarrassed by the dampness beginning to show through the bodice of her dress. She folded her arms and pressed them against her bosom, but the old woman had seen. She did not hesitate to unwrap the infant and carry him across the tepee to Jesse.

Jesse looked away, pretending not to understand, but the wail persisted and she turned to look at the child. The wail stopped momentarily when the child's eyes met hers. Jesse whispered, "I am not who you want," but even as she spoke, she instinctively reached out to stroke the velvety cheek. The tiny head turned to seek out her fingers to suckle.

Instinct took over. Jesse reached for the infant and cradled him on her lap as she unfastened her bodice. Put to her breast, the child sighed, nuzzled gently, and began to nurse greedily. He lay quite still, his tiny dark hand posed against her white skin. Then he stopped, looking up. As his eyes searched her face, milk trickled out of his mouth. He burped loudly and began to nurse again.

Weariness overtook Jesse, and she sat looking dumbly about. Through the flap of the tepee, she caught glimpses of Indians moving about as twilight approached. The fire in the center of the tepee was burning low. A lazy wand of smoke circled upward and out the hole at the top of the tepee. Jesse's eyes followed the smoke upward, and she saw a star twinkling in the fast-darkening sky.

The old woman intervened again, taking the child from Jesse's arms. Carrying him closer to the fire, she unwrapped him and laid him on a buffalo robe near the fire. Legs and arms flailed the air. Jesse watched as the old woman ministered to the infant, murmuring softly as she massaged his body with some kind of lotion.

The old one left the newborn then and moved to the side

of the tepee opposite Jesse. Grunting loudly she dragged a bedroll across to where Jesse sat. Returning to the opposite side again, she unrolled two more skins, obviously preparing beds for the tepee's inhabitants.

As dusk arrived, the Indian came back. He glanced Jesse's way and turned abruptly to speak softly to the old woman. He tipped a skin that hung on a pole near the center of the tepee. Fresh water spilled out and he washed his hands, then drank deeply. Jesse watched fearfully as the head tilted back to drink. The muscular neck was set onto powerful, broad shoulders. The hands that held the water skin were large. In the growing darkness, the glow of the fire gave the Indian's skin an eerie redness. Jesse shivered as he finished drinking and turned toward her.

But it was the infant who commanded his attention. Kneeling by the child he stroked the dark hair, softly chanting,

a wa wa wa
Inila istinma ma
a wa wa wa
wablenica.

He padded a skin hide with something white and fluffy taken from a leather bag. Then he wrapped the baby in the hide diaper and returned him to Jesse. He motioned for her to lie down on the buffalo robe the old woman had unrolled. Jesse gratefully lay down, the child at her side. In spite of her fears, sleep came. The baby slept in her arms, waking to nurse greedily several times that first night.

In the morning, when the old woman tried to awaken her, Jesse was vaguely aware of being prodded to rise, but she could not respond. The bruises and the aching muscles, the fear and the sleepless night of the storm, had taken their toll. The sleeping infant was lifted gently away and his fawnskin diaper changed. Jesse King slept away most of her first day as a captive in a Lakota village.

Chapter 7

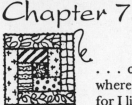

. . . cause me to know the way
wherein I should walk;
for I lift up my soul unto thee.

Psalm 143:8

For as long as he could remember, life had been unkind to Howling Wolf. His father had been killed in a raid on the Brule tribe. The new husband who took in his mother had instantly disliked Howling Wolf, chasing him off until the young man quit coming back and scrounged for his own livelihood. He managed to survive, but his luck was always bad. Once he had acquired a fine mare, but she had gone lame the morning after he stole her from the Pawnee. Mounted on old, poorly kept ponies, Howling Wolf rarely succeeded in the buffalo hunt. His tepee was small and sparsely furnished. He had only two ponies. Still, he was a handsome brave. Recklessly fierce in battle, he won the respect and admiration of many of his peers.

Howling Wolf usually hid the bitterness in his heart. But the tribal elders saw his quick rages and shook their heads in disgust. Four Skies waxed eloquent over more than one campfire on Howling Wolf's behalf. "I am certain that time will calm his heart," and here Four Skies paused and winked at those around him, "time and a good woman." The other elders shrugged their shoulders and hoped that Four Skies was right.

As he grew older, Howling Wolf's fortunes did not change much. He always seemed to have just enough to get through each winter, but there was never an abundance. He remained restless and fierce, yearning to grasp success from the wind and become a leader of his people. When Prairie Flower cast her first womanly glances in his direction, Howling Wolf was astounded. She was the daughter of a well-respected elder.

Prairie Flower's father warned her against Howling Wolf's uncertain temperament, but Prairie Flower became even more determined to woo him. She was captivated by both his beauty and his rebellious and fierce nature. Her own loveliness transformed Howling Wolf's surliness long enough for him to wrap her in his buffalo robe outside her father's tepee and claim her as his bride.

Their youthful exuberance soon wore itself out. Prairie Flower became the excuse for Howling Wolf's continued bad luck. He ridiculed and blamed her, destroying her youthful affection before it could mature into a love that would endure his fits of temper. When he returned from hunting with only a meager catch, she took it without a word of complaint. He interpreted her silence as accusation and blamed his poor catch on a lame pony—or anything he could think of. The fact that he had risen late or been impatient and scared game away was never brought up, and Howling Wolf went through life blaming others for his own shortcomings.

Prairie Flower tried to be a dutiful wife long after her affection for Howling Wolf had died. Her mother was a great comfort, encouraging her that if she remained faithful in her duties, Howling Wolf would one day settle down and appreciate her. But day in and day out, Howling Wolf continued to fail. Failure turned to bitterness, and the very beauty of his wife became a reminder of his own failures. Howling Wolf was caught in a downward spiral that Prairie Flower refused to join, and he hated her for it.

It was late during their first year of marriage that Prairie Flower finally realized she had made a terrible mistake. Her father, Talks a Lot, sympathized, but he gave his daughter the same advice as her mother had—stay with Howling Wolf and give him time to grow up. Talks a Lot also added the Lakota version of an "I told you so" speech to his advice. Prairie Flower determined not to bring up her disappointments to her parents again.

In the fall of that first year, something happened that would forever change Prairie Flower's life. Rides the Wind's wife died, leaving him with an infant son to raise. A week later, Prairie Flower watched with her friends when he came riding into the village with a white woman on his pony. Howling Wolf brought his wife a strange white blanket that he said they had found in the broken pieces of a white man's cart. Prairie Flower said nothing, but Howling Wolf saw her glance toward Rides the Wind's tepee as she accepted the blanket. She thought, *Rides the Wind brings a woman . . . Howling Wolf brings a dirty piece of white cloth. And it will always be this way. Howling Wolf will always bring what no one wants.*

Howling Wolf watched jealously as Rides the Wind ordered the white woman inside his tepee. When she scrambled inside, he smiled, enjoying the thought of what he imagined would ensue.

But Rides the Wind came outside and rode away almost immediately after following the woman inside his tepee. Howling Wolf watched in disbelief and then shoved his own wife inside his small tepee to demand payment for his gift.

The next morning, Prairie Flower laughed with the other women as they talked about the arrival of the new woman.

"What is she like?" they demanded when Old One arrived to join their berry-hunting expedition.

Old One shrugged her shoulders. "You see. She is white."

"Will she stay?" came the question.

"My son says this is a woman to feed his son." Old One added, "She was found by one of the strange carts the whites bring. Rides the Wind says they found things for a papoose. The hunting party watched when this woman and her husband put their papoose in the ground."

"They put him in the *ground?*" The women were horrified.

"He was stepped on by the strange cart. They put their dead ones in the ground."

The women muttered their disbelief. They had heard of such things, but never had one of them actually witnessed the whites doing such a thing until now.

Prairie Flower spoke, "So if her papoose has gone to the other land, she must have milk for the child of Rides the Wind."

Old One nodded and cackled, "She has much milk. She did not want to give it, but I made her." The old woman's eyes softened, "I think she likes the child. Rides the Wind has named him Two Mothers. She will stay." At that, Old One said, "Enough! You will see her for yourself. You decide what you think. I have talked too long, and my son will have no food if I do not get to work.

It was early afternoon when the old woman finally succeeded in waking Jesse. Motioning for her to follow, she scooped up the baby and left the tepee. Jesse followed the old woman to the nearby creek where she watched as the woman unwrapped the infant and bathed him. After the bath, the firm little body was massaged with leaves. The old woman pointed to a nearby weed. Jesse pulled off a leaf. Instantly, it gave off a sweet, pungent fragrance.

When the woman had finished with the baby, she replenished the diaper lining with tufts of milkweed fluff, rewrapped him in the fawnskin diaper, and gave him to Jesse. The fragrance of the wild plant hung on the air. Jesse snuggled the infant in her arms, longing for Jacob's smiling blue eyes and happy greeting.

The old woman watched carefully. She saw Jesse's wistful smile as the gray eyes blinked back tears. The old woman patted Jesse's arm gently.

The infant nuzzled to be fed and Jesse complied, sitting at the water's edge, oblivious to the Old One's comings and goings. When the child's hunger abated, Jesse heard footsteps behind her. She looked up to see the Old One spreading an elkskin shift on a serviceberry bush nearby. Moccasins were set below the dress.

Jesse leaned over to see her reflection in the water and was horrified by what met her gaze. Her face was filthy, her stringy hair caked with dust.

Old One took the baby and Jesse knelt at the water's edge, dipping her hands into the current and splashing her face with the cool water.

Stepping into the stream, she waded to a spot where overhanging bushes afforded some privacy and sighed as she fumbled to unfasten her wet buttons and stays. Cool water rushed over her skin. She scrubbed her hair vigorously and crept back near the bank to quickly don the clean shift.

Wading back to retrieve her own clothing, she rinsed it as best she could and spread the multitude of petticoats out to dry in the sun.

Well, Father, she thought, *here I am, little Jesse King . . . Indian maiden.* She grinned at the ridiculous picture she would make dressed in the elkskin dress the Old One had brought. Still, she was grateful for anything clean, and she welcomed the comfort of the garment. With no stays squeezing in her waist, and no petticoats catching on the grasses as they walked back to the tepee, Jesse felt pounds lighter.

Back in the tepee, the Old One produced a strange sort of comb made from quills. She watched Jesse struggle with it for a few moments and then took it from the inexperienced hands and patiently combed the long, thick hair until it hung straight and silken.

Old One said something again, and made motions for Jesse to braid her hair. The task completed, Jesse quickly exited the tepee and ran to the edge of the stream to look once again at herself. She chuckled at the strange woman who appeared in the water. Her skin was white, her eyes were still gray, but the red hair was braided neatly and hung down her shoulders. The soft tawny color of the dress she wore made her hair glow.

Well, now, Lord, you know the number of the hairs upon my head . . . so you must be able to recognize me, even in this unbelievable garb. Jesse's calico dress and petticoats still lay spread across the bushes. Women began to congregate and exclaim over the petticoats. Jesse was horrified to watch them help themselves to whatever struck their fancy. She had intended to keep her clothes but, unable to communicate, and afraid to defend her possessions, she watched the pieces disappear, one by one, into the tepees of the other women.

Supper—stew cooked over the tepee fire—was taken in silence by the two women. The baby's father made no appearance. *"Be not afraid"* seemed to be whispered by the wind as Jesse settled onto her buffalo skin pallet that night. The baby who was not Jacob snuggled close, and Jesse slept soundly.

∽

After breakfast the next morning, Old One strapped the infant's cradle board to Jesse's back. Jesse followed her obediently outside the tepee, her heart racing. They joined a group of women on a foraging expedition. Unaccustomed to the weight of a cradle board on her back, Jesse stumbled along, fascinated by the women's knowledge of what grew on the prairie. They dug up roots and gathered berries until their skin bags bulged. Jesse began to see the prairie in a new light. On the trail, she had admired the flowers, but the wide expanse of scenery had soon taken on a sameness. Indeed, once or twice even Homer had fallen asleep while he drove, lulled by the monotony of the land. He had sworn about the worthless land.

"Just look at it, Jess. You see anything *worth* lookin' at? No woods for lumber—how's a man to build a house out here? Nothin' to build a decent fence, neither—not even enough rocks fer that! No rivers to float yer crops to market. No way to build up a trade. It's a desert, Jess—a worthless desert. Let the Injuns have it, I say!"

Homer, Jesse thought. She wondered at the lack of emotion she felt at the thought of him. He had been her husband, but he was gone now, and she found herself in such an unbelievable situation that all her energies were used to cope with it. The Indian obviously meant for her to stay and feed his child. *Surely the others will look for us,* she thought. *But perhaps not. Except for George and Lavinia, we had no friends there ... and the storm ...* Her thoughts whirled round and round, until the child in the cradle board cried to be fed, and she stopped to nurse him.

The women stood about her in a circle, watching and giggling. One insolent girl poked Jesse's arm, prodding at each freckle that dotted the wind-burned skin. Old One finally came hurrying up and scolded them all, shooing them away and sheltering Jesse from their curious eyes with the cradle board. Jesse looked up into the wrinkled face. "Thank you," she said. Old One could not understand the language, but the appreciative tone meant much. Old One pointed to the child and said, *"Wablenica."* Jesse repeated the word. She pointed a finger at herself. *"Wakanka."* Jesse parroted the word.

Prairie Flower witnessed this scene, and something stirred in her. The white woman was trying. Was she lonely? She certainly looked bewildered. Yet, she had not flinched when they poked and prodded her strange white skin with the brown spots. She had looked back at them with her cool, gray eyes.

When the child finished eating, Old One helped Jesse rewrap the baby and take up the cradle board once more. Prairie Flower left the group of women who laughed and giggled at the white woman's clumsy ways and approached Jesse to offer her digging tool to her. Jesse took it, but looked about in confusion. She had no idea what to dig. Prairie

Flower walked along, indicating plants, showing Jesse where and how to dig. Jesse was soon finding her own plants and roots. Prairie Flower nodded her encouragement.

"Tinpsila," she said, pointing to a root already in her own bag. Jesse tried to say the word, but the new sounds were difficult. Prairie Flower went on patiently. Digging up another root she said, *"Pangi."*

Jesse found one and called out, *"Pow-gay!"* The women looked up and laughed at her, but Prairie Flower corrected her and smiled encouragement.

Jesse remembered only one thing from that first day among the other women. They could be unbearably cruel as they laughed and made fun of her. But Wakanka—the Old One—was kind. And the beautiful one with the gentle eyes seemed to like her.

That night Old One showed Jesse how to cook what they had collected. Rides the Wind arrived, ate, and departed without a word to either woman. He seemed not to notice Jesse at all, except to grunt with satisfaction when he saw her feed his son.

It was late when the door flap opened and he entered the tepee. Jesse, who had been asleep, woke when he touched her shoulder. She sat up, her heart pounding, but the Indian only moved to another part of the tepee, opened the box made from skins, and returned to her side, placing a bundle on her lap. He motioned for her to unwrap it, and she obeyed, gasping in amazement at what she saw. The edges of its pages gleamed gold in the firelight. It was a small Bible.

Jesse picked it up with a quiet cry of joy and held it to her. She bowed her head, and a tear spilled down her cheek. *Oh, Lord,* she prayed, *how can I ever thank you for this miracle?*

It seemed, however, that this was to be a night of miracles, for the Indian abruptly sat before her and said in a low voice, "You tell words in book?"

Jesse was dumbfounded. Had she really heard her own

language? *No,* she thought, *it was only the wind . . . or my own dream . . . or . . .*

"You *tell words* in *book?*" It was repeated, with accents on different words, as if he thought she had not understood him.

Jesse looked at the Indian in wonder. She did not answer his question but rather stammered, "You speak *English?*"

The Indian gave one brief nod. "Many moons ago. I forget much." He paused before saying, "In your tongue I am Rides the Wind." He pointed to Jesse.

"King," she stammered. "I am Jesse King."

The Indian reached up to grasp the gold cross still about Jesse's neck.

"Jess-e-king know book?"

Jesse nodded.

"Jess-e-king know Jesus?"

Again, she nodded.

He reached for the Bible and opened it, pointing to the page. "You tell book."

Jesse could only sit and stare dumbly at the hand that covered half the open book. Veins stood out in relief along its back. The fingers were long, and the nails were cracked and rough.

When she remained silent, Rides the Wind made a fist and placed it over his heart. Slowly, he spoke. His voice was gentle and low. Jesse was reminded of the way her father had spoken once when they had come upon a deer in a clearing. His usually gruff voice had become gentle as he tried to avoid frightening the wary fawn.

The Indian thumped his chest with his fist and repeated, "Know God here." Opening the fist, he touched his temple. "Need God here. Missionary say this book teach God. You teach."

Jesse fumbled with the pages of the worn Bible, praying for guidance. Rides the Wind waited patiently. The pages fell open to the first Psalm. Jesse finally began to read, her voice shaking,

Blessed is the man that walketh not in the counsel of the ungodly, nor standeth in the way of sinners, nor sitteth in the seat of the scornful. But his delight is in the law of the LORD; and in his law doth he meditate day and night. And he shall be like a tree planted by the rivers of water, that bringeth forth his fruit in his season; his leaf also shall not wither; and whatsoever he doeth shall prosper.

She stopped reading and sat fingering the pages of the book.

Rides the Wind, too, was quiet for a moment. Then, he said, "Tree by stream grows strong."

Jesse nodded her agreement.

He took the Bible from her, wrapped it carefully in skins, and handed it back to Jesse. "When the stars come again, you tell book for Rides the Wind."

Jesse nodded.

After a moment he asked, "Jess-e-king have brothers?"

"No."

"Sisters?"

"Yes, I have a sister."

He started to speak and then stopped abruptly, struggling for the right words. Finally, he asked, "Sister of Jess-e-king sorry she stay with Lakota?"

Jesse thought about the question. Would Betsy grieve? It would be years before Betsy even realized that something was amiss. Other than the Woods, she and Homer had had no friends on the trail. Homer had no family. No, no one would miss her. The truth hurt terribly, but she told Rides the Wind the truth. "No, she will not be sorry. She will not know."

He was quiet for a long moment, then he said, "*Wicatokapa* need milk. Jess-e-king has milk. Rides the Wind needs more God. Jess-e-king knows God-book. You give milk to my son? You teach book?"

"As newborn babes, desire the sincere milk of the word." The apostle's words came into her thoughts as Jesse pondered his question. In the darkness, she smiled at the odd way in which she would be able to obey the mandate if she stayed. *If I stay,* she thought in wonder. *Lord, am I really being given a choice?*

As if in answer to her thoughts, Rides the Wind said, "Jess-e-king want to go, Rides the Wind will take her to her people."

Lord, how can I make such a decision when so much has happened? She was dismayed by the impossibility of deciding tonight. Then she was amazed to realize that she was actually considering staying instead of instantly demanding to be returned to her own people.

How can I possibly be considering staying with these savages? she wondered. *But if I go back, where would I go?* Painful memories reminded her how relieved her parents had been when she finally married.

Rides the Wind waited.

Jesse avoided answering directly. "You are Rides the Wind. Does the child have a name?"

"Lakota call him *Wablenica*—'mother gone.' I call him *Wicatokapa*—'first son.' He will have new name if Jess-e-king stays."

"A new name?" Jesse asked softly.

"If Jess-e-king stays, *Wicatokapa* will be called Two Mothers."

The infant stirred in his sleep, and as Jesse moved to feed him, the sounds of his eager nursing filled the tepee. He nuzzled Jesse's warm skin. Reaching down to take a tiny hand in her own, Jesse felt five fingers close tightly about her thumb. The baby didn't let go. Jesse whispered, "His name will be Two Mothers."

Rides the Wind smiled and retreated to his own pallet across the tepee.

You should smile more often, Jesse thought. *I'm not so afraid of you when you smile.*

❧

The next morning Jesse woke when Rides the Wind left the tepee. Rising immediately, she stirred the fire. Old One woke with a start, smiling her approval at Jesse. She joined her in morning duties, correcting Jesse's clumsy attempts to make the morning meal. Seeing the smoke rise from the vent at the top of his tepee, Rides the Wind reentered his home, nodded to the women, ate without a word, and left.

When the village women met again to go foraging for roots and berries, one wore the petticoat Jesse had spent hours trimming with handmade lace. The other women laughed and joked among themselves, and the petticoat's owner soon discarded it in disgust because it kept catching on the plants as they foraged.

Once again, the beautiful young squaw took the role of teacher. She taught Jesse to say Prairie Flower in Lakota and was obviously pleased to see that Jesse had remembered what some of the edible plants and roots looked like. She patiently repeated the names of the plants until Jesse could remember a few of the new words. Once, when Jesse reached to dig up a plant, the young woman stopped her, grabbing her hand and making a face. Jesse found another example of what she thought she was digging, and her new friend carefully pointed out the differences in the leaves of the two plants. One, edible, had a longer stem than the other. Jesse nodded her understanding.

Old One had not come on this expedition, and when Jesse returned to the tepee, she proudly presented the older woman with her small contribution to the next meal. One by one she laid the items out, trying to remember their Lakota names, and dutifully correcting her pronunciation when Old One corrected her. At evening that day, they ate alone, for Rides the Wind had left again with a hunting party and would be gone for several days. He had told Jesse in her own language, but he had used as few words as possible. "Jess-e-king," he had said, "I go hunt. Go many days. Old One, Prairie Flower teach you."

Jesse waited for his return, trying all the while to learn how to fit into her new role. For every kind act by Old One and Prairie Flower, there were myriad jeers and cruel jokes from the other women. Unable to communicate except with signs to either of her friends, Jesse longed for Rides the Wind to return. In his absence, she read the small Bible by the hour, searching for passages that would have meaning to him. She wondered about his ability to comprehend the old language of the Bible, and despaired of her own abilities to explain anything.

She prayed, asking the Lord to guide her to the right words, asking for patience with the unkind women of the village, *and please, Lord,* she added each time she prayed, *please help me not to be so stupid and slow about all the new things I must learn. Help me to understand what they say and to imitate what they do so that I can serve while I am here.* She knew that she would be leaving as soon as Two Mothers no longer needed her, but she was eager to fit in until that time.

Just how much there was to learn became apparent two days later when the village suddenly became a hive of activity. Women shouted, children screeched, dogs barked, and everyone hurried about as tepees were brought down, fires doused, and things packed up. Old One somehow made Jesse understand that the activity had something to do with food, but Jesse remained ignorant, fumbling about and getting in the way until finally even Old One grew frustrated and forced her to sit on a travois and hold Two Mothers.

Chapter 8

> . . . I have learned, in whatsoever
> state I am, therewith to be content.
> *Philippians 4:11*

The women and children streamed out of camp. As soon as Old One had everything packed, she motioned to Jesse to take hold of the horse's jaw strap and lead it along. Jesse recoiled in fear. Old One insisted, strapping Two Mothers' cradle board to the side of the animal where the child could watch the activity around him.

Still, Jesse hesitated. At last Old One grabbed the jaw strap herself and, in disgust, started out across the prairie. Jesse followed along, humiliated, but unable to overcome the fear she had always had of horses.

They had walked only a few miles when they came to the site of the buffalo hunt. Old One unloaded the travois and began to re-erect the tepee. First, she took the four longest poles, laid them on the ground, and tied them with a leather strap. With Jesse's help, she raised the four poles and spread their ends apart. The framework for the tepee formed, the two women added more poles, completing a circular framework. Old One showed Jesse how to order the process so that the poles would lock into one another. When the poles were set, Old One brought out the tepee cover. It had been folded so that it was easy to lash its middle to the last pole by straps sewn along the length of the cover. Once this was done, Jesse and Old One lifted the last pole and set it in place. They each took a fold of the cover and walked about the framework of poles, meeting where the door opening would be. Above the opening, the edges of the cover were fastened together. Finally, a stake was thrust through a loop at the edge of each side of the doorway and into the ground.

Jesse stepped back to survey their handiwork. Old One patted her on the shoulder and smiled encouragement. They both took the buffalo skins that served as their bedrolls inside, prepared a fire pit, arranged Rides the Wind's parfleche and their few other belongings and were soon ready to join Rides the Wind at the side of his freshly killed buffalo.

Jesse stood helplessly by, ignorant of what she might do to help. At one point, Old One motioned to her and laughed. Rides the Wind turned his face away, but Jesse caught the expression of disbelief on his face.

Rides the Wind skinned the buffalo, but not until he had cut open its side and, reaching in, removed the beast's liver and, to Jesse's horror, bit into it with relish. He offered her a bite, but she shook her head and turned away. He shrugged and continued his treat before finishing carving up the buffalo, placing each piece of meat on the hide. Once the job was completed, he caught up the four corners of the hide and used it as a sack with which to carry his catch back to camp.

Running ahead to the village, Jesse hurried inside the tepee. Eager to be of help, she had decided that she would start the first fire. She had watched Old One do so several times, and although Old One used sticks instead of the flint and iron Jesse had used on the trail, she still felt confident that she could accomplish this "simple" task.

Looking around for the long case that held the firesticks, Jesse emptied its contents. Laying the narrow cedar splint on the ground, she held it firmly in place with one foot. Taking up the small bow, she wound the firestick in its strong sinew and placed one end of the stick on the cedar splint. With her left hand she placed a hollowed-out rock on top of the firestick and began to saw with the bow, intending to spin the firestick as she had seen Old One do. With the first movement of the bow, her hand bobbled, the stick was dislodged from the indentation in the rock and flipped into the air.

Jesse repeated the steps again, changing the way the firestick was wound into the sinew. It stayed in place—until her hand wobbled and the stick again came out of the indentation in the rock.

Patiently, she set up the paraphernalia again. This time, as she sawed with the bow, everything stayed in place, but the fringe on the hem of her dress became entangled in the sinew. She gasped with impatience. Something made her turn around. Several of the village women were watching through the tent opening. They giggled, pointed at her, and talked among themselves.

Jesse's face flushed red with anger and embarrassment. She tossed the firesticks aside and turned to face them, but they were gone, scurrying away as Rides the Wind set his load of buffalo meat down outside the door. Jesse sat in the dust, the firesticks at her side, fighting back tears. She looked up angrily, picked up the sticks and handed them over.

"I wanted to help—but I don't know how." Her voice was miserable.

Rides the Wind took the sticks and patiently demonstrated the art of making a fire. As he worked, she asked, "What were they saying?"

Rides the Wind shrugged and ignored her.

"I want to know." She was kneeling next to him, trying to work the sticks as he had shown her.

Reaching over to steady the hand that held the rock, Rides the Wind said slowly, "The women gave you a name."

"I have a name. My name is Jesse King."

"That is not Lakota. It means nothing."

"Then what name do they give me?"

"Woman Who Makes No Fire." Jesse flinched and turned away to hide the tears that threatened to spill over.

Rides the Wind offered no comfort. He continued to demonstrate the starting of the fire. Jesse sawed the little bow back and forth rapidly, angrily, and the force of her anger brought success. A tiny, glowing coal was finally created at the base of the cedar splint. Rides the Wind deftly tossed it into the tinder in the fire pit and blew on it steadily to encourage the flame to grow. In a few moments, smoke rose from the tepee's opening.

The village women observed the smoke, but they did not change Jesse's name. A few of the more eligible young women wondered how long it would be before Rides the Wind realized his mistake and returned the clumsy woman to her own kind.

Yellow Bird said it aloud. "The child does not need her. I would feed him buffalo soup and cherry juice. He would grow strong. He needs a mother from the people, not this woman who will teach him strange ways."

Prairie Flower surprised herself by defending Jesse. "If Rides the Wind had wanted a woman from the village, he could have had one. Many hoped he would wrap his buffalo robe about them. He did not. It is our custom to be kind to the weak. We should help her if she wants to learn our ways. You have seen that she tries to learn. She cares well for the child of Dancing Waters and Rides the Wind. I have seen her tears for her own child." Prairie Flower took a breath and looked at Yellow Bird as she added, "Think how it would be if *you* were among the *whites,* Yellow Bird!"

Yellow Bird retorted, "Rides the Wind has *not* wrapped her in his robe. There has been no feast. She is *not* his wife! She is only a slave. And, Prairie Flower," she added hotly, "I would *die* before I would stay with a strange people!"

Prairie Flower demurred. "I do not know why she stays. Perhaps Rides the Wind will not let her go. Perhaps she has nowhere else to go. She does not seem to care for him. But she stays. If she wants to learn our ways, I will help her."

Yellow Bird and her friends were already walking away from Prairie Flower, hurrying to their own tepees to begin the work of butchering and cooking their own kills. Prairie

Flower's defense ended abruptly as Howling Wolf pulled her away, scolding her for neglecting to erect the frame over their fire to cook their buffalo meat. He had erected the frame himself and brought in the small buffalo's paunch. Filled with water, the paunch was hung on the frame over the fire. Soon, hot rocks and meat were added and allowed to boil.

While some of their meat boiled, Old One showed Jesse how to cut other meat into thin strips, which were hung on a large frame to dry in the sun. Pointing to the drying meat, she said, *"papa"* and Jesse repeated the word. Later in the day, they pounded thin-cut meat with marrow and choke-cherries. *"Wakapapi,"* Old One called it. Jesse was surprised to find that she liked it.

That night there was a huge feast. Dancing and singing ran late into the night. Jesse watched as Rides the Wind sat among his friends, telling some story of the day's hunt, his hands waving the air as he re-created a scene for them all.

Howling Wolf sat at the edge of the group, listening in stony silence. When the group joked about the size of Rides the Wind's kill compared to his, Howling Wolf rose stiffly and stalked away without a word. When Rides the Wind protested and went after him, Howling Wolf refused the hand of friendship.

Still, there was great happiness in the village, and they all ate until they could eat no more. Jesse watched the dancing with lively interest. Dressed in their finest dresses, the women stood about the edge of the fire, hopping about slowly from left to right, then right to left. Each dancer stepped out with her left foot and then dragged the right to meet it, then the direction was reversed. Drums played by the men seated in a circle inside the dancers provided the rhythm for the dance.

She saw Old One with a band of crones and Prairie Flower smiling softly at a friend's whispered secrets. Quietly, she slipped away from the campfire to the tepee of Rides the Wind. Two Mothers slept, but she scooped him up anyway. When Rides the Wind missed her and left the celebration to search, he found her sleeping soundly, Two Mothers' tiny head nestled in the crook of her arm.

∾

In the days that followed, Jesse learned that nearly all of the buffalo would be used by the Lakota. Horns were made into ladles and cups, hair from the scraped hides was collected and used to stuff pillows. The ribs were kept for the children to use in games, and Old One claimed the bladder as a pouch for storing some of her precious herbs.

Tanning the hide took all of Jesse's strength. First, the skin was stretched on a large frame and allowed to dry in the sun. Once their hides were dry, the women began fleshing them, scraping fat and tissue away with an elkhorn scraper. Jesse worked hard, ignoring the aching shoulder muscles that complained about the new workout. The first scraping done, the skin was left to dry again, and in a few hours became stiff, dry rawhide. Still more scraping was needed to remove the hair from the hides.

Jesse inwardly recoiled from the next step in the tanning process, but she tried not to show it. Buffalo brains were cooked and, when cooled, spread over the skin until it was totally covered with the paste. Then, round, smooth stones were used to work the mixture into the skin. Finally, everything was covered with the broth that the brains had been cooked in and allowed to age for the rest of the day. The hides were then soaked in a mixture of water and pounded yucca roots. They took on a sweet smell. Remounted on their frames, the hides were stretched again and the water was worked out.

At Old One's instruction, Jesse stretched and worked the hide over and over. Her shoulders and arms ached and she panted with the effort, but still Old One instructed her to continue working the hide. Finally, the two women pulled and stretched the drying hide over a braided buffalo sinew rope that had been attached to a tree limb high off the ground and stretched to a stake that had been pounded deep into the ground. The two women pulled and tugged with all their might as the hide was drying. To Jesse's amazement, when it was finally dry, it was as soft as velvet.

At last, Rides the Wind took the softened hide and staked it over a slow-burning fire. As it was smoked, the hide turned a soft brown color. He explained to Jesse that smoking would keep the hide soft it if got wet.

Jesse helped Prairie Flower sew many hides together, using the long tendons from the buffalo's back as "thread." Howling Wolf smiled at the prospect of a new tepee and set to work decorating the outside with skillfully drawn pictographs. Jesse was amazed by his artistic ability, and her opinion of him softened as the beauty of the tepee grew. *Surely there must be a good side to a man who has such artistic abilities.*

Jesse watched and learned as the women of the village transformed their buffalo hides into tepee covers, moccasin tops, dresses, leggings, and cradles. Feathers, porcupine quills, and dyes made from berries or roots were constantly in view as the women worked to create beautiful things for their families. Rawhide provided moccasin soles and parfleche boxes for storage. As they worked they sometimes roasted a large buffalo bone over a cottonwood bark fire. Every few minutes, someone would turn the bone so that it would cook evenly and thoroughly. When it was done, the women cracked the bone and ate the brown, tasty marrow.

One morning Prairie Flower signed that Jesse should begin a pair of moccasins. Jesse nodded her agreement and became a willing student. However, when time came to decorate the moccasins, she quickly displayed her own artistic skills, wielding the awl easily and creating an intricate beadwork design for Prairie Flower to admire.

When the moccasins were at last ready, Prairie Flower smiled coyly and suggested that Jesse give them to Old One. Old One accepted the gift with a warm smile and kind words.

Pointing at Jesse that night when Rides the Wind had joined them, she showed him the moccasins, and motioned for him to translate what she said.

"Among the people, it is the custom for a new wife to make moccasins for the husband's mother. When the mother accepts the gift, she welcomes the new wife into the family."

Jesse blushed at the message her innocent gift had sent to the old woman. Rides the Wind watched Jesse carefully as he concluded, "My mother accepts the gift you have given. She says that she welcomes you as my wife."

His dark eyes met hers briefly, but then he picked up Two Mothers and said, "My son and I will say good night to Sun, now." Jesse was left behind to watch as Old One donned her new moccasins, clucking her appreciation.

As the days went by, it became a habit for Rides the Wind to seat himself next to Jesse outside the tepee just at sunset. Holding Two Mothers, he would demand that she read from the "God book."

Jesse struggled to know just what to read, until Rides the Wind solved the problem. One evening, as the village women looked on and smiled knowingly at one another, Jesse thumbed the pages of the Bible. Rides the Wind covered her hand with his own.

"Is not *all* of it from God?"

Jesse answered, "Yes, it is all from God."

"Then you tell it all."

So Jesse began reading, *"In the beginning God created the heaven and the earth."*

Rides the Wind listened attentively. Jesse had no way of knowing what he did and did not understand, for he never interrupted her. Obediently, she read until he would stand up abruptly and say, "It is enough."

Then he would hand over Two Mothers, return the Bible to his parfleche, and leave to check on his horses. He rarely returned to the tepee until long after Jesse was asleep.

Chapter 9

He paweth in the valley, and re-
joiceth in his strength. . . . He
mocketh at fear.

Job 39:21–22

Jesse was almost asleep one evening a few weeks
later when Rides the Wind entered the tepee, sat
beside her, and asked abruptly, "Why do you fear horses?"

When she did not answer, he said, "Old One's horse is a
kind and gentle pony. Old One says you fear her. Why do
you fear?"

Jesse remembered Old One's laughter as she and her son
had butchered the buffalo. She remembered the look of
disbelief on Rides the Wind's face.

"Has a horse ever hurt you?" he asked.

"No."

"Your family?"

Jesse shook her head and said, "I have always been
afraid—for no reason." She shrugged her shoulders, feeling
stupid for her groundless fears.

The Indian searched her face, trying to understand. Whatever he saw there, he said no more, but retreated to his own
buffalo robe. Turning his back to her, he seemed to fall
instantly asleep.

Jesse had just finished feeding Two Mothers the next
morning when Rides the Wind came into the tent, took her
hand, and led her outside. They walked quickly along the
edge of the camp. Rides the Wind seemed to be trying to
avoid being noticed. Jesse followed unquestioningly, her

curiosity piqued by his unusual behavior. They were headed away from the camp. Tall grasses waved in the morning sun.

Once, Rides the Wind crouched down quickly, pulling Jesse down beside him. He pointed toward a hill in the distance, calling her attention to several elk, grazing undisturbed. He whispered, "Soon I will bring you fine elk skins."

But Rides the Wind was not intent on hunting today. A few hundred yards across the prairie from them stood the objects of his interest. His own horse was grazing peacefully, and not far from him was a lovely little mare. Jesse didn't know to admire the breadth of her chest, the angle of her hocks, or the smallness of her feet, all of which combined to make this pony a dependable, swift mount. Jesse did, however, notice the flowing red mane and tail, made all the brighter by the contrasting white spots that spread across the mare's stout neck and back in an intricate pattern. A dark red star nearly hidden by her forelock explained the pony's name.

Rides the Wind whistled, a low sound that gradually rose in pitch until the horses lifted their heads and started toward him. Seeing Jesse, the two ponies stopped a few paces away and watched Rides the Wind. When he didn't move, they dropped their heads to graze again. Holding Jesse's hand, he approached the two horses. He felt Jesse stiffen nervously.

"You have fear because you do not understand how the horse thinks. I will teach you. Your fear will go." He added solemnly, "The women in the village will not laugh."

Taking two jaw straps from the leather pouch at his side, Rides the Wind handed one to Jesse, demonstrating how it was to be held. Quietly he walked to his own horse's side, lifted the pony's head, and put the jaw strap on. The pony danced a bit in anticipation of a morning run. Jesse grew more tense.

"Wind is a hunter's horse," Rides the Wind explained. "He is swift and ready to do what his rider desires. He dances for the joy of the run, not because he wishes to hurt you. We are friends, he and I. Soon Red Star will be your friend too."

Jesse tried to quiet her fears and walked up to the mare. To her amazement, Red Star willingly lifted her head from the grass and stood quietly while Jesse fumbled with the jaw strap. Rides the Wind had bridled Wind in one quick motion. It took Jesse several attempts before she successfully slipped the noose over Red Star's lower jaw and up over her neck. Through all the clumsiness, though, the mare stood quietly.

Jesse relaxed. Red Star turned her head toward Wind, staring at him when he snorted and pawed the ground. Jesse wondered if she were saying, "Calm down, you fool. Don't you see this woman is nervous?"

Jesse reached up to pat Red Star's neck. To her delight, the mare curved her head around Jesse's arm. Jesse beamed with pleasure, and Rides the Wind said, "She is a wise horse. She tells you not to be afraid. She says, 'Let us be friends.'"

Rides the Wind demonstrated how to mount bareback. Red Star stood quietly while Jesse tried to spring up onto her back. Jesse succeeded after several tries.

Riding lessons began. Mounting Wind, Rides the Wind took Jesse's reins in his own hands, explaining, "I will lead her. You must learn to feel her move. Feel her turn." Jesse concentrated on Red Star's movement as Rides the Wind led them in a wide circle.

"See how she moves in this way," he said, and they made a second wide circle in the opposite direction. For nearly an hour, Rides the Wind led Red Star about, instructing Jesse to grip her pony with her knees, explaining how to apply pressure against the mare's sides to signal her to turn.

Finally, Rides the Wind dismounted, handed Jesse the reins to her own mount, and ordered her to ride away from him, guiding the mare only with leg pressure. To Jesse's dismay, Red Star did not seem to understand anything. Try as she would, Jesse could not get the mare to go where she wanted. Signaling a turn in one direction, she would be dismayed to see the head turn the opposite way.

Ordering a halt, Jesse began again. Again, the mare turned in exactly the opposite direction. Jesse's frustration mounted as Red Star continued to display what seemed to be a very stubborn temperament. Signaling the mare to stop, she succeeded only in having her back up. Trying to get the mare to turn left, she was helpless as they began a wide circle to the right. Finally, anger won out. "Turn *right*, you stupid horse, *right!*" Jesse shouted, kicking the mare's flanks.

Red Star obeyed the kick and jumped ahead to a canter. Jesse was dumped into the dust. The moment she felt Jesse leave her back, Red Star stopped, dropped her head, and began to graze.

Rides the Wind ran to Jesse. She sat, her forehead on her knees. "You are hurt?" he asked, concern in his voice.

She lifted her head, and he saw tears on her cheeks. "No!" she exclaimed.

"Then you must try again."

Jesse's shoulders stiffened, and she stood up slowly. Anger blazed in her eyes. "I *hate* horses!" she shouted. "I hate horses, and I *can't* learn to ride!" She turned to stride away. He laid a hand upon her shoulder and insisted.

"You must try again." Then, more kindly, he added, "You can learn. Try again."

Jesse began to cry. Rides the Wind folded his arms and waited for her to stop. At last she lifted her head. Staring at the distant horizon, she vented the frustration of the last few weeks.

"I am so helpless," she moaned. "I cannot cook without help from Old One. I cannot find food without Prairie Flower. I cannot raise the tepee. Everything is hard. Everything is new. I am treated like a child, and they are right. I am a child. I know nothing of your ways. I cannot even talk, because I do not know your language. Old One must teach me how to cook. And you must teach me to ride a horse so that I do not shame you. I am *tired* of being stupid!" Her voice trembled as tears threatened to come again.

Rides the Wind gripped her shoulders hard and spoke slowly. "It is true, you have much to learn. But if you wish it, you will learn. You will learn to ride and to cook and to speak my language. I will learn about God as you read the book to me." He added, "Two Mothers will call you *Ina*—'mother' in your tongue. If you want to be part of my people, get back on Red Star and learn to ride."

Jesse looked into the stern, dark eyes. The feathers that hung from his braids moved in the breeze. He dropped his hands from her arms without dropping his eyes from hers.

Jesse got back on Red Star. At last, a few turns were successfully executed. When her legs ached until she thought she could stand no more, Rides the Wind came alongside. "It is enough." He ordered her to dismount and to return to the village on foot. "We need no watching eyes while you learn."

Jesse nodded obediently and headed back to the village. She picked a few flowers along the way, hoping that the bouquet would explain the reason for her early morning walk. A few women made comments as she walked by, and for once Jesse was glad that she didn't understand.

When she entered the tepee, Old One chuckled and invited Jesse to rest her tired legs by sitting near her.

Jesse wondered, *How is it, Old One, that you always know my secrets?* She gestured until Old One understood. Old One grinned broadly, revealing the spaces left by two missing teeth. Wrinkling her nose, she made Jesse understand that she smelled of horses. The two women laughed together and shared the first of many secrets.

❧

During the days that followed, Jesse and Rides the Wind left camp early every morning. Jesse learned to ride and found that her young muscles adapted quickly and the soreness soon disappeared. She did not notice when the change occurred, but one morning she suddenly realized that the approach of the great animals no longer inspired uneasiness on her part. Rather, she eagerly anticipated the morning lessons. Whether it was the male or the animal companionship that she enjoyed, she did not think through.

One special morning, Red Star raised her head and nickered a welcome. It was a soft, low rumble, and it barely reached her across the prairie for the morning was unusually windy. But at the sound, Rides the Wind said, "Now you are friends. Red Star welcomes you." At the sound of his voice, Wind jerked his head up from grazing, tossed his head, and trumpeted a spirited welcome.

That day as Jesse cantered Red Star smoothly in a wide circle about him, Rides the Wind said, "You have gained the friendship of your horse. Watch her ears. She will tell you what she sees or hears or smells. You must ride every day until you know what she is telling you. Always watch for the things that might frighten her. She has one way to protect herself— that is to run away. Do not fear. Understand."

Rides the Wind was standing on the prairie as he talked. Suddenly, he gave a piercing whistle. Wind came running to him, mane and tail flying. Jesse watched in admiration as Rides the Wind took a few running steps, grasped Wind's mane, and sprung into the air. Lifted by the motion of his running horse, Rides the Wind was carried onto his pony's back. The pony shot away from Jesse and Red Star, his body stretching out as his hooves pounded along the ground.

Rider and pony worked together smoothly, until Wind made a quick turn, and Rides the Wind disappeared from view. Wind turned quickly again, revealing his rider clinging to his side, one hand twisted in the flowing mane, the tip of one foot hooked over the pony's back.

As the two raced past Jesse, Rides the Wind righted himself again, only to slip to the other side. Wind wheeled about abruptly and ran toward Jesse, halting only a few feet away from where she sat astride Red Star.

Rides the Wind caught his breath and held Wind in with a tight rein as he cautioned Jesse, "Know what you can do. Know what you cannot. Then you will do what is best for you and your pony."

They rode back to camp that morning, Jesse trotting Red Star alongside Wind. As they paraded through the middle of camp, she thoroughly enjoyed the stares of disbelief from the women. She glanced at Rides the Wind. He caught her eye. She thought she saw a faint glimmer of a smile.

Is he proud of me? she wondered. She dismissed the thought, reminding herself that she was, after all, only a convenience brought into camp to feed his baby and read the book he was curious about.

They stopped outside the tepee of Rides the Wind. As they dismounted, Prairie Flower ran up and patted her arm, chattering and smiling encouragement. She demanded that Rides the Wind translate.

With no expression he said, "The woman says that you have been given my favorite mare."

Jesse looked up at him. "Is this true?"

Rides the Wind shrugged, "Red Star is a good mare. Whether she is my favorite, I cannot say." Before Jesse could thank him, he took Red Star's reins from her and walked away, turning his broad back to the group of women who giggled and pointed at them both.

Chapter 10

... our God whom we serve is able to deliver us from the burning fiery furnace.

Daniel 3:17

As the weeks passed, Jesse grew to understand more of the people's ways. She learned to think of them as Lakota rather than Indians. Their language took on a familiar cadence, and she found herself mimicking the sounds when she was alone. She obediently repeated whatever words Old One taught, and remembered many, but her innate shyness precluded her trying to say much on her own. She learned to understand a great deal more than she could say.

If they knew how much of what they say I understand, she thought, *they would not be so cruel.* She wanted to believe it, and yet she wondered. Open taunts had decreased since Rides the Wind had given her Red Star. However, at Jesse's first attempts to speak with them they began to laugh. Only Prairie Flower and Old One were truly kind. Jesse grew to love them, and consoled herself with their growing friendship.

Two Mothers began to coo and grin at sight of her. She continued to read the Bible to Rides the Wind. He was kind and patient. On days when he did not hunt, he willingly took care of Two Mothers, proudly carrying the growing boy through the camp. Jesse saw that Rides the Wind was respected by his people. She also noticed the hungry eyes of a few single young women when he turned his broad back and limped away. Had it not been for the crooked leg, Rides the

Wind would have been much desired by the young women of his tribe.

The summer had grown hot and dry, and camp moved again, seeking fresh water and grazing for the considerable herd of ponies owned by the band. Jesse was glad for the shade of the tepee. Her fair skin burned and peeled and burned again until she despaired of its roughness. Old One gathered a plant that she instructed Jesse to chew, forming a paste to spread over the rough, inflamed skin. It helped, but Jesse continued to seek the shelter of the tepee whenever possible. Anxious not to appear lazy, she worked hard to soften the hides of the buffalo Rides the Wind had killed. She worked at it by the hour until even Old One ordered her to stop before she wore the skin out.

"But Old One, I know *nothing*. I do nothing. People call me *wagluhe*." Jesse flinched at the thought of how broken the language was, how infantile she must sound.

Old One understood and, handing Jesse a sewing awl, demonstrated how to stitch skins together.

Jesse was working on her sewing project one morning when she heard concerned voices outside her tepee. Prairie Flower rushed in and pulled her outside to view the horizon. What she saw made Jesse clasp Prairie Flower's hand in her own and cry out in fear.

Billowing black smoke leaped into the sky and rushed toward them. The alarm was sounded. Older boys rounded up the grazing ponies to herd them across the creek. The ponies, frightened by the scent of burning grass, fled willingly, and the boys scuttled back to help move the camp.

Hastily the women gathered up what belongings they could before heading for the creek. Jesse snatched up Two Mothers. Giving him to Old One, she motioned for her to run toward the water, and she rushed back into the tepee. She grabbed Rides the Wind's parfleche and ran out. Already, they could see flames roaring across the prairie toward them.

Ahead, the women were wading across the creek, some carrying buffalo robes, others empty-handed. Jesse looked across and located Old One and Two Mothers, already safe on the opposite bank. Holding the parfleche high, she splashed across and dropped to the earth beside Old One, gasping for breath and hugging Two Mothers. The scent of the burning prairie filled her nostrils and stung her throat.

Then, from the crowd of women came a shriek. A young squaw Jesse knew as Rain rose and held up her hands to the sky in disbelief. Oblivious to the inferno behind him, her child sat on the opposite hill, sorting pebbles from a carefully arranged pile beside him.

It was Hears Not. He had straggled behind the group, and Rain, occupied with her twin infants, had failed to notice when the toddler let go of her dress. Now he sat, unaware of the flames that had already begun to lick at the knoll above him.

Suddenly the wind shifted, sending a blast of smoke and heat swirling about him. He looked about and in one motion was on his feet. His young face worked with effort as he tried to control the impulse to cry out in terror. Already, the value of bravery had been impressed upon his young mind. Eyes wide, he started for the creek bank, looking for a way across. His mother, overcome by fear, could only stand with arms raised to the sky, wailing his name over and over again.

Jesse never remembered dumping Two Mothers onto the grass, nor did she recall plunging across the creek, but suddenly she was running up the hill toward Hears Not. Thick smoke burned her throat. The stench of burning hair filled her nostrils, but still she ran on. Finally she reached Hears Not and, sweeping him into her arms, she hunched over to protect him as much as possible. The flames were at them now, as she ran toward the creek. She was aware of a searing pain across her shoulders.

Hands reached out to take Hears Not, and Jesse sank down onto the prairie, unaware of the buffalo robe that was thrown across her to put out the flames that had consumed the back of her dress.

And now Jesse lived in a new world. She heard her own cries echoing down the long dark tunnel of pain. It engulfed her and carried her along until she felt she was drowning in it. Then, just as she did drown, she mercifully fainted. But in the agony there was something else—quiet voices and tender hands, singing, and the sound of rattles, and then pain again as something foul smelling was smeared on her burned shoulders.

Over and over she heard the voice of Medicine Hawk chanting the song of the sun:

> *Wanka tan han he ya u we lo*
> *Wanka tan han he ya u we lo*
> *Mita wi cohan topa wan la*
> *Ka nu we he ya u we lo*
> *Anpe wi kin he ya u we lo*
> *A ye ye ye yo*

She lay in agony for days, and while she struggled to come out of the tunnel of her pain, Old One lovingly tended her. Medicine Hawk came to invoke his gods to heal this brave woman who had saved a child. The women in the village took care of Two Mothers. And Rides the Wind hunted with savage energy, killing buffalo for a new tepee. Returning late each day to the camp, he crouched by Jesse's writhing form and watched as Old One tended the wounds. He brought fresh water to Jesse's lips and held her head in his hand as she drank. And he prayed to his God to heal this woman.

When the day came at last that he knew she would live, Rides the Wind rode out at dawn to thank his God. Raising his arms to the sky, he shouted his joy and sang the words she had first read to him from the holy book. He called for the village herald to announce a feast of celebration. When he returned, Jesse was sitting upright, her hands fingering the exquisite beadwork on a pair of moccasins in her lap. She looked up and smiled weakly, explaining "from Rain."

Rides the Wind nodded and said, "You danced with death for Hears Not."

"I only remember his terrified eyes. Then we were in the fire." Jesse flinched as she reached out to take the drink he offered her. "Where is Two Mothers . . . how long?"

"The sun has set ten times since the fire. Two Mothers is well. Another tepee will be his home until you are able to tend the fire."

Rides the Wind abruptly ended the conversation, rising to leave. He was at the tepee's opening when he heard a low cry. Turning he watched as Jesse felt about the singed frill on her scalp. Her eyes filled with tears as she moaned, "My hair . . ."

Rides the Wind walked back across the tepee. Kneeling before her, he cupped her chin in his hand and raised her face so that their eyes met. "It will grow again. Until then, hold your head high, for all to see that Walks the Fire has given much to become one of our people."

"Walks the Fire?"

"You have earned a new name among the people."

The words were spoken tenderly, and Jesse's heart lurched as she watched the powerful form go to the opening of the tepee. He bent to leave and then turned back a moment. The sunlight fell across his face, lighting one bronzed cheek and one dark braid. A gentle breeze stirred the eagle feathers dangling from his hair. But Rides the Wind said nothing, and in one silent movement he was gone.

Chapter 11

. . . Entreat me not to leave thee, or
to return from following after thee.
Ruth 1:16

Prairie Flower was the bearer of the news. When
she said it, Jesse stared in disbelief. Prairie Flower
repeated it, wondering if Jesse had understood.

Jesse denied it. "He does not care for me. He brought me
to the village to feed his child."

"He gave you Red Star."

Jesse denied its significance. "That was only so that I would
not shame him."

"He brought many skins for a new tepee. He brought you
elk skins for a new dress."

Jesse explained. "We needed those things because of the
fire. All of the people needed new tepees, new clothing."

"He sits with you every evening outside the tepee."

"That is so I can read from the Book."

Prairie Flower grew impatient. "Walks the Fire! I tell you
truth. Rides the Wind wishes you to be his wife. You know
nothing of Lakota ways. I will tell you!"

Jesse started to protest, but Prairie Flower interrupted. "No!
You listen! When a man wishes to show he wants a woman, he
dresses in his finest clothing and comes to her outside her
tepee. They sit and talk. He gives gifts to her parents. Not every
custom is followed, because you are not a young Lakota woman.
But I tell you, Rides the Wind cares for you.

"After the fire, when Medicine Hawk came—when you
were as one dying—you did not see him. *I* saw him. Rides the

Wind did not eat. He did not sleep. He thought only of Walks the Fire. He hunted healing herbs. He hunted the elk for your dress. He took Two Mothers to Yellow Bird's tepee so that his cries would not disturb your rest. He trusted no one but Old One, and himself, and me to care for you."

Jesse hid her face by drawing up her legs and bowing her head low so that her forehead rested on her knees.

Finally, she whispered, so quietly that Prairie Flower almost could not hear the words, "You are my friend, Prairie Flower. If I tell you what is in my heart, will you promise never to tell?"

Prairie Flower laid a hand on Jesse's shoulder, pulling it away quickly when her friend flinched in pain. "I will not betray my friend."

Taking a deep breath, Jesse lifted her head. "When Rides the Wind comes near to me, my heart sings. But I do not believe that he cares for me. I am clumsy in all of the things a Lakota woman must know. I cannot speak his language without many childish mistakes. And . . ." Jesse reached up to lay her hand on her short hair, "I am nothing to look at. I am not . . ."

Prairie Flower grew angry. "I have *told* you he cares for you. Can you not see it?"

Jesse shook her head.

Prairie Flower spoke the unspeakable. "Then, if you cannot see that he cares for you in what he *does,* you must see it in what he *has not done.* You have been in his tepee. Dancing Waters has been gone many moons."

"Stop!" Jesse demanded. "Stop it! I . . . just don't say any more!" She leaped up and ran out of the tepee—and into Rides the Wind, who was returning from the river where he had gone to draw water.

Jesse knocked the water skins from both of his hands. Water spilled out and she fumbled an apology then bent stiffly to pick up the skins, wincing with the effort.

"I will do it, Walks the Fire." His voice was tender as he bent and took the skins from her.

Jesse protested, "It is the wife's job." She blushed, realizing that she had used a wrong word—the word for *wife,* instead of the word for *woman.*

Rides the Wind interrupted before she could correct herself. "Walks the Fire is not the wife of Rides the Wind."

Jesse blushed and remained quiet. A hand reached for hers and Rides the Wind said, "Come, sit." He helped her sit down just outside the door of the tepee. The village women took note as he went inside and brought out a buffalo robe. Sitting by Jesse, he placed the robe on the ground and began to talk.

"I will tell you how it is with the Lakota. When a man wishes to take a wife . . . " he described Lakota courtship. As he talked, Jesse realized that all that Prairie Flower had said seemed to be true. He had, indeed, done nearly everything involved in the courtship ritual.

Still, she told herself, *there is a perfectly good explanation for everything he has done.*

Rides the Wind continued describing the wedding feast. Jesse continued to reason with herself as he spoke. Then she realized the voice had stopped and he had repeated a question.

"How is it among the whites? How does a man gain a wife?"

Embarrassed, Jesse described the sparsest of courtships, the simplest wedding. Rides the Wind listened attentively. When she had finished, he said, "There is one thing the Lakota brave who wishes a wife does that I have not described." Pulling Jesse to her feet, he continued, "One evening, as he walks with his woman . . . " He reached out to pick up the buffalo robe. He was aware that the village women were watching carefully.

"He spreads out his arms . . ." Rides the Wind spread his arms, opening the buffalo robe to its full length, "and wraps it about his woman," Rides the Wind turned toward Jesse and reached around her,"so that they are both inside the buffalo robe." He looked down at Jesse, trying to read her expression. When he saw nothing in the gray eyes, he abruptly dropped his arms.

"But it is hot today and your wounds have not healed. I have said enough. You see how it is with the Lakota."

When Jesse still said nothing, he continued, "You spoke of a celebration with a min-is-ter. It is a word I do not know. What is this min-is-ter?"

"A man who believes in the Bible and teaches his people about God from the Bible."

"What if there is no minister and a man and a woman wish to be married?"

Jesse grew more uncomfortable. "I suppose they would wait until a minister came."

Rides the Wind insisted. "What if a minister did not come?"

"I don't know. I never thought about it."

Rides the Wind went inside the tepee and brought out the Bible. "Read what God says about man and wife."

They sat down again and Jesse read every passage she could find while he listened.

"I hear nothing of min-is-ter."

She grew defensive. "No—but—God says to obey the way of the people. Among the whites, the way of the people is with a minister."

Rides the Wind took the Bible from Jesse's hands and held it as he said, earnestly, "You live among the Lakota now. Would God say you cannot be a wife without a minister?" He answered his own question. "I think God would say a man and a woman were made to be one. I think God would find a way without a minister."

Rides the Wind abruptly tossed the Bible and the buffalo robe inside the tepee, grabbed the water skins, and strode toward the creek.

Yellow Bird saw and smiled to herself hopefully.

Old One heard and clucked with regret.

Prairie Flower saw and sighed in exasperation.

Jesse watched him walk away with a singing heart. *He cares for me . . . He cares for me . . . Prairie Flower was right . . . He cares!*

Several evenings later after the fire burned low, Jesse lay awake, trying to sort her muddled emotions. Two Mothers had returned to their tepee and he slept beside her, his breath sounding a rhythmic whistle. Through the hole at the top of the tepee Jesse could see the stars. A psalm came to mind. *"When I consider thy heavens, the work of thy fingers . . . what is man, that thou art mindful of him?"*

Indeed, Lord, she thought, *what am I that you should think of me? Yet you have always been there for me. When little Jacob died, you gave me comfort through Homer. And when I felt that I had lost everything, you put me in the tepee of Rides the Wind. Truly, Lord, you have cared for me, but in such unexpected ways! And now, Lord, what am I to do? There is no minister, there will never be. Is there some way?*

Jesse raised up on one elbow to look into the face of the sleeping child. He was different from the child she had yearned for, and yet his existence had, in many ways, given her back her sanity and her faith in a loving God. *Surely, Lord, there is a way.*

From across the tepee she sensed the presence of Rides the Wind. His actions had proven that he cared for her. Now, as she lay in his tepee, she realized that she felt at home. *Adam and Eve had no minister, Lord. If I read from your Word—if we shared vows—could you not bless us, Lord?*

Quietly she padded across the darkened interior of the tepee toward Rides the Wind. The embers of the fire cast her shadow on the skins of the hide walls. Her foot inadvertently kicked his parfleche. Rides the Wind was instantly on his feet, knife in hand, a cry of warning in his throat. It died there as he gazed into Jesse's eyes. She smiled stupidly and shrugged her shoulders in embarrassment.

From across the tepee Two Mothers whimpered a moment, then quieted. Flames blazed up from the fire to light the interior. Still, Rides the Wind gazed at Jesse.

In a rush she realized that a chance for unspeakable happiness stood before her. Inspired words came to mind,

And the Lord God said, It is not good that the man should be alone; I will make him an help meet fit for him. . . . And the Lord God . . . made . . . a woman, and brought her unto the man. . . . Therefore shall a man leave his father and his mother, and shall cleave unto his wife, and they shall be one flesh.

As the words sounded in Jesse's heart, uncertainty fell away. She whispered to Rides the Wind. "I think that if there is no minister, God would understand. As long as he is part of the celebration. As long as everyone knows that the man and the woman promise for life—to be joined—in his name."

Moving closer to him she leaned against his chest. His heartbeat quickened as they stood together. His skin was warm. He put one arm about her waist and stroked her short hair. Reaching down to pick up his own buffalo robe, Rides the Wind wrapped her in it and held her close, whispering, "We will find a way to please God, Walks the Fire."

Abruptly he dropped the buffalo robe and backed away.

"I cannot stay here longer tonight." He grabbed his weapons and fled outside.

The next morning the entire village woke to see Rides the Wind leading Red Star toward his tepee. The mare's mane and tail had been braided and about her neck was a garland of sunflowers.

Prairie Flower ran quickly across the compound, a white bundle clutched in her arms. She jumped in front of the tepee door.

"Rides the Wind—you wait here!" she ordered as she

disappeared inside. Jesse heard the words just as she finished feeding Two Mothers.

Prairie Flower giggled and announced, "There is a Lakota brave outside with a pony. He means to carry you away, but I have told him he cannot, for you are not ready. You must wear these things." She hesitated and made an apology. "They were not made for you—as is our custom—but still, they are beautiful."

Jesse caught her breath as Prairie Flower unrolled the bundle to reveal her own elaborately decorated wedding dress and leggings. From across the tepee, Old One called, "I was preparing your dress, Walks the Fire, but my son is impatient. He woke me this morning and said there was to be a feast today . . . for he would take you as his wife."

Prairie Flower interjected, "So you see, Walks the Fire, your heart sings when he is near, and his heart answers the song. You did not believe me, but it is true."

The women helped Jesse get dressed and led her out the door of the tepee. Rides the Wind lifted her onto Red Star's back and prepared to lead her through the village. Suddenly, she slid down again and hid her face against his shoulder whispering, "I cannot."

He misunderstood. The village had gathered in anticipation, and now he flushed with embarrassment. Jesse pulled him inside the tepee.

"You do not wish to be my wife?" he asked brusquely.

"I do! But to be led before the entire village . . . to have everyone watching . . ." Jesse wrapped her arms about the broad shoulders. "I have given you my heart. But I cannot tell the village how I feel. It is in here," she put his open palm over her heart. "It is for *you* to know. It is not for *them*." She stared up at him, her eyes pleading.

Rides the Wind stepped outside, and she heard him say, "You saw when Walks the Fire came to the village. I brought her on my pony as a warrior brings what he takes from his enemy. I brought her to care for the son of Dancing Waters.

I brought her to teach me about the God who created all things. She has done this. She has saved Hears Not. She has earned a place among the people. Today I tell you she is no longer only the woman who tends the fire in the tepee. *Mitawicu.* I take this woman for wife."

There were murmurs of approval.

Rides the Wind continued, "I will hunt for many days. There will be a feast."

He came back inside and reached for Jesse. "Now the people are satisfied. We follow the custom. What can we do to please God?"

Jesse reached for the Bible. Turning to Genesis, she read the creation of man and woman. Turning to Ephesians she read the duties of husband and wife.

Last, she turned to Ruth, reading the beloved passage, *"Entreat me not to leave thee, or to return from following after thee: for whither thou goest, I will go; and where thou lodgest, I will lodge: thy people shall be my people, and thy God my God: Where thou diest, will I die, and there will I be buried."*

When she had finished, Rides the Wind demanded that she repeat it. Three times he asked her to repeat the passage. Then, setting the Bible aside, he took her hands in his own and said, never taking his eyes from hers,

Where Walks the Fire goes, there will I go.
Where Walks the Fire lodges, there will I lodge.
Her people shall be my people.
Her God shall be my God.

Looking up, he said, "God who created all things. I thank you for sending Walks the Fire. I take her as my wife. I ask you to be pleased. You make all things. You make her heart sing for me. You make my heart answer back. You give your Son to die for us. We have no min-is-ter, but you know us. We are Lakota. We are husband and wife. We are yours."

Thus Rides the Wind and Walks the Fire were joined in

holy matrimony. And there was no minister, but God was there. And he was pleased. And the two became one.

∾

A few days after their wedding celebration, Jesse padded across the tepee to scoop up a whimpering Two Mothers. Returning to Rides the Wind's bed, she covered herself with his buffalo robe. Two Mothers lay between them, eating noisily until he fell back to sleep. Jesse lay awake, listening to morning. Propped up on one elbow she gazed down at the cinnamon-colored face beside her, stroking the soft cheek. In a rush of emotion she leaned down to kiss the smooth forehead, inhaling the scent of the child.

"What is this strange touch?"

With a start Jesse realized that Rides the Wind had awakened. He lay watching her closely. Feeling shy she pulled the buffalo robe up under her chin, answering softly, "My people say 'kiss.'"

"And who gives this 'kiss'?"

"Parents to children, husband to wife."

"Show me." As he said it he leaned toward her. Jesse obediently placed a kiss upon the wind-hardened cheek.

He kept his face near hers and the dark eyes searched hers. Then a knowing smile curled up the edges of his mouth. "When Marcus Whitman met with Running Bear and the traders, Rides the Wind was there. I saw many things. I saw this touch you call 'kiss' between man and woman. It was not here," he tapped his cheek, "but here." His finger indicated his mouth.

Jesse felt her face flush and wondered if the early morning light revealed her embarrassment. She assented, "Yes, for some it is so."

"Did Jesse King and Homer King touch in this way?"

Jesse looked hard into the searching eyes. They returned her stare with honest interest. "My people do not speak of these things."

Rides the Wind was quiet for a moment, pondering her response. "If the white man speaks not of what is here," he laid a hand flat upon the tawny chest, "he must be very sad." Rides the Wind dressed and went outside.

Light was streaming through the door now, and Old One had risen to stir up the fire and begin the morning meal before he returned. Jesse dressed and went outside. Leaning over the creek she washed her face. She didn't hear Rides the Wind approach, but as the ripples in the water smoothed out she started to see his face looking down into the water beside her own.

He sat back on the earth awkwardly, folding his crooked leg under him. Jesse noticed a pouch in his hand. It was ornately beaded, obviously the work of a skilled woman. Seeing her eyes upon it, Rides the Wind opened it, taking out the contents and arranging them carefully upon the grass.

First, he picked up two bone needles. "Dancing Waters used these to decorate the cradle board of the child to come." He laid them back and held up a digging tool.

"While Rides the Wind hunted, she used this to gather food."

Jesse asked, "What happened to her?" She watched his face intently as he prepared to answer. It revealed nothing of his feelings.

He replied, "When the child came she was silent. We did not know how it hurt her. Old One cared for her well, but she did not rise again."

After a moment Jesse moved to return to the tepee, but Rides the Wind stopped her. Lifting the last item from the pouch he stood behind her and began to comb her short hair. Then, from another pouch laced to the belt about his waist, he produced a strange sort of woven headband, decorated with feathers and shells. He wrapped it about her head.

Jesse submitted to his ministrations, grateful for any way to hide her singed hair. When Rides the Wind had finished, he placed the tools back in their pouch and handed it to her. Taking off a small knife that hung about his neck, he put it over her head.

"When Dancing Waters was Rides the Wind's woman, these things belonged to her. Now they are Walks the Fire's."

Jesse leaned over the water again to see her newly done hair. At the strangeness of the reflection she laughed a short, embarrassed giggle.

Rides the Wind inquired harshly. "Does Walks the Fire find my gift so?"

She turned to see hurt in the dark eyes although his jaw was tense with apparent anger. A shadow had appeared under each cheekbone.

"No," she protested. Laying a hand on his arm, she felt the muscles relax.

Looking across the creek to the distant hills, Jesse took a deep breath and began to speak of things she had never shared with another human.

"It is that Rides the Wind has made me feel as I never felt among my people. I .   " she bit her lip and could not continue. Seeing smoke rise from the air hole in the tepee she said, "Old One cooks. Two Mothers may need me."

"Old One will not expect you back so soon." As Jesse began to protest about Two Mothers, he added, "He will wait. Now you speak of how it is with your people."

His gentle urging opened a flood of memories, and Jesse struggled to organize her thoughts. Then she began again, "I am not one to speak of these things. It is hard for me. I laughed because you have made me feel beautiful. And yet I know that I am not. When the time came for me to marry, men did not come seeking." Her face flushed with the admission, and her voice trembled with shame as she blurted out, "Homer King only took me because my sister refused him. He needed a woman to help him on the way west. When Betsy said no, he asked me. My pa was glad for a chance to get me married off. That's how I became Mrs. Homer King."

Once finished she looked up at him defiantly, "I know I

am not beautiful. I laughed at myself for thinking such impossible things."

Rides the Wind was quiet for so long that she wondered if her rush of words had overreached his abilities in English. But just when she started to question him, he turned his own face to the horizon so that she could view only his profile.

"When Rides the Wind was young, he danced about the fire like no other brave. It was then that Dancing Waters came to be his woman. She would watch, and her eyes danced with the flames. But one day Rides the Wind went to hunt. His pony fell and crushed his leg. Marcus Whitman fixed the leg, but it would not grow straight. Rides the Wind could dance no more. The fire died in the eyes of Dancing Waters." He encircled her with his arms before continuing. "Walks the Fire sees Rides the Wind when he walks like the wounded buffalo. She sees, but the fire does not die in her eyes. Beautiful is in here," he placed his hand over her heart. "So do not laugh when you think you are beautiful. Rides the Wind sees the fire in your eyes. And to him, you are beautiful."

Jesse reached for his hand and, holding it palm up, she kissed it.

He growled, ". . . and so you give me more of the white man's ways."

In a moment of uncharacteristic abandon, Jesse stood on tip-toe and placed a less-than-chaste kiss upon the mouth of her husband. She smiled in spite of the resulting blush on her cheek, reaching up to tug childishly on his flowing hair.

Then, to his delight and amazement she spoke the Lakota words: "*Mihigna*—my husband—Walks the Fire is an obedient wife. If he wishes her to stop this strange touch, he must tell her. Walks the Fire will obey."

Rides the Wind took her hand, and they started back to the tepee. As they climbed the hill together he replied, "Many of the white man's ways must be forgotten to live among my people . . . but not all."

Chapter 12

Fret not thyself because of evil men. . . . For there shall be no reward to the evil man; the candle of the wicked shall be put out.

Proverbs 24:19–20

It was spring again. Jesse had been with Rides the Wind for two years. At last she spoke Lakota well enough to translate the Bible as she read, hoping that Old One would show an interest in the message too.

Two Mothers toddled about, jabbering as he tossed rocks into the dust. Once when he walked too close to the fire, Jesse moved quickly to scoop him up and out of harm's way. Old One reached out to stop her. "One must learn from the bite of the fire to let it alone."

Jesse made herself watch as Two Mothers toddled nearer and nearer the fire. Finally, one toe got too close, and he whimpered in pain. Jesse washed the burn and spread it with healing paste, being careful not to make more of the small wound than was needed. Two Mothers must learn to be brave, to withstand pain with as little complaint as possible. Someday, the survival of his people might depend on his ability to be silent in the wake of danger or discomfort.

Jesse's friendship with Prairie Flower had grown, and Howling Wolf's resentment of Rides the Wind continued. His wife's friendship with Walks the Fire irritated him. The two women shared every task possible, from cleaning new buffalo skins to foraging for food. Nearly every day something happened to emphasize the difference in their husbands and, thus, the differences in their lives. Prairie Flower was stoic about her unhappy choice of a husband. She did everything in her power to keep Howling Wolf happy. She suffered his abuses without complaint and worked hard. Howling Wolf was unappreciative. Sadly, children had not come. Unable to blame his poor position in the tribe on his wife's laziness, Howling Wolf pounced on their childlessness.

"Without sons," he would say, "we are disgraced among the people."

Everyone knew that Howling Wolf's own laziness and poor disposition had earned him the poor position he held in the tribe. Still, he refused to accept responsibility. Rides the Wind tried to help him by hunting with him. They joined together with a small band of braves, riding south through the Buffalo Gap, and soon picked up the trail of a large herd of elk. They followed the trail for many days, and Howling Wolf learned by watching Rides the Wind interpret the tracks.

"The leader is wounded," he said, showing Howling Wolf how one leg was dragging slightly as the great beast moved along.

"He was challenged by a younger buck here. See how the snow shows the great battle."

"Do you think I know *nothing?*" snapped Howling Wolf.

Rides the Wind refused to be drawn into a fight. "Howling Wolf, I know that you had no father to teach you. This is not your fault. If you do not know, I mean to help you. You are a fierce warrior—much better than I. You can teach me in war. I can teach you in the hunt."

Howling Wolf was mollified, but when they neared the herd, he urged his pony to run ahead, eager to kill the biggest elk and take honor for himself. He pictured the triumphant return to the village, the women singing around the campfire. *They will sing for me,* he thought, *a song that says:*

> Come and see Howling Wolf,
> Come and see, all who hear,
> The great hunter returns,

He has captured his brother the elk,
And we all will feast,
Howling Wolf returns,
Come and see, come and see.

Howling Wolf grinned to himself at the thought of the village women honoring him with their song. He dug his heels into his pony and eagerly galloped up the hill ahead of the other riders. Rides the Wind watched him go in disgust and turned Wind back toward the Buffalo Gap.

When the others in the group called to him, he gestured angrily toward Howling Wolf, "That wolf runs like a fool. He will scatter the elk, and there will be no kill today. Let him go, I return to the village. We will all be empty-handed and our women and children will be hungry." Rides the Wind urged Wind to gallop away toward the village.

His prediction came true. Lost in his vision of greatness, Howling Wolf charged his pony up the rise and came upon the elk herd. Surprised by their proximity, he was unprepared to shoot. The elk tore away, their breath rising from their nostrils in great puffs. Not one elk was shot that day, even though the other hunters tried to round them up for a second try. The promise of an oncoming snowstorm forced them all to give up the hunt, and they returned to the village empty-handed and tight-lipped.

The women wondered what had happened. Only Prairie Flower knew the answer, for Howling Wolf was not among those who returned in the daylight. He waited until after dark before skulking into camp and into her bed. He complained once again about the lack of sons, his lack of luck, and his unresponsive wife.

Early one morning not long after the failed hunt, Prairie Flower stepped outside her tepee to braid her own hair. Howling Wolf still slept and she was eager to join Jesse and the other women. Today they were to begin decorating new garments with beads and shells and porcupine quills. Jesse had promised to show Prairie Flower a design used from her days in the world of the whites. Prairie Flower had long admired Jesse's abilities with a needle. For her part, Jesse welcomed the opportunity to repay Prairie Flower for her many kindnesses. If learning a new design for beadwork would please Prairie Flower, it was a small thing to do. The two women had planned to meet as early as possible so that the morning could be dedicated to their project.

As Prairie Flower faced the rising sun and braided her hair, White Eagle strolled by. He had glanced her way many times. Today he stopped. "Howling Wolf did not come to check on his ponies this morning."

"He sleeps."

White Eagle smirked. He reached up to touch one of her braids. "If I had such a beautiful woman in my tepee, I would not sleep while she braids her own hair." He walked on without a backward glance. But Prairie Flower thought of him often that day. Each time his face appeared in her mind, she tried to force it away, but Howling Wolf's insolent smile was often replaced by the handsome face of White Eagle.

Prairie Flower did poor beading that day. The village women noticed that her mind was not on her work. Jesse worried that she was ill, but Prairie Flower only shook her head when Jesse pressed her to share her thoughts.

∾

It was the Moon When the Chokecherries Are Ripe when Rides the Wind woke Jesse one night. Laying his finger over his lips, he led her outside and onto the prairie. As they walked quietly away from the soft glow of the village fires he whispered, "You must see the sky . . . it is on fire."

He pulled Jesse down beside him and they lay on their backs, all attention drawn upward. The night sky was ablaze with stars and was so clear that even the hazy band of the Milky Way was visible. Taking his wife's hand in his, Rides the Wind whispered, "Tell me again the words from God's Book about the heavens."

Jesse recited, *"When I consider thy heavens, the work of thy fingers, the moon and the stars, . . . what is man, that thou art mindful of him?"* As she quoted the familiar psalm to Rides the Wind, a burst of light shot across the sky. Only seconds later, the first streak was followed by others, and the couple gasped in wonder.

The two of them had been watching for nearly an hour when Rides the Wind sat up, cocked his head to one side, and listened. Jesse heard it, too, from near the river. They rose and warily crept through the tall grass toward the sound.

When they saw the herd of ponies grazing peacefully, they both relaxed a little. The ponies would be restless if an enemy were near.

As they approached the river, the sound stopped. Then, coming from behind thick brush growing along the banks, they saw the source. White Eagle and a young squaw scurried toward the village.

Rides the Wind made no attempt to overtake the two lovers. He put his arm about his wife and led her toward their tepee at a leisurely pace.

Jesse relaxed against his arm, praising God for sending her to a man so well suited to her own nature. *He is so solemn in public,* she thought. Prairie Flower was a bit afraid of him. It made Jesse smile to see her friend, usually so outgoing and friendly, become unusually quiet and reticent around Rides the Wind. Yet, she secretly enjoyed the knowledge that part of Rides the Wind belonged only to her—and Two Mothers and Old One. The rest of the village saw only the skilled hunter, bent on providing food for the village, limping out early each morning, unable to participate in the dances of celebration, seeking no deep friendship with any other brave.

They knew that he loved to tell stories, but if they had seen him retelling his expeditions to his family, they would have been amazed. The stern face softened, the eyes crinkled with broad smiles. He delighted in entertaining his young son with tales of the hunt. Crouching on all fours, he would paw and spit like a buffalo, charging Two Mothers and making him tumble head over heels. Father and son wrestled about on their buffalo skins until Two Mothers gasped for air and begged for him to stop. Then Rides the Wind would turn to Old One, respectfully requesting her advice about some new project. For Jesse, he reserved all his tenderness. The love of God found a willing vessel in Rides the Wind, whereby it could flow to Jesse.

The morning after the meteor shower, Prairie Flower and Jesse had just begun quillwork along the front of a new elk-skin dress when Howling Wolf burst into the circle of women. Shouting and cursing, he grabbed Prairie Flower by the arm and pulled her up. Her face went pale, and she tried to pull free. Enraged, Howling Wolf slapped her across the face, shouting accusations about White Eagle.

The women scattered immediately, and Jesse ran for Rides the Wind. She found him working with a new colt. He had led the colt into chest-high water and was preparing to mount him for the first time.

Gasping for breath, Jesse cried out, "We must do something! Howling Wolf—" She gave the details, ending with a plea that Rides the Wind intervene. He continued soothing the nervous colt and made no move toward the village.

After a long silence Rides the Wind said, "It is a matter between Howling Wolf and Prairie Flower."

Jesse protested, "But he is so angry . . . he may kill her!"

"I do not think that even Howling Wolf would be so foolish. Prairie Flower is a beautiful woman, and she is the only good thing that he has. He will not kill her."

"But he slapped her so hard!"

"Yes, and that is his right. It is the way of the people."

He slid up on the colt's back. The colt thrashed about madly in the water, rolling its eyes and trying to rear up, but the deep water prevented it from unseating Rides the Wind. The mad splashing went on for a few moments, but not for long. The colt was intelligent, and soon realized that its rider was determined and able to stay on its back. At last it stopped thrashing about and stood, shivering, in the water. Rides the Wind slid off its back and patted its neck, whispering in the colt's ear and patting its side until the shivering subsided and the colt stood quietly, head bowed.

Rides the Wind turned to Jesse. "Prairie Flower must decide what she will do. Howling Wolf must decide what he will do. I can do nothing. It is for them to decide."

He ended the conversation abruptly by leading the dun colt up the bank of the river and toward the herd. Jesse bustled angrily back to her tepee.

Just as Old One had begun to explain the Lakota outlook, Prairie Flower charged into the tepee. She was howling with pain, her hands held up to her face, blood flowing between her fingers. Jesse grabbed her and pulled her bodily down onto a buffalo skin. The woman rocked and wailed with pain.

Old One instructed Jesse to hold Prairie Flower down. Jesse straddled her friend, grasping one wrist in each hand, forcing the thrashing woman's body back with all her weight. At last, Prairie Flower lay still, trembling and crying with pain.

Old One wiped away the blood, revealing a deep gash across the bridge of Prairie Flower's nose. Cleansing the wound, she pressed until the flow of blood had nearly stopped. Then, without a word to Prairie Flower, she got her sewing kit and did her best to close the wound. In spite of Old One's best efforts, it was done awkwardly, and would leave a horrible scar on the once beautiful young woman's face.

Jesse demanded, "Did Howling Wolf do this to you?"

Prairie Flower made no answer. Moaning, she turned her face to the wall of the tepee. Old One intervened.

"The husband has the right to avenge himself if his wife is unfaithful. The village has known for many moons that White Eagle planned to steal Prairie Flower away from Howling Wolf. Howling Wolf has learned of this and punished his wife." Old One spoke the words matter-of-factly.

Jesse refused to believe it. She repeated to Prairie Flower, "Did Howling Wolf do this to you?"

Her face still turned away, Prairie Flower whispered, "Yes."

"Then he must be punished."

Jesse rushed outside, mounted Red Star and rode away, thinking all the while of the savagery of Howling Wolf. He must be punished. He must not be allowed to get away with this treatment of her friend.

That evening, Prairie Flower returned to her tepee. Jesse watched while she threw everything belonging to Howling Wolf outside. "The tepee belongs to *me*," she shouted for the benefit of the entire village, "And I say that Howling Wolf goes!" It didn't take long to rid the interior of every trace of Howling Wolf. The last thing Prairie Flower grabbed to throw outside was the white quilt he had brought home the day Jesse had been dragged into camp.

Prairie Flower started to throw it out, too, but something caught her eye. In the quilting she recognized the design that Jesse had been helping her bead on a new dress. Prairie Flower looked up, "Walks the Fire made this?"

Jesse nodded. Prairie Flower folded the quilt up and whispered, "Then Prairie Flower will keep." She emptied the largest parfleche of Howling Wolf's dress regalia, threw it out the door, and put the quilt in its place. Satisfied that she was rid of her cruel husband, Prairie Flower began to prepare her supper.

"You should go now, Walks the Fire. I will never forgive Howling Wolf. But I was the crazy one who waited for him to change. My father warned me not to marry him," she said sadly. Jesse longed to comfort her, but there were no words. At last, she returned home where she demanded, again, that Howling Wolf be punished.

Rides the Wind was impervious to her demands. "It is the way of the people," he responded again and again. "I will not interfere. Howling Wolf did what he thought would keep his wife."

Jesse was outraged, "And if I looked at another handsome brave, would Rides the Wind cut off my nose?"

Rides the Wind stared at her solemnly. "God's book has said that you must be faithful to me. We do not live as Howling Wolf and Prairie Flower." After a moment he added, "And if you were unfaithful to me, I would cut off your beautiful red hair, not your nose. For it is your hair that makes you beautiful."

Jesse refused to be distracted from the conversation. Finally, Rides the Wind became exasperated with her insistence. "Walks the Fire, it is enough," he almost shouted. "You say that Howling Wolf must be punished. He will be punished. For all the days of his life he will have to look at the scar where he has hurt his wife. All the days of his life he will have to endure the sadness he has caused. And all the days of her life, Prairie Flower will remember when she was young and beautiful. White Eagle has left. It is over. We must pray for them, for they do not have God to help them. But I will not punish Howling Wolf for doing what is his right among the Lakota. He will answer to God for what he has done. He does not have to answer to me."

Rides the Wind rose from the fire and left, returning only when he was certain everyone was asleep. But Jesse was not asleep. She lay awake for hours, praying for the power to understand her husband's decision. At last she fell asleep with no answer to her questions.

Chapter 13

... the God of all comfort; ... comforteth us in all our tribulation, that we may be able to comfort them which are in any trouble.

2 Corinthians 1:3–4

In the tepee of Howling Wolf, Hepzibah Miller sat shivering. It was a lovely spring day, but to Hepzibah the world had become a dark and terrifying place. She had only meant to gather a few wildflowers that morning. Rising before her family, she had dressed and slipped away from camp, thrilled by the adventure of a lone trek on the wild prairie.

"You all stay close together," Elder Smith had warned them before they left their winter camp. "Once we leave the states, the Indians aren't quite so peaceful. A lone white man makes an easy target. A lone woman . . ." Elder Smith didn't finish his sentence. The glowering of his eyes from beneath bushy eyebrows sufficed.

Hepzibah had heard the warning as a challenge. The old urge to be free from all the rules stirred again. *Oh why,* she thought, *why can I not be meek and obedient like Melinda?* Hepzibah glanced at her lovely sister, who sat in the meeting, hands folded demurely. When Elder Smith issued his warning, Melinda flushed and bit her lower lip. Her hands clasped tightly. Melinda was frightened enough by her imagination to settle her response to the warning—as always, she would obey Elder Smith without question.

But Hepzibah met Elder Smith's warning with a slight lift of her chin and an unblinking stare. Trying to hide the rebellious questioning in her heart, Hepzibah smiled. Elder Smith was not comforted. He made a mental note to watch this youngster carefully and to warn her father of the spiritual problem he had detected in young Hepzibah.

However, the warning was not taken too seriously by Brother Miller. Always jolly and not too pious, Brother Miller had responded, "Now, now, Ezra. Hepzibah's young. She just hasn't settled yet. She'll be fine. Soon as I can get her promised to her young man she'll settle right down." Overwhelmed by the task of readying his large family for the trek to Utah, Brother Miller set the concerns about Hepzibah aside.

Hepzibah entered into the preparations with all her young energy. She cleaned and sorted and quilted and cooked. On the walk west she continued to bustle about, helping carry her brother Caleb for hours at a time, bedding down the little ones and binding up their scratches without complaint. But Elder Smith's warning lay beneath all the activity, prodding Hepzibah.

They left the states and entered the vast prairie. The tall grasses and flowers danced in the wind, and Hepzibah longed to dance. Wild game raced along the horizon, and Hepzibah longed to race with them. The "flat water" they followed raged with spring flooding, and Hepzibah raged against the rules set for women in her community.

After all, what harm could lie in rising early to take a walk and gather a few flowers? Indeed, didn't the Bible talk about a godly woman rising before dawn? So Hepzibah rose and slipped out of camp when the last stars were shining against a dawn-streaked sky. Striding briskly up a small rise, Hepzibah was entranced by the specter of thousands of blue flowers blooming on the next ridge. Unaware of the true distance to that ridge, she walked toward the mass of blue. The sun was nearly up, now—she knew she must get back quickly. A few of those white blossoms to fill out the bouquet, and . . .

A shadow fell across the very blossom she reached for. Hepzibah looked up in surprise. There stood Howling Wolf, his morning catch of prairie hens dangling from one hand. Hepzibah's heart lurched, but she straightened up and looked into his eyes. Her glance never wavered. One hand grasped the bouquet as the other reached up to touch the brim of her bonnet.

Howling Wolf reached out and pushed Hepzibah's bonnet away from her face. It fell back to reveal a tumble of glossy black hair. Dropping the prairie chickens Howling Wolf bent slightly, and in one motion hauled Hepzibah up and over his shoulder.

Hepzibah became a ball of fury. She screamed and kicked and flailed at the man's back. He walked on. She prayed and swore and wrestled. The man's grip tightened and he walked on. Finally, Hepzibah dug her short nails into his back. He threw her into the dust. The wind knocked out of her, she lay helpless while Howling Wolf slowly wound a leather thong about her wrists and ankles. He hauled her up again. Hepzibah yelled and screamed and tried to roll off his shoulder.

Howling Wolf was not a patient man, and he had had enough. He threw Hepzibah to the ground, shouting and slapping her face. Elder Smith's words came back to her: "A lone white man is an easy target. A lone woman . . ." For the first time in her young life, she had been struck. Her cheeks flamed with the sting of the blow and the shame of her situation. But the blow had accomplished more. It had transformed her rebelliousness into terror. Hepzibah nodded assent to the warning and meekly submitted as she was once again picked up and carried away.

Where is he taking me? she wondered. She watched the ground beneath her for a while. It was still early. The sun was barely up. It was cool. Her head began to throb. Hepzibah closed her eyes for a moment, wondering if her father had discovered her absence yet. A new sound caught her attention—*children laughing!*

Howling Wolf strode into camp, shouting about his successful hunt. He dumped Hepzibah in the dirt by a tepee and grinned at the joke he had just made about the giant bird he had found fluttering in the field of blue flowers nearby.

"I have a new prairie flower," he laughed. Hearing her

name, Prairie Flower left her cooking pot and looked outside. A white woman lay in the dirt. She was lovely. Her dark hair hung in a mass down her slender back. Her eyes were the color of the sky.

Howling Wolf looked his new woman over. He glowered at Prairie Flower. "Feed her. I may want to keep her." He walked away, still laughing.

Prairie Flower had broken her ties to Howling Wolf. She did not have to obey him. But she had to think of a way to protect this innocent girl. Carefully she untied Hepzibah and urged her inside. With Howling Wolf out of sight, Hepzibah refused. Prairie Flower dragged her inside. The girl turned away from the food offered her, pushed herself away from the fire, and sat staring dumbly about her.

She inspected Prairie Flower carefully. The woman must have been beautiful once, but an ugly scar ran across the bridge of her nose and one cheek. Her hair was parted and braided neatly. Each braid was decorated with beads and feathers. She was clean, not at all the picture of the Indian squaw Hepzibah had been told about. Still, she shivered, put her head on her knees, and began to sob.

Will they find me? she wondered. *Will they even look?* In her misery she questioned whether the others would even think her worthy of the effort to form a search party. *Why must I always disobey? What is it in me that always wants to go the other way?*

As Hepzibah soberly contemplated her sinfulness, Prairie Flower bustled about the tepee, rolling up the bedding. She set aside the other tasks she had planned that morning in the wake of this new event. Howling Wolf had found another woman. He had even called her New Prairie Flower.

Prairie Flower tied Hepzibah's hands again. Calling a young girl from across the camp to keep watch at the door, she hurried outside.

There was no sign of Howling Wolf. Others told her he had ridden off with two or three ponies in tow. Prairie Flower knew this meant he had gone to trade for the new woman. He intended to keep her.

Jesse was cleaning her own tepee when Prairie Flower stuck her head in the door and hissed, "Walks the Fire—come and see."

Jesse followed her friend without question. The young girl left to watch Hepzibah skittered away and left the two women staring down at Hepzibah, who lay sleeping, exhausted by her ordeal.

"Howling Wolf calls her New Prairie Flower," Prairie Flower moaned. Jesse took her friend's hand, not knowing what to say. It was apparent the young woman was exhausted and would sleep for a while.

"Stay here—I will talk to Rides the Wind," Jesse whispered. "Send for me as soon as she is awake. I must help her understand we will not hurt her."

Jesse hurried away, her heart pounding.

Rides the Wind watched from among his small group of ponies as Jesse hurried toward him. Her hair shone bright red in the morning sun. She ran lightly to him, and his heart stirred as he slipped down from Wind's back. The pony danced about impatiently.

"Come near," Rides the Wind called out. Seeing Jesse hesitate, he loosened the strap from Wind's jaw and walked to her, wrapping the strap about his hand. "What has happened?"

"Prairie Flower came to me. Howling Wolf has taken a new woman."

"It is the way for some men," he answered.

"But it is a young girl he has chosen," Jesse added. "She is white. He found her near the Blue Hills. She is frightened. We must take her back to her people." As she spoke, Jesse reached out to lay her hand on Rides the Wind's forearm.

"If Howling Wolf found her, we cannot interfere."

"But he wants to keep her."

"Prairie Flower was unfaithful. Then, he was thrown out

of her tepee. Howling Wolf is angry. He must regain respect. A new woman is one way to do that."

Jesse withdrew her hand from Rides the Wind's arm. "You don't believe that. You can't."

He stared at her, unblinking. "It does not matter what I believe. This is Howling Wolf's business." He turned to remount Wind.

Jesse felt her anger rising. Could he really stand by and do nothing? She tried again, "But, Rides the Wind—the young girl is terrified. She wants to return to her people. She should not be forced to stay."

He was quiet for a long while. Then, slowly, Rides the Wind responded. "You were terrified when I brought you to my tepee. But you stayed. Perhaps now you wish you had told me to take you back."

Understanding quieted Jesse's anger. "It is not the same. I was not a young girl. I was a woman. My family was gone. We don't know about this young woman. She may have a husband who grieves for her even now. And I . . ." she reached for Rides the Wind's hand, and he let her take it, "was rescued by a man who loves my God and who came to love me. Howling Wolf is . . . " Jesse hesitated, but then said it anyway. She used a Lakota word that Rides the Wind did not even think she knew.

He studied her face and asked, "What would you have me do?"

"Trade something for her." Jesse knew she must plan carefully. "It will save his pride. Tell him I need a slave. Tell him I want one of my own people to help me. Oh . . . tell him *anything*, just get that girl away from him!"

"I will try, Walks the Fire, but Howling Wolf is proud. You had better pray."

Hepzibah woke with a start and sobbed miserably the instant she realized where she was. The tent flap opened at her first sound. Two women entered the tepee. The sun shining behind them obscured their features. Hepzibah watched them approach without sitting up.

"Are you awake?" Hepzibah was too startled to reply. She had heard her own language from these savages! As her eyes adjusted to the new light, she saw the women. One was the scarred-face one. But the other! Gray eyes, red hair—and white skin! Freckles stood out on the hands and arms. She was white! Dressed like a squaw, but white—and speaking English! Hepzibah stammered a reply.

Jesse smiled, "It must be quite a shock to awaken in an Indian's tepee and see someone like me." Hepzibah nodded and sat up.

"You have been brought to us by Howling Wolf. He says he found you in the Blue Hills."

"I . . . went to pick flowers. I went for a walk. Elder Smith warned us to stay close, but I just went for a walk. I didn't think," she paused, "Oh, I just didn't *think*."

"Where are your people?"

"I don't know. I didn't walk far. They must be looking for me. Oh! You won't—you won't *hurt* them, will you?"

"*I* certainly wouldn't hurt them," Jesse replied. "But we must think of a way to get you back to them. Howling Wolf rode out just a while ago to find your people and trade for you. He wants to keep you."

The realization sprouted new terror in Hepzibah. She gasped. "Oh, no! I can't . . . oh, don't say it . . . I couldn't live . . ." Jesse's Indian garb confused her, "But you . . ."

Jesse explained, "I have lived with these people many years. I have no one else. My family is here now. But *you*," she smiled warmly, "are a different story altogether. We will try to see that you go back where you belong."

"Oh, thank you!" Hepzibah stammered. She turned to Prairie Flower and managed a smile. "Thank you. I don't know what I would do . . ." Hepzibah began to cry.

"Hush, now. Let's get you cleaned up. And you *must* eat.

My friend here is one of the best cooks in our village, and you will like her food."

Hepzibah managed a little uplifting of the corners of her mouth. The knot in her stomach relaxed a bit.

Jesse and Prairie Flower presented her with a bowl of stew for breakfast, and Hepzibah was surprised to find that she was hungry. She wanted to ask the white woman more questions, but as soon as she had begun eating, Jesse had left. Hepzibah remained alone with Prairie Flower, who tried to bridge their language gap by smiling and urging Hepzibah to eat more.

Rides the Wind leaped up on Wind after Jesse left him. With three of his best ponies in tow he started out toward the Blue Hills. He had taken great care to single out one mare that Howling Wolf had always watched with envy. The mare was in foal now to Wind, and she would make a desirable trade.

Riding swiftly, Rides the Wind caught up with Howling Wolf just as he crossed the Blue Hills. Smoke from campfires could be seen in the distance. Howling Wolf heard the approach of Rides the Wind and turned. When Rides the Wind was within earshot, he shouted, "So you come to trade for a new woman, also?" He added a coarse jest about Jesse's childlessness. Rides the Wind's silence and stony glance silenced further comment, and Howling Wolf waited for him to speak.

"You have found a new woman among the Blue Hills," he said.

"Yes, a New Prairie Flower to replace the old hag your wife finds so helpful."

Rides the Wind ignored the comment. "It is my wife of whom I am thinking now, Howling Wolf. She is a good woman, but she is clumsy in the ways of our people. She needs help with so many things. I would like this girl to be her slave."

Howling Wolf eyed Rides the Wind suspiciously. "If Walks the Fire is clumsy in the ways of our people, how can another white woman help you? Better to take another wife from among our people." He added another coarse jest.

Rides the Wind hastened to close the haggling. "You have always liked this mare. She will bring you a foal after the snows. A foal from Wind. I will give you these other two in addition. Walks the Fire does not give me rest, asking for help. I am tired of her complaining." He hated the deception but had grown tired of the game.

Howling Wolf looked at the horses greedily. The addition of four ponies to his meager band would raise his status in the tribe considerably. And a foal out of Wind in the spring was especially tempting. He thought about the white girl and how she had fought him when he carried her to the camp. Perhaps she would be more trouble than she was worth. He could just as easily take another woman from among his own people, and perhaps that would be simpler, after all. Let Rides the Wind add another white woman to his tepee. People might not like that. Perhaps it would lower him in their eyes and make Howling Wolf appear wiser.

Howling Wolf nodded and accepted Rides the Wind's offer.

Rides the Wind quickly handed over his ponies. "I will help you drive them back to your herd," he offered. Howling Wolf accepted, and the men rode back to camp in silence, Howling Wolf rejoicing at his wise trade, and Rides the Wind troubled by what would happen next.

When they re-entered the village, Rides the Wind trotted quickly to his own tepee. He entered and said only, "She is yours. Do what you want with her." He left quickly, remounted Wind, and was about to canter away when Jesse laid her hand on the horse's neck and asked, "Do you not wish to meet her?"

Rides the Wind shook his head. "I have done as you wished. She is yours. I do not wish to see her."

Jesse wondered at his lack of curiosity, but she did not press the matter. Instead, she headed for Prairie Flower's tepee, realizing too late that she had not even thanked her husband for his help.

Hepzibah sat up expectantly when Jesse came back. "Well, my dear," she said, "it seems that you are now my property."

"Yours?" Hepzibah questioned.

"Yes, my husband has arranged for you to be my slave." At the fear in Hepzibah's eyes, Jesse quickly added, "So now I can do with you as I please. And it pleases me to take you back home. Let's get started before your family follows you here and causes more trouble."

Hepzibah was on her feet, "Oh, thank you! Thank you! How can I ever thank you?! But . . . " she added, "don't you want to come back too? We would make you feel very welcome, you know . . . and you could go on the journey with us. I'm sure Elder Smith would give his permission."

Jesse shook her head. "No. My only family is here. I have a husband and a son. I am quite content here, my dear. Now, quickly, come along! What is your name?"

"Hepzibah. Hepzibah Miller." Jesse said the name slowly.

"What's your name, ma'am?" Hepzibah questioned. "If you don't mind my asking."

"In English I would be called Walks the Fire," Jesse responded. She was surprised to hear herself use her Lakota name. She added, "Before I came here, I was known as Jesse King."

Hepzibah was full of questions, but Jesse quieted her by leading her outside into the blazing sun. They crossed the village. Everyone stared and grinned as Walks the Fire led her new slave to her own tepee. A few children ran up to touch Hepzibah's long dress. Feeling cotton for the first time, they pronounced it thin and useless for prairie life. When they entered her tepee, Jesse introduced Old One and Two Mothers and ordered Hepzibah to stay with them until her return.

"Can you ride a horse without a saddle, Hepzibah?" she asked.

"I never tried."

"Then, I will show you how, but we must try to move quickly before Howling Wolf gets back. If he learns that we have tricked him out of his New Prairie Flower, he will be very angry, and we will be obliged to return you to him." At the prospect of being once again under the power of Howling Wolf, Hepzibah's willingness to ride bareback doubled. When Jesse returned with Red Star, Hepzibah clambered up behind Jesse and clutched at the pony's sides with all her young strength.

Jesse headed for the Blue Hills immediately, unaware of the lone rider that followed at a distance.

As they rode along in the morning sun, Jesse answered Hepzibah's questions as briefly as she could. She found the girl's exuberance a bit wearying. She could not, after all, explain in a short ride all that had happened to transform her from a white settler into the wife of Rides the Wind. She found that she really did not care to defend herself or her adopted family's ways to this young, foolish woman.

It was not long before Jesse saw the dust of a large number of riders in the distance.

"Your people are coming for you," she said to Hepzibah, pointing at the horizon. Hepzibah raised one hand to shade her eyes. "Slide down and wait here. I will be watching to make certain that they find you. Good-bye."

Hepzibah did not slide down. Instead, she said, "but you must wait so that we can all thank you. Please wait."

Jesse shook her head. "To know that you are with your own again is thanks enough. And," she added, "to know that perhaps now you will obey Elder Smith and not go searching for wildflowers when you should be working in camp."

Hepzibah blushed. Obediently, she slid down from Red Star. Jesse turned and cantered Red Star away, stopping behind the first hill. Dismounting, she crawled back up a few feet until she could peek over the rise and watch the reunion that took place only moments after she left Hepzibah's side.

A party of a dozen or more riders thundered toward

Hepzibah. Her blue calico dress bobbed up and down as she waved and called to them. One heavy-set man jumped from his horse and swept her up in a great bear hug. The entire party looked in Jesse's direction as Hepzibah gestured. Soon, she was hauled up behind the man who had hugged her, and they pounded away, lost from view.

Jesse smiled to herself and turned to go. Rides the Wind was standing behind her, having dismounted from his own horse.

"I did not thank you. What did you have to promise Howling Wolf to buy your poor wife a slave?"

He shrugged, "Only three ponies . . . "

Jesse cried out, "Three ponies! You are kind, Rides the Wind. It was a great price to pay to help a young girl, and you did not even meet her."

He looked down at her in amazement. "I did not give away three ponies to help a stupid white girl. I gave three ponies to help Walks the Fire. She is gone?"

Jesse said softly, "She is gone."

He brought up the subject again. "Do you sometimes wish to return to your people?"

Jesse didn't hesitate to reply, "I lived among the whites for twenty-one of their years. As they count time, I have been among the Lakota for four more years. The day you took me as your wife, we promised, 'Wherever you go, I will go, and wherever you lodge, I will lodge; your people shall be my people, and your God, my God.' This promise was forever. I wish to be with Rides the Wind, among his people for all the time that God gives."

Rides the Wind and Jesse walked back to the camp together. Howling Wolf patted his new ponies and watched them enter the village, wondering at the stupidity of a man who would pay so much for a slave and allow his wife to give her away. And if Howling Wolf thought that Rides the Wind entered his tepee to beat his wife for her ungrateful attitude, nothing was said to convince him otherwise.

Chapter 14

... her husband ... praiseth her.
Many daughters have done virtu-
ously, but thou excellest them all.
Proverbs 31:28–29

No children came. Jesse waited hopefully for each
moon's passing. But still, no children came.

Rides the Wind loved to tell stories and delighted in the
myriad questions asked by his growing son. He shared leg-
ends that had been handed down through generations of
Lakota, skillfully weaving God into them so that even Jesse
and Old One listened, fascinated. A favorite became the
story of a hunter who fell onto a cliff and escaped by tying
himself to two grown eagles and flying off. Two Mothers' eyes
would grow wide as Rides the Wind built up to the dramatic
moment when the hunter stepped off the cliff with only the
power of the eagles to save him.

"But it was not the power of the eagles that saved him,"
Rides the Wind would remind his son. "It was God who gave
the eagles strength."

He told stories to help Two Mothers overcome childish
fears. "Now, my son, why do you fear the storm? It is only the
warriors of thunder and lightning. When you are tempted
to be afraid, remember that God tells the lightning where it
may go. Pretend that the noise and the light are from two
warriors called Thunder and Lightning. They ride beautiful,
swift ponies and carry lightning in their hands. As they race
the wind, their ponies' hooves strike the clouds. That is
thunder. When they throw their lightning sticks, it flashes
brightly in the sky. When God says 'Enough!' the warriors

ride down to the earth, bringing the rain to water their ponies."

"Have you ever seen the ponies, Father?"

"Once, when I was hunting in the Black Hills, I thought I caught a glimpse of them. But before Wind and I could catch them, they rose again into the sky, taking the thunder and lightning with them to another place."

When Two Mothers was six, Jesse had long since begun to speak her new language fluently. She thought of herself as Walks the Fire and was often surprised at some reminder that she had lived most of her life as part of another culture. The reminders came less frequently as she adapted to the ways of the Lakota. Now she could start a fire quickly, whenever it was required. She rode Red Star without a thought of the old fears. She tanned hides and decorated clothing for her family. But she longed for the opportunity to begin a new cradle board, to fashion tiny moccasins, to have the village women give her advice as they did every expectant mother among them.

Two Mothers raced his friends in footraces, threw rocks at every available target, and pretended to hunt with the bow and arrow fashioned by Rides the Wind. In winter he coasted down hills on a sled made from buffalo ribs, "skated" over the ice in his fur-lined moccasins, and stalked hapless rabbits across the snow-covered prairie.

Rides the Wind told stories of bravery. "We returned victorious, but I was sad, for I had been forced to leave Wind on the battlefield where he had fallen under the enemy's arrows. He could not rise again."

"But, Father, Wind is here with us now . . . "

"Ah, yes, but I left him that day on the battlefield, for I thought he was dead. And so, when I rode into camp behind White Eagle, I went to my tepee with great heaviness in my heart. My best friend had been lost. I knew that praises would be sung about the campfire for the lost pony, but still, my heart was sad.

"The feasting lasted for days, and then the other villages began to fold up their tepees and return to their own hunting grounds. At last, everyone was gone, and my village returned to quiet living. All was well. Evening was coming, and I had just finished working with my newest pony when I saw in the distance something that I could not believe. It seemed that a ghost-horse was coming to me across the prairie. For there, in the distance, was Wind. He was walking slowly and his head was drooping. The people all came from their tepees to watch. He came to me, and I saw that a terrible wound still ran along his side. I could not believe my eyes, and yet, I must believe it, for my faithful horse had come back to me.

"Remember, my son, that when you have such a friend it is a rare gift from the Father. Ever since that day, Wind has been my best friend." Rides the Wind paused and looked across the fire at Jesse. "Until, of course, I found a certain white woman on the prairie."

He stared at Jesse, who answered playfully, "My dear husband, what an honor it is to know that I rank above your horse."

Two Mothers looked from one face to the other. He had often heard the story of how Walks the Fire had come to live among the Lakota. Sometimes he was teased about his mother's fair skin. But in the tepees of some of his friends, he had heard shouting and ugly words. He was grateful for the affection between his father and mother. It didn't matter that she was white. She was a good mother and a good wife.

As Two Mothers grew, Rides the Wind joyfully took on the task of teaching his son. He had held his infant son in front of him as they rode Wind and had fashioned a tiny bow and arrow for him from soft woods that grew along the creek. As the boy became older, Two Mothers learned to scramble up on his own pony. Then began the serious business of learning to ride. He fell so many times that Jesse despaired of his welfare, but Rides the Wind refused sympathy and insisted that he always try again. Jesse remembered her own experience of learning to ride, and Rides the Wind's stony reaction to her tears. She decided not to interfere with the training of her Lakota son.

One evening Two Mothers came in, his face and arms covered with scratches. He grudgingly admitted that he had fallen off his new pony and had rolled down a steep bank covered with thorny bushes. Jesse cooed sympathy, but Two Mothers would not have it. He was ashamed for having fallen, and Jesse thought she detected a little fear at the prospect of mounting his spirited pony again the next day.

Rides the Wind examined his son's wounds carefully, removed a few thorns, and then proceeded to paint each scrape with red paint. "Now Two Mothers appears as a brave warrior returning from defeating the enemy." He squeezed the boy's shoulders. "And tomorrow you will ride the pony again, and everyone will know that you are the bravest of the sons in our village."

Two Mothers rose early the next morning, having slept little in fearful anticipation of the day. But he successfully controlled the willful pony's dashes for freedom, and he did not fall off again. That evening, the campfire in their tepee illuminated the faces of one very tired Lakota boy and three very proud adults.

"You were right to insist that he try again," Jesse whispered when Rides the Wind stretched out beside her in the dark. Rides the Wind buried his face in Jesse's long hair and inhaled deeply.

"You gathered *Sikpe-ta-wote* today, my wife . . . its sweetness lingers in your hair. Let us talk no more of our son's riding," he whispered. "Let us talk no more."

By the time Two Mothers was seven, Jesse's longing for a child had become a burden that she carried through every day. She counted the moons and when each one passed with no sign of pregnancy, she grew despondent. Old One concocted foul-tasting teas to help, and Prairie Flower advised Jesse to seek the help of the medicine man. Jesse could not bring herself to do the latter. She carried her longing to the Lord. "Father, I am nearly thirty years old—please, Father, a child for Rides the Wind." When it seemed that His answer was *no*, she thought she could not bear it.

Rides the Wind sensed her unhappiness and misinterpreted it. He waited for her to speak of her sorrow, and when she said nothing, he believed she was longing to leave the village. The tension between them mounted until, one night, he reached out for her and she feigned sleep. He got up abruptly, strapped on his hunting gear, and strode out of the tepee. Jesse waited for him to come back, but it was three days before she saw Wind back in the herd. Even then, Rides the Wind did not join his family at the fire.

On the evening of the third day, Jesse walked away from the village at twilight. In the west the horizon glowed a deep pink that faded upward into a pale blue. The blue darkened to a rich violet and there, in the sky, shone one bright star. It was a still night, and no moon was visible.

Lord, Jesse prayed, *you said, "Children are an heritage of the Lord and the fruit of the womb is his reward. . . . As arrows are in the hand of a mighty man; so are children of the youth. . . . Happy is the man that hath his quiver full of them." Why, Lord? Why do you not give us children? I try not to ask for too much. I have tried to be content. But, Lord, is it too much to ask for a child?* She heard a coyote howl, the sound of the ponies munching grass and stamping their feet, but no answer. She expected some verse of Scripture to come to mind to bring her comfort, but nothing came to mind except her own longing. The emptiness of the prairie and the vastness of the sky were reminders of her barrenness. She wept quietly, and sat in the dirt, holding her bowed head in her hands.

Footsteps behind her in the dark startled her out of her

misery. She automatically reached for her knife, but a familiar voice broke the stillness.

"The stars say that it is not safe for women to be out alone." He did not sit down beside her, but waited for her to get up.

Jesse straightened her back, wiped away tears, and stayed seated. "I needed to be alone . . . away from . . . I needed to pray."

"Then I will leave you to your prayers." Something was gone from the well-known voice. Gentle concern had always been there for her. Where was it, now, when she needed it so much?

He had already turned to go. She knew he would not go far. He would wait out of sight, watching to see that she was safe. But she did not want him out of sight. "No, I am finished. I . . ." her voice wavered. "There is no answer to my prayers."

"There is always an answer. But the answer is not always what we want to hear."

The truth of the simple reply cut deep. The answer to her plea for children was *no*. She couldn't understand it. She didn't want to accept it. But for years, now, the answer had been there. She knew it, but she couldn't bear it. Tears welled fresh in her eyes. He couldn't see them. The dark offered protection and enabled Rides the Wind to speak his fears.

"I have had prayers too. I have prayed that you would learn to be happy among the Lakota. But you tell me of the white man's count of years. You talk of all the time that you have been here. I have not wanted to hear the answer to my prayers. The answer is *no*. I have prayed to know how to make the smile return to your face." The voice grew so quiet that she could barely hear the words, "Now I see that I cannot. You must tell me what you wish. Two Mothers is grown, now. You have done well among the people. You do not need to fear telling me that it is time for you to go. I am not like the others . . . I will not make you stay." He cleared his throat and forced the words out calmly. "The line of your people crossing the prairie never stops. We are a small band. We have tried to stay away from them. Now, I will take you to them."

Jesse could find no words to bridge the darkness between them. He had seen her unhappiness and wrongly blamed himself. She had sensed his distancing himself from her and had wrongly guessed her childlessness to be the cause. Words failed, but she found a way to bridge the darkness. He had turned to go, but she was there, wrapping her arms about him and laying her head on his shoulder, her own body shaking with the effort to hold back her tears.

His arms held her, but there was little warmth in them until she managed the words to tell him how the absence of children plagued her . . . how she had failed him . . . how useless she felt. The broken words poured out and the chasm was crossed. Loving arms enfolded her. His head bowed low as he placed his own wind-hardened cheek next to hers and waited for her to spill out the cause of her sadness.

As she shared her grief, Rides the Wind's heart was made glad. He interrupted the torrent of words. "This is nothing, Walks the Fire. My anger came when you would not speak of your sadness. I thought you longed for the whites, that you cared nothing for us, that you feared telling me. To have many sons would be a wonderful thing. I cannot lie about that. But if having many sons means I must take another woman, then I would choose no sons and keep Walks the Fire in my tepee. Your heart cries out for children . . . my heart cries out only for you, best-beloved."

The vastness of the prairie and the wide expanse of sky had been reminders of her emptiness, but she was no longer empty. God had filled the emptiness with his love poured out through Rides the Wind. In the days that followed God began to heal the wound. Jesse still prayed for a child, but the desperation was gone. She began to find fulfillment in Two Mothers, in her friends, in her husband. Something approaching contentment grew within, and the smile that Rides the Wind had longed to see returned to the face of Walks the Fire.

Chapter 15

 Even the youths shall faint and be weary, and the young men shall utterly fall: But they that wait upon the LORD shall renew their strength; they shall mount up with wings as eagles; they shall run, and not be weary; and they shall walk, and not faint.

Isaiah 40:30–31

When Two Mothers turned eight, Rides the Wind presented him with an elk horn bow. The boy had watched his father fashion it with glowing eyes, not daring to presume that he would merit such a fine bow. The horn was boiled until soft and then split into shape, the pieces joined together at notches. Wet sinew was wound about the joint of the bow. It contained a natural glue, and when it dried, it glued itself in place. Joined in this way, the joint was stronger even than if the nails used by the whites held the pieces together. When Rides the Wind had finished the bow, he strung it with a fresh buffalo sinew and presented it to his son without ceremony.

Two Mothers was barely able to contain his excitement. He stammered his thanks and prepared to rush outside to show the gift to his friends. But Rides the Wind stopped him. "There will be time to boast when you bring home your first deer . . . let us make new arrows before we hunt. Let us see how you have grown since the last moon."

Rides the Wind measured his son's arm. The distance from the elbow joint to the tip of the middle finger and then back to the wrist would be the length of Two Mothers' arrows. Together they searched for suitable feathers, fastening them to the arrows with sinew. Two Mothers looked longingly at the turkey feathers that adorned his father's arrows, but turkey feathers were scarce. He would have to be content with the offerings from the duck and the prairie chicken.

Early the morning after the new bow and arrows were finished, Rides the Wind announced, "My son and I are ready to try out the new bow." With great ceremony they prepared for their hunting trip, for with the presentation of the bow, Rides the Wind had announced that he would begin training his son in earnest, sharing his secrets so that the tribe could gain another fine hunter.

"God has given each animal a manner of living, my son. You must learn to watch these ways and to respect them. By watching the animals, you will learn much that will help you in the hunt." They stopped along a familiar trail, and Rides the Wind pointed to deer tracks. "Is this a recent track or an old one? Was the deer running or walking? If the deer was running, then we must look for other tracks. Perhaps there is an enemy nearby who is hunting. These are all things we must know to be good hunters."

A familiar cry caused them to look up from the tracks. Soaring high above were a pair of eagles. Father and son watched for many minutes before Two Mothers ventured, "My father, you have your eagle feathers . . . could I not make preparation and hunt for mine?"

Rides the Wind pondered the request before replying, "The taking of an eagle is a serious and dangerous thing, my son. Three men were required when I captured the eagle. Today there are only two." He was careful not to call Two Mothers a child.

The son gazed longingly up at the soaring birds. He bargained for time. "Perhaps we could follow these two. You could teach me the way of the eagle. Then, when my time has come, I will be ready."

It was a reasonable argument, and Rides the Wind nodded

his assent. "By the way they circle, I would say that they have a nest, and they are trying to get the young one to fly with them. I have seen the mother sometimes push her young one out of the nest and over the edge of the cliff to make it fly. Sometimes, the young does not know how, and it flaps its wings, but it falls toward the earth. The mother bird flies beneath her child and catches it and takes it on her back to the nest, to safety."

Two Mothers listened, fascinated. "And then what happens, my father?"

"Again, the young one is pushed off the cliff. This time it flies better, but if it still cannot fly away, the mother catches it again and again until it learns and flies back to the nest on its own."

"Perhaps we could find the eagles' nest," interjected the boy. "Just to see if the young ones are fully feathered." His heart yearned to return from his first hunt with the most prized of all prey.

Rides the Wind smiled patiently. "Never among our tribe has a boy of your age succeeded in bringing home eagle feathers from his first hunt." At the downcast expression on his son's face, Rides the Wind was urged to speak some comfort. "But perhaps God has saved his best eagle for Two Mothers and Rides the Wind."

The downcast expression changed instantly, and the young boy nodded his head emphatically. He thrust out his chest and blurted out, "Yes, I will be the first . . . and the people will sing my praises."

Rides the Wind smiled and studied Wind's mane as the pony stood motionless. Seeming intent upon arranging each hair of the mane until it flowed perfectly, he recited from the book, *"There be three things which are too wonderful for me, yea, four which I know not . . ."*

"Do you remember what the first is my son?"

Two Mothers answered, *"The way of an eagle in the air."*

"It is always good, my son, to remember that God is the

one who decides the way of the eagle and the ways of men. Let us ask him to help us find your eagle . . . if he agrees. We should never boast of what we can do, for he may not agree, and then we will seem to be fools."

Two Mothers' shoulders slumped a bit and he blushed. "I only meant . . . "

"You meant that your heart is bursting with the desire to hunt these eagles. I understand. There is no wrong in the desire." Rides the Wind picked up the reins to his pony and urged him forward as he finished the thought. "Just remember that we must always make our desires one with those of the heavenly Father."

The two climbed steadily, their ponies scrambling over rocks, their eyes ever watchful of the eagles. Finally, after what seemed like hours, they reached the top of the cliff where Rides the Wind dismounted and advanced to the edge, peering over. He motioned for Two Mothers to follow.

Perhaps twenty feet below them was the eagles' nest. In it, side by side, sat two fully feathered eaglets. The temptation was too much. It took only a few moments for him to decide what must be done.

"We will kill a deer and return here. We can cut the hide into strips to make a rope. I will lower you to the ledge, and you will capture one of the eaglets."

"But, Father, the lodge, the sacrifice to the Great Mystery . . ."

"All my life, I have served the Great Mystery, my son. Long ago, when my leg was broken and wrapped by the man of God, I learned that the Great Mystery had a name and that he cared for all people, that he came to this earth to show his caring. Since Walks the Fire has come to our tepee, we have heard the words of God. He does not require sacrifice before he gives to his children, and he will be pleased if we thank him for his help when you have gained your prize. We will pray for his help. I do not think that the ceremony is important."

Two Mothers accepted the answer in respectful silence. Still, his mind was filled with doubt. It did not seem wise to so quickly change the ways of the people.

It was not long before they spotted the tracks of an elk, and Rides the Wind returned to the role of teacher as he and Two Mothers tracked their prey. Clouds had begun to gather in the western sky, and it was late afternoon before they succeeded in bringing down the huge buck. They worked quickly to skin the animal and pile the meat onto Two Mothers' pony. Rides the Wind plucked two teeth from the elk's mouth and tucked them into the pouch at his side. He had been saving elk's teeth for months, and these two would furnish exactly the number needed.

The wind blew harder as they headed back to the edge of the cliff, and black clouds scudded across the sky. The two eagles were no longer in sight, but as Rides the Wind and Two Mothers peered over the edge of the cliff, they saw that the eaglets had huddled down into the nest in preparation for the storm. As they watched, one grown eagle soared over their heads and lighted on the edge of the nest. Spreading her wings over her young, the female settled onto the nest and awaited the storm.

Two Mothers' heart sank. With the storm coming, they would have little time to capture their prey. Rides the Wind, however, had become determined to have his son succeed. Quickly he slashed the elk's hide into thin strips, tying them together to form a rope just long enough to reach the ledge below.

"You must move very slowly. Speak to the eagles as a friend. Tell them what you are doing. Do not thrash about and frighten them. If you do this right, they will watch you and allow you to join them on the ledge. Then you must sit down—slowly—and wait. They will watch you carefully. Still, you must wait. If you make no move toward the young ones, she will settle down. The storm will come, and still, you must wait. I do not think it will last long. When it has passed, they will go to hunt, or they will push one of the eaglets out of the nest and begin to teach it to fly. Either way, you will have your chance to capture one of them. Reach slowly, like this. . . ." Rides the Wind demonstrated his own movements from years ago, grasping an imaginary leg just above the claw, then tightening his hold on the leg and sliding the hand slowly up the feather-line on the thigh. "He will not struggle. But then, you must bring your other hand up and break his neck. When you have done this, climb slowly back up to me. If the old ones return, I will throw stones to keep them away while you escape."

It sounded simple, but as they talked, the storm moved closer. Thunder rolled on the clouds and lightning flashed. No moisture had poured from the clouds. "Perhaps it will go over us," Rides the Wind muttered hopefully. "If not, you will have to wait through the storm down there on the ledge. Are you certain you wish to do this today, my son?"

Two Mothers bristled at the idea that he might not be brave enough to earn his eagle feathers. His answer was unspoken as he tossed the elk-skin rope over the edge of the cliff and prepared to slide down it. Rides the Wind nodded his approval but stopped the boy with a reminder. "This is a dangerous thing that you are doing, my son. You are brave, and that is good. But do not be foolish. In a few years this can be done . . . when you are stronger, and when there is no storm. No one needs to know that we even thought of this today."

Two Mothers' dark eyes flashed as he took up the challenge. "Everyone will know, my father, for we are riding back to the village with our ponies adorned with eagle feathers!"

With that, he pushed himself over the edge of the cliff and started his descent. Rides the Wind had been correct about the behavior of the eagles. They lowered their heads and watched carefully, but showed no signs of alarm. Two Mothers moved slowly and deliberately—until the fresh elk-skin rope broke and he landed with a thump at the side of the nest.

Rides the Wind watched, his heart pounding. The storm was approaching quickly, and the eagles lashed out to protect their young from the intruder. Fierce talons ripped at the young flesh, powerful wings beat the air and the beaks began to work furiously as the two grown eagles tore at Two Mothers in fury.

Rides the Wind acted immediately. Lowering himself as far as he could on the remaining portion of the rope, he dropped to the ledge beside his son. Two Mothers had done his best to fight, but two enraged adult eagles were too much. Deep gashes bled freely along his back. One talon had ripped into his left cheek.

Rides the Wind stood over his crouching son. The storm broke, pouring rain and blowing fierce gusts against the side of the hill. Lightning illuminated the side of the cliff, but Rides the Wind noticed nothing as he slashed at the eagles with all his might. One blow plunged his knife into the breast of the male bird, but the female seemed to be everywhere at once, slashing and beating, impervious to the weather. The eaglets joined in, but were thankfully less skillful in their own defense.

The female ended the battle. One great talon found the neck of the fierce warrior. Held in her grasp, Rides the Wind saw her breast stained with his own blood and knew that he was gravely wounded. He grabbed one of her legs with his left hand, trying to free himself with his knife.

The cloudburst passed, and Rides the Wind staggered back, no longer able to protect his son. The flow of his own blood was telling, and he realized that he was losing the battle. Just as he began to lose consciousness, he was aware of a loud cry—was it his own?—and then the terrible pain at his neck seemed to stop. He reached again for where the eagle's talons had been holding him but felt only air. As he fell to his knees he realized that Two Mothers had dealt the death blow and was now battling the eaglets. At his feet lay the bodies of the adult birds. It was a valiant fight, but Rides the Wind realized as he fell against the cliff wall that it was useless. Too much blood had been spilled.

The sky was suddenly a brilliant blue. The storm had left a great rainbow in its wake. It arched from one end of the prairie below to the other, and all things sparkled. Back in camp, Jesse looked up at the rainbow and smiled, wondering where her two men had sat out the storm. She stirred up the fire and began the ritual of preparing for the evening meal, wondering if they would return that night, hoping that on his first hunt, Two Mothers would not be disappointed. *Please, Father, if it pleases you, let him return home with meat for the family. It would make him so happy.*

But at the moment Walks the Fire was praying for her son, he was in the fight of his young life. The eaglets turned on him with all their fury, and as they beat upon him with their wings, Two Mothers realized that they must be very near the day of leaving the nest. One glance behind him told him that he was in a desperate situation. Above him, too far away to be of any help, were Wind and Stormy Day, the latter loaded with meat. They had been tethered to a tree. They would undoubtedly break loose and return to the village, but not before it was too late for Rides the Wind. The dark stain on the ground was growing with every passing moment.

Two Mothers did a foolish thing. It should have plunged him to his death. Miraculously, it did not. *If you are truly there, God of my mother . . . if you are truly the maker of all things . . . then help me, now. My father lies dying. Help me down from this place or let me die now!*

Somehow, he managed to grasp the legs of each frenzied bird and tottered to the edge of the cliff. As they went over the edge, Two Mothers cried aloud, "God of my mother, help me!" His heart seemed to stop beating. Squeezing his eyes shut, he held his breath and waited to plunge to his death. A great gust of wind rushed up from the earth. The young eagles spread their wings and beat the air in an attempt to escape. Down, down, they spiraled, beating their wings and screeching at the thing that held them to let go. He would not. Down, down, they went, into a deep pool of water formed by a spring at the base of the cliff. The birds had not borne him up, as did the eagles in the legend he had heard so many times, but they had broken his fall.

As he sank below the surface of the water, Two Mothers felt the muscles in the legs of the two birds go limp. He let go, and came up, gasping for breath. The two drowned birds floated on the surface of the water. Two Mothers swam to the edge and dragged himself into the grass, panting. He looked down, unbelievingly, at the deep gashes on his arms. When he touched his cheek, his fingers were covered with blood.

But Two Mothers had no thought for himself, now. He must get help for his father, and quickly. The dark stain in the earth about his father's unconscious body . . . was it still growing?

Two Mothers staggered to his feet and began the run of his life. *How far did we come?* He knew the direction to run, but had no idea how far they had come as they watched the eagles earlier in the day. Climbing the cliff again to reach the ponies was out of the question. *I am swift. God of my mother,* came the plea, *make me swifter.*

There was no miracle in the answer to this prayer, but still, an answer came. Hardened by the countless hours of running with his friends, Two Mothers was strong. He covered the ground efficiently, his moccasins beating a steady rhythm as he ran toward the village. He watched carefully for cactus, leaping over those that came in his way. His breath came hard, and his legs ached. Still, he ran on. The blood on his cheek dried and crusted over. Tears of fatigue came to his eyes. Still, he ran on. Back there, on that ledge, lay his father. The picture of the crumpled body, the empty eagle's nest, the dead birds, haunted him. And he ran on.

How long he ran, he did not know, but when he thought his heart would burst and his legs would crumple, he staggered into the village, shouting for help, pointing the way, and finally crumpling into a heap just outside Medicine Hawk's tepee. Jesse heard the disturbance and peeked outside. She saw men mounted on ponies charging out of camp.

Just then, Two Mothers was carried to her. A deep gash had reopened along his cheekbone and bled freely. The marks of the attack of some animal were everywhere. Her heart lurched. *Where was Rides the Wind? He would never have allowed this if he were safe. No, I must not think that. If I think that, I will panic. I must not think it. Dear God, don't let me think it. I must help Two Mothers. Oh, God, let them find him . . . bring him back to me.*

"Call Medicine Hawk," she screeched to the women who huddled nearby. She held open the tent flap for the men to carry her unconscious son inside. They laid him by the fire. Old One darted about the tepee, carrying water to wipe the wounds, scrambling for her healing herbs.

Jesse knelt helplessly by her unconscious son. Old One touched her arm.

"Wash the wounds, my daughter." Jesse moved to obey. She was numb with fear, but she obeyed. Two Mothers' eyes opened. Through the opening above he could see that it was still daylight. Slowly, he moved his head to look about him. *Home. I am home.* Gentle hands were washing his wounds, and he saw the red hair of his mother as she bent low to tend his wounds. Old One held a compress to his cheek, clucking in sympathy as she occasionally removed the compress to check the wound. "We will need to sew it shut," she muttered to herself. "And there will be a scar."

Two Mothers saw tears sliding down his mother's nose. She worked quickly, but her hands shook, and she looked often at the doorway.

Two Mothers croaked, "My father?"

Jesse started at the sound of his voice. Her voice trembled. "They have gone for him." It was all she could say.

He struggled to explain. "The eagles . . . the storm . . ."

Old One interrupted him. "Hush. This cut on your face must be held together before you talk more." Already, she had her finest sinew and her smallest needle ready. Even as the last word was spoken, she took the first stitch. Two Mothers flinched, but pressed his lips together and did not cry out. In the set of his mouth, Jesse saw Rides the Wind. She finished cleansing the wounds of her young son and sat back to watch as Old One skillfully sewed up the gaping wound on her son's cheek.

"Will he be all right?" she asked anxiously.

Old One nodded, "We will apply healing salve. I will show you how to make it. He will have a scar, but we will keep it clean, and he will be fine." Her eyes, too, looked toward the door.

It was not long before they came, bearing Rides the Wind. Jesse's legs would not carry her to him. She sat beside Two Mothers, frozen with terror. Rides the Wind was pale, and his head was thrown back, showing a horrible gash on the side of his neck. Tendons were bared, and the wound still bled. The braves lay him before her and scuttled away. Medicine Hawk carefully pressed the neck wound shut, bending to listen to the chest, which seemed still. Other horrific wounds gaped open, and it seemed to Jesse that Rides the Wind was bathed in his own blood.

Two Mothers raised himself up on one elbow to watch. He saw his mother's white face. Never had he seen such an expression of desperation before. The air in the tepee felt heavy. The tinkling of the bells from Medicine Hawk's garb filled the air. Old One finished her ministrations to Two Mothers and moved to Rides the Wind.

"More water!" she shouted to Prairie Flower, who watched from the opening to the tepee.

Jesse jumped at the sound of the order, leaped to her feet,

grabbed the waterskin from its place on the ridgepole, and fled to the creek. As she ran the short distance, she was aware of a great weight that pressed against her ribs. She could not catch her breath. Her mind filled with the sight of her son and her husband who lay dying in her tepee.

With the skin full of water, she ran back to the tepee, heedless of the women who had gathered outside. As she ran past, they offered encouragement,

"He is strong, Walks the Fire . . ."

"He is a great hunter . . . "

"Old One is a good nurse . . ."

"It will be all right . . ."

"We will celebrate their hunt . . ."

Jesse didn't hear what they said as she ducked inside the tepee again, but the sight before her calmed her nerves. Two Mothers sat by the fire, surveying his wounds with something approaching pride. And Rides the Wind lay, motionless, but breathing. The medicine man had stopped the bleeding and Old One was ready with soft deerskin to cleanse the wounds.

Seeing his chest rise and fall brought Jesse back from desperation, and she knelt by the unconscious man and began to gently wash his body. There seemed to be no place left unscathed by the animals.

"What did this to you?" she finally asked.

"Eagles . . . we were hunting eagles," Two Mothers whispered.

"You are too young for hunting eagles!" she snapped.

Two Mothers was quiet. Respectfully, he answered back, "My father did not think so." Just as he began to try to explain, a party of braves entered the tepee and silently laid the carcasses of the four eagles by the fire. They shot admiring glances at Two Mothers and Rides the Wind, but one look at Jesse and they left without saying what shone in their eyes.

"I don't want to hear it!" she almost shouted, "I want," she worked steadily as she began to cry softly. All the anger was gone from her voice when she spoke again. "I only want you to be well. And I want your father . . . to live."

Rides the Wind stirred, pushing her away with his arm. Medicine Hawk muttered, "He still fights the eagles . . ." and leaning over, he said to Rides the Wind, "Stop fighting, my brother. You have won. The eagles are no more. Two Mothers is safe. You are back with the people."

Rides the Wind's arm dropped to his side. He took a deep breath, but he did not open his eyes. The wounds were cleansed and sewn up and then dressings were applied. The medicine man sang a song of healing before leaving the tepee. Two Mothers forced himself to stand.

Crossing the tepee, he had grabbed two of the birds by their legs before Jesse said anything.

"My mother, I want only the feathers. I must finish what my Father and I began." Jesse stayed with Rides the Wind. Two Mothers' friends—indeed, every man in the village, watched with open admiration as the boy plucked the feathers he would need from the bodies of the great birds, painted their heads red, placed a bit of meat in the beaks, and laid the bodies on a beautiful white buckskin outside the tepee. He was too weary to do the rest, but the next morning Two Mothers rose early to return the bodies of the eagles to the foot of the cliff where the struggle had taken place.

"Great Mystery, God of my mother, whatever your name— I humbly thank you for the gifts of these eagles. Now, I return them to you." He turned to go, but then once more faced the cliff and added, "And I ask that it may be in your plan to make my father well." With that, he returned to the tepee where Rides the Wind still lay motionless.

Two Mothers was exhausted and lay beside his father on his own buffalo robe until the sun stood at its highest point. His father showed no signs of awakening. Walks the Fire redressed his wounds, moistened his lips with fresh water, and hummed softly. She left his side only to prepare meals.

Watching her anxious vigil, Two Mothers was tempted to

be jealous, but just when he had decided that she blamed him for everything, she seemed to awaken.

"My son, I have been praying for wisdom," she said. "I do not understand why the eagle was so important. You are young, and you have many years to prove yourself to the people. But I am proud of what you have done. You have saved your father's life. And," she looked warmly at him and smiled, "I am grateful to God that you are all right. Losing either one of you would bring me such pain—I do not think my heart could endure it."

A familiar voice whispered into the silence between mother and son. "Does my son have his eagles' feathers?"

Two Mothers looked quickly at his father's face. A familiar half smile curved up the corners of the mouth.

"He does, my father."

"Then we must hold a celebration." Jesse protested, but he silenced her by laying a hand on her knee. "But the celebration must wait a few days so that Rides the Wind can attend. We must call Medicine Hawk to cry out the news. And I think that I must give away one horse for every eagle."

Exhausted by the effort of the speech, Rides the Wind fell asleep again, but as he dozed off, he was aware that his hand had been lifted to meet a soft cheek dampened by tears of gladness.

Two Mothers and Rides the Wind rested several days. When Rides the Wind was able to sit up and eat, the celebration was announced and preparations began. Jesse finished a new dress and spent long hours with Old One and the village women gathering what would be needed to prepare a great feast.

On the day of the celebration, Rides the Wind walked on weak legs out of his tepee and climbed stiffly onto the back of Wind to ride to his herd and select the ponies that would be given away.

Returning from that task and a visit to a nearby tepee, his eyes twinkled with pride as he offered a tiny rawhide pouch full of elk's teeth to Jesse. She caught her breath. Only two teeth were saved from each elk, and to be able to decorate an entire dress with teeth would put her in a position of envy in the tribe. "How long have you been saving these?" she asked.

"I am a skillful hunter . . . it is nothing," came the proud reply. "I only had to get them back from Running Bear. He has been keeping them for me."

Jesse worked all afternoon to add the elks' teeth to her new dress. She scolded herself for her pridefulness, but when she and Rides the Wind attended the celebration, she could not contain her happiness at the admiring glances that came her way. Rides the Wind could not have said what made him prouder—the wife he believed to be beautiful or the brave son who had earned the name Soaring Eagle.

Chapter 16

... the LORD gave, and the LORD
hath taken away."

Job 1:21

Rides the Wind and Soaring Eagle's adventure
had earned Soaring Eagle a place with the hunting parties. His friends admired him and tried not to be
jealous. Rides the Wind often reminded his son to bear the
new name with dignity and humility. "Never forget that God
sent the winds that bore up the eagles. He is the one who
saved you. You cried out to him, and he heard. It is by his
strength that we still live—not by our own."

Month followed upon month, and the routines of life
continued in their familiar cycles. The Lakota worried over
the endless stream of wagons that crossed their lands. Farther west, bands of the people united to fight the white men
and won a great victory.

Jesse was affected little by the momentous political affairs
involving the land she lived in. Rides the Wind's band was
inclined to avoid conflict and tried to stay far to the north,
away from the roads the wagon trains followed. Jesse was
grateful, content to care for her family.

However, their dependence upon nature eventually
forced her band to move farther south. A drought had
ravaged the countryside the previous year, and the threat of
hunger weighed heavily on everyone's mind. The scarcity of
buffalo forced them to range farther south.

Rides the Wind and Soaring Eagle had been gone with a
hunting party for several days when word finally came that a

small herd had been located and the camp could move. The village was jubilant, and as the women began breaking camp, Jesse watched the horizon for the hunting party to return. She expected Rides the Wind and Soaring Eagle to be among the first hunters to ride back, and she wanted to pack quickly and be on the way to meet them.

She knew she could fit the travois to the pony without help, but taking down the huge tepee alone was a concern. Old One's age had begun to affect her mobility, and the size of the tepee made it difficult for only one woman to handle it. It was considered "women's work," but Rides the Wind didn't care. He was usually nearby to help. Now, it seemed she would be left to herself as the others busied themselves packing their own households.

Jesse fed the long poles through the sling across Red Star's back. The litter was formed and ready. "Come, Old One, sit and I will do the rest," she urged. Old One panted with the exertion of packing and seated herself gratefully.

The line of march was forming and Jesse noted with dismay that all the other tepees were down. She moved quickly to pile their bundles in proper order on the litter, forming a snug nest where Old One could ride in comfort.

It was Prairie Flower who brought the news of the accident. She came running across what had been the center of camp, her braids flying out behind her. Jesse felt a rush of relief, thinking that she had come to help with the tepee. Then, something in Prairie Flower's expression caused the greeting to die in her throat. Prairie Flower paused, dust swirling about her feet, leaving a light coating across the beadwork on her moccasins.

"Rides the Wind . . ." she began, then stopped, not knowing how to continue.

Jesse's heart thumped wildly. The sounds of camp faded away, and she stood staring down at Prairie Flower's moccasins, noting a missing bead. Unconsciously she reached up to touch her own thick braids—the braids Rides the Wind had decorated for her only that morning. Jesse became aware of Talks a Lot sitting mutely on his pony behind Prairie Flower. "I will take you to him," was all he said.

Jesse nodded and turned to mount Red Star. But Old One was already seated on the litter strapped to the mare. Jesse hesitated. Talks a Lot beckoned to her and pulled her up behind him on his pony.

Prairie Flower told her, "You go, Walks the Fire. I will see to the tepee—and to Old One. She will be with me when you return."

Jesse nodded, clutching tightly to Talks a Lot's shirt. She found herself praying desperately. No verses came to mind to comfort her, but a phrase repeated itself in cadence with the pony's stride: *Be not afraid . . . Be not afraid . . . Be not afraid . . .* When had this happened before? Jesse remembered another horse from long ago, and the same rhythm of the words, the smell of war paint, the unfamiliar sway of a body she must press against lest she fall.

The pony lurched to a halt. Jesse slid to the ground and saw Wind, his head twisted back and impaled on the horns of the massive buffalo that lay atop him. The huge, dark mass completely covered the once swift pony's body. Only the noble head and a few wisps of tail could be seen.

Talks a Lot led her around this grotesque scene, and she saw that the hunting party had erected a makeshift shelter to protect Rides the Wind from the sun. War spears held up a ragged blanket. One edge had come loose and fluttered in the breeze.

A cry of grief died as Jesse saw with relief that Rides the Wind's chest rose and fell. But then a spasm of coughing and a yelp of angry pain ended her joy. Blood trickled from the corner of his mouth, and his left hand clawed the air as if trying to push aside the waves of pain. His right arm lay useless, and as she knelt at his side, Jesse saw that the right side of his jaw was crushed.

Jesse looked up at Talks a Lot. Sadly, he explained, "He

was beneath the buffalo. We pulled him out, but . . ." He shrugged and looked away.

"Walks the Fire." A voice said it, but it was not the well-beloved voice. This was a whisper from deep in the chest, gurgling out between clenched teeth, ending as if cut off not by choice, but by a knife that cut the sound from the throat.

"I am here. I am here, best beloved." Jesse heard the sing-song reply and realized she must have said it, and yet she could not recall making the effort to speak. Lost in the scene about her, she seemed to be watching what was happening rather than living it.

Rides the Wind opened his eyes and stared up at her. A light gleamed in his eyes, but the damaged face lay still. His left hand reached up and touched her red braid, traced along the edge of the cheek, fell into her lap, and lay still.

Jesse clasped the hand, groping for self-control, mute with fear. Tears rolled out of her eyes, dripping onto his hand. Weeping openly, she raised it to her lips and held it there, tasting the salt of her own tears as she kissed the open palm.

Feeling the warmth of her breath on his hand, Rides the Wind once more made an effort to speak, but before he could utter a sound, he inhaled sharply and began to gasp for breath. He struggled to rise, but barely lifted his head from the earth.

Jesse slipped her arm beneath his head and clutched him to her. Her body began rocking slowly, and as she did so Rides the Wind lay still again. His chest rose, the nostrils flared, and with great effort, he whispered through clenched teeth, "I will come for you." Jesse wanted to cry out, to stop the words, to hold back his farewell. But she sat clutching him to her, rocking. "I will ask the Father. And I will come for you."

A last gasp for air, a tightening of his fist about her hand, and he lay still.

For a moment Jesse clutched him to her, moaning. Then, from somewhere there was a whisper and a prayer, *Lord God,*

Lord God, HELP ME! Be my rod. Be my staff. Comfort me! Grief washed over her. Jesse shuddered and cried. She rocked the motionless body gently, all the while groping for direction. What to do? What to do?

The answer came from the nights before the fire, reading the Book to Rides the Wind. One after another, the phrases came back: *"Sorrow not, even as others which have no hope. . . . Yea, though I walk through the valley of the shadow of death, I will fear no evil, for thou art with me. . . . The LORD gave, and the LORD hath taken away. . . . Blessed be the name of the LORD."*

At last Jesse laid the body down and rose from the dust. She turned and walked to where the hunting party stood maintaining a respectful silence. Jesse approached Talks a Lot.

"I will need help to care for Rides the Wind."

Chapter 17

... God my maker ... giveth songs
in the night.

Job 35:10

Talks a Lot gestured toward the approaching villagers. "We will do it. The people come." As they
neared, the cries of the mourners could be heard bounding
over the prairie. The almost inhuman wails pierced the air
until Jesse could stand them no longer. Running at them she
screamed, "Stop it! Stop it!"

The women, amazed by her outburst, stopped wailing and
watched as Jesse turned to rush back to the band of hunters.
They had begun to erect a burial pyre for Rides the Wind's
body. Jesse tore the stakes from their hands. "No . . . No! I
will not leave his body so. It must be *my* way!"

Jesse realized that she must seem demented. Her friends
watched her without a word and waited for her to calm
herself before proceeding. Catching her breath, she felt an
unearthly calm returning. She knew what she wanted to do,
and as the plan took shape, her breathing slowed, and she
regained her dignity.

The women of the village stood nearby murmuring their
disapproval. She was not, after all, one of them.

"Please, Talks a Lot," Jesse said persuasively. "You were his
friend. You know he read the Book. He believed in the one
God and his Son, Jesus. Please . . . I want to bury him as my
people bury those they love." Tears began streaming down
her cheeks again, but she wiped them away stubbornly.

"Please," she repeated, "I cannot leave him to the birds. I cannot."

Talks a Lot came close and murmured, "But his spirit must be allowed to soar to the new hunting ground, Walks the Fire. The people will never understand."

"His spirit is already with the Father, Talks a Lot. That is what the book we read together teaches. I must do this last thing for Rides the Wind." She turned to look down upon the body. "I *will* do it!" Her eyes flashed as she hurried away to repeat her words to the elders who had assembled. Then she ran to her own litter where Old One sat.

"Old One," Jesse said, dropping down to look up into the aged woman's clear eyes. "Will you help me bury him?" The old woman sat still for a moment, considering this request to turn against the traditions of her people. A moment passed, then another. The village watched and listened. Then the aged hand reached out to cup Jesse's chin in a gesture of tenderness. "This I will do—for you, my daughter." The villagers muttered their disapproval, but none moved to stop the two women as they carefully unwrapped Rides the Wind's ceremonial dress.

With loving hands, the two women dressed Rides the Wind, placing his ceremonial headdress on his head, his hands across his chest. They wrapped the body in buffalo robes.

Jesse hesitated. *How could she dig a grave?* The people had no need of shovels. It would be grueling work, but she knew how. Reaching into her leather pouch for her digging tool, she dropped to her knees beside Rides the Wind and began to scrape the hard earth. Old One knelt beside her, and together they worked. The tools designed only for digging up the roots and tubers they used for stews made hard work of the task, but the two kept on scraping the earth.

The women of the village began to look about, wondering what should be done. The leaders huddled silently. None of them approved of Jesse's actions, yet they did not move to stop her.

He was young, but Soaring Eagle stepped out of the crowd and approached the council. He had been struggling to control his own grief, and now a new purpose helped him. Respectfully he addressed the elders. In the quiet, dignified manner of his father he began, "Walks the Fire is a good woman. She is white, but she has been among you for many years now. She was a good wife to Rides the Wind. She is a good mother to me. I remember your tales of how he hunted after she walked the fire to save Hears Not. When she was well, he held a banquet in her honor. You were all there to share his joy." Coming from the mouth of a youngster, the short speech carried added weight. The elders murmured their agreement with what Soaring Eagle had said. His speech given, the young boy walked gravely to the travois and seated himself.

Talks a Lot spoke next. "For many years, Rides the Wind cared only for Walks the Fire. Together they read this Book she speaks of. My daughter has told me of this. Walks the Fire would tell the words in the Book. Rides the Wind repeated them, then he would tell how the words would help him in the hunt or in the council. Walks the Fire listened as he spoke. She respected him. She did as he said."

As Talks a Lot spoke, the people remembered the years since Walks the Fire had come to them. Many among them recalled kindnesses beyond the saving of Hears Not. Many regretted the early days, when they had laughed at the white woman. They remembered Prairie Flower and Old One teaching her, and many could recall times when some new stew was shared with their family or a deerskin brought in by Rides the Wind found its way to their tepee.

Prairie Flower's voice was added to the men's. "Even when no more sons or daughters came to his tepee—even then, Rides the Wind wanted only Walks the Fire." She turned to look at Running Bear, another elder, "Even when you offered your own beautiful daughter, Rides the Wind wanted only Walks the Fire. This is true. My father told me. When he walked the earth, Rides the Wind wanted only Walks the

Fire. Now that he lies upon the earth, you must know that he would say, 'Do this for her.'"

Jesse had continued to dig into the earth as she listened. When Prairie Flower told of the chief's having offered his daughter, she stopped for a moment. Her hand reached out to lovingly caress the dark head that lay so still under the clear sky. Rides the Wind had never told her of this. She had been afraid that he might take another wife when it became evident they would have no children. Now she knew that he had chosen her alone—even in the face of temptation.

From the women's group there was movement. Prairie Flower stepped forward, her digging tool in her hand. Defiantly she sputtered, "She is my friend . . ." and stalked across the short distance to the shallow grave. Dropping to her knees beside Jesse, she began attacking the earth. Ferociously she dug. Jesse followed her lead, as did Old One. They began again, three women working side by side. And then there were four women, and then five, and six, until a ring of many women dug together.

The men did nothing to stop them, and Running Bear decided what was to be done. "We will camp here and wait for Walks the Fire to do what she must. Tonight we will tell the life of Rides the Wind around the fire. Tomorrow, when this is done, we will move on."

And so it was. Hours later Rides the Wind, Lakota hunter, became the first of his village to be laid in a grave and mourned by a white woman. Before his body was lowered into the earth, Jesse impulsively took his hunting knife, intending to cut off the two thick, red braids that hung down her back. It seemed so long ago that Rides the Wind had braided the feathers and beads in, dusting the part. Had it really been only this morning? He had kissed her, too, grumbling about the white man's crazy ways. Jesse had laughed and returned his kiss.

A hand upon her shoulder brought Jesse back to the awful moment. She stared down upon her husband's body and whispered a prayer. *"Sorrow not, even as others which have no hope."* Jesse dropped her braid and put Rides the Wind's hunting knife into her own belt.

The women lowered his body into the grave. The leaders might allow this to take place, but they would not help put their respected brother to rest as a white man.

Jesse pushed the earth atop Rides the Wind's body. Even the women could not bring themselves to do this strange and awful deed. When it was done, Jesse sat, exhausted, looking about her. Once again the villagers watched in uncertainty. Then Jesse rose and began collecting stones, piling them atop the grave. The women helped her in this, and soon the grave was marked.

Returning to her litter, Jesse dug out the Bible. She opened it and began reading aloud.

Most of the tribe had not heard Jesse speak in her tongue for years. The foreign words were meaningless to them. It was only in the face of the reader that they could discern the comfort the words must speak of. *"The Lord is my shepherd, I shall not want. . . ."*

When Jesse had stopped reading, she bowed her head. Her lips moved in a prayer. From across the years, she remembered a hymn and found herself singing it.

Amazing grace, how sweet the sound that saved a wretch like me.
I once was lost, but now am found, was blind but now I see.

She went on to the last verse:

When we've been there ten thousand years, bright shining as the sun
We've no less days to sing God's praise than when we'd first begun.

Her voice cracked and failed several times, but she struggled on to complete the song.

As the final note died out, Jesse turned away from the grave. Her shoulders sagged, and she would have stumbled had Prairie Flower not been there to hold her. She led her to the litter, then walked back to the grave, where the other women circled and began the keening. When the cries had subsided, Prairie Flower turned to see Jesse sitting, head in hands, on her litter. Soaring Eagle stood at her side. The loss of his father meant that he was the leader of the family now, and he took his new position seriously, not allowing himself to show any grief, eager to prove his manhood.

Prairie Flower helped Jesse up. "You will sleep in my tepee tonight, Walks the Fire. And Old One too. And Soaring Eagle." Jesse allowed herself to be led away like a child. With relief she realized that Prairie Flower's invitation meant she would not have to struggle to erect her own tepee for shelter tonight.

The people moved about quietly, raising their tepees so that each one faced the east. Soaring Eagle wandered off by himself. The sun was setting, and fires were started. Supper was prepared and taken in a subdued manner. Occasionally a baby whimpered or a dog barked, but most of the evening was spent in unnatural quiet. Families whispered of the strange things they had witnessed that day or shared a memory of Rides the Wind. Many wondered how his white woman would fare among them now that he was no longer alive.

When Jesse finally sank onto her pallet in her friend's tepee, the drums had broken the silence, calling the village to dance and sing and tell the life of Rides the Wind. Jesse listened, alone, and wept quietly. Shadows danced about her on the walls of the tepee. The fire crackled, and Jesse longed for the shadows to take the familiar form of Rides the Wind coming to her. She wept, her body shaking with each new wave of grief.

At last, the sounds of the village slipped away and Jesse slept. As she slept, her hand came to rest over her abdomen. The child within had stirred.

Chapter 18

Hear my cry, O God; attend to my prayer. From the end of the earth will I cry unto thee, when my heart is overwhelmed: lead me to the rock that is higher than I.

Psalm 61:1–2

Then there was the grieving. She had buried a child and lost one husband, but this was different. Sadness brooded over her, a dark, heavy presence that covered every act, every word. At times she felt breathless from carrying the weight of it.

Old One cautioned Jesse not to travel too far from the tepee. "You might see something that frightens you—the child would be marked." When Soaring Eagle hunted and brought in rabbit, Old One refused to cook it for fear the baby would be born with harelip. Duck was forbidden lest the baby have webbed feet. Jesse complied with the superstitions, too weary with grief to protest.

When Jesse grunted with the effort to bend and cook, Old One took over tending the fire. "Eat much meat—cook little. We do not want the child to go back to the hills." The familiar saying used to describe the death of a baby made Jesse flinch. She fled outdoors, hoping to find someplace that death would not haunt her, but her feet swelled in the heat of the day, and Prairie Flower forced her back inside her tepee, insisting she rest. She encouraged her to make clothing for the baby and brought plentiful supplies.

The kindnesses of her friends brought little comfort. All their attention could not fill the emptiness.

Over every day, in every moment, the absence of Rides the Wind presided. When Jesse fled the tepee to walk in the open, there was Red Star, hurrying across the landscape to nuzzle her shoulder. But Red Star's welcome hung in the air, unanswered by the shrill neigh that had always followed it. Wind was not there.

When Jesse returned to her tepee, she was faced with the conquests of Rides the Wind painted on the outside. Inside, there was his parfleche, oh, why had she kept it? Why hadn't she buried it with him?

Jesse picked up his parfleche, running her hands along the edges, feeling the rawhide thongs. *His parfleche . . . his stitching . . . his tepee . . . his mother . . .* one hand fell to her swollen abdomen. Something pressed against her hand. Jesse pushed against it. It pushed back. She looked about the tepee. *His tepee . . . his parfleche . . . his baby.*

She should be planning for the baby. She should—but no, not today—perhaps tomorrow. But tomorrow the grief was back, covering everything. Jesse pushed it aside, took a breath, and started another day. She carried the grief, carried the growing baby, carried wood for the fire. Just carrying it was all she could do. Beating it down into something she could carry took all her strength. When the evening fire died and her strength waned, the grief loomed up and won. It carried her into the night and filled her dreams. It denied her rest. She woke and listened for his breathing. She reached out to feel the emptiness next to her. She inhaled only smoke from the fire. There was no scent of war paint and animal skins and warm flesh.

Soaring Eagle returned from hunting with his friends. His father's death had matured him, seemingly overnight. He was tender with Jesse, no longer her little boy, but a young man who wore the mantle of manhood willingly and took pride in his ability to provide his two women charges with meat. His care brought little comfort, for in the line of his jaw, Jesse saw another's face. When he spoke, the inflection of another's voice hung in the air. And the grief came rolling in.

Jesse fought it desperately. It seemed bent on smothering her very will to take breath. Still, she clung to life. She marked every sunrise without Rides the Wind by inserting a black bead into the design on the dress she was decorating. When thirty black beads had been worked into the design, the dress was finished. But the grieving was not.

Howling Wolf watched Prairie Flower help her friend prepare for the baby. He sat in his empty tepee at the edge of the village and replayed scenes from the past until he convinced himself that the white woman's arrival in camp had been the start of his worst troubles.

In his eyes, when "Woman Who Makes No Fire" had arrived in camp, Prairie Flower's attentions had turned from her own tepee. She had been caught up in teaching the woman. She had forgotten her own husband.

Was it not her helping the white woman that had forced Howling Wolf to start his own fire the day of the buffalo hunt?

When "Woman Who Makes No Fire" had become Walks the Fire, Prairie Flower had deserted him for many nights to tend her wounds.

Then, Walks the Fire had tricked him out of the lovely new wife he had brought to camp.

Sitting alone in his tepee, Howling Wolf went over and over each incident. Each time his resentment for Jesse grew. He began to believe that ridding the tribe of the white woman would enable him to regain his position with Prairie Flower. If he regained his wife, the people would no longer call him *canniyasa,* the derisive term they used that meant he had shown himself unfit as a husband.

A plan began to form. When it was complete, he kept it to himself, going over and over the details. *Soaring Eagle will go to hunt as soon as we make winter camp,* he thought. *Then I will repay the white woman for all she has done to me.* He watched Jesse furtively, smiling to himself.

The village joined thousands of Lakota moving through *Pte ta tiyopa,* the "Gate of the Buffalo," and into winter camp in *He Sapa,* the Black Hills. Heavily wooded with dark pines, the hills hid countless pure springs. Abundant wood and game and shelter from winter storms made it a favorite winter camp for both the Lakota and the buffalo.

When Jesse and Old One tore down their tepee, Jesse reverently carried Rides the Wind's parfleche to the travois and took great care to see that it was firmly strapped in place.

Her heart ached as they walked along the narrow stream bed that marked the trail. *Only last year,* she thought, *he had me look up to see how the trees almost touch at the tops of the cliffs.* Jesse stopped abruptly, pretending to have a rock in her moccasin so that her tears would not be seen.

Arriving at winter quarters, the people set up camp and settled in. Jesse moved quietly through the days and Old One worried. Talks a Lot offered a new cradle board for the coming child. Prairie Flower stayed nearby and watched her friend closely. Howling Wolf leered at them from across the camp. He watched Jesse's growing belly with quiet delight, plotting and waiting.

Working with her hands kept Jesse sane. She opened her Bible each evening out of habit, but Rides the Wind was not waiting to absorb the beloved words, and they lay dead on the page, lost in a stream of tears.

It had been her habit to greet each day with Rides the Wind. Together they would face the rising sun and pray. He had often used the very words she had read by the previous night's fire. Now, no words came. The wound of his death lay fresh, and she had no words for the pain. Raising her empty palms to the sky, she waited for the sun to rise, wordlessly offering her emptiness to God.

Not until she lost count of the black beads in her work did Jesse find words for her grief. Even then, they were not her own, but those of an ancient who had also known the deepest sense of loss.

Hear my cry, Oh God; attend unto my prayer. From the end of the earth will I cry unto thee, when my heart is overwhelmed: lead me to the rock that is higher than I.

The psalms began to tumble from her mouth, giving voice to the hurt.

Save me, O God; for the waters have come in unto my soul. I sink in deep mire, where there is no standing: I have come into deep waters, where the floods overflow me. I am weary with my crying: my throat is dried: mine eyes fail while I wait for my God.

Jesse read the same words again and again. And the living thing that had held her under a weight of darkness began to lift.

Lord, I cry unto thee: make haste unto me; give ear unto my voice, when I cry unto thee. Let my prayer be set forth before thee as incense; and the lifting up of my hands as the evening sacrifice.

And then one morning the grief quieted. It lay curled on the horizon as dawn broke. It prowled along the edges of her day. But it let Jesse breathe and move through the day without the constant battle. Old One saw her smile at Soaring Eagle. A soft light returned to the gray eyes. Howling Wolf noted the change, too, but decided to wait until spring to avenge his hatred.

Only once after that did the grief nearly overpower her—at the water's edge. She looked down and saw the absence of the face that should be reflected beside her own. She tamed the grief by slapping the water's surface, destroying the image. It retreated. Life went on.

By the Moon of Strong Cold Jesse had grown large with child. Prairie Flower brought her the softest, whitest skin Jesse had ever seen.

"It is the skin of an unborn buffalo calf," she explained,

adding shyly, "I was saving it for my own child . . . but now
. . ." Tears stung her eyes, and she brushed her hand over
her scarred face.

Jesse wondered why the kindness of a friend should bring
the grief prowling back from the shadows. Managing a
whispered thanks, she clutched the skin and fled across the
camp to her own tepee where Rides the Wind was not; his
coming child pushed the very breath from her body as she
panted from her short run. The baby churned and kicked.
A tiny foot pushed against Jesse's ribs and she pressed against
it. The foot kicked back, harder, and she whispered, "Your
child insists on his own way, best beloved."

And then, one morning, Jesse raised her palms heavenward and found her own words tumbling out in place of the
psalms she had been reciting.

The grief retreated to the fringes of her day. It still surprised her at times, leaping out with fresh attacks when she
was least prepared. But time had begun to heal the wound.
When she woke to the absence of Rides the Wind, she filled
the emptiness with his favorite passages of Scripture, reading
them over and over until they became part of her.

Soaring Eagle spent the winter months gentling a new
pony. He had taken over the care of his father's herd and
tended the animals with genuine tenderness, proving that
he had learned his father's lessons well. Jesse watched as he
faithfully gained the trust of the young horse, teaching it to
run swift and straight as its rider slid sideways until only one
knee was visible to the pretended enemy. The two would
chase around a meadow again and again until great clouds
of frosty steam rose from the pony's gaping nostrils. Then
Soaring Eagle would slow the pony to a walk and carefully
cool him down before turning him out with the other horses.

Jesse praised her son for his skill as a rider and was grateful
to be able to watch his demonstration without losing her
battle with grief. A pang of regret was there for the father
who could not know of his son's accomplishments, but it was

manageable and the pain was duller. Jesse had grown to accept it as a permanent part of her existence. She kept it at arm's length and worked every waking hour, helping other women in the village as much as possible, chattering away the hours of each day as she waited for the birth of her child.

She was troubled, though, with more than the ever-present grief. It seemed that wherever she went, Howling Wolf was not far away. When she spoke of it to Prairie Flower, the woman shrugged and said, "Howling Wolf is a worthless man. He pleads with me to come back to him. The other women do not want him. He only seems to be watching you because we are together so much. But I do not want him. He will not give up. Only last week he offered a new buffalo robe as a peace offering." Prairie Flower paused a moment and unconsciously touched the scar his knife had left across her face. Then she whispered, "As if a buffalo robe could heal *this* and take us back to the days when we cared for one another. I will never go back to that *canniyasa!*"

Jesse kept her concerns to herself after that. Still, Howling Wolf seemed to be watching her, and the hatred in his eyes made her shiver.

In the Moon When the Geese Lay Eggs, the signs of spring were everywhere and the people grew restless and ready to move from winter camp. Jesse grew concerned about the move, knowing that her time to deliver her child was growing near. Prairie Flower offered encouragement. "Old One is good *hoksiacu.* She has brought many babies into our band. You need not fear when your time comes."

Soaring Eagle left with a hunting party, joking that when he returned he would have meat for his new brother.

When Soaring Eagle left, Howling Wolf decided to act. Jesse and Old One were asleep when he prowled into their tepee, knocking Old One unconscious with one blow. He leaped across the campfire and grabbed Jesse by the throat, menacing her with his knife. Jesse clutched at his hand and struggled to scream, but the rage Howling Wolf had nursed against her gave him such strength that she had no chance. He hissed at her. "You white demon—now I will have you! You turned Prairie Flower against me and taught her white ways. You schemed and stole the new woman I brought into camp. There is no Rides the Wind to protect you now. And Soaring Eagle is far away. Cry out to your God—he will do *nothing*. The spirits give *me* power. . . . You have ruined me in the eyes of my people, and now you will pay for all you have done!"

Jesse gasped for breath as he gagged her and tied her hands behind her back. He pulled her backward across the tepee, slitting the skins, forcing her through the hole. He began alternately dragging and pushing her toward the creek. Her feet grew icy cold as they trudged through the melting snow. She winced and stumbled. Howling Wolf jabbed her belly and forced her on. Fear for the unborn child kept her quiet. Panic kept her moving.

When they reached the creek, Jesse saw Red Star tethered next to a strange pony. Howling Wolf shoved her up onto Star's bare back and leaped onto his mount to lead her away. He went slowly at first, careful not to rouse the camp. Jesse gripped Star's sides with her knees as tightly as she could.

The next few hours they rode along the stream, back through the Gate of the Buffalo. Jesse clung to Star's sides with agonized muscles, desperately praying to stay mounted. Her great belly threw her off balance as they lurched along, and she bounced hard against Star's spine, unable to move with the familiar rhythm of the pony's stride.

Howling Wolf stopped only to water the ponies. Each time, he checked the ropes that held Jesse's hands behind her. Each time, he shoved the gag back into her mouth with a filthy hand.

Near dawn, they struck out across the open prairie. At last, Jesse saw their destination. Rising from the earth—indeed, made from the very earth, was a cabin. From its only window came the feeble glow of a lamp.

Caution had kept Pierre Canard inside his soddy as he watched the approach of two unfamiliar horses. He crouched peering over the window sill, rifle in hand, and waited. The ponies moved slowly and the trapper scratched at his graying beard and squinted his eyes to learn all he could by observing the visitors. As the sun rose and the riders approached, he whistled his amazement that one of the riders was a white woman, bound and gagged and obviously very pregnant. She had also received very rough treatment. Her tangled red hair hid most of her face, in spite of her efforts to shake it back over her shoulders.

Howling Wolf dismounted and strode to the door of the cabin, pounding loudly to awaken the inhabitants. He ignored Jesse.

Canard made the immediate assumption that here was a captive to be rescued and returned to her family at whatever cost. He opened the door and stepped lightly outside, conversing with Howling Wolf in sign language. Gagged, Jesse could only watch the conversation. She raged inwardly, powerless to contradict Howling Wolf's lies.

The trade was made quickly. Canard was eager to rescue the helpless captive and rid himself of the greedy savage before his friends showed up to protest the meager reward Canard had offered. Howling Wolf grudgingly accepted the two scrawny ponies Canard offered in trade and demanded Canard's rifle as part of the bargain. Canard shook his head defiantly and retreated inside the soddy to rummage for a substitute. He came back out with a bottle of whiskey. Howling Wolf guzzled it before handing over the reins to Red Star and staggering over to bridle the two ponies that were part of the trade. In a few moments, he had departed with the two ponies and the whiskey, forgetting to take Red Star back with him. Canard laughed to himself about the savage's stupidity even as he lifted Jesse down from Red Star and unbound and ungagged her.

Jesse gasped for fresh air and rubbed her hands together,

not knowing what to say. Canard broke the silence, "Please, madame, come inside. I will make you coffee, bring water for washing. Whatever you need, Pierre Canard will try to supply. I am only a trader, alone in this house, but you are welcome and I will help you. You need have no fear. When you have rested, we will go to the fort and I will help you find your family."

Jesse interrupted him. "My family is back in the Lakota village, my son, my mother-in-law, my friends." Canard stared dumbly at her, his brain slow to process the amazing fact that this woman actually wanted to return to the very savages that had brought her here.

"I have lived with the people for . . . " Jesse stopped. How many years had it been? She had lost count. "I have lived with the people for many years, now . . . "

"But," Canard interrupted, "he said that you were a slave, that he needed horses more than a worthless woman who would no longer work. . . . He said . . . "

"He is a liar. He is my enemy. My husband is dead, and he has been waiting to attack me. My son went out with a hunting party, and I was stupid. I thought that Howling Wolf had given up his schemes. I was wrong. Please! Help me return to my people." Jesse grew desperate. "It's all I have, all I know. I wouldn't know how . . ." She was crying now, tears running down both cheeks.

Canard took the reins to the pony that stood waiting patiently. "Please, madame, you go inside, sit by the fire. I will take the pony to the corral and bring you fresh water. We will talk. I will help you. Please, do not cry."

But Jesse could not stop the tears. She nodded at him and plodded inside the strange cabin and sat obediently by the glowing fire, but the angry tears continued.

The trapper bustled about outside and hurried in with a full bucket of fresh water. Jesse washed her hands and her face and tried to tame the tangle of her hair while Canard stirred the fire and boiled water for coffee. He bustled about efficiently while Jesse sat wearily on the floor, her head nodding in spite of her efforts to stay awake.

She did not know how much time had elapsed when the once familiar aroma of coffee filled the air and Canard touched her hand gently. "Madame, we haf' breakfast now, and we talk. And Pierre Canard will help you all he can."

Jesse allowed herself to be led to the rough-hewn table where she was presented with a tin cup of steaming liquid. She stared in wonder at the fresh biscuits before her and looked up at Canard. Kind blue eyes twinkled as he said, "I am a man alone, but I am a good cook! You eat for the baby, eh?"

The reminder of the baby's welfare encouraged her to eat. She lifted a biscuit to her lips, and the aroma of sourdough made her mouth water. She ate greedily, washing down two biscuits with the steaming coffee. It revived her, and she tried to smooth the torn elkskin dress, tucking her cold feet back underneath the chair as far out of sight as possible. The warmth from the fireplace soothed the aches from the night-long ride. Her weariness receded.

Canard joined her at the table, consuming a half dozen biscuits and as many cups of coffee, trying to fill the silence with activity. At last, he pushed his chair back from the table and looked out the window. The sky was gray and threatening.

"It looks like we may have a storm coming, madame. I go to tend the horses. The foolish man who brought you here did not know that the good horses I keep inside at night, to protect them from the likes of him. So I put the little pony inside too."

At mention of Red Star Jesse found her voice. "She's mine. Her name is Red Star . . ." her voice trailed off. "She was a gift from my husband. She is a good pony . . . " Jesse looked up into the kind eyes and decided he would not laugh at her. "She is a good friend."

Canard smiled. "Well, then, this good friend must have

shelter inside, also, from the storm. You see, it comes even now." Indeed, snowflakes had begun to fall and the wind had begun to sound a low, threatening wail.

Canard bustled outside and tended to his stock. His eyes searched the horizon, and he did not like what he saw. Tying one end of a rope to a corral post, he walked to the well in the yard, and then to the soddy, where he pulled the end of the rope through the door-latch hole and tied a knot to keep it in place. "It looks like this will be a bad storm, madame. Now, I can find my way to the horses and to the well, even if the worst comes . . . which, I hope it does not."

But the wind moaned louder, and the snow came down mixed with pellets of ice that beat against the one window of the soddy. By noon, the grass was coated with ice and the shorter buffalo grass had disappeared under a blanket of white. Jesse sat at the table and watched the storm, praying it would stop so that she could be away. Weariness overtook her, and she curled up near the fire and slept, refusing Canard's urgings to lie down on the rope bed in the corner.

She awoke with a start at the desperate howl of the wind. It had grown eerily dark outside and she knew that she could not find her way back home today. The blizzard would destroy any trail that Howling Wolf had left. She realized with grim satisfaction that the blizzard might destroy the drunken Howling Wolf, as well. And she wondered about Soaring Eagle and the hunting party. Would they have returned to the village by now, or had they, too, been caught by the storm? How long would it be before Soaring Eagle would even know what had happened? How long would it be before he would try to find her?

Her thoughts were interrupted by Canard's repeated urgings that she rest on the rope bed. She refused, choosing instead to make a pallet on the floor in a remote corner of the soddy. Canard gave in to her stubbornness, and hung a tattered quilt across that corner to give her some privacy.

"Thank you," she managed. Then, she said softly, "I am

sorry that I cannot explain to you, but it is all so muddled. I don't know where to begin . . . and," she sighed, "I am so very tired."

Canard interrupted her. "This storm will give you many days to think. And if you choose to tell me your story, then I will listen. But, madame," and the blue eyes glowed warmly, "you need say nothing if that is what you wish. I will listen if you wish to talk . . . if you wish to be silent, I will understand. And, madame," he added awkwardly, "I am in a land of many godless men, but I am a God-fearing man. I will not harm you. Perhaps God has sent you here so that I can help . . . please, do not fear me." He seemed to be groping for more words, but he said no more.

Jesse only nodded as she tried to grasp the implications of his speech. She raged in anger that she had been torn away from the Lakota. She did not want a new future. She wanted to go home where Soaring Eagle and Prairie Flower and Old One waited. If a return to the whites was God's will, then for once, she did not want God's will. Rides the Wind, Soaring Eagle, Prairie Flower, Homer, horses, wagons, ponies, Old One, images and memories swirled and danced even as the snow swirled outside, destroying any hope of her following a trail back to the Lakota.

Chapter 19

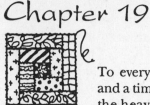

To every thing there is a season, and a time to every purpose under the heaven. . . . A time to weep, and a time to laugh; a time to mourn, and a time to dance.

Ecclesiastes 3:1, 4

They came to her in the night. For the first couple of hours, she slept fitfully, wondering in semi-consciousness why the sounds of a blizzard should cause her such alarm. The stomach cramps did not subside, and Jesse awoke in misery. Her breathing came in short gasps as she struggled to rise from her pallet. Groping about in the darkness she reached to light the lamp she had left on the floor. A gush of warm liquid revealed the cause of her discomfort.

"Oh, my Lord," she whispered aloud, "My Lord—not tonight—not here—please, Lord."

The answer to her prayer came in a new wave of contractions. *Yes, my child—tonight.* Jesse breathed deeply and readied herself for the next onslaught.

Yes, Jesse—here. The answers were not audible, and yet her heart heard, *and I will be with you, just as I was with you when you walked the fire, just as I was there in the valley of death, just so, I will be here.*

Jesse's mind grew calmer. The contractions lessened and she thought clearly. She would need clean water, a knife, something to wrap the child in.

The child, she thought in wonder. Tonight she would hold Rides the Wind's child in her arms! A particularly strong contraction came and Jesse cried out—a low whimper that grew as the contraction intensified and ended in a shrill "oh."

She bit her lips to silence herself, but it was too late. Canard had heard. He was standing uncertainly just on the other side of the ragged quilt he had hung for her privacy.

"Madame, what is it?" he asked anxiously. "You need help?" His voice was warm with concern.

Jesse took a deep breath. "I am fine," she gasped. "I am to have my baby tonight, it seems."

Canard stood on the other side of the partition, unwilling to move it without her permission.

"Do you know how to do this thing?" was the next question.

Jesse waited through another contraction before answering. "This is not my first; years ago I had a son. He died—a baby—fell off the wagon. I have helped among the Lakota. I will be all right." Another contraction cut short her reply. She moaned softly.

Canard asked again, "What can I do?"

Jesse silently called to the Lord for help. To Canard, she replied, "Water, a knife, paper, and s-s-s-some-thing-to-wrap-the-ba-by." The last words came out in short gasps. She had expected a long labor. It was not to be.

Canard moved quickly. Beneath the hanging quilt she saw shadows dance as he, too, lit a lamp. The soddy door opened and closed. Two contractions later a pail of fresh water was slid under the quilt. Something was moved on a shelf, and neatly folded brown paper and a knife appeared. Finally, a bar of lye soap and a soft cloth were added to the row of things on the floor. *Thank you, Lord,* Jesse thought, *for supplying what I need even before I ask.*

Two more contractions came, one upon the other. Jesse was forced to her pallet.

There was little respite after that. At one point, Canard peeked around the edge of the quilt. His face showed genuine concern, but Jesse rejected his help. Entirely consumed by her own body, engulfed at once by physical pain, longing for Rides the Wind's presence, and a desire to be elsewhere, Jesse clung to her privacy. "I-don't-want-you-here!" she spat out between clenched teeth. Canard mumbled an apology and was gone. He paced violently up and down the length of the cabin, totally immersed in the miracle occurring just the other side of the tattered quilt.

She came at dawn. Howling immediately and waving her tiny fists, a girl was born in the sod cabin of Pierre Canard, the trapper. Shaking with fatigue and delight, Jesse whispered familiar words to the baby, *"Hoksicala wan icimani hi,"* a baby traveler has arrived. Soaring Eagle, you have a sister.

She managed to cut the cord, clean herself, and wash the child before collapsing. Canard threw back the quilt that had walled him out, swooped upon the mother and child, and tended both. He produced a clean comforter for Jesse's pallet and lifted her back onto it to rest. Jesse stirred and was amazed to see him deftly dressing the tiny infant in a gown. He tied a bonnet over the thick dark hair before wrapping her in a small quilt and handing her to her mother.

Jesse whispered her thanks and asked, "But where . . . ?"

Canard did not let her finish. "I am not so old as I look, Madame. These belonged to my wife, to Suzette. We dreamed together of a family, a home. Five more years of trapping, and we would return home to St. Louis. But my dreams, they die. Suzette—our baby." His voice shook. He shrugged and ended his tale, "Still, I keep the trunk full of memories, full of dreams that have died. You take for this little one what she is needing. My Suzette, she love to sew. She make many baby things. Take, too, what is there from my Suzette. Whatever you need. She would be happy to know she helps. She always was busy that way—helping others."

His voice failed him and Canard rushed outside, returning later to find Jesse and her daughter asleep.

When Jesse woke a few hours later, it was to the wails of a hungry baby and the smell of strong coffee. Canard bustled about the cabin cooking and cleaning as if readying his home for a royal guest. Hearing the baby cry, he approached the quilt and inquired, "Is Mama hungry too?" Jesse said yes, and quickly found herself presented with "enough flapjacks to choke a mule." She smiled grimly at the memory that had resurrected the phrase from long ago. Homer had used it when he demanded his breakfast the morning after Jacob's birth. Jesse had climbed out of bed and complied.

This birth, however, and the blizzard, had placed her at the mercy of Pierre Canard. He seemed bent on showering the mother and child in his care with all the attention he had stored up for his own wife and child, and never used. But Jesse would have none of it.

"Nonsense," she replied to Canard's insistence that she rest. "The Lord has blessed me with health and strength. I will not be a burden to you. As soon as the storm is over, we must return to the people. My son will be looking for me." Even as she said it, Jesse's head swirled, and she found herself scooting back down under her comforter.

Canard said softly, "The Lord has blessed you, yes—and you must ask, too, to be humble, madame. Perhaps God has sent you to me, so that I can help you. What do you say to that?"

The blizzard raged, hurling so much snow against the soddy's door that Canard was barely able to squeeze outside to tend the horses. Jesse realized that returning to the village anytime soon would be impossible.

When her baby was two days old, Jesse found the courage to sort through the trunk Canard had moved to her corner. It contained enough baby clothes to keep her child in clean linen for several days. Two calico dresses in good repair were hauled out and washed for Jesse. By letting out the waists, letting down the hems, and ignoring the too-short sleeves, Jesse partly regained her appearance as a white women. She left her hair braided, though, and refused Canard's offer of a pair of his shoes when they discovered that Jesse's feet could not be forced into Suzette's tiny shoes.

"I hate them, anyway," she reasoned. "Moccasins are so much more comfortable. Besides," she added, "these were a gift from someone very dear." Canard dropped the subject of shoes and returned to admiring the baby, whose grunts and sighs sounded from the crate he had fashioned into a cradle.

"And what is this lovely little girl's name, eh?" He questioned.

"I haven't a name . . . yet," Jesse answered quickly. "She came too soon."

The blizzard finally abated on the third day of her daughter's life and Jesse ventured outside. The world was a sea of brilliant white. From the corral she heard a familiar nicker. Red Star stood watching her, eyes and ears alert. The flood of emotion she felt at the sight and sound of her pony surprised Jesse. She buried her face in the red mane and sobbed. Canard peeked out the door and nodded. "Good," he mumbled, "it is good—she cry, she feel better."

Embarrassed by her emotional display, Jesse hesitated to return to the soddy, but a hungry wail precluded further privacy. Jesse hurried in, grabbed the baby, and retreated quickly to her corner. Canard pretended he had not seen her tears, and she offered no explanation.

As time passed and Jesse recovered physically, she grew restless. There seemed no way to leave the trapper's soddy. The people would have moved to their spring camp. Soaring Eagle would search—but was there any chance he would find her? Canard was a gentleman, it seemed, but the thought of staying alone with him filled her with dread. With no idea what to do, Jesse stayed on and prayed for answers. It seemed she heard only silence. As the days passed, she lost all joy in her child. To look upon her dark eyes and hair was to look into the face of Soaring Eagle, who looked so like his father.

Canard cooed over the child, making himself ridiculous. He coaxed Jesse with suggestions for a name, but she would not decide. Jesse fed the baby and cared for her, but once the infant's needs were met, she put her back into her cradle-crate and either sat in a chair near the window to stare outside or she fled outside to spend fresh grief with Red Star. Her eyes searched the horizon for a sign of Soaring Eagle.

Canard waited for Jesse to recover, but recovery did not come. Instead, she sank into an ever-deepening mire of depression and indecision. She slept often, worked little, and did only what she had to to keep her child alive. *Lord where are you?* she prayed. *I cannot help myself . . . why won't you help me? Where is Soaring Eagle—why does he not come?* The words seemed to hit empty air and fall back to the cabin floor. She finally tired of sending them up.

Canard watched her downward spiral and grew increasingly desperate to force a change. He cooked well and tried to tempt Jesse with creative dishes. She ate whatever he made without relish, and continued to lose weight. He sang and danced with the baby, but Jesse turned away.

At last, his patience spent, Canard grew angry, and by accident discovered a way to help Jesse recover. He began storming about the cabin, scolding Jesse. "You tell me you have a heavenly Father who will help you with the birth of this baby, eh? And where is he now, eh? He goes away now and leaves you to be so sad, poor madame, eh? You have a baby, madame! You have a healthy baby, no? Oh, yes, the husband, he is gone . . . but *look* what he give you! My Suzette, when she leave, she take the baby with her! Pierre, he get *nothing!* Well, look, madame," Canard rushed over to the trunk. He opened it and began tossing things out. "I tell you I will help you find these people—if that is what you wish. We will look until we find your band—your son. I tell you I will help you find a new life—if that is what you wish. But you sit and say nothing. Look here, madame. You want to die, Pierre has the coffin, just for you. See, here." He measured its length, holding his arms apart as he approached Jesse. "You fit just fine. So you die, madame—you no care for baby anyway. I raise this child. I will love her. *You!*" he pushed Jesse back onto her cot, now piled with the contents of the trunk. "You go ahead. Die! Die now!"

Canard huffed over to the sleeping infant, picked her up, crate and all, and took her outside. Jesse paid no attention to him. Rather, she stared about her at the bits of cloth Pierre had scattered in his anger. Mechanically, she began picking them up. Some were cut into diamonds. Others were narrow strips. Then she found it. It was half hidden by a mended camisole, but she uncovered it. *A Log Cabin patch,* she thought. *Just like my Log Cabin quilt back home. . . . Home?* Her brain shut out the painful memory. She began to sort the remnants around her.

Jesse rushed over to the trunk and rummaged about feverishly. *There! In the corner.* It was a bit rusty, but it was a needle. *Thread,* she thought, *I need thread.* She picked out the basting from the discarded camisole. The project consumed her. She sorted and folded, and sorted, and put away. And somewhere, in the work of sorting, God began his work of covering over her pain.

Hours later, when Pierre returned, he found Jesse seated by the window, stitching. He saw no trace of the trunk's contents, except for the few piles of what Pierre called rags. They were sorted by color and shape, and they were the beginning of Jesse's healing.

Bad weather continued. Spring was late that year, and Jesse was glad. It provided an excuse for the absence of a search party. It prevented her from having to make a decision about where she would go. She waited to be found. Pierre became a treasured friend. They haggled over baby names, drank gallons of coffee, and hummed lullabies.

Jesse pieced a quilt. It began as a Log Cabin, but then she ran out of logs and added a border and a row of the diamonds. Too soon she was out of the patches Suzette had cut. Pierre offered a few more precious bits of cloth so that Jesse could keep working. She added them to the quilt.

As the patchwork grew, Jesse's spirits soared. She sang lullabies to the baby, beginning with the one she had learned from Rides the Wind.

a wa wa wa
Inila istinma ma
a wa wa wa
Be still, sleep.

One crisp, cold morning, she went out to see Red Star and was surprised to realize that the mare's greeting no longer caused her anguish. In its place there was a peaceful joy at the familiar sound. The memories rushed in, but Jesse smiled through them and stroked Star's soft muzzle. "Star," she said aloud, "Soaring Eagle has not come. I cannot find my way alone. Pierre tells me of the white greed for land. They battle the Lakota, which they call the Sioux. I wonder what it will bring to us."

As her grief retreated, Jesse's certainty grew that in the spring she would return to white society. Soaring Eagle had not come, and she began to believe that Howling Wolf had been the instrument God used to guide her into his will for the new baby. Jesse stitched, and cooked, and prayed for answers. They did not come all at once, but she no longer felt that her prayers went unheard.

She began to think of the child as Daughter of the Wind. But when she finally shared her decision with Pierre, the name that came out was not Daughter of the Wind. Jesse was surprised to her herself say, "Her name is LisBeth W. King. LisBeth for my grandmother."

". . . and the W.?" Pierre asked.

"Just W. Someday I'll tell her. She was almost named for the wind."

Chapter 20

If any of you lack wisdom, let him
ask of God.

James 1:5

In the spring of 1855, Corporal Gavin Donovan
was off duty when Pierre Canard rode into Fort
Kearney with three pack mules in tow. His arrival would have
gone fairly unnoticed if it were not for the fact that he was
accompanied by a woman and an infant. Leaning against the
corner of the sutler's sod building, Donovan whistled lowly
and sent a stream of tobacco spewing toward the trapper's
mules before saying, "Well, if it ain't Kay-nard. Looks like ya
had yerself a good winter, Frenchie."

"Trapping was not so good this year—too much snow. I
have trouble keeping the traps set. Too many storms."

"Trappin' ain't exactly what I was thinkin' 'bout," drawled
the Corporal with a telling glance at Jesse and LisBeth.
Pretending not to hear, Jesse sat straighter in the saddle and
avoided looking at Donovan.

Canard ignored the coarse joke. He held LisBeth while
Jesse dismounted and accompanied him into the sutler's
building. A few meager provisions lined the shelves in the
sod hut. Moses Shipman complained about the poor freight
service he had received all winter and apologized to Pierre
for the lack of provisions. "If you can wait a week, they's a
freight train due through here. I'll be stocked up then."

"A week is no problem. I can wait." Turning to Jesse, he
said, "If you will wait outside, Madame King, I will request to
see the captain."

The picture of Donovan's company for even a few moments repulsed her. "Please, Pierre, I can speak for myself." As she completed the sentence, Donovan's barrel-shaped form filled the doorway to the sutler's. He made an exaggerated bow as Pierre and Jesse, with LisBeth held tightly to her body, squeezed by.

Coming outside into the sunshine, Jesse took a deep breath of fresh air. Across the square parade ground, soldiers were pouring out of the commissary and lining up for the morning's drill. Jesse followed Pierre to the building next to the sutler's, where he requested to see Captain Woodbury.

Having partaken of too much blackberry cobbler the evening before, Captain Angus Woodbury had been awake most of the night suffering severe indigestion. When he learned that Pierre Canard had requested an audience, he was irritated. But then he had not accounted for *Mrs.* Angus Woodbury, who had controlled her passion for blackberry cobbler the previous evening in hopes of still fitting into her one good dress at the officer's ball.

Libby Rose Barber and Angus Woodbury had been married in the parlor of the grand house that represented Rosewood Plantation to the surrounding county. Blushing just enough to appear ladylike, she had congratulated herself on landing the most handsome graduate of West Point from the county. She had packed her dowry—including her great-grandmother's porcelain tea set from England—and set up housekeeping in the tiny new home that she was sure would be replaced by lavish officer's quarters in no time.

Angus did not disappoint her. He excelled in the military and was promoted readily. What did disappoint her, however, was his passion for the frontier. Libby stared in wide-eyed, speechless dismay the day Angus came home with the news that they were headed west, to Nebraska Territory, where he had been awarded the command of Fort Kearney.

"Just think of it, Libby. We can make a difference there! We'll be protecting the emigrants that pass through, providing a place for them to pause and reflect, to get their bearings, to recuperate. We'll assure their safety and do our part in helping this country grow." Angus beamed with enthusiasm. Libby was not amused. But Libby Rose Barber was wiser than her years. She feigned excitement, pretended to share his enthusiasm, packed her great-grandmother's porcelain tea set, and headed for the frontier without complaint. Thus, she began to grow the love and commitment that would hold her marriage together through fifty childless years of military life. Thus she sealed her promise that she would remain faithful to Angus until death required that she lay him in God's arms.

Just at the moment that Canard requested to see the Captain, LisBeth decided she was hungry and let out a demanding wail. Squirming unhappily she refused to be quieted. Libby Rose heard LisBeth's hungry wail. Jesse was sitting on a hard, narrow bench in the commander's office, wondering how to find a private place to nurse her baby when a tiny woman burst through the door behind the desk.

"Oh, a *baby*," she exclaimed with delight. "May I *see* him?" And when Jesse complied and pulled the quilt away from LisBeth's face, she exclaimed more pleasure and swooped the baby up in her arms, covering the squalling face with kisses. She was lost for a moment in her enthusiasm and then stopped short. Still holding LisBeth, who had stopped crying, seemingly made breathless by the attention, Libby gushed, "Goodness. You must think me a fool! I'm sorry. I didn't even introduce myself, did I? I'm Libby Rose, the captain's wife."

Jesse rose and nodded her head, smiling a hello. "Jesse King, ma'am. Pleased to meet you."

"And you are here with Pierre?" She cuddled LisBeth, who had miraculously gone to sleep in the stranger's arms.

Jesse found herself unable to explain. She stammered and was relieved to see the door open again and the Captain enter the room. Pierre came in behind her, and the four looked at one another momentarily before the Captain invited explanations.

"You requested to see me, Mr. Canard?" He stomach still felt disagreeable and he rang for an officer and ordered tea.

"Thank you, sir. I have, as you see, a traveling companion this spring. Mrs. King came to me the day before the last blizzard." Pierre had asked Jesse's permission to give an abbreviated account of her story to satisfy the curiosity of strangers. He repeated what they had agreed upon. "A Sioux warrior brought her, bound and gagged, to my cabin. He wanted only a few horses in exchange for her. Of course, when I saw that she was captive, I immediately made the trade. The child, she came the very night they arrived. Thanks to God both mother and child are well. With the bad weather, so many storms, there has been no chance to travel this far until one week ago, when finally the thaw came. I wanted to get her to safety before the rivers swelled with spring thaw. I have told Mrs. King that she will find only sympathy with her plight here. I am hoping that you will be able to help her find her way, as God wills."

While Pierre talked, Jesse looked from the captain to his wife. Libby's face expressed horror, then compassion. Tears welled up in her eyes as she gazed down into LisBeth's face. She placed another kiss on the infant's cheek and smiled warmly at Jesse. Clearly, this was a matter for women to handle.

"Angus, dear," Libby said in a low voice. "As always, I defer to your wisdom in matters affecting the military . . ." Then her eyes flashed and she seemed to come to life. "But Angus, honey, we've just got to help this poor woman! Just look at this precious face. Why, when I think what they've been *through*. We must help. Angus, what can we do?" Clearly, Libby Rose had taken Jesse King under her wing and intended for her to stay there until it was certain that she and her baby were safe.

Angus thought his options through carefully. Libby Rose

had no patience to wait for him to do so. She felt that further urging was required. "Just think, Angus, if it were *me*—if *I* had been taken by the Indians—what if *I* were being returned to the care of some military officer! How would you want *me* to be treated, Angus?"

The last thing Angus wanted to ponder was the fate of his Libby Rose in the hands of the Sioux. He hastened to speak, lest the image remain too long in his mind. "Mrs. King, we will do all that the military can do to help you locate your family and return to them. Please, give me their address. We'll have a communique sent immediately. And while you make arrangements to return home, you'll be afforded shelter . . ."

The question of shelter was a hard one. The few frame structures were all occupied by officers or commissioned men, the sutler, and the teacher. Only crude sod buildings completed the relatively small square of structures that surrounded the parade ground and it's focal point, the flagpole. There was barely room enough for those assigned regular duties at the fort. Adding a guest would not be an easy task.

Jesse broke the silence and solved the difficulty. She also closed off her past and finished the separation from her family in Illinois that had begun the day she had been carried off by Rides the Wind. "Truth be told, Captain, I have no family. At least none that would welcome me home, now."

Captain Woodbury cleared his throat. The specter of the poor woman's experiences with the savages rose up and forced him to take immediate action to protect her. "Mrs. King," Woodbury said quietly, "God forbid that anyone I love be called upon to endure the hardships you have known. This government is sworn to protect its citizens, and, as its representative, I offer you everything in my power that will assist you in reclaiming your rightful place in our society."

It was a pretty speech, but still, the captain had no idea how to help her. Libby saved him.

"Angus . . . perhaps she could *work* here at the Fort. The

men have been complaining that there aren't enough laundresses, and with the dragoons arriving in the fall . . . "

Jesse spoke up quickly. "I'd be grateful for any work, sir." Her calm gray eyes met the captain's. "The Lord has blessed me with good health and a strong constitution. He seems to have declared that I'll need to make my own way in the world. I'm not afraid of hard work, if it will provide the means for me to make a home for my daughter."

The daughter in question woke and without warning began to squall again. Libby was unable to quiet her this time and reluctantly returned her to her mother, then ushered Jesse into her own drawing room for privacy.

When the two women were alone, Libby remained warm and concerned. "The laundresses' quarters are sod right now, but Angus has plans to rebuild as soon as possible. Most of the other laundresses are the wives of enlisted men. They're not rough or undesirable at all, and some have children too. I think you'll be comfortable."

"I'm grateful for your help, Mrs. Woodbury." Jesse took a deep breath. "But of greatest concern to me is this: Can I depend on you to help me protect my child?" Cool gray eyes and stormy green eyes met and understood one another. But Jesse would not be content with unspoken promises. "Obviously, LisBeth is not Pierre's child. I was among the Sioux, as you call them, for many years. I was returned here against my will. But after a long spring of constant prayer seeking God's will, I feel that he has a plan for us that does not include our staying with the people. Tensions mount every day. I know the power of the government and the will of the Lakota. There will be trouble, and for LisBeth's sake, we should not be with the Lakota when hostilities break out. I owe it to her and to her father to do my best for her. So, against my own desires, I have come here, seeking a new life." Jesse's eyes had not left Libby's for the entire speech. "Will you help me build a new life—for the baby's sake?"

Libby Rose Barber Woodbury stretched to her full

height—which was not quite five feet. Earnestly, with her hands clasped, she said solemnly, "Mrs. King, I promise you at this moment, on the memory of my beloved father, that your secret will go to the grave with me." She was the perfect portrait of a child acting the dramatic climax of a play. Her promise seemed genuine, but it was her next words that truly comforted Jesse and enabled her to trust this stranger. "God's Word says that the Lord hates a lying tongue. Mrs. King, I try to obey his Word with all my being. Your secret is safe with me."

Jesse finished feeding LisBeth and was ushered once again into the captain's office, where Pierre Canard and another soldier waited. Woodbury bowed formally to Jesse and extended his hand. "Mrs. King, may I officially welcome you to Fort Kearney. Private Dennison will escort you to your new quarters and introduce you to Gilda, the head laundress. If there is anything we can do to help you get settled, please do not hesitate to make your needs known."

Jesse followed Pierre and the soldier past the sutler's quarters and the hospital to a long, low sod building. At one end of the building was a closed door. The soldier swung it open to reveal the dusty room that was to become their new home. At the look of dismay on Jesse's face, the soldier stammered explanations. "Don't fret, ma'am. Captain gave orders for three of us to clean it up for ya', and we'll be doin' that right away—bringin' in some furniture too. It won't be fancy, but it'll be cozy. Sod don't look like much, but it's cool in the summer and warm in the winter. And we'll be buildin' a new place for ya' soon, leastways, that's what Ma'am says." The soldier grinned at Jesse. "And one thing we all learn real quick around here is that she's tiny, but when Ma'am speaks, it gets done."

Ma'am had apparently spoken about the quarters for the new laundress. Pierre arrived with his pack mules and unloaded all of Suzette's things that he had been able to convince Jesse to take. Together, they walked across the compound to stable Red Star and the mule train. Pierre would stay a few days until the wagon train arrived with fresh provisions.

Having seen to the comfort of their animals, Jesse and Pierre stopped in again at the sutler's, where Pierre insisted that Jesse allow him to trade a fine beaver pelt for several yards of richly colored madder-brown calico, muslin, a new pack of quilting needles, and several half-yard pieces of various colors of cotton cloth.

"I saw how the needlework heals you when you are lonely," said Pierre "This is my gift to you, for the little one." Jesse accepted the gifts with warm thanks.

By the time they had walked the short distance back to her new quarters, the three soldiers assigned the duty had swept her room clean, set up two cots and a table, and laid out a plate, cup, frying pan and tea kettle near the fire. A rocking chair, "compliments of Ma'am" sat by the fireplace. Jesse sank into it gratefully, and rocked LisBeth before laying her, sound asleep, on the cot in the corner.

Pierre cleared his throat and turned to go.

"Surely I will see you before you . . .?"

"Of course, I will stop by to see how you are settled. Just now, if you wish to meet this Gilda, the head laundress, I will stay with LisBeth." He felt awkward in her room and encouraged her to leave.

Jesse searched out Gilda, who stood scrubbing the collar of a filthy shirt over a steaming pan of water.

"So, yer the one who's causin' all the commotion t'day," was her terse welcome. Jesse hesitated at the doorway.

"Where's the baby?"

"She's asleep. Mr. Canard said that he would watch her."

"How you gonna' work with a baby in tow?" She did not look up, did not pause in her attack upon the shirt collar.

"I'll manage."

"Don't want you expectin' no favors."

"I won't."

"Fires need to be started and roarin' hot by 5 A.M.—that's when the water brigade fills the tubs. You know how to start a fire?"

Jesse smiled at the irony of the question. "I know how."

"Then that's yer job from now on."

Two days later, Pierre Canard had traded his furs for provisions and headed home. Before he left, he clasped Jesse's hands warmly in his own. "The sewing that helped you not be so lonely . . . perhaps I should have had you teach me, eh?" He cleared his throat, kissed Jesse on the cheek, rumpled LisBeth's thick dark hair, and walked briskly away.

Chapter 21

Thy testimonies . . . are . . . my counselors.

Psalm 119:24

As LisBeth grew into a toddler, Jesse often longed to confine her in a cradle board the way she had Two Mothers. She had thought it cruel when she first lived among the Lakota, but now she appreciated that most sensible way of keeping a young babe out of harm's way. Somehow she managed to keep LisBeth away from the dangers of the laundry room. She rigged up a sort of play area, with boundaries created from a mix of branches and broken chairs. But when LisBeth began to scale the walls of her prison, Jesse took it down, afraid it would fall. Then she tied a cord about LisBeth's waist and her own, ignoring the teasing of the officers who called LisBeth Jesse's pet. Once in a while, someone would offer to help with the child, but Jesse always refused. She was never quite sure whether she didn't trust the potential care-givers, or simply could not bear to have the child out of her sight. Whatever the reason, LisBeth grew up literally tied to her mother's apron strings. But as soon as she was old enough to roam safely, she ran free, proving to be obedient even when out of her mother's sight.

Life at Fort Kearney fell into a monotonous routine. Up at 4 A.M., Jesse dressed in the dark, wrapping her thick braids around her head with no thought to style. Lighting a small fire, she prepared biscuits and hot mush for breakfast and set a little bowl close to the flames to keep it warm until

LisBeth wakened. In a few moments, Jesse was out the door and across the compound. Entering the laundry room, she repeated the fire-building process, warming the huge tubs of water that were filled each morning by cavalrymen.

As she grew older, LisBeth had the luxury of sleeping until she chose to waken, which was usually soon after sunrise. By the time she was seven, her morning routine was well established. After making her bed, she helped herself to breakfast, washed her cup and bowl in the bucket of water just outside the door, then followed her mother's footsteps across the compound.

When LisBeth arrived, Jesse would always pause for a moment to hold her daughter's hands and say a quick prayer for the day before them. The ritual brought them both comfort, as Jesse committed her daughter to the Lord's care, asked for his help in her work, and thanked him for their home. Her thankfulness never wavered, and LisBeth consequently never saw herself as deprived. She seemed not to notice that her life was far different from that of the other children who had large families at the fort.

Jesse often despaired of more time to spend with her daughter. She needed time, she thought, to teach her the many things that a young girl needed to know. But the work never let up, and there was never time for more than the most basic lessons. LisBeth learned to read, sounding out and memorizing one word at a time from the Bible—their only book. She learned to keep house by watching her mother, late at night, sweeping and doing their own laundry. As soon as she was able, the young girl took over many of those chores. She was quick to see the weary lines in her mother's face at day's end, and in her little girl fashion, LisBeth strove to lighten the burden.

The ritual of morning prayers taught LisBeth the importance of regular worship. The quick prayers she often heard her mother send heavenward taught her the dynamics of a living faith. Whatever the problem, Jesse always took it to her

Lord. She would break into the middle of a talk with LisBeth to say, "Now we'll just have to ask the Lord about this, LisBeth." And without even bowing her head, Jesse would turn her words heavenward, "Father, we need fabric to make LisBeth a new dress." Or, "Father, please make Jimmy see that it hurts LisBeth when he doesn't play nice." And sometimes, "Father, we don't really *need* it, but we sure would appreciate a new lamp to light our room at night." LisBeth learned that God was not a stranger far away in the sky and that he was interested in her problems. LisBeth learned about the God who is "a very present help."

"We don't have Papa here to take care of us," Jesse would say, "but our heavenly Father knows and cares, so we'll just tell him about it and wait to see what he thinks needs to be done."

After the long day of toiling over laundry tubs and flat-irons, Jesse would drag herself back across the compound and lie down for a few minutes. She was only forty, but she was beginning to feel aged.

Once Jesse had risen and begun to prepare their supper, LisBeth would begin her string of tales from the day's adventures. She explored every corner of Fort Kearney, knew every soldier's name, petted every horse's neck, and never complained of being bored. Jesse often thanked the Lord for having given her a child so able to entertain herself and so capable of the few chores demanded of her. Indeed, it had seemed that since she was an infant, LisBeth had been a blessing. As a baby, she would lie for hours, watching her mother hard at work, squirming only when hungry. Jesse would hear her first peeps and look over to see two dark eyes following her about the laundry room. She was reminded of another pair of dark eyes that had followed her every move just as eagerly, waiting to be fed.

After every supper, as the evening light dimmed, Jesse would place her Bible on the scarred tabletop, open it to a favorite passage, and read aloud. This was one of the few times she would be stern with LisBeth.

"Having God's own words in a book is an awesome thing, LisBeth," Jesse would remind her daughter at the first sign of a squirm. "We must cherish it. But more important, we must obey what it says. Now, let's see what the Lord has for us today." Jesse favored the Psalms and the end of Job, where God displayed his might in nature.

"Your pa loved this part of the Bible," Jesse would say, and LisBeth's eyes would sparkle at the thought of her imaginary papa reading the same book that her mother held.

"He never learned to read it himself," Jesse explained, "but he had me read it to him every night. And he especially liked this part about God controlling the wind and the wild animals." Then Jesse would read. She was careful not to read for too long. She did not want to tax her young daughter's attention span. She longed for her daughter to look forward to rather than dread the reading.

LisBeth did her part, sitting quietly and listening to the words.

"It isn't much, Lord," Jesse would pray, "but you promised your Word wouldn't come back void. I'm doing my best to share it with my daughter. Please bless it. Put it in her heart so that someday, when she needs it, your word will come to comfort her and guide her."

Day in and day out, Jesse's and LisBeth's schedules remained the same. There were few interruptions in the routine of life. Sunday was the one day when the two had respite. They began the day with church. Jesse would have been embarrassed had her daughter realized that it was not church that refreshed her mother's soul. Many Sundays Jesse only endured the sonorous sermons, waiting for the true highlight of her week: the opportunity to escape the fort, to return to the prairie, and to remember.

After services, they would change into older clothing, saddle up Red Star, and amble across the prairie. As the walls of the fort grew smaller in the distance, Jesse's spirit soared. Heading for the nearby river, LisBeth and Jesse would dismount and eat their meager picnic on its banks.

After lunch, Jesse's heavy braids would come down so that LisBeth could play with her mother's hair. They picked flowers, sang hymns, walked along the edge of the water, and talked and laughed. Most Sunday afternoons, Jesse brought along a bit of needlework or mending. She diligently taught her daughter basic stitching and piecing. Together they cut out squares from discarded uniforms, and LisBeth happily pieced a doll quilt for the ragged doll she loved. It was a simple Nine Patch pattern, and the seams were uneven so that one edge was longer than the other, but Jesse praised it and stitched LisBeth's name and the date along one edge.

As they picnicked and sang and stitched, Jesse's eyes searched the horizon. Shadows seemed to dance in the prairie grasses about them. Had LisBeth seen them, she would have been afraid, but Jesse was comforted. Her long hair flowed down her back, and she drank in the fresh air. *He would be nineteen now,* Jesse thought, imagining Soaring Eagle hunting with his friends. The time always went too quickly. LisBeth would watch in fascination as her mother deftly rewrapped her hair about her head. Slowly they would ride back to the fort to begin another week of soap water and rinse water, of scrubbing and toiling.

If Jesse noticed how lonely their existence was, she never spoke of it. If LisBeth longed for a dear friend, she never spoke of it to Mama. LisBeth began to notice that Mama had two smiles. There was the gentle smile of every day—the one that barely showed and left her gray eyes solemn. But there was another smile that wreathed her mother's face in joy and lighted something in her eyes. *I only see that smile on Sunday,* LisBeth thought, *I wonder why.*

LisBeth sat outside the laundry room where Jesse worked. Her legs dangled over the edge of the bench, and her tiny feet pummeled the earth angrily as she stomped and muttered to herself. Her chubby hand defiantly swiped at the tears that she could not will away. "Not gonna cry . . . not gonna cry," she muttered to herself.

Sitting down beside LisBeth, Jesse said, "You're back early. Was it too hot for the game?"

LisBeth nodded and turned her head away. But Jesse had already seen the tracks the tears had left on her daughter's dusty cheek.

"Why, LisBeth," Jesse said gently. "What happened? Did you fall? Did you hurt yourself?"

LisBeth shook her head no. She hugged her knees and studied her toes, waiting for her mother to leave. But Jesse was not put off so easily. "LisBeth," she said, "you must tell Mama what happened."

It all came out in an angry tumble, "I hate that Jimmy Callaway. I just *hate* him! He thinks he's really somethin'. Thinks he's better'n me."

Jesse waited for the little voice to regain its control. LisBeth continued, "Said he didn't want me on his team. Said I got no pa." LisBeth stared up into her mother's eyes. "He called me a *name*."

Jesse's arms encircled her child as she whispered, "Jimmy Callaway is just a little boy, LisBeth. He doesn't know anything about us. You *do* have a papa, LisBeth. But your papa's in heaven—that's all."

LisBeth slipped out of Jesse's firm grasp. "Tell me about him, Mama. Tell me about my papa," she pleaded.

Jesse had gone through the story dozens of times with her daughter. Every time she told it, she meant to tell it all, but something always held her back. She had gone over it in her mind dozens of time. *This child deserves to know,* she would think, *she should know all about her father.* But then she thought about the word *half-breed* and the general spite of those around her toward Indians. Her fears of how they would be treated rose, and somehow, caution would win out and they would go another day with LisBeth assuming that Homer was her father. Jesse meant to correct the memory. She meant to tell LisBeth that her father was Rides the Wind, a Lakota Indian. But somehow she never did.

"Your papa was the kindest, gentlest, bravest man I ever met," Jesse said. "He had dark hair and dark eyes, and he walked with a funny limp because he'd hurt his leg before I met him. He could ride a horse and hunt . . ."

LisBeth's voice chimed in, "And he loved you very, very, much."

"That's right, honey," Jesse said. "He loved me very, very much."

LisBeth added, "And you were very, very sad when he died."

"I was very, very sad for a long, long time," Jesse agreed, "but then *you* were born, and you looked so much like your papa it was as if he had come back to stay with me. We moved away from the home that I had shared with Papa. And we came here to Fort Kearney. God has given us a new home. We have plenty to eat, and clean clothes to wear, and a nice room. And we must thank God for his blessings."

Jesse held her daughter's shoulders and stared solemnly into the young eyes. "Now, you go back to Jimmy Callaway, and you tell him about your pa. Don't be ashamed, LisBeth. And don't run away. It's when people don't understand that they say mean things. Jimmy may not know Jesus like we do. I know it hurts when people talk that way, but if you ask Jesus to help you, he will help you be kind to Jimmy."

Jesse gave LisBeth a little push in the general direction of the children's games and turned back to her work. A little voice sang back to her:

He don't know Jesus
and he don't know 'bout my pa,
So Jimmy Callaway
Don't know nothin' at all.

LisBeth skipped away delighted with her new rhyme. Jesse returned to work, attacking the stains on Corporal Donovan's dress shirt with unusual energy. She smiled pleasantly to her coworkers and turned the incident into an amusing anecdote to share over the hot, soapy tubs of laundry.

But underneath the smile and beneath the laughter lingered a wish for the courage to tell the story that had not been told.

Chapter 22

A friend loveth at all times, and a brother is born for adversity.

Proverbs 17:17

It was on a particularly monotonous day the year that LisBeth was twelve that Jesse's past rumbled into Fort Kearney on a battered freighter wagon. Jesse had stepped outside and was fanning herself with her apron. The overhang outside the laundry-room door shaded her face. It had been nearly twenty-five years since she had seen him, but George Wood still stepped lightly as he climbed down from his wagon.

Removing his trail-worn hat, he beat the dust out of it against the wagon seat. Carefully replacing its crease, George put the hat back on, pulled the brim down to shade his eyes and glanced around the compound. Jesse stood motionless, the tips of her apron poised in midair. Recognition, followed by surprise and then dumb amazement appeared on George's face. He strode briskly across the few feet that separated them.

"Jesse? Jesse King? Is it you? Is it really you?" Then, without waiting for a reply, "I don't believe it! After all these years!"

Jesse extended her hand. "George . . . George Wood."

Where Jesse stood speechless, George sputtered to fill the silence with words. "Jesse . . . how? We looked for you! When you didn't join up with us that night, we went back. We found—we found Homer—the horses—but you were gone. Vinnie nearly worried herself to death. There wasn't a trace of your trail after that rainstorm. How did you . . . Where did you . . . ?"

Just then LisBeth ran up and grabbed Jesse's hand. As Jesse introduced her daughter, George looked down at the dark-haired little girl. Her wavy hair flowed halfway down her back. Her skin was tanned by the hot Nebraska sun. In seconds, he had estimated her age and filled in the details of what had become of Jesse King after they had given up the search. He was miserable. "Oh, Jess—I'm sorry. We should never have given up. We should have looked until . . ."

Jesse interrupted him. "The Lord always provides for his own, George." Her gray eyes looked steadily into his as she tried to send an unspoken message. For the first time she was guilty of a deliberate deception. "After LisBeth's papa died, the Lord provided for us. We've been well cared for by kind people, and I have no complaints. You needn't feel guilty, George. God worked all things out for my good."

Understanding shone in George's eyes. He changed the subject. "I sure wish Vinnie could be here to see this. She wanted to come with me, but I told her there's too much Injun trouble. Made her stay on the place. We've got a homestead in the Willamette Valley, Jesse. She'll never believe it when I tell her I saw Jesse King."

"Can you come for supper?" Jesse asked. "Our little room is just over there. It won't be fancy, but I sure would like to hear news of everyone."

"Did you know my papa?" LisBeth interrupted.

Jesse looked down at her daughter and spoke before George had a chance to answer, "No, LisBeth, Mr. Wood never had a chance to get to know Papa, but he's coming to supper tonight, and we can talk more then." Jesse looked at George hopefully, and he nodded his assent.

LisBeth ran off happily with the anticipation of a dinner guest. This was something new. They had never had a friend for dinner. They had never had a friend, really. LisBeth liked the idea.

After she was out of earshot George said, "I'll just see to my team, Jesse. When you're done here, let me know. I'll be over at the sutler's for a while. And Jesse," he added, "your secret's safe with me."

"Thank you, George. We eat about six o'clock."

Supper had to be simple, but Jesse did her best. She put a cloth on the scarred tabletop. LisBeth had gathered a few wildflowers, and they served as a centerpiece. George dominated the suppertime conversation. Urged on by countless questions, he was in his element, laughing and joking as if the trip west had been a hilarious adventure. Lavinia was in good health; the children were growing strong. They had come through a bout of fever, and little Esther had nearly died. "But the Lord pulled her through," George said. "The Lord always seems to pull us through."

"Yes," Jesse agreed, "sometimes in ways that we don't expect, but he always pulls us through."

George was headed back east to try to convince Lavinia's sister and brother-in-law to join them in Oregon. He sang the praises of the new territory, and Jesse was reminded of Dr. Whitman's persuasive speeches.

"Did you hear about Dr. Whitman?" George asked. When Jesse said no, he told the sad tale. Dr. Whitman and his lovely wife and their coworkers had all been killed by the Indians they had gone to serve. George ended the story, "What a waste . . . such young lives ended that way."

"Lives poured out for God are never wasted, George," Jesse reminded him. *"Now we see through a glass, darkly."*

Uncomfortable with the aspect of a theological discussion, George rose to leave. "Jesse," he said, holding out his hands to take hers, "when Vinnie hears that you survived, you'll probably hear the 'Hallelujah!' all the way from Oregon. You got plans?"

"Only to raise my daughter, George," was her answer.

"I'll be back through here in a few weeks with the rest of the family. Why don't we do one better than me just tellin' Vinnie 'bout you? Why don't you and LisBeth come west with us? You can make a home there. You'll have friends. You was closer to Vinnie than her own sister, anyway. You won't be just a friend. You'll be family. What do you say?"

When Jesse hesitated, George urged her, "Well, think about it! You don't have to give me an answer now, but when I come back through, I'll be looking for you, hoping you got your trunk packed and your bonnet tied on."

"I don't know, George, I'll let you know when you come back." George left, LisBeth went to bed, and Jesse lay awake until long after midnight thinking about the possibility of joining friends in the Oregon Territory.

What shall I do, Lord? she prayed. In the early morning hours, Jesse felt she had her answer. The prairie had claimed the life of the man she had loved, and there had been times when she had been bitter and had hated it. But faced with the prospect of leaving it behind her, Jesse was surprised to learn that she had come to love the land around her. It was cruel at times, when blizzards blew, or the hot sun blazed. Yet, there was something here, something in the panoramic views that held her heart. It was her adopted land, but it was her home, and she had no desire to leave it for the woods of the northwest.

Jesse did not realize until later that George's invitation to Oregon played a great part in the next major change in her life. Although she had determined never to leave the prairie, she had come to realize that as LisBeth grew, there would be a need for ties to others. There would be a need for a more settled life than what was possible here in the fort. The possibility of moving on had been planted, so that in the weeks ahead, Jesse became convinced that God had a new plan for her and her daughter.

One morning not long after George's departure for the east, Gilda rushed in to work with news of a skirmish between the Sioux and a scouting party. There had been casualties, mostly "the thievin' Sioux," but one young lieutenant had been seriously wounded.

"Corporal Donovan's just rode in with the prisoners. Says he's goin' back and clean out the rest of the troublemakers," Gilda blurted out.

Jesse glanced out the door of the laundry room just as the soldiers herded the group of prisoners past. At the rear of the little band of aged warriors straggled a middle-aged squaw dressed in a tattered doeskin dress. Stealing glances at the whites, she hid her face behind the corner of the blanket she huddled in.

Jesse had been dipping sheets slowly into the steaming vat before her. When she caught sight of the squaw, she quickly dropped the sheets and grabbed her apron to wipe her eyes. The squaw had lowered her blanket, revealing a once-beautiful face marred by an ugly scar across the bridge of the nose.

Jesse gasped in disbelief and was instantly out the door. "Prairie Flower!" she called out in Lakota. She pushed her way past one of the soldiers and touched the squaw's shoulder.

Wheeling about, the squaw stammered, "Walks the Fire! It is you?!"

The soldier whom Jesse had pushed by interrupted them. "Mrs. King . . . you know this squaw?" He questioned her in disbelief, forcing his considerable bulk between the two women.

Jesse realized that she must explain herself in a way that would protect LisBeth.

"Why, yes, Corporal Donovan . . . I do. Years ago, when we were crossing the prairie, my husband and I met an unfortunate accident. We were overtaken by buffalo, our wagon destroyed. A hunting party proved uncommonly helpful. Prairie Flower was among their band. She showed me much kindness. Indeed, I have never forgotten her."

Donovan smiled. It was not a pleasant smile. "Prairie

Flower," he repeated the name. "Sure ain't much of a flower now, is she?—just a dirty old scarred up squaw taggin' along after some beat-up Injuns. And a sorry group they are, at that." Donovan shoved one of the warriors. He moved away, careful to hide the rage blazing in his dark eyes. The brave looked at the ground and muttered, "You white dog—I will feed you to the eagles."

Donovan turned to the Pawnee guide who had accompanied the soldiers on their mission.

"What's he say?"

Jesse interrupted before the Pawnee could reply, "He says that he wishes to see the leader of the brave men who fought today."

Donovan looked surprised, but when his Pawnee scout remained silent, Jesse explained, "We were among the Lakota long enough for me to learn a little of their language and their customs. They value bravery above all else. You must have impressed them as very worthy opponents for this one to request to see your leader. It is a sign of great respect." Jesse prayed that Donovan would believe her and that God would forgive her lies.

Donovan turned to his Pawnee scout. "Is she telling the truth?"

The scout looked long at Jesse and then at Prairie Flower. He stared into the eyes of his enemy. Finally, he answered, "She speaks truth. The people value bravery."

Donovan looked at Jesse again. He stared at her moccasinned feet and scribbled in the dirt with his quirt as he drawled, "Well, now, just suppose you tell these here fellers to behave and not cause any trouble, and they just might get to meet the captain yet today."

Jesse turned to the warriors and for the first time she recognized Talks a Lot, Prairie Flower's father. She addressed him slowly. It had been years since she had spoken Lakota. The words came with difficulty. "This white dog says you must be patient. He is an arrogant good-for-nothing, but

I will try to find a way to get the leader to come to you soon. The captain is a fair man."

Even as she said the words, Jesse wondered how she would fulfill the promise. How could a camp laundress hope to get around the Corporal to command any influence with the Captain?

Talks a Lot remained expressionless, but Jesse noted the flicker of thanks in his eyes.

Donovan nodded in agreement with her speech and smiled confidently. Prairie Flower ducked her head to avoid smiling at his foolishness.

"Good," Donovan said, smacking the palm of his hand with his quirt. "Now, let's go." His unit shoved the Indians across the compound.

"Corporal," Jesse asked, "could not the woman stay with me?"

"Mrs. King," Donovan sneered, "these here are official pris'ners of the U.S. Government. I can't be handin' 'em over to just anyone who feels sorry for 'em." He paused a moment and looked Jesse over, "'sides, I don't know just how friendly you was with them Injuns a-fore. How'd I know you wouldn't help 'em escape?"

Jesse's cheeks flushed at the veiled insult, but she controlled her temper. "Surely as a gentleman you wouldn't expect a lone woman to remain locked up with the men."

Donovan's lips curled up. "Ma'am, these is Injuns we're talkin' about. I don't think it'll be a problem to keep 'em all together. It's not like they was white folks with real morals and all." Donovan enjoyed the return of the angry flush to Jesse's cheeks. His curiosity was piqued. It had been a boring spring, and he had relished fighting Indians. Now this woman's relationship with the Sioux added a new dimension to the whole affair. Things were looking up.

Donovan stared down again at Jesse's moccasins. Involuntarily, she tucked her toes back under her skirts.

"Good-day, ma'am," he said to Jesse, touching the riding

whip to the bill of his cap and turning his rotund back on her. Jesse saw Prairie Flower cover her scarred face from the curious eyes of the fort residents who had gathered to stare at the Indians. Talks a Lot walked proudly along, his long gray hair flowing over his shoulders, his head held high.

Jesse returned to her work, hushing LisBeth's questions with unusual sternness as she wondered how she could help her friends. She wondered and prayed for the rest of the day as she worked in the laundry. No answer came. She continued to wonder and worry through supper with LisBeth, who noticed that her mother was unusually quiet.

As the sun went down, Jesse settled into her rocker by the fireplace, reached for her quilting, and prayed desperately for wisdom to reason out how she might help Talks a Lot and Prairie Flower. *And Lord,* she added, *give me time to ask about Soaring Eagle—Lord, I must know.*

"Mama, how did that Indian get the scar on her face?" LisBeth's voice interrupted Jesse's musings.

"I'll tell you another time."

"Mama, do you know the one with the long gray hair?"

"Yes."

"How did you learn to talk like them?"

No answer.

LisBeth had never been shut out from her mother's thoughts so completely. Bewildered, and a little angry, she noisily made preparations for going to bed. She huffed and puffed and rattled about the small room, finally settled onto her cot, and surprised herself by falling immediately asleep.

As soon as she saw that LisBeth was asleep, Jesse jumped up and went to the door. The horizon was fading to pale pink, and above the rim of the sunset in the violet-blue sky hung one star and a crescent moon. *The giant in the sky sleeps . . . but look, he has opened one eye to peer down at us.* Jesse leaned against the door to her room and sighed as she remembered how Rides the Wind had once described the moon to Two Mothers before that awful day he became Soaring Eagle.

Memories of her other life assaulted her, jumbling her thoughts and making it difficult to plan. She longed for the hostility between the whites and the Indians to end. She wondered how to help her old friends, and she prayed for a way to introduce LisBeth to her true heritage without jeopardizing her future.

Taking another deep breath at the impossibility of it all, Jesse turned toward the low fire, sat down again in the creaking rocker, and reached for her sewing basket. Her fingers pressed the seams of a few quilt blocks flat as she thought about her predicament. Rescuing a scrap of cloth from the floor beside the sewing basket she folded and cut a tiny calico triangle and began stitching it to the end of the long row of triangular pieces already in her lap. The monotony of stitching soon calmed her, and she began to think more clearly, assessing her new situation, planning how to proceed when daylight came.

The last few stitches in the row had been taken and Jesse had bent to fold the row of patchwork back into her basket when Prairie Flower burst through the door. Sobbing, the woman threw herself at Jesse's feet. The sound of boots stomping the hard earth just outside the door preceded Corporal Donovan's appearance. His swaying form filled the doorway. Drunken voices from the group of soldiers with him added to the din.

Jesse stood up, her wide skirt partially hiding Prairie Flower from view. She had taken in enough of her friend's gasping cries to understand.

Calmly, Jesse bent over to pick up the quilt pieces that had fallen to the floor. Steady hands belied her pounding heart. LisBeth had awakened and lay wide-eyed, staring over the edge of her coverlet. Her dark eyes went from Prairie Flower, to Donovan, then to her mother.

Jesse collected the quilt pieces slowly. A glint of steel reflected in the light from the fireplace. She picked up her sewing scissors and straightened to face Donovan. At her side was a fist clenched around the scissors. Donovan could see the knuckles of her right hand whiten as she held tightly to the scissors, pointing the blades upward like a weapon. Her voice was steady.

"Corporal Donovan. Is there a problem?"

The drunken men behind Donovan were suddenly quiet, and the Corporal's rumbling voice drawled out a reply. "Only problem here is that squaw . . . what don't know her place in the worl' . . . and what runs away when we wuz jus' tryin' to be frien'ly."

Prairie Flower shuddered and muttered an oath under her breath. Jesse's gray eyes looked coolly at each man standing behind Donovan. Finally, after a long silence, her eyes met his. "Perhaps she has seen the white man's attempts at friendliness in the past. Perhaps she does not wish to be friends with you."

Donovan belched loudly, scratched under his arm and swore a reply. Jesse was aware of LisBeth's moving as she drew her feet up beneath her. The child curled up into a tight ball beneath the covers and covered her face. Prairie Flower's sobs quieted, and she sat listening.

"Is this woman a prisoner of the Army?" Jesse asked.

"Pris'ner? . . . No, she ain't no pris'ner. She jus' straggled along when we brought in that worthless bunch a savages."

"Then she is free to go if she wishes? Surely the Army does not require that you guard an innocent woman. Surely the captain would not wish you to detain her against her wishes." Jesse mentioned the commander's name deliberately. Donovan thrust his jaw out and squinted at her.

"Why d' you care 'bout a dirty ol' squaw, anyhow? She ain't no prize catch, neither . . . face all scarred up. You want her, you can have her fer all I care." He turned his great form sideways and said it louder. "I don' care nothin' fer a dirty ol' squaw anyhow." The men with Donovan began to disperse.

Jesse's heart lurched and she prayed that Donovan could

not see her hand tremble as she gripped the scissors more tightly. She remained standing, staring at the corporal, listening as he tried to talk himself out of the confrontation. The threat to report him to the captain had worked. He might be drunk, but he was no fool, and he knew that his future in the army depended on the opinion of his commanding officer.

Jesse ended his ramblings with, "Good evening, Corporal. Thank you for bringing Prairie Flower to me. I will see that she has a comfortable place to rest tonight, and we will certainly meet you in the morning at the commander's office to decide on her future. You are to be commended for your interest in improving Indian relations." As she spoke, Jesse stepped forward, grasped the back of the heavy door to her room, and threatened to shove it shut in Donovan's face. He retreated with a noncommittal oath at his men. Jesse closed the door and leaned against it, trembling.

The air in the room was stale, filled with the stench of Donovan's unwashed body and the liquor he had spilled on himself during the night's drunken party.

LisBeth sat upright, lowered the coverlet, and stared at Prairie Flower. The woman returned her stare. Then, understanding lit her eyes. They glowed warmly as she said softly, "This one has the eyes of her father."

Jesse understood, but was slow to answer. "Yes, the eyes of her father. And when she laughs, sometimes I think I am hearing Soaring Eagle."

LisBeth started to speak, but Jesse stopped her. "LisBeth," she ordered, "you must be still now. Prairie Flower and I must talk of what can be done. I cannot translate for you. It has been too long, and I cannot remember the words well enough. It will be hard for me to talk, and you must be quiet."

Jesse crouched on the floor beside Prairie Flower and whispered, "I must know, Prairie Flower. Tell me of Soaring Eagle. *Why* did he not come for me? What has become . . ."

Prairie Flower interrupted her. "When Old One awoke and sounded the alarm, the storm had already begun."

Jesse rejoiced—Old One had not been killed!

Prairie Flower continued to talk. "Soaring Eagle and the other hunters were trapped by the blizzard. It was many days before they returned. Still, Soaring Eagle mounted a fresh pony and vowed to bring you back. The snow was so deep in the Gate of the Buffalo that his pony could find no way through. He tried again and again to break through. At last, the elders convinced him that as soon as the snow melted, a search party of our finest trackers would be sent out."

Prairie Flower paused and smiled grimly, "Many days later the melting snow uncovered Howling Wind. We thought then that he had killed you and Red Star. There was no trail to follow."

Jesse begged for more. "Tell me of Soaring Eagle. Tell me of my son." LisBeth hugged her knees and watched the two women. Never had she heard such a tone in her mother's voice. She sounded happy, and sad, and almost desperate, all at once. *What could they be talking about?*

"When he thought that you were lost, when we thought that you were lost, we mourned greatly, Walks the Fire. Soaring Eagle cut off his braids and sang the mourning song."

Jesse eagerly asked more questions. "And now? Where is he? Was he in the battle? Does he fight the soldiers?"

Prairie Flower held up her hand to hold back the barrage of questions. "He is a hunter—not a warrior. But now the whites take more and more. Many hunters must become warriors. Soaring Eagle remembers that a white woman was his mother. It is hard for him."

With a glance toward LisBeth, Prairie Flower continued, "I will tell him of his sister and of Walks the Fire. You can tell her," Prairie Flower said, nodding toward LisBeth, "that Soaring Eagle her brother has become a great hunter, like her father."

Jesse whispered reluctantly, "My friend, I have not told her that she is one of your people." She hurried to defend herself, "We are among the whites now, and they would not be kind to her if they knew."

Prairie Flower's soft brown eyes blinked rapidly as she replied, "There is no shame in being the daughter of Rides the Wind. There is no shame in being the sister of Soaring Eagle."

Jesse faltered. "I know, but . . ." Then she tried to make an excuse. "I *do* tell her of her father. I do not mention the people, that is all."

Prairie Flower exclaimed, "She thinks her father was *white?* She thinks her father was that man you were with before you came to us?"

Jesse nodded.

"So. You have taken the memories that belong to Rides the Wind and given them to a worthless *white man?*"

Emotions Jesse had struggled with for years, emotions she thought she had long since forgotten, welled up. Memories she had prayed that God would take away flooded the room. Jesse pushed them away, one by one, into the tiny cubicles reserved for the past in her mind.

Jesse wanted to ask more. She wanted to know about Old One. But LisBeth had been quiet for as long as she could. "Mama, how do you say her name?"

Grateful for the change in subject, Jesse helped LisBeth pronounce the Lakota words. Then she pronounced Lis-Beth's name for Prairie Flower, who smiled and offered her hand to the child as she said, "LisBeth."

"Mama," LisBeth asked, "do you think the captain will help Prairie Flower? Will he let her friends go?"

"The captain is a good man, LisBeth, but Talks a Lot and the other braves were fighting with the soldiers. I fear he will be forced to punish them. Prairie Flower has done nothing wrong, but she will never leave her father alone here."

As she talked, Jesse retrieved her tiny quilting needle from her sewing basket and began trying to mend the rip in Prairie Flower's garment. It was useless. The tiny needle couldn't begin to puncture the deerskin. Jesse pulled her only other dress off the hook where it hung behind the door and offered it to her friend. Prairie Flower shook her head, but Jesse urged her.

"It was *your* dress I wore when I became the wife of Rides the Wind. Now I return the kindness."

Prairie Flower hesitated between her abhorrence for anything from the whites, most of which was connected in her mind with their cruelty, and the kindness of this woman who had been her friend.

Necessity won out. She accepted the dress and donned it awkwardly, struggling with the detailed closures, muttering against the flowing skirts and long sleeves.

When she was dressed, the two women stood looking at one another. Prairie Flower spoke first. "The man you speak of—this captain—if this man were kind, he would not be defending the people who take the land where we have hunted. He would know that the Great Mystery gave us the land. He would not send his men to kill women and children. I will go to Talks a Lot now. They have put him and the others behind a door that will not open. I must find a way to get them out so that we can make our way back to the people." She was out the door and had disappeared into the darkness before Jesse could stop her.

Jesse had no time to reason it out or pray it through, but she knew what she would do. Gathering up her own quilt, she folded it deliberately and lay it on her bed.

"LisBeth," she said, "get dressed. Gather up what you can. Roll it up into this quilt. Only enough to fit into the quilt, now. And don't forget my Bible. Wait here until I come back."

Something new in her mother's voice prevented LisBeth's usual barrage of childish questions. Mama was very serious tonight, and LisBeth nodded obediently and slipped out of bed, beginning to dress even as Jesse stepped outside.

Jesse's moccasinned feet padded noiselessly along the edge of the laundresses' quarters. Feeling her way in the darkness, she stepped cautiously toward the storeroom where she knew Talks a Lot and the other warriors had been locked up.

There was no sign of Prairie Flower, but she knew that the daughter would not be far from her father's prison. She prayed that Donovan's drunkenness would prevent any further encounters. The man was loud and abusive and overly confident. Surely he would not be expecting an escape attempt tonight.

Jesse nearly tripped over the sleeping form of the guard who was supposed to be on duty. Reaching into the pocket of her apron, she felt the key and smiled grimly at the irony that of all the women in the fort, Gilda had chosen her to keep it.

"I know you don't want the responsibility," Gilda had said, when Jesse had tried to reject the key, "but the Captain said that somebody ought to have an extra. And you're the most dependable one on the place. So that's it. You take the key and don't lose it."

Dependable, Jesse thought as she reached to unlock the door. The sleeping guard snorted and her heart lurched. But he only scratched his nose and settled into slumber, snoring loudly.

Peeking out from around the corner of the storehouse, Jesse saw Prairie Flower. As the door to the storeroom inched open, a strong hand grabbed Jesse and jerked her inside. Another hand clutched her throat and began to squeeze. Jesse struggled noiselessly to tear the hand away, frantically signing "friend" over and over as she prayed that in the darkness someone would see the sign and save her from choking to death. There was a faint rustle and she sensed that she was surrounded by the small group of warriors who had been planning their escape.

Talks a Lot reached out to tear the hand from her throat. No spoken word was needed to communicate their plans. Furious signing went back and forth in the gloom of the storehouse interior. In seconds the warriors had slipped out of the storeroom, stepped soundlessly across the body of the drunken guard, and disappeared into the darkness. Only Talks a Lot remained. Prairie Flower came to his side. She signed to Jesse, "You come. Bring child."

Jesse shook her head from side to side. Impulsively, she reached up to unclasp the gold cross that had hung about her neck for so many years. It had never left her, but she took it now and laid it in her friend's palm, closing Prairie Flower's long fingers about the metal and squeezing her hand.

Prairie Flower tried to refuse. This was the thing that had made Rides the Wind bring Jesse into the camp. Jesse had used it to tell her of a man who died long ago. She had said that the man came to life again. Prairie Flower doubted that, but she had seen that their belief in this man and in the strange book they read had created a strong bond between Rides the Wind and Walks the Fire. She had envied the bond between the two. But she had always refused to believe it for herself. It was only a nice story to tell about the campfire.

And now the cross, the only thing Walks the Fire still had from her time among the people, was being offered to Prairie Flower. In the feeble light, Jesse saw that Prairie Flower held the cross in one clenched hand as she crossed her wrists in front of her and brought them to her heart, signing "love." Seconds after the gesture, Prairie Flower and Talks a Lot slipped away into the night.

Chapter 23

Great peace have they which love
thy law.

Psalm 119:165

Jesse ran swiftly back to her room to find LisBeth
dressed, sitting obediently at the foot of her bed,
the brown quilt rolled up at her side. Jesse checked only to
see that her Bible was in the bedroll. Gripping LisBeth's
hand, she moved across the compound to the stables. A few
horses stamped and snorted when the two entered, moving
restlessly in their stall. Jesse whistled low, and they quieted
to the familiar sound. From the far side of the row of stalls
came a soft, welcoming nicker.

Quickly Jesse saddled Red Star. She lifted LisBeth into the
saddle and led the old mare out, running now, desperate to
put the fort as far behind them as possible before the escape
was discovered. They were far from the fort before Jesse spoke.

"LisBeth, Mama has done something you may not understand. But I had to do it. I have helped my friends escape, and
now we must get away quickly before I am discovered. If we are
caught, God will take care of us . . . but I am praying that we
will not be caught. For some time, now, I have felt that we
should leave the fort. I was planning for us to go west with Mr.
Wood when he returned. But I cannot wait for Mr. Wood. We
must hurry tonight, and pray that God will protect us."

LisBeth pondered her mother's words before answering.
Then, looking back over her shoulder she said, "I'm glad
we're leaving, Mama. I don't like it there anymore. It's too
windy, and too dusty, and they don't have trees. I want to go

where there are trees and where we can have friends . . . and be like all the others." She hesitated, then, and asked, "But, Mama, *where will we go?*"

"To Dobytown," came the reply.

"Dobytown?!" LisBeth had only heard stories about their destination, but still she could not imagine her mother ever consenting to set foot in the place.

Only two miles from the fort, Dobytown's reputation had spread much farther. Inhabited largely by gamblers, lewd women, and criminals, Dobytown was shunned by the God-fearing and sought out by the sin-loving.

And that, Jesse thought, *is exactly why we must go there.* No one at Fort Kearney would think to look for her there. First, they would search all the immigrant camps at the opposite side of the fort. It would buy them precious time and enable them to perhaps . . . well, Jesse didn't have a plan beyond Dobytown, but she knew that their best opportunity to escape lay there.

"Lord," Jesse said aloud. "Lord, we need your help. Please send us someone to help us get away. Make Donovan—and anyone else—go the other way." She stopped, afraid to say much more, for her heart was beating fast, and the fear that she would be caught and separated from LisBeth was building. *If anything should happen to me, Lord,* she prayed silently, *what would become of LisBeth?*

She wondered where the bravery that had helped the Indians escape was now. But was it bravery? As Red Star trotted across the open prairie, Jesse's fatigue grew. LisBeth clutched her mother's sides, and lay her head against her back. *What could I have been thinking?* Jesse wondered. *What a fool I've been.* And yet, she could not bring herself to regret helping her friends.

Be not afraid . . . Be not afraid . . . The words came again, in rhythm with Red Star's gait. The words echoed from the past, and, as always, reassured her. Jesse was able to pray again. Her thoughts turned again to LisBeth. Where, indeed, in this Nebraska territory, could a single woman make a life for her child? She needed schools, and churches, and friends. She needed a society that wasn't divided between the "officers' children" and "the others."

Red Star stopped and snorted, staring straight ahead. Her tiny ears flicked forward and back, trying to catch a sound from the light ahead. With dismay, Jesse realized they had somehow missed Dobytown.

A man hunched over his fire. At the sound of Red Star's snort, one of his horses whinnied. He rose quickly, grabbing the rifle that lay next to him. His deep voice boomed into the darkness, "Who goes there?"

When Jesse said nothing, the voice called out again. "Who goes there? And what business have ya' in the night? If yer an honest man, speak up right now, or else my gun'll be doin' some talkin.'"

LisBeth had awakened and clutched her mother's sides fearfully.

"Don't shoot!" Jesse called out. "It's a lone woman and her child. That's all. Please, don't shoot!"

The rifle came down off the shoulder. The voice called out again. "And how do I know yer tellin' the truth, and yer not some good fer nothin' from Dobytown just plannin' to rob and murder?"

"I promise by the Lord God who made heaven and earth, it's only me and my daughter."

"Then walk into the campfire where I can see ya'."

Jesse urged Red Star forward where the man could look them over.

LisBeth clung to her mother, but whispered loudly. "Mama, that man is black!"

The man raised one eyebrow and looked down at his massive forearms. Stretching out one hand, he held it up in the firelight and examined it. "Well, I'll be . . . " he exclaimed in mock surprise. "I shorely am! Now, how d'ya suppose that happened?" He grinned at LisBeth, and Jesse relaxed a little.

Then LisBeth answered, "My mama says God made people

all colors so's the world wouldn't be dull. We know white folks, and we've got some brown friends, but we've never had black friends before. We've got to run away now, 'cause we helped our brown friends, and they might catch us and take my mama away."

Jesse hushed LisBeth. "My daughter and I were headed for Dobytown. My name is Jesse King. My mare must have taken the wrong way and . . ."

The man grasped the crown of his hat and set it farther back on his head. "*Dobytown?* What you be lookin' for *Dobytown* for? Dobytown's no place for a woman and her child . . ."

"Yes, I know that . . . and under normal circumstances I'd never . . . but . . ."

"Somebody lookin' fer you?"

"I'm not sure. But if they were . . ."

He interrupted. "But if they were, they wouldn't be lookin' in Dobytown. That it?"

Jesse wondered if God would have answered her prayer for help so quickly. She answered, "Exactly."

"Who're these 'brown people' you been helpin'?"

"Lakota. At the fort. Friends of mine. I unlocked the room they were held in and helped them get away."

The man added, "Then *you* best be gettin' away too." Approaching Red Star, he turned his attention to LisBeth. "You hungry, little lady? Help yourself. Shot a rabbit earlier. They's a few pieces left in that skillet by the fire." He lifted LisBeth down, and for some reason Jesse did not move to resist. She climbed down and stood holding the reins as Lisbeth scampered to the fire.

"Seem to have forgot my manners, ma'am," he said. "Name's Joseph Freeman. I'm a blacksmith. Been workin' over to Dobytown fer some weeks, now. But I'm leavin'. Sick of the swearin' and carryin' on. Ain't no place for a man who . . . well, who cares about the things of the Lord and all. They's a new town bein' started up near the Salt Creek. Name of Lancaster. Figure every good town needs a blacksmith. Guess I'll settle there a while and see how I like it."

All the while he talked, he was leading Jesse to the fireside, helping her settle onto the ground, unsaddling Red Star, rubbing her down, checking her feet with sure hands before he hobbled her with an extra set of hobbles he fetched from his wagon.

His voice was pleasant, and Jesse settled comfortably near the fire as an inexplicable peace settled over her.

Joseph Freeman rambled on about his plans. "They's a widow there, Miz Augusta Hathaway. That Miz Hathaway, she's a real good woman. A real Christian woman. Never heard nothin' but a kind word about her. Folks say that new town'll be growin' fast. Sure Miz Hathaway'll help you get settled. You got no objections to ridin' with a colored man, I'll be happy to have you come along. It just ain't right for you to go into Dobytown. No, ma'am . . . it just ain't right."

Freeman stopped short. The woman was asleep. Her child lay at her side, cuddled into the crook of her mother's body on the ground.

"Man alive, Joseph . . . when you goin' to learn to shut up? You done talked this woman to sleep!" He smiled at himself, and withdrew his bedroll to a respectful distance from the campfire. Unrolling the woman's quilt to cover her, he dropped her worn Bible into the dust. He picked it up, wiped it off, and set it where the woman would see it as soon as she woke.

Jesse and LisBeth woke the next morning to the aroma of coffee boiling and biscuits baking. LisBeth was quick to exclaim over their new friend's kindness. Freeman accepted her chattering good-naturedly and explained to Jesse, "You'all fell to sleepin' so quick last night, I didn't think you'd mind if I covered the girl up. The Bible fell outta' the bedroll, ma'am. I sure hope it didn't come to any harm."

Jesse picked up the Bible and rubbed her stiff neck. "It's fine, Mr. Freeman. Thank you for your kindness."

Freeman offered her coffee and as she took the steaming

cup he said, "If you don't mind, ma'am, I'd sure love to hear a few words from that book. That is, if you don't mind, ma'am."

The request helped Jesse feel at ease with the stranger. Whatever his background, if he loved God's Word, she felt that they could be friends. Long since used to Bible reading, LisBeth instantly plopped onto a log by the fire and waited for her mother to read.

"Do you have a favorite passage, Mr. Freeman?"

"Oh, no, ma'am, I ain't never learned to read. Anything'll do. I just love hearin' the words." He had removed his hat and stood, head bowed, as if awaiting a benediction.

Jesse thumbed the worn pages and read aloud, *"In thee, O LORD, do I put my trust . . ."* She read the psalm quietly; Joseph stood drinking in the words. When Jesse finished the passage with *"Be of good courage, and he shall strengthen your heart, all ye that hope in the LORD,"* Freeman whispered a hearty "Amen!" He shoved his hat back on his head and, with sudden energy and few words, rounded up Red Star and his own team. Harnessing the team, he turned to Jesse.

"As I said last night, ma'am, I'm headed for the Salt Creek, 'bout 150 miles from here. They's a widow there, Miz' Augusta Hathaway, a good Christian woman who'd be happy to have you stop by, I'm sure. It ain't much, only about thirty folks settled in, but whoever might be looking' fer ya' sure wouldn't be lookin' there."

"We'd be indebted to you if we could accompany you, Mr. Freeman. I haven't any way to pay you for your protection, but it seems that the Lord has sent us to you, and if you think Mrs. Hathaway wouldn't mind two pilgrims alighting on her doorstep, then we'll go with you."

As she talked, Jesse mounted Red Star and motioned for LisBeth to join her, but LisBeth had her own ideas of how she preferred to travel. "I don't wanna' ride that old horse, Mama. I wanna' ride in the wagon with Mr. Joseph!"

Embarrassed by her daughter's forwardness, Jesse tried to

hush her, but Freeman interrupted. "I'd be honored to have her ride with me, ma'am, if you think it's all right."

Jesse hesitated. Freeman misinterpreted the hesitation. He turned to LisBeth. "Little lady, it ain't fittin' for you to be ridin' next to a man you don't know too well, and your mama's right to be concerned. So now you just scramble up on that little pony and don't give your mama no more trouble."

LisBeth protested again, and Freeman took action before he thought. "My mammy used to switch me good when I acted the way you actin' up. Now, you be a lady like your mama and get up on that hoss!"

Not waiting for LisBeth to obey, he swept her up in his great arms and deposited her on Red Star's back where she sat sullenly but quietly. They headed off across the prairie as morning's light began to touch the tips of the brush that dotted the open plain.

For most of her life Jesse had been carried along, an often unwilling participant in many of the events that had shaped her life. The encounter with Prairie Flower had changed that. With no time to consciously ask the Lord's guidance and wait for a reply, she had chosen to do something that would change her life permanently. As she rode behind Freeman's wagon, she had time to contemplate the results of her actions. It seemed that God had blessed her decision. He had, after all, provided Joseph Freeman to lead her to a new village and a new life, and he had granted his peace.

As the morning passed and Jesse and LisBeth followed along behind Freeman's wagon, Jesse felt more and more that she was in the center of God's will for her life. Accompanying Joseph Freeman to the village on the Salt Creek seemed right. Her heart swelled with a sudden, inexplicable happiness, and she began to hum. Freeman heard the tune, picked it up, and hummed along. It wasn't long before they were singing the familiar words. Jesse's hoarse alto and Freeman's rich bass resounded across the prairie.

Amazing grace, how sweet the sound . . .

LisBeth recovered from her tantrum and began to sing too. Red Star's ears worked madly, first pricking forward to hear the bass voice coming from the wagon and then flicking back to the familiar voices she had known for so long.

As the music continued, something happened. Unseen hands reached between the travelers. They were tentative, not touching, but still there, open to whatever might be offered. As the morning passed and the miles were covered, the unseen hands grew closer. A spiritual bond was growing, created by their shared belief in Christ.

When they stopped for lunch, Jesse hopped down happily from Red Star's back, sent LisBeth to the nearby creek for fresh water, and asked Freeman how she could help.

"Just read some more, ma'am. That'd be help enough. I got plenty of hard tack and jerky . . . a little extra water will make the coffee last until we get there. . . ."

"But I want to do my part, to repay you in some way for your kindness."

"Well then, ma'am, you read from the Good Book and let me cook."

They ate quickly and were ready to be on the move again. As Freeman climbed onto his wagon, Jesse called out, "Mr. Freeman, sir, if you don't object, could LisBeth ride with you this afternoon?"

He had his back to her, but at the question, she saw the huge shoulders relax, and he turned about with a warm smile on his face. Winking at LisBeth, he answered, "I'd be honored, Mrs. King." There was more to be said, but he held it in and helped LisBeth scramble up beside him. Together, they bounced and jolted along. The unseen hands came together in a firm grasp and held on.

Blessed be the tie that binds our hearts in Christian love,
The fellowship of kindred minds is like to that above.

The old hymn became real as the days passed. Jesse rode alongside the wagon instead of behind it. They sang every hymn they knew. By the end of the week, Jesse had stopped fearing pursuit from the fort. Three strangers had joined together in a unity that those who did not know their God could never understand.

At last, over an evening campfire, Jesse told Freeman the details of their flight from Fort Kearney. He listened without much reaction and failed to offer some of his own history in turn. The silence had become uncomfortable when LisBeth asked, "You talk different from the people at Fort Kearney, Joseph. How come?"

"*Mr. Freeman,* LisBeth!" Jesse corrected.

Freeman smiled. "That's just fine, LisBeth. You can call me Joseph. Guess partners on the trail don't need to be so formal, after all." He backed away from the fire into the shadows before he answered LisBeth's question. "Well, now, LisBeth. I talk different 'cause I'm not from around here. I talk the way folks talk where I grew up."

"Where's that?"

"South Carolina."

LisBeth looked at her mother. "That far away, Mama?"

"Very far away, LisBeth."

"Farther away than Illinois?" LisBeth looked from Jesse to Joseph. When her mother nodded, LisBeth blurted out, "Mama says she and Papa came all the way from Illinois, and it was a terrible hard journey and took months and months. Then Papa died, and we had to stay here in Nebraska Territory and work for the soldiers. Mama says the Good Lord made her strong to work hard and she could take care of us just fine with the Lord's help. She didn't want another husband after Papa died, and so that's why we stayed." LisBeth took another breath. "So why'd you come all the way to Nebraska from South Carolina, Mr. Joseph?"

"LisBeth! Mr. Freeman doesn't need to tell us his personal

affairs. And *you,* young lady, have blurted out our personal affairs without a bit of good manners!"

Freeman broke in, "That's all right, ma'am. They ain't much to tell 'bout me. I joined up in the war and dug trenches and the like for near four years. Got in a fight one night, got hit in the head. When I come to, I was layin' in a hay stack in a field. Headed west. Didn't stop till I got to the Missouri River. Kept working my way west, and here I am."

LisBeth was not satisfied. "Is your family gonna come out here when you get settled?"

"LisBeth!" Jesse nearly shouted.

LisBeth defended herself. "Well, Mama that Corporal Donovan said that when he got settled he was gonna have his wife and kids come out west, and I thought maybe Mr. Freeman was too!"

At the mention of family, Freeman's face became a mask. The tolerant smile left his face, and he looked down at his hands. Still, he answered LisBeth honestly. In a whisper, he said, "Had a wife. Had two boys. They was sold off the place before the war."

Jesse's heart ached for the man. She stood awkwardly, waiting for him to stop. She didn't want to hear his story, but he seemed to need to tell it. He looked steadily at LisBeth, who stared back, unbelieving. She had heard about slavery, but it had never touched her. The war had come and soldiers had left the fort in droves. Volunteer recruits from Iowa had come to take their places. It had had little effect on her life. But here, before her, was a man—a nice man—who had lost his family. Freeman went on. "The Massah promised he'd never do it, but times got tough, and he went back on his word. Guess they all do, sometime. When the war came, I ran off first chance I got . . . lookin' for Mattie and the boys. It was no use. It was like they disappeared off the face of the earth. I hope they got away. There was some folks who helped us when we run away." Freeman's eyes clouded over. Then he whispered to himself, "I hope they got away." He had returned to a past world that LisBeth and Jesse would never understand or know.

Inhaling sharply, he brushed his hand across his forehead and looked again at LisBeth. There was no smile, but she heard the kindness in his voice as he said earnestly, "You be thankful that God borned you right where he did, LisBeth. You've had some hard times, I know. But you've been free. You never had to fear that your mamma'd be sold away from you—never had to fear *you'd* be sold away. You be grateful."

LisBeth nodded solemnly. "Mr. Joseph, sir," she offered, "I'll pray for your Mattie and your boys. Mama says the Lord cares for all his children. Mama says we're gonna see Papa someday in heaven. Sometimes at night when I wish I had a papa, I just think about heaven and how I'll see him, and I pretend he's hugging me tight, and then I feel better. Maybe you could think about heaven too . . . and maybe that . . ." the young voice wavered. She was too emotional to continue.

A slight smile came back to Joseph's grief-stricken face. "You know, LisBeth, that's just what I do. When it hurts so bad that I just can't bear it no more, that's when I look to God for help, and he always seems to have a way of helpin'. Tonight, he helped me by havin' you say those nice things. You helped me remember that the Lord knows where Mattie and my boys are, and someday, I'm gonna go in that gate and just inside, they's gonna be three dark faces just smilin' and shoutin' and glory!" He almost shouted it out, "We shore gonna have us a party then!" He slapped his knees and stood up abruptly. Jesse jumped at the sudden noise.

The travelers scurried about checking on the horses, spreading out bedrolls, rinsing coffee cups in the nearby creek. As coyotes howled, Jesse and LisBeth lay beneath their shared quilt, watching as the camp fire died down. Jesse pondered the future while LisBeth could think only of the past—of families torn apart, of fathers separated from their children, and of men selling other men. The evil called slavery had a face now. It had a name too. Joseph Freeman.

Chapter 24

Trust in the LORD with all thine heart; and lean not unto thine own understanding. In all thy ways acknowledge him, and he shall direct thy paths.

Proverbs 3:5–6

On the morning of the ninth day of their journey, three weary travelers topped a rise on the prairie and paused under a blue sky to survey what lay before them. Joseph Freeman was familiar with the scene.

"That's the salt flats."

The vast, treeless prairie was punctuated by a large area of blazing white. Smooth as glass, it looked like polished marble. The land was parched and barren and covered with salt two or three inches deep. Someone had tried to harvest it and had left the wrecks of two old salt furnaces and two cabins.

"Where's it come from, Joseph?" LisBeth demanded.

"See them cracks there?" Joseph pointed to gaping cracks in the dry earth. Pulling his team to a halt, he jumped out of the wagon and reached down into one of the cracks. It was so deep his arm went in up to his elbow. "Now you see why we're travelin' *around* the basin instead of *across* it. I'd lose a whole wagon wheel if it fell into one of these cracks. Funny thing, though. I heard about it and I didn't believe it till I saw it happen. Twice a day—just like clockwork—this here basin floods. Shallow water—only a couple of inches deep, but when it sinks back into the cracks, it leaves the salt behind. Folks come from all over to scrape it up. Sometimes it gets two or three inches deep."

Jesse pondered the future of the Salt Flats. Joseph told of the thriving salt industry that all the settlers expected to spring up and fuel the growth of Lancaster. Jesse saw the potential. Being part of a growing community would provide benefits for LisBeth she would never have had at Fort Kearney.

They traveled to the southeast, seeming to descend into a shallow saucer. They saw a few trees—one giant elm and a few honey locusts punctuated by plum thickets. When the village of Lancaster came into view, Jesse's heart sank. The only buildings in sight were a two-story structure of red sandstone, two log cabins, a house with a sod roof, a small stone building, and a dugout! Closer inspection revealed two stores, one shoe shop, six or seven houses, but no main street, no trees, no churches. They crossed several dry creek beds. A coyote trotted into view, stopped, looked in their direction and then continued on its way, unhurried.

A small crowd had gathered outside one of the larger cabins. Joseph pulled his team up in the shade of the cabin. No one seemed to have noticed the arrival of three strangers. All attention was on a tall bearded man giving a speech.

"Gentlemen . . . and ladies . . . while this is not an official announcement, I feel it is our duty to inform you that the commission has met in closed session and unanimous choice has been made for Lancaster to be the capital city of this great state . . . the state of Nebraska." Cheers went up from the twenty or so people who had been listening intently to the speech. A few of the men threw hats into the air in their enthusiasm. A group of boys, apparently coming from the nearest fishing hole, wandered by with the morning's catch on their line. Pausing momentarily, they quickly lost interest in the spectacle and continued on in the direction of the dugout just visible toward the southeast, near the only trees in sight.

As soon as the speech ended, a large woman dressed in

black descended upon them. Her mellow, matronly voice called out, "That you, Joseph Freeman?"

"It's me, Miz Hathaway. Brung some poor souls along with me."

As Augusta Hathaway looked them over, Jesse shifted nervously in her saddle. The woman was a keen observer. Her eyes moved from LisBeth's face—was that a wink or just the glare of the sun causing her to squint?—to Jesse's, to Red Star and took in their clothing, the bedroll, and Jesse's moccasinned feet. Jesse felt as though she had been weighed in a scale and found wanting.

But then the round face crinkled into a wide smile, the eyes warmed up, and, yes, that really had been a wink she had proffered LisBeth. "And a motley crew you are, Joseph! Well, just go along to the cabin. There'll be plenty of lunch for you all," she turned to Jesse, "and then you can tell me how on earth you happened to team up with this miserable wretch!"

Augusta Hathaway was apparently accustomed to being obeyed. Before Jesse could reply or introduce herself—indeed, before even LisBeth could blurt out a word—the portly woman had picked up her dusty skirts and was striding away from them in the direction of a two-story log cabin at least a hundred yards away. Upon their arrival at the cabin, Jesse dismounted stiffly. Augusta Hathaway swooped down upon her, pulled her into the cabin, pushed her into a chair at a long table, plopped a plate full of steaming food before her, chucked LisBeth under the chin, and then, hands on her hips, demanded that Joseph Freeman tell her exactly what he meant by lighting on her doorstep with two extra mouths to feed and no explanation?

Before Joseph could reply, Augusta turned to LisBeth, "Drink all the milk you want, honey. The pitcher's full and the cow's out back, and there's plenty more where that came from."

Joseph started to reply, but Augusta interrupted again,

this time talking to Jesse. "This man is the best blacksmith I ever saw, and I tried to get him to believe me when I told him that Dobytown was no place for the God-fearing but, just like a man, he wouldn't believe me . . . had to find out for himself. Just like a man!" Without expecting a response from Jesse she turned to Joseph again. "Well, speak up, man! What in tarnation you plan to do now? You finally see the reasonableness of my offer? You gonna stay and be a part of this new city? Did you hear? It's gonna be the state capital. Now *that's* somethin' to be part of, Joseph! This here's a place with a future. You listen to me, and I'll see to it that you make a way for yourself!"

Jesse was beginning to wonder if Augusta Hathaway ever waited for an answer to any of her questions.

Augusta went on, "Goodness me, Joseph, set yourself down and eat somethin'. I got so caught up in the future I plumb forgot to dish up a plate for you. Sorry about that." While she talked, she ladled a plate full of the roast meat and potatoes that bubbled on the iron stove in the corner of the cabin. Plopping it on the table without ceremony, she handed Joseph flatware wrapped in a spotless white napkin. Joseph sat down and began to eat.

"Well, I guess *he's* not going to tell me a thing, so, my dear, how did you come to Lincoln. That's the new name, Joseph, Lincoln. They tried to get the vote against statehood— thought the Democrats would never vote for statehood if they knew the capital would be named for our dear departed president," Augusta dabbed an imaginary tear from her eye out of respect to the slain President. "Humph! Just like a man. They'll use anything to try to maneuver their way. But it didn't work. No sir, it didn't work! We've got ourselves into the Union as a state, and Lincoln will be the capital. And, Joseph, you'll be interested to know, that in Nebraska, the Negroes will be able to vote!"

Joseph looked up in disbelief. Augusta assured him it was true. Jesse waited to be given permission to answer the question. Now, just which question should she answer if she were ever given opportunity to speak? As usual, LisBeth took the initiative and said, "We got lost in the dark, and Red Star took us to Mr. Freeman's campfire. I was scared at first, 'cause it was dark, and he was black, and he had a gun. But then he smiled and I knew he was gonna be my friend. I like people with big voices. You've got a big voice, too, Miz Hathaway, but you winked at me, and you said I could have all the milk I wanted, and I think you're gonna be my friend too!"

Augusta chuckled. "Well, it appears that my fierce exterior has failed to fool *you,* young lady. I must practice my demeanor more. Never let it get around that Augusta Hathaway is an easy mark!" She winked broadly at LisBeth and turned with a great smile to Jesse. Jesse suspected that Augusta Hathaway had yet to convince anyone that she was a woman to be feared. In spite of the booming voice and the bustling manner, she exuded kindness like a great comforter ready to be spread over those around her.

At last, she asked Jesse's story, and waited for a response. Seating herself in the rocker that stood by the kitchen fireplace, she folded her hands over her ample lap and waited for Jesse to speak. Jesse looked down at her work-worn hands. She rubbed them together and reached up to tuck a stray curl back into the roll at the nape of her neck. Joseph gulped coffee noisily, clearly uncomfortable in the silence that had suddenly descended upon the cabin's interior. LisBeth crossed and uncrossed her legs under the table and sipped milk daintily. Augusta waited patiently. At last, Jesse collected her thoughts and spoke.

"My daughter and I have lived at Fort Kearney for many years. I've been a laundress there since LisBeth was an infant. My husband was killed before LisBeth was born, and we were forced to fend for ourselves. We fled Fort Kearney in the night when our safety was threatened, and God directed us to Mr. Freeman's campfire. He agreed to let us accompany him here. We need a new home. Joseph seems to think that Lancaster—Lincoln—will be a great city someday. I must think of my daughter. A city could perhaps offer schooling—and a chance for a better life."

Augusta Hathaway wanted to know more. But the gray eyes that met hers were veiled; they warned her not to ask too much. Still, they looked directly at her, not wavering. The woman had gumption, Augusta decided. Gumption to pick up and leave a bad environment, gumption to travel for days, gumption to start a new life. She said as much to Jesse.

"Gumption? No, Mrs. Hathaway. I have no courage of my own. I've always had difficulty making decisions, but the Lord seems to have cared for us in spite of my weaknesses. Coming here just seemed the right thing to do."

Augusta interjected, "Was it also the *only* thing you could do?"

Jesse answered honestly. "No. In fact, when we left Fort Kearney, we were waiting for the arrival of an old friend who had invited us to accompany his wagon train to Oregon. But we couldn't wait. And I had decided we wouldn't go, anyway."

"Why on earth not, if you had friends there?"

Jesse struggled to find words to explain her decision. "I don't know, really. It just didn't seem right, somehow. Lis-Beth was born here, on the prairie." Jesse gazed over Augusta's shoulder and into the distance. "There's just something about the prairie. It grows on you—gets into your blood, I guess." She looked back at Augusta and blushed, embarrassed. "It sounds silly and trite . . ."

Augusta interrupted her, "It's all right, dearie. I feel it too. I grew up in Minnesota with trees everywhere—right up to the house. You couldn't see a thing of the land. It closed a body in and kept you guessing about what might happen next. The minute I set foot across the Missouri River I knew this was the place for me. Nebraska's a place where you can see clear to the horizon and on into the future." The voice grew mellower and dropped a few decibels, "This land took my husband and my sister and her children . . . cholera . . . I ought to hate it here, but I don't. It suits me. Lincoln's gonna be a great city someday, and Hathaway House Hotel is gonna be part of that city!"

Joseph's interest was kindled afresh. "Hathaway House, ma'am?"

Augusta's energy returned and she stood up abruptly, her broad hands gesturing expansively. "That's right, Joseph, Hathaway House. They'll be all sorts of people arriving in Lincoln soon: stonemasons and carpenters and all kinds of people to build. They'll need a capitol building first, and then there'll be more—a university, a penitentiary, churches, schools. I already feed a half dozen bachelors supper every night. They're here lookin' for claims out in the countryside. I can cook and clean with the best of them, and Hathaway House is going to be the best hotel on the plains! Now, Joseph, are you or are you not going to put up that lean-to like we discussed and open your blacksmith shop? Since you've been gone, I've expanded the plan too. Why not a livery stable?"

Joseph grinned broadly at Augusta's ever-expanding plan for his future. "Miz Hathaway, I spent lots of hours thinkin' 'bout your plan. Seems like I couldn't find a better chance to make my own way anywhere else. And if they're gonna let me vote in this here state, then I'd say that Nebraska's home from now on! And hooray for Lincoln!"

Augusta turned to Jesse. "Mrs. King, a hotel is a prodigious amount of work. You been a laundress for the infernal military, so you know all about hard work. If you care to join up with me, I'll offer you and LisBeth a room and meals and a salary—although a mighty small one at first—in return for your help with the laundry and housekeeping and whatever else comes up!"

LisBeth's face brightened and she looked eagerly at her mother. Jesse paused only momentarily. The prospect of more days traveling to find another town to settle in was not one she relished. "I'd be honored if you'll have us, Mrs. Hathaway."

"There's just one requirement you may find difficult." The woman folded her arms across her bosom.

Jesse looked up with apprehension at the suddenly stern face.

"You may *not* continue to call me Mrs. Hathaway. I'm just plain Augusta to all thirty of the illustrious citizens of Lancaster-turned-Lincoln, and I'll not have you puttin' on airs with all this Mrs. stuff. You call me Augusta and I'll call you Jesse and that's that! And *you,* young lady," August turned to LisBeth, who sat up straight and looked suddenly serious. "*You* call me Aunt Augusta. *That* will hush any overcurious souls who just can't mind their own business."

June 22, 1867, is recorded in Nebraska history as the day that the capital was chosen. Nowhere is it written that another important ceremony was witnessed on that day. Of course, the only witness was a recently freed slave. It was, however, a most significant day for Jesse and LisBeth King, recently of Fort Kearney, Nebraska. Adopted into the family of Mrs. Augusta Hathaway, the well-known hostelier, the very *un*known King women began a new life.

Chapter 25

And whatsoever ye do, do it heartily, as to the Lord, and not unto men.

Colossians 3:23

Augusta and Joseph were right about the potential growth of the village of Lancaster. New residents came pouring in, swelling the population and bringing Jesse and Augusta more work than they had anticipated. They cooked stew, put up preserves, and bedded down travelers, working from sunup to sundown with little time to spare. Augusta kept up with current events by reading the articles in the local *Commonwealth* aloud with no admission charged for her editorial commentary.

Fifty miles away, in Omaha, the *Republican* sneered, "No one will ever come to Lincoln . . . no river, no railroad, no steam wagon, nothing . . . fifty miles from anywhere." Augusta took the slight personally, "Hmph! Just sour grapes, that's all. They wanted the capital for themselves, and now that they've lost, they just can't say anything nice. "

Augusta had barely finished her commentary when a fine carriage pulled up outside the hotel. Three gentlemen dressed in top hats and well-tailored suits descended and paused to survey Market Square. One finally broke away from the trio and entered the hotel, dusting off his top hat carefully as he asked, "Would there be a possibility of supper being served three extra boarders this evening?"

Never one to turn away business, Augusta assured him that Hathaway House would be pleased to serve him and his companions a fine dinner—in about two hours.

The man bowed stiffly and left to inform his companions.

"Hmph!" Augusta blustered, "he practically wrinkled his nose when he came through the door. Doesn't think Hathaway House is good enough for him!"

"Augusta," Jesse chided. "That's not fair—you don't even know the man."

"*Know* him?" Augusta retorted, "I know him all right. That's Jonathan Daniels from Omaha. He's the one who threw such a fit when they secreted the state records out of Omaha in that snowstorm last winter. Would I ever like to know just what he's got up his sleeve! Think quick, Jesse! What can we serve for supper that's—elegant? If that fellow has one tiny excuse to put down Lincoln, he'll do it. One of those other men is probably a reporter, and I'm sure they'd just love to write a nice little article about how impossible it is to even get a decent meal in the west! Now, Jesse, say what you will, but it's our civic duty to feed those men the best meal they've ever et."

Jesse couldn't argue with civic duty. Joseph was requisitioned to go hunting prairie chickens.

"LisBeth, come along!" Jesse called. "Augusta, we'll be back in a little while. I've got some ideas." Grabbing their bonnets, the two were out the door before Augusta could ask too many questions. Heading away from the village, Jesse began gathering—a root here, a few leaves there.

"LisBeth, look for a bushy plant with bright orange flowers—there! Over there! That one! See how the butterflies flock to it? Dig down deep and bring up a few roots. We'll use that to flavor the soup. Now . . . a few more of these," Jesse stripped some leaves off a plant and stuffed them into the already full muslin sack she had brought along.

"Mama, where on earth did you learn about all these plants. You never cooked with these before."

Jesse smiled. "Remember when I told you how the Lakota had helped me and Pa? Well, they taught me about plants, too, and these things are all edible. And they taste wonderful.

I don't think those gentlemen from Omaha will have experienced quite the same taste ever before."

LisBeth looked at her mother. Jesse grinned. "I also learned how to cook dog meat stew." LisBeth grimaced and Jesse added, "but I don't think we'll put *that* on the menu tonight . . . although, actually, it tastes quite good."

Back in the kitchen, LisBeth plucked the birds while Jesse made a salad of wild greens and onions. The birds were roasted in the oven alongside a wild plum upside-down cake.

"We'll make leadplant tea instead of coffee. Just tell them it's imported." Jesse whispered.

"Mama, you taught me never to lie," LisBeth chided.

"Well, it *is* imported—from the prairie!"

Just as the cake came out of the oven, Jonathan Daniels, Timothy Price, and Pythias Young were seated at their table—a few feet away from the regular boarders, as requested. They conducted their important business while the kitchen help served them.

Pythias Young was the first to notice that things were not quite right. Looking down at his plate, he poked suspiciously at the greens. But hunger won out. With a sigh, he muttered, "I guess I shouldn't have expected a proper meal out here on the frontier," and took a bite. He took another bite. Then he tried the wild carrots. By now, Jonathan and Timothy, the less timorous members of the party, had attacked their prairie chickens with gusto.

The planned meeting was forced to wait as the three gentlemen from Omaha had forgotten that they were genteel and must set a good example for the rough-hewn pioneers of Lincoln.

Augusta and Jesse served up huge platefuls of the food to all the boarders, who acted as if they ate in such grand style every evening at Hathaway House.

Jesse could have hugged scrawny Tom Mason when he commented—just loudly enough to be overheard, "Another excellent meal, Mrs. King. I always say, 'Hathaway House in Lincoln surely knows how to serve fine fare to one and all.'"

"Thank you, Mr. Mason," Jesse replied matter-of-factly. Her eyes sparkled. Augusta thumped him on the back and offered him more tea.

"Tea?" Jonathan Daniels asked from across the room.

"Imported!" barked Augusta as she poured him a cup. "Goes with the dessert better than coffee. See if you don't agree!" And she set a huge piece of cake down at his place.

The gentlemen from Omaha were softening toward Lincoln. Pythias began to think that perhaps his editorial might not be so brazenly negative, after all. Jonathan despaired of having the brilliant anecdotes he had hoped to share at the club upon his return.

"Uh, just what was the delicious soup you served this evening, Mrs. King?" he asked in his smoothest voice.

Jesse could not resist. "Dog meat stew, sir. It's a specialty of Hathaway House."

The three men from Omaha were aghast. Pythias gripped the edge of the table with both hands and forced himself to retain his supper. Jesse pursed her lips, arched one eyebrow, and allowed a tiny smile to curve up the corners of her mouth. From the kitchen doorway, LisBeth giggled.

The gentlemen looked at Jesse, then at one another. "Ah, a joke, a frontier joke, how amusing!" They smiled broadly— laughing to cover their sighs of relief—and Jonathan, the clever one, guffawed, "Dog meat stew, specialty of the Hathaway House! Great! I love it." Jonathan had his anecdote for his next evening at the club. He warmed toward the Hathaway House and Lincoln. The little village was coming of age, after all.

Having eaten enough cake to "kill a mule" according to Augusta, the gentlemen mounted the stairs to their rooms. The other boarders joked and mimicked them while Jesse sincerely tried not to enter in, and failed. When the last boarder had left the dining room, the three women shared triumphant smiles.

The next morning, Jonathan, Pythias, and Timothy left on the 7 A.M. stage for Elkhorn and on to Omaha. The *Republican* carried a short article some days later that Tom Mason rushed over to Augusta.

The proprietors of The Hathaway House in Lincoln do nothing by halves. They serve the finest meals, making use of the bounty of the prairie to create delicacies this writer found completely palatable.

"I guess he did!" snorted Augusta when she read the article to LisBeth and Jesse. "He ate two platefuls of greens!" The article concluded:

The author is most impressed by the rapid growth of Lincoln. Thanks to citizens like those encountered at The Hathaway House, and with the development of the salt industry, it will, no doubt, develop into a fine city.

❧

In spite of the grudging praise from Omaha, however, Lincoln still had its problems. The commissioners failed in their first attempt to raise the $50,000 needed to build a Capitol.

Augusta went to the first land sale and hurried home, the proud owner of the lot adjacent to her claim. She boasted of the bargain price of just twenty-five cents over the appraised value of forty dollars and lamented the foolishness of those who refused to speculate. But hers was the only purchase made that day.

"It's a well-thought-out city, Jesse," Augusta argued. "They've set aside blocks and lots for schools, parks, churches, a market square. Why, they've even allowed for three lodges! Folks'll come from all over. I just don't understand why these fool men don't see it. Just like men—they get their own way and then they're afraid to get on with it! Why on earth don't you buy yourself a lot? I'll certainly loan you the money!" Augusta was expansive in her desire to share the future of her beloved Lincoln.

"I don't argue that someday Lincoln will be a great city, Augusta. It's just that I'm content." Jesse replied. "The more a person owns, the more you have to worry over. LisBeth and I have enough."

Augusta couldn't understand. LisBeth, who was stirring a kettle of apple butter, secretly questioned her mother's wisdom. But Jesse would not be moved. Augusta stopped scolding and tried to empathize.

"I tend to go overboard sometimes, Jesse. So, I guess we'll balance each other out. You don't seem to want *anything*, and *I* want to own the whole town! You keep me from going too far—and maybe I'll force you to think of LisBeth's future a bit more."

Jesse bristled visibly. "Augusta, the Lord is perfectly able to take care of LisBeth's future. I don't think my acquiring material wealth is the way to teach her security. I want her to put her whole faith in the Lord. He always takes care of his own."

"The Lord helps those who help themselves, Jesse!"

Jesse smiled and quoted, *"My help cometh from the LORD, which made heaven and earth."*

"That's the trouble with you, Jesse, you always have an answer to everything. And it's usually from the Scriptures, which makes me sound like a heathen if I try to argue!" Augusta changed the subject abruptly, going to the door and staring across the open land. "Now where's Joseph with that string of fish he promised me for supper? All these newcomers can't have fished Willow Bend dry yet!"

Joseph arrived soon with the promised string of fish in

hand. Twelve regular boarders now dined at Hathaway House morning and evening, with a lunch available to those who required it at a minimal extra charge. Most of the boarders were the skilled laborers recruited to help build the new Capitol. Some had come from as far away as Chicago, and their opinions of the prairie city provided lively debate at most meals.

"Know what, Miz Hathaway," Tom Mason would begin, delighting in stirring up trouble, "I heard today that the railroad is headed clean around the salt flats—won't come near Lincoln for fear some Sioux on the warpath will scalp the crews."

Whatever the device used to "rile Miz Hathaway," it always worked. Augusta bristled. "Tom Mason, you and I both know there hasn't been an Indian scare in these parts in years. And tell your 'source' that around here all we have are Pawnee, and they've been peaceful for a long, long time!"

A sod dormitory was erected on the Capitol grounds. Boarders from the east grumbled about living in dirt houses, and Augusta defended again. "I suppose you easterners would have just laid down on the prairie and died before now. Got no gumption! Well, Nebraskans know how to make do, and if the Good Lord don't provide trees, Nebraskans just look around and use what he *has* provided. Our sod houses will still be standing when your children have children!"

All the while Augusta argued and defended, she moved around the table, taking up plates, refilling coffee cups. Jesse worked just as hard, but very quietly. Both women kept LisBeth busy in the kitchen, out of sight and sound of the men. "For your own good, dearie," insisted Augusta. LisBeth was fast becoming a young woman, and neither Jesse nor Augusta wanted it noticed.

Augusta was wrong about Jesse's lack of ambition for LisBeth. When Jesse saw Hortense Griswall's ad in the *Commonwealth,* she was one of the first to respond.

Miss Griswall's select school will open October 1 on 10th Street. Come to the first door south of Dr. Patton's Drug Store. Tuition per term of 12 weeks: Primary Grades, $4, High English and Latin, $7, French and Music extra. Tuition to be paid half in advance.

"LisBeth, look at this," Jesse called out the first night the ad appeared. LisBeth laid her knitting down and peered over her mother's shoulder at the ad.

"Oh, Mother . . . I'm too *old* for school!"

"Nonsense, LisBeth. 'High English and Latin.' We have enough for that. Now I wonder how much extra music and French are."

LisBeth wrinkled up her nose and returned to her knitting. "I don't *need* to go to school. I know all I need to know to do sums for Aunt Augusta's bookkeeping. I know how to cook and clean . . ."

Jesse interrupted her, "And you don't know how to do a thing else."

"But, Mother, I don't *want* to do anything else. All I want out of life is a home and a family." Seeing that her pleading was making no headway with her mother, LisBeth changed her attack. "Mother, you've said that God's highest calling is to be a wife and mother. Did you suddenly change your mind?"

"Of course not, dear. It's just that . . ."

"It's just that you're afraid I won't be able to meet the *highest* calling, so I'd better get busy and prepare for something else. That's it, right?"

"That is *not* it," Jesse retorted, feeling defensive. LisBeth changed her strategy again.

"Mother, if we trust that the Lord will do what's best for

me, then why should I need a secondary plan to his *best* plan? Why not just be patient for him to work it all out? That's what you've always told me to do. Be patient. He makes all things beautiful in his time . . ."

Jesse's mind whirled for an answer. She went to retrieve her sewing basket from her room, buying time to concoct a reasonable answer. By the time she returned, God had provided it.

"LisBeth, of course we wait for God to answer our prayers. However, that doesn't mean we do *nothing* while we wait. Do you remember when Joseph shared about the brick wall with us? He said, 'There's a brick wall, and the Lord says, "Joseph, now I want you to go through that." I ain't going to say, "Lord, I can't. I've got nothing to do with that." All I have to do is push against the wall, and it's the Lord's business to put me through.'

"LisBeth, the future is a brick wall. Only God can put you through the wall into a happy marriage. But you have to step up to the brick wall and push against it. You have to put yourself into society. And to be in society, there are certain things a young woman needs to know . . . things I've never had a chance to learn. Things Augusta never learned. We've both been too busy surviving to worry about them. But you don't have to worry about surviving, LisBeth. I'll provide for you. You *can* learn all those things, and I want you to. God has provided the opportunity. We must not neglect to push against the brick wall!"

"All *right,* Mother," LisBeth sighed. "I'll hang up my fiddle. I'll go to Miss Griswall's school," she added, "but she'd better be *nice!*"

Hortense Griswall was nice. She was really nice. The first day of classes, she wore a nut-brown calico dress adorned with a gold clasp engraved with the initials H.G. in fine script. Expertly sewn tucks covered the entire bodice of the dress from the high neck to the perfectly fitted waist. The hem swept the floor at just the right length.

Unfortunately, in spite of her meticulous wardrobe and perfectly coiffed hair, those who described Hortense with Christian sensitivity could only expound upon her being so nice, so well groomed. Bobby Miller, who at the age of six had sported no Christian sensitivity, had said it when Hortense, also aged six, had smiled at him in hopes that he would invite her to the May Day celebration. "You're real nice, Hortense, but I don't wanna go with you. You're just too ugly."

But she *was* nice. Hortense never complained. Although she found primary classes a bore and young children very trying, she was an excellent teacher.

Only a little older than LisBeth, Hortense wanted to resent LisBeth's loveliness. But she found she could not, for the girl was unpretentious and, after her initial grumblings to her mother, honestly eager to learn.

So Hortense Griswall plodded through elementary grammar with her five small students, refreshed her toilet at noon, and then swept into the afternoon, her energies renewed for the conjugating of Latin and French verbs with LisBeth.

❧

One night long after LisBeth had gone to bed, Jesse and Augusta were startled by an urgent tapping at the door. "Who's there?" demanded Augusta, reaching for her husband's rifle, which she kept over the door.

"Tom, ma'am, Tom Mason."

The rifle was returned to its place over the door, and Augusta let Tom in.

"Land sakes, Tom, you nearly scared us both to death! What do you want at this hour?"

Tom looked down, embarrassed. "Miz Hathaway . . . you got any more rooms? Any room at all? I'm sick to death of the varmints that we gotta share that soddy with! I went to turn in tonight and a snake done fell outta the ceiling and curled up right on my cot! Please, ma'am . . . anything'll do. Even a bedroll on the floor . . . just so I don't have to sleep in no dirt houses anymore!"

Jesse was already moving the rockers away from the fireplace. Augusta read her meaning "Well, now, Tom, all the beds are taken, but if you're set on it, you can sleep here by the fireplace." The young man nodded gratefully and reached outside the door to grab what proved to be his bedroll. He had known Miz Augusta would never turn him away.

The two women bid him goodnight. When they came down at dawn to begin breakfast preparations, Tom was out back milking the cow while LisBeth put on coffee and mixed up biscuits.

Augusta chortled, "Well, now, this may be a man that's worth somethin' after all! First one I ever met," she said, adding abruptly, "except, of course, for Mr. Hathaway."

"And Joseph," LisBeth reminded her.

"And Joseph," Augusta agreed.

When breakfast was finished and the diners scooted their chairs back to head for their work at the Capitol, Augusta proffered a plan. "Any of you men interested, I'll provide free room and board in turn for your starting my addition. Joseph'll have all the timber cut by next month. I need a two story addition on the back, here . . . you can all have room and board and your choice of a new room for as long as you like if you decide to stay in Lincoln."

"I'll set up the foundation, Miz Hathaway."

"I'll help Joseph cut timber if he'll tell me where to find him after supper."

"I'm good at carpentry . . . hangin' doors and such."

By the time the men had gone out the door, Augusta's addition was well underway. She nodded with satisfaction. "We'll cut a door here," she said, outlining the new doorway on the back wall of the cabin. "Narrow hall, three rooms down, three rooms up. Stairway right on the other side of this wall—convenient for you and me. When the addition's done and the rooms are all rented, we'll bump out the other side of the kitchen for you and LisBeth to have new rooms, then I'll take over your room for my private sittin' room. It'll be kind of a hodgepodge building, but it'll serve us well."

"Augusta," Jesse said, "I appreciate your being so generous, but as hard as I can work, I'll never be able to pay for the construction of a wing just for LisBeth and me. Please, don't feel obligated to do such a thing."

"Now, Jesse King, you listen to me. You two are the closest thing to family I have, and if I want to see you comfortable, you just hush and let me be happy doin' it! Sometimes I'm all bristles and quills, but don't think I don't appreciate them prairie flowers that LisBeth brings in for every supper table. And don't think I don't know that you put extra care in them quilts and comforters you made for all the beds in this place. Land sakes, woman! You more than earned a new room," Augusta turned her back to Jesse and swept the floor vigorously as she croaked. "You've both earned a special place in this old hard heart. So you just hush and let me do what I want. I own this place, and I'll build on to it if I want to!"

Jesse patted Augusta's ample back and said softly, "You don't fool me one bit, Augusta Hathaway. You're all bluster and bother, but I see through it. Inside there's a golden heart just waiting to show itself. I thank the Lord for letting *me* see it."

Augusta was suddenly serious. "I wish I could see inside *you*, Jesse King. You're all civility and manners. You never raise your voice. It drives me crazy. Haven't you ever been so mad or sad you wanted to scream? How is it you're always so . . . far away?" Augusta's clear blue eyes met Jesse's. Jesse looked over her friend's shoulder. On the back of her rocker by the fire was the quilt that told her story: the log cabin, the broken dreams, the wagon wheels, the Indian tepees, the True Vine who had carried her through it all.

226 • STEPHANIE GRACE WHITSON

She whispered, "Oh, I've had my moments." Loneliness made her yearn to share the story with Augusta. Fear held her back. What would Augusta think? Would she understand? Jesse looked back at the unflinching blue eyes that still questioned. She stiffened her shoulders, lifted her chin, and shut Augusta out. The blue eyes smiled and Augusta dropped her hands from Jesse's arms with a sigh, "But you can't talk about it, can you? Your kind never can. There's fire behind those gray eyes. I see it, Jesse. I'm a good judge of people, and there's a lot more to you than you let on." She sighed again before abruptly changing the subject. "Now we've got to get to those chokecherries or the men'll have twenty-minute chokecherry pie for lunch."

"What's that, Aunt Augusta?" LisBeth came in with a bouquet of flowers for the table.

"Why, that's chokecherry pie with the pits left in. It takes twenty minutes to eat one piece!" Augusta's laughter boomed.

Jesse's eyes crinkled at the corners and she winked at LisBeth. "That's one way to keep the boarders from eating more than their share!"

The three women joined in the now-familiar preparations that they would repeat day after day, week after week, month after month, while Lincoln's boom continued, Hathaway House grew, and Joseph Freeman's livery stable and blacksmith shop met the needs of travelers from near and far.

Chapter 26

A naughty person, a wicked man, walketh with a froward mouth. He winketh with his eyes. . . . Frowardness is in his heart, he deviseth mischief continually.

Proverbs 6:12–14

By 1868 the population of Lincoln had grown from thirty to five hundred. Augusta crowed, "One hundred forty-three houses, Jesse, and we've got our first bank now. God bless James Sweet and N. C. Brock and their new stone building!" The newspaper rustled and Augusta leaped out of her chair. "And Hathaway House needs a change too. Enough of this frontier log cabin, Jesse. We're going to have brick! And a fancy dining room, not just these plank tables anymore." Augusta grabbed a pencil and began making notes in the margin of the paper.

Jesse and LisBeth smiled at each other over Augusta's bowed head.

"Joseph!" she shouted, "Joseph!" Joseph came hurrying in mopping his brow. Augusta began to share her plans. "Now, when you have time, Joseph, could you locate that stonemason that's been working for George Atwood and ask him to stop in?"

"Happy to, Miz Hathaway. I just finished shoeing the bay mare. She's rented out tomorrow, and she seemed to be draggin' that off hind foot a bit. Got her all fixed up. She'll put on a fine show trottin' through town."

Augusta scowled. "I suppose Winston Gregory again?"

"Yes'm."

"I wish that varmint would take his business elsewhere!"

"Well, Miz Hathaway, his money's just as green as anybody's." Joseph was uncomfortable. He knew where the conversation was leading.

Jesse chimed in, "He treats you like a slave, Joseph."

"Where he come from, Miz King, I *was* a slave."

"But you're free now, Joseph," Jesse answered.

Joseph stared back at Jesse levelly and bared just the tiniest piece of his soul. "You know it, and Miz Hathaway knows it, but they ain't many others that seems to remember it, ma'am. I may be free, but I ain't free enough to turn down a white man's business just 'cause he's high-falutin'."

Jesse knew it was true. Joseph snapped his exposed soul shut and left to hunt down the stonemason. Jesse returned to her quilting, Augusta to reading the paper aloud. LisBeth sat at the table pretending to darn socks, but her mind was not on the task at hand, for LisBeth had been up town today, and upon exiting Patton's Drug Store, she had been the recipient of a Winston Gregory smile.

&

"Winston! Winston Gregory, come here!" the shrill voice could be heard up and down the block, and no doubt Winston Gregory heard his mother's summons well before he answered. He was, however, absorbed in the dime novel he had secreted in the barn out back. "Mother can wait," he told himself, "after all, I'm not her slave!" He inwardly lamented the loss of their slaves. The last two had been sold in Nebraska City because the stupid Nebraskans wouldn't abide slavery in their territory.

"Such a sensible institution," his mother had complained, "but then your father thinks we simply must take advantage of a new city. Although how I'll ever keep up without Betsy, I'll never know." Lillia Gregory had waved her lace-edged handkerchief in despair and closed her eyes, a martyr to her husband's wishes.

Winston's father, Randall Gregory, had been a vigorous, ambitious lawyer, with plans to make a great name for himself. He had inherited wealth from his father's landholdings but wanted to make his own way. Nebraska Territory held the key to future social position that he could earn on his own merits. So Randall broke his mother's heart, took his ample inheritance, packed up his whining wife and their spoiled son, and headed for the "wild west." He had the good sense to settle in the boom town of Lincoln and the bad fortune to die shortly after erecting an imposing mansion on the corner of 13th and J Streets.

The instant her husband's funeral was over, Lillia Gregory began packing her trunks and making plans to return to civilization. All that remained was to sell the house, and a land agent had assured her that that could be settled by mail. Winston shared his mother's passion to return to "real society," but then that dark-haired beauty outside the drug store caught his eye.

Winston had smiled. She smiled back. He followed her home and sniffed audibly when he saw where she lived. Too bad. The daughter of the maid at Hathaway House. His prospects brightened. *Not material for a wife but maybe perfect for a little fun before leaving town. Why not?*

On Sunday Winston Gregory amazed his mother by offering to accompany her to church. He was dashingly handsome in his best suit and hat. Just as he was helping his mother down from the rented carriage, Jesse and LisBeth walked by. Winston tipped his hat and bowed. LisBeth blushed. Jesse nodded, pressed her lips together, and hurried inside.

Sitting in their usual pew, the two women waited for the service to begin. Winston Gregory ushered his mother to the same pew. "Ladies, may we join you?"

Jesse forced a smile and slid down to make room. Lillia sat

stiffly and offered no greeting. It was, after all, not necessary to acknowledge the existence of the servants in town. Winston sang much too loudly and gave too much when the offering plate was passed. Jesse put in her meager gift and was miserable.

Back at the Hathaway House, Jesse and LisBeth joined Augusta in preparations for the early afternoon meal. Hathaway House offered only one meal at 3:00 on Sundays, in deference to the Lord's Day and at Jesse King's insistence. Augusta's faith wasn't a bit threatened by the earning of money on the Sabbath, but Jesse insisted that they somehow honor the Lord. Augusta had flatly refused to close the hotel kitchen.

"You just can't do that, Jesse. It's not good business."

"Good business honors the Lord, Augusta. Anything else is worthless."

Augusta had long since learned that Jesse's cool exterior was easily ruffled in matters where her faith in what was right before God was challenged.

"Compromise, Jesse," Augusta urged. "We won't close, but we'll offer only one meal. Didn't the Lord eat on the Sabbath? Surely he'd understand that we can't just let our boarders go hungry!"

"We could fix a cold lunch on Saturday to serve on Sunday."

"And lose every single boarder to Cadman House! Not on your life, Jesse King! Now, I'll accommodate your piety when I can, but business is business and I won't give it away. We'll offer one hot meal at 3:00 on Sundays, and it'll be a great one. We'll do something special every Sunday. But only one meal."

Augusta would not be moved. *She's set her jaw,* Jesse thought, *just like Homer.*

Thus, the announcement in the *State Journal,* at twenty cents per line, read:

In an effort to honor the Lord's Day and provide all with a day of rest, boarders at Hathaway House are hereby notified that only one meal will be served on the Sabbath. Boarders are invited to dine at 3:00 P.M. in the hotel dining room. A sumptuous feast will be provided.

Much to Augusta's surprise, not one boarder complained. She attributed it to the "sumptuous feast" provided. Jesse attributed it to the hours she had spent on her knees, asking God to understand, and to make a way for her to honor his day.

Winston Gregory's time was running short. The stage was to depart in only two days, and he had not yet managed to kiss LisBeth King. He had rented the best carriage from Joseph Freeman for the evening, and now he presented himself at the Hathaway House just at the hour when LisBeth was setting tables for the noon meal.

Winston cleared his throat and LisBeth jumped, wheeled about, and blushed.

"I was pleased to see you at church yesterday morning." He saw the pitcher of water tremble as LisBeth tried to appear casual and continue pouring water into glasses. She spilled some.

"I wondered if you would be available for a carriage ride this evening after dinner?"

LisBeth blushed. "I . . . I'd have to ask my mother."

Winston smiled patiently. "Of course." LisBeth sailed out of the room, through the kitchen, and out back where Jesse was harvesting carrots from the garden.

"Mother! Mother! Winston Gregory's inside and . . . and . . . he wants to take me for a carriage ride tonight!"

Jesse stood up abruptly, shaking garden dirt off the carrots. "LisBeth King, you're only thirteen years old!"

"But, Mother, *he* doesn't know that. I act older. Everyone says so. I'm mature for my age." LisBeth grew defiant as she saw her mother's expression. She knew what the answer was going to be.

It came in a kind voice, but it was still difficult to accept. "There's plenty of time for you to be grown up, LisBeth. Enjoy being a girl for a bit longer. I'll tell Winston no for you." Jesse moved to pass LisBeth, but LisBeth held out her hand and said, miserably, "No, Mother . . . I'll tell him. I knew I shouldn't." The dark eyes glistened, "But, Mother, it's nice to be noticed and . . . to be asked. Can't you remember when you were a girl, and the boys noticed . . . wasn't it nice?"

The question was innocent, but it brought back old pangs of loneliness, the feeling of rejection from a lonely young womanhood when no boys had noticed, and no one had asked.

Jesse cleared her dry throat and lied, "Of course, dear . . . it's nice. But it's too early. Tell Winston you're too young," Jesse corrected herself. "No, you don't have to tell him that. Just tell him I said no, that you must work in the kitchen after the boarders eat, and when you've finished it will be much too late for you to go out riding." Jesse smiled. "Make me out to be an ogre. And you needn't tell him you're only thirteen. I know you don't want him to think you're a baby."

LisBeth gave her mother a quick hug and whispered, "I didn't really want to go, anyway. It's a little scary, growing up, Mama. Thanks for saying no."

"LisBeth, that's what mothers are for. You use me anytime you need an excuse to say no and still save face with your friends. Don't lie, but you can make me out to be as mean as necessary if you need help."

LisBeth retreated to the dining room where Winston waited expectantly.

"Thank you very much, Winston, but," LisBeth sighed dramatically, "Mother insists I do the dishes after the boarders have eaten. Of course, it would have been lovely."

Winston turned his hat around in his hands and thought of an alternative. "Then walk with me after you're finished. I'll go out in the carriage, and when I bring it back I'll just hang around the stable, waiting. Come out back when the dishes are done and your mother's asleep."

LisBeth hesitated. "Come on, LisBeth. I'm leaving day after tomorrow. I just want somebody to talk to. It's been lonely here . . . and, gee . . . I thought you'd understand."

LisBeth's heart softened momentarily, but Jesse came to the door. She had overheard, and she was angry. Green highlights blazed in her gray eyes, "We may be working class, Mr. Gregory, but that does *not* mean that my daughter is to be used for one night's amusement when you have nothing better to do. She does *not* go out unchaperoned, sir, and I suggest you remember that, or . . . ." Jesse cut him with sarcasm, "I'll tell your mother what you've been up to!"

Winston Gregory flushed with anger, stuffed his hat on his head, and retreated. LisBeth tried to be angry with her mother, but one look after Winston and she burst out laughing. "Oh, Mama, he was acting so grown up. I thought he was such a man, but look at him, hustling off down the street, just because you threatened to tell his mama! What a sight!"

In a burst of affection, LisBeth hugged her mother. "Thank you Mama, for protecting me from 'ghoulies and ghosties and long-legged beasties and things that go bump in the night.' And from Winston Gregory!"

Jesse was serious. "LisBeth, somewhere, God has a husband for you. I'm certain of it. I've prayed for him since you were little. When he comes, we'll know it. Until then, you must be very careful that you never give away anything that you should be saving for him. Don't give away your dreams or your inner thoughts or your affection until you have the man who's right."

"Did you save your dreams for Papa?" LisBeth asked.

Jesse pondered the question and avoided answering it directly. "There's someone deep inside every woman, Lis-

Beth, just waiting to be loved into the light. She was there, inside me, but I didn't know it until I met Papa."

LisBeth saw her mother's face change. That other smile— the one from Sundays at Fort Kearney—almost came back. LisBeth hadn't seen that smile in a long time, and it made her ache inside. It made her want a father. Jesse knew.

"Oh, dear LisBeth, just remember, when you feel lonely for Papa, you can always tell the Lord. He has promised to be your father. He will be your guide, and he will never, ever, leave you."

"Sometimes it doesn't seem enough, Mama."

Jesse squeezed her daughter's hand. "I know, honey. Sometimes it doesn't seem enough for me either. But I just take a deep breath and do the next thing, and somehow it is enough. The Lord gives me the grace to go on." With scarcely a pause, Jesse added, "When the right man comes along, LisBeth, he'll fill up that place inside you that Papa left empty. It'll fill up and overflow until you're just bursting with the love inside you. In the meantime, don't you give any of LisBeth King's heart to the likes of Winston Gregory, or I'll take a switch to you!"

Jesse attempted humor to hide sentimental tears. LisBeth was nearly grown up. Men would be calling on her and she would someday be leaving—for where?

With one arm around her daughter's waist, Jesse added, "Now let's get supper cooking. I promised Augusta that we'd take care of everything tonight so she could attend that meeting up at the bank. Let's get to it!"

Winston Gregory and his mother departed on the 7 A.M. stage on Wednesday morning for Marysville, Kansas, where they were met by Lillia's family and carted back to Missouri and civilization. Somehow, Nebraska carried on without them.

Chapter 27

Now unto him that is able to do exceeding abundantly above all that we ask or think, according to the power that worketh in us, unto him be glory.

Ephesians 3:20–21

"It's finally getting syrupy, Mama," LisBeth called, wiping her forehead and continuing to stir the huge pot of boiling purple liquid. Jesse hastily wiped the rims of the last few canning jars and hurried over to the stove. Together, the two women ladled elderberry syrup into the jars, sealed the lids, and stood back to survey their work with satisfaction.

"Now, see, aren't you glad we went along to help Joseph harvest elderberries?" Jesse asked. "There's nothing quite as rewarding as a larder full of preserves!"

"... unless it's a hope chest full of quilts!" LisBeth finished the sentence for her mother.

Jesse laughed. "I suppose I've said *that* enough times, haven't I?"

LisBeth smiled wistfully. "Every time you added a quilt to my hope chest, Mama, and there are twelve now, and all hope is nearly gone."

Jesse's attempt to encourage the daughter who had witnessed the weddings of each of her classmates in the past few months was interrupted by Augusta's booming voice. "Get in here! Look at this . . . I never!"

Jesse and LisBeth hurried to the front room of the hotel where Augusta peered outside. The sun had gone behind a dark cloud, and the building was shaken by violent winds that came on suddenly with the roar of hailstorm. But there was no hail. As the three women watched, the black cloud passed by and the wind quieted. In the distance, they could see the cloud seem to descend from the heavens. A few grasshoppers appeared in the road.

"Odd," Augusta murmured. The three women returned to their chores and gave the cloud little thought until the next morning, when homesteaders began arriving in town with their unbelievable tales.

"In two hours, they were four inches deep on the ground . . ."

"I'm wiped out. They et the onions right out of the ground . . ."

"All that's left of my garden is holes where they was beets and carrots . . . "

"They climbed up my dress . . . ate the stripes right out of the weave before I could beat them off and get back into the house!"

"The curtains are hanging in shreds at the windows . . ."

"The livestock all went crazy and ran off . . . "

Jesse and LisBeth prayed for the homesteaders and were thankful they were in town. The worst of the horde had passed Lincoln by, but it was the final calamity for hundreds of homesteaders. Beset by prairie fires during a drought, and floods when the drought broke, having battled tornados and hailstorms, they were finally wiped out by an insect. Only a few days after Hathaway House inhabitants had witnessed the cloud going over the town, droves of homesteaders began arriving to take the railroad back east, back home, out west, up north—anywhere.

One poor woman got on the morning train that week weeping hysterically and shouting to the disembarking passengers, "Turn back, turn back! I've spent a winter and a summer here. God help you all if you stay in this cursed place!" Her embarrassed husband pulled her up into the train car and gently lead her to a seat, his arm about her shaking shoulders.

On Friday of that week, a rickety wagon pulled up outside Hathaway House. MacKenzie Baird shouted an unnecessary "Whoa" to his ancient team—which had already stopped to drink from the horse trough on the street—and slowly climbed down from his rig. He stood for a moment, both hands on the side of the wagon, seeming to inventory its contents.

LisBeth looked out the dining room window and watched carefully. The man's head was turned away from her. She couldn't see his face, but she saw his shoulders rise as he took a deep breath. She saw the dusty hat removed and shaken angrily in one hand while the other hand made a fist that pounded the side of the wagon.

Before he turned to face the hotel, MacKenzie Baird clamped the slightly oversized hat back on his head and pulled the brim down over his eyes. He scraped the mud from the bottom of his boots along the edge of the board sidewalk. Then he made elaborate inspection of the worn harness that held his team to the wagon. With a final attempt to slap the dust out of his flannel shirt, MacKenzie strode into the hotel and rang the bell for the clerk.

Augusta answered the bell immediately, sweeping into the small office from her sitting room "in the back."

The voice that LisBeth heard from her conveniently out-of-sight location in the dining room was mellow, deep. She would describe it in later years as the sound of a deep river rolling gently along a rocky gorge. *I wonder if he looks as good as he sounds,* she thought, and blushed. *LisBeth, you're not a flirt . . . stop being so dramatic!* Having scolded herself properly, she continued to eavesdrop.

The voice was steady, but slightly strained. "Do you have any work available that would enable me to pay for a room, ma'am? Joseph Freeman said to check with Hathaway House as soon as I arrived in town." The young voice faltered.

MacKenzie cleared his throat, hooked his right thumb in his suspenders and continued, "I, uh, we—that is, the grasshoppers wiped us out, and as soon as things are settled on the place and I earn enough for a new rig and team, I'll be moving on." He rushed to finish, "I'll do anything honest to earn my way. I'm strong and a hard worker, but the fact is, I've got no way to pay for the room or the meals unless I get work."

Advancing age had not dulled Augusta's ability to appreciate abundant black hair, deep blue eyes, fine teeth, and an undeniably handsome face. Age had, however, taught her to measure her kindnesses carefully to those who merited them. Augusta later assured herself, Jesse, and LisBeth that MacKenzie's beauty had had nothing to do with the fact that he was immediately taken in. It was, rather, his use of the "password" that had resulted in countless folks finding shelter at Hathaway House. MacKenzie Baird called Joseph Freeman a friend. When Joseph Freeman sent someone to Augusta, Augusta helped.

So it was that moments after his struggle to state his case in a mature, controlled way, MacKenzie Baird found himself ushered into a spotlessly clean hotel room by Jesse and being handed clean linen by her lovely dark-haired daughter who told him dinner would be served in two hours and then blushed and practically ran down the stairs and out the front door of the hotel.

LisBeth paused just outside the front door. An early morning rainstorm had turned the streets of Lincoln into a nearly impassable quagmire. The board sidewalk ended at the end of the "block" occupied solely by Hathaway House, and Joseph Freeman's Livery Stable. Glancing down at her new shoes, LisBeth turned left, toward the Livery Stable. Lifting her calico skirts high, she picked her way through the mud and ducked into the stable. Once inside, she closed her eyes and inhaled the wonderful aroma of recently curried horses and fresh hay. From overhead, Warbonnet, the chief cat on the block, stared down regally.

"Warbonnet, here kitty-kitty!" LisBeth coaxed. Warbonnet ignored her. LisBeth scurried up the ladder to the loft as quickly as her abundant petticoats would allow and tumbled into a pile of fresh straw. The cat flicked one ear in her direction and yawned.

"Oh, all right, Warbonnet, so I don't have any milk with me today. Still, you have to listen." LisBeth dropped her voice and confided, "It's the greatest news in all the world, Warbonnet. I've *met* him! I've met the man I'm going to marry."

Warbonnet was not a very good friend. At the first sound of LisBeth's voice, he had seen the movement of a mouse on the opposite side of the stable—along the floor. With a flick of his half-missing tail, he had leaped down and engaged in hot pursuit.

LisBeth would not be discouraged. "Fine . . . don't believe me. But I know what I know, and someday, you old cat, you'll see. Mama and I have quilted and sewed until my hope chest is brimming over with lovely things. I'd nearly lost hope, but not anymore! MacKenzie Baird . . ." She tried the name out loud several times. Then footsteps sounded below and she was forced to be quiet or be discovered.

It was Joseph, bringing in MacKenzie's team.

"But, Joseph . . . I can't pay for this either. I'll just take them to the edge of town and let them graze. Shoot! I saw cattle grazing on the lawn of the Capitol building earlier. No one's going to mind a couple of aged draft horses at the edge of town. You don't want to take up your stalls with my team."

"Mac, you just hush," Joseph replied. "I done tol' you that I'm gonna help you. It's a horrible thing that's happened to us all. It'll be all right. I got the livery and my land. Crop's ruined for this year, sure, but I done proved up on the place, and it can just set for a year while I run the livery. What happened out there on your place—that should never happen to nobody, son, and the Good Lord done tol' me to help you all I can. So you just hush up and let this ol' black man len' you a han'!"

In the privacy of the stable, MacKenzie Baird broke down. The kindness being poured out was too much. He had steeled himself against the horror of what he had found when he had returned from searching for the livestock the night before. But he had not prepared himself to handle kindness.

Caught with no way to escape from the loft, LisBeth listened to the broken dreams of the young homesteader being poured out onto the wide shoulder of a former slave. "Why'd he do it, Joseph? I'll never understand what made him do it. We could have started over. We could have taken care of everything . . ."

Joseph interrupted the young man. "Don't know why anybody takes his own life, son. They's never any answer. Just leaves the folks behind with a big hole in their heart and a whole load of guilt."

"Maybe it just took too much out of him, Joseph."

"Losin' your ma last winter—he took that real hard."

LisBeth peeked over the edge of the loft. MacKenzie was wiping his face with a faded kerchief and nodding his head. "Yep—when Ma died, Pa just didn't seem to have the interest anymore. He's been going downhill ever since, but I never thought . . . I never suspected . . . I never would have gone and left him alone . . ." The voice trembled again, threatened to break down. Joseph put a thin hand on the boy's shoulder.

"Stop it, boy. You did what was right. Somebody had to see if they was any livestock to be rounded up. Somebody had to pick up and get on with it. You done right. Your pa took the wrong way out, son. That's just it. The wrong way. Life handed him some hard stuff, but the Lord always helps his children bear up. Look here, Mac—you don't know nothin' 'bout me, and I ain't tellin' you much, either. What's past is past and it ain't good to be dredgin' it up. But I'll tell you somethin', I been through lots worse than floods and grass-hoppers. I lost a wife—and it wasn't no sickness that took her 'cept the sickness of one man thinkin' he can own another and buy and sell 'em as if they was animals. I lost two boys the same way. Thought I was gonna go plumb crazy when it happened. But I didn't. I just sung and prayed my way to freedom and I sung and prayed some more, and finally, it didn't hurt quite so bad. . . ."

MacKenzie looked into the earnest dark face and croaked, "How long was it before you could quit singing and praying to keep going, Joseph?"

"Don't know, MacKenzie, don't know."

The blue eyes questioned.

"Don't know 'cause I'm still singin' and prayin' to keep going. That kind of hurt just don't ever go away, son. But it gets bearable. It fades. And yours will fade too. You just keep prayin' and singin.'" Joseph paused. "Say, can you read, boy?"

"Pa was sending me to the university next year. Yeah, I can read."

"Then you pray and you sing and you read the Bible. You keep doin' it every day, and you'll see. The Lord will pull you through. And when you need it, son, you come to the livery stable and you let old Joseph Freeman hear your troubles. Only the Lord can solve 'em, but sometimes you just needs to tell someone."

"Who'd *you* ever tell, Joseph?"

Freeman was quick to respond. "Only met two people I ever cared to tell. You met 'em both. LisBeth and her mama heard it a long time ago. Miz King, she ain't never forgot. I see it in her face every time she looks my way. That's a woman what don't show her feelin's much. Still, I know she cares."

"How can you tell?"

"Oh, she ain't much for words, Miz King ain't. She just does what's right and keeps her mouth shut. Last week, one of the poor coloreds died. Family didn't even have money to bury him. We got ourselves a fine new cemetery northeast of here—named it *Wyuka,* 'Place of Rest' in Sioux. Funny ain't it, white man callin' his graveyard that when he ain't givin' the Injuns a place to rest in all this land that used to be theirs. Anyway, ol' Jubilee Jamison up and died, and his family's got no way to pay the undertaker. They's hollerin' and carryin' on somethin' awful. Comes a knock at the door, and there stands Miz King. She don't say a word, just hands over an envelope and then leaves. She's already halfway across town when here comes Jubilee's widow after her. Miz King turns about and says, real quiet like, 'The Lord has provided for Jubilee, Harriet. Don't tell another soul or he might be upset with us all for flaunting our good works!' And that's that. The undertaker gets a call, and Jubilee Johnson had a real nice buryin', after all. Now, you ask Miz King about that, she'd just look out the window and smile and say she 'just don't know what to say about that, but ain't it wonderful how the Lord provides?'

"She heard my story, and she ain't never forgot. I can tell her anything, and she cares to listen. It's a healing thing, MacKenzie, sharing with another human being all the hurts life deals out. You've had a heap of hurt for your young years. When you need to spill it out, you always know where Joseph Freeman is!"

Joseph ended the encounter. "Now, scoot! Miz Hathaway don't take long to find work for anybody, and she's shorely got a job for you by now. Go fin' out what it is and get to it!"

Chapter 28

In the end it was Jesse, not Augusta, who helped MacKenzie find work. His industrious search for work and his genteel manners won over the three women of Hathaway House. Jesse and Augusta agreed that he was a "fine young man." When Sunday arrived, and MacKenzie requested permission to accompany the women to church, Jesse's approval soared almost as much as her daughter's heart. Although it was Augusta that MacKenzie chose to escort personally, and although he sat at the opposite end of the pew from her, LisBeth was unable to concentrate on the Reverend Samuel's exposition of the Scriptures that day.

Her daughter's infatuation with MacKenzie did not go unnoticed by Jesse. When LisBeth dished up supper, MacKenzie received the biggest portions, the fluffiest dumplings, the freshest coffee. If he happened to look directly at her, the usually vivacious young woman blushed and fumbled a reply.

He had been in Lincoln only two weeks when MacKenzie announced that as soon as he had saved enough for a new outfit, he was headed to the Black Hills to try his luck in the gold mines. Jesse had "spoken a word" to J. W. Miles, owner of the dry goods store in town, and MacKenzie had worked for him since the day after he arrived in town.

"Lincoln's a fine city," he said, with tactful deference to Augusta, "but I'm just not cut out to live in the city. I grew up in the open air, and I couldn't abide being cooped up in a store for long."

Turning to Jesse he added hastily, "That's not to say I'm not grateful for all you've done to help me, Mrs. King."

Augusta interrupted him, "The Black Hills gold mines are not exactly the safest place to make one's fortune, MacKenzie."

Jesse agreed. "I certainly understand your love of the outdoors, MacKenzie. But why not return to the family homestead? Mr. Miles says you're a fine worker. Build up credit with him to outfit your farm. Owning land is a wonderful way for a young man to get started. Why, you're halfway to being able to support a wife and family already." Jesse stopped short. "I mean, if a family is in your plans for the future." She felt awkward broaching such a personal subject, and quickly went back to Augusta's subject. "The Lakota have been pushed so far already . . . prospectors coming into their lands are going to be in a very precarious position."

Uninvited, other men in the dining room joined into the conversation.

"Yeah, that massacre back in '66 made 'em think they could push us all around!"

Another voice boomed, "Carrington sure botched that job, all right. Shoulda been court martialed."

"They oughtta hang ten of the murderous savages for every one of our boys they butchered."

Jesse's face flushed with anger. Her mouth opened, but the angry retort went unspoken. As quickly as she had opened her mouth she snapped it shut, excused herself from the table, and hurried into the kitchen.

Augusta took note. *Pots and pans sure are rattling louder than usual out there.* She jumped at the sound of a plate crashing to the floor.

As the men continued to opine about the "Indian situation," Augusta followed Jesse into the kitchen where she found her always calm, never emotional friend slamming things about with gusto, muttering to herself, mopping either angry tears or sweat off her face. LisBeth scuttled about, trying both to help and to stay out of Jesse's way.

Another plate hit the floor, and Jesse stamped her foot angrily. "Tarnation!" she whispered vehemently.

"Jesse!" Augusta exclaimed.

Jesse looked up, startled. Augusta and LisBeth stared back, speechless. It grew very quiet in the kitchen. Joseph broke up the uncomfortable silence as he came in the back door with an armload of firewood.

"Land sakes!" he exclaimed. "You ladies finally done it! I been wonderin' how long three women could live in such close quarters and not have a scrap. So what's it all about?"

Jesse closed her eyes, looked up to heaven, and took a deep breath. "Joseph," she said, her mellow voice once again under control, "I have made a fool of myself and broken two plates. Would you mind sweeping it up while Augusta and LisBeth serve dessert?"

She turned to Augusta. "I'm sorry, Augusta, but I cannot go back into that dining room with *that* conversation going on and remain civil. If we do not want to be forced to close Hathaway House due to the insanity of one of the 'staff,' you had better serve the dessert and let me get some fresh air."

Jesse didn't wait for Augusta to answer. She swept by Joseph and slammed the back door as she stomped across the back lot. Augusta hurried to slice up the hickory-apple cake Jesse had hauled out of the oven. Joseph didn't ask any more questions. Wondering what had happened and assuming that LisBeth and Jesse had had some kind of argument, he helped Augusta by working in the kitchen as LisBeth and Augusta hurried back and forth to serve her customers.

When the last paying customer had left, MacKenzie quickly rose from his seat to help clear the tables. When Jesse made no appearance to help with the dishes, he rolled up his sleeves and thrust his callused hands into the hot dishwater. Joseph wiped the tables, and Augusta and LisBeth dried the dishes and straightened up. Joseph and MacKenzie talked about nothing to avoid talking about what interested them most. Augusta and LisBeth set a personal record for silence.

When the last dish was clean, the floor swept, and tables were set for breakfast, the two men left Augusta sitting by the fireplace reading. LisBeth had hurried off to her own room, seemingly troubled by her mother's outburst.

MacKenzie heard Joseph's reassuring voice as he went out the back door, "I'll watch for her, Miz Augusta. If'n she don't show up directly, I'll hitch up the old mare."

Augusta murmured her thanks, and MacKenzie went upstairs to his room where he watched from his window until he saw Jesse returning to the hotel, walking from the west. Her graying hair had either fallen or been taken down, and she held a loose bunch of flowers in her left hand. Before she came inside, MacKenzie saw her pause and look up at the full harvest moon that hung low on the horizon. She bowed her head for a minute, and then MacKenzie heard the door creak and the sound of voices. He listened carefully. Unable to decipher actual words, he still heard what he listened for. The murmur of the voices was low-pitched. There was no anger. The tones were mellow and comfortable. After a few moments, only one voice could be heard. The voices continued until MacKenzie fell asleep, the lamp at his bedside table still lit.

Augusta accepted Jesse's apology with a hearty, "Nonsense! No apology necessary! I been waiting a long time to see you get mad, Jesse King. Did my heart good." With a grin, Augusta bid Jesse "good night" and headed for her own quarters. Jesse put the flowers she had collected in a vase, turned down the lamp, and walked down the hall toward her room. Muffled sobs sounded through LisBeth's door. Jesse opened it quietly. LisBeth was lying in her bed, clutching the lace-edged pillow that Jesse had recently embroidered.

As soon as she felt her mother's hand on her shoulder, LisBeth quieted and whispered, "Mother, he can't leave! He just can't! If he leaves now, he'll never know how much I care."

Jesse patted her daughter's arm and collected her thoughts. With a silent prayer for wisdom, Jesse answered. "A young man has to make his own way in the world, LisBeth. You wouldn't want him to do anything less than to make his own way."

LisBeth sat up abruptly on the bed, crossed her legs, and slapped the pillow on her lap to support her elbows. Resting her chin on her hands, her dark eyes earnest, she answered, "Of course I want him to make his own way, Mama, but if he goes away . . ."

"LisBeth," Jesse sighed, "MacKenzie is a fine young man. I could wish for none finer for you—if the Lord has chosen him for you. But, dear, " Jesse tried to soften her voice, "he doesn't seem to have . . . I mean, he hasn't asked my permission to court you."

LisBeth was defensive. "Of course not, Mother! MacKenzie would never ask to court a girl when he has no way of supporting a wife."

"He has his family's homestead."

"He'll never go back there." The young voice trembled with feeling.

"Why on earth not? Joseph says it's acre after acre of rich land."

LisBeth's eyes filled with tears. "Oh, Mama, it's just too terrible. It's just so sad, but he'll never be able to go back." She spilled it out, her retreat to the loft of Joseph's stable, MacKenzie's emotional sharing, his father's suicide. Jesse's heart swelled with sympathy and affection for the young man who had been so early exposed to heartache and failure.

Before LisBeth finished the telling, Jesse had reached out to cover her daughter's young hands and squeeze them affectionately. The gesture gave LisBeth courage to continue after she had told MacKenzie's history. "Mama, I can't explain it. Of course I felt sorry for him, but when I heard the words—when I saw how he felt—I just had to love him! Do you think it can happen like that, Mama? Can a woman really, truly love someone so quickly? Is that how you fell in love?"

In characteristic fashion, Jesse's gray eyes looked away as she pondered her response. "I don't know, LisBeth. I don't remember. "

Impulsively, LisBeth interrupted her, "Oh, Mother! You're always so, so, *analytical*. Honestly, I don't remember ever seeing you upset—until tonight. Please don't be hurt, Mother, but sometimes I wonder if you can possibly understand how I feel."

Jesse got up abruptly and crossed the room to look into the mirror. LisBeth noticed for the first time that her mother's hair streamed loosely down her back. Jesse reached up with one hand and began to wind one graying curl through her fingers.

"You think I don't understand how it feels to be young and in love. Well, perhaps I *have* forgotten some things. But, just now, do you know what I was thinking?"

Jesse turned to face her daughter. "I was looking in the mirror and wondering, 'Who *is* that old woman come to interrupt my talk with LisBeth?'" Jesse searched her daughter's eyes and found willingness to listen and try to understand.

"You see, LisBeth, when I think of myself, I don't think of that woman I just saw in the mirror. Sometimes, I am a young child, running out to the well to pump fresh water for *my* mother. Then another time, I am a young wife, shopping to fill a wagon for a trip across the prairie. I'm scared to death, but I'm doing what I have to do. Sometimes, I am a sad woman, grieving the loss of her husband. But never, LisBeth, never do I think of myself as the old woman you see. It just seems so short a time ago that I was young. Oh, I was never so beautiful as you, and certainly never so impulsive, but I was young. And I am still young—inside. Yes, dear, I *do* remember what it was like and, yes, I do have strong feelings. I've just had lots of practice at covering them up so that others won't see them. . . ." Jesse hesitated before she added, "So that others won't see *me*. LisBeth, dear, don't always accept what you see because if you do, then you won't see *me*. I know that I'm usually soft-spoken and very private, but I remember quilting a hope chest full of quilts . . . and waiting . . . and waiting . . . and no one came to fulfill my hopes. I remember hurting and then learning to love someone I never chose for myself and then hurting again, more than I ever thought possible. I learned to trust the Lord in all those things. There's a Bible verse, LisBeth, *'He hath made every thing beautiful in his time.'* I've learned the truth of that verse, and now," Jesse's hands trembled as she parted and loosely braided her thick hair, "now, I think it's time that you learned about your mama, and yourself. Wipe your tears, and wash your face, and meet me in the kitchen."

Jesse left and LisBeth splashed her face, went to the kitchen, stirred up the fire, and settled into one of the rockers, her heart pounding.

When Augusta answered the soft knock at her door, Jesse whispered, "Thank the Lord," and then said quickly, "Augusta, I'm about to do something I may regret, but I've got to do it before I lose heart. Will you come to the kitchen with me and just be there while I tell LisBeth something?"

Augusta saw fear in her friend's eyes. She grabbed her duster and followed Jesse into the kitchen where LisBeth waited.

Jesse cleared her throat, and then courage failed her. "Wait here," she said, and left again. Augusta and LisBeth exchanged quizzical glances and waited. When Jesse re-entered the room, she was carrying the ragged quilt that had always covered her bed. LisBeth had tried to replace it countless times, but Jesse would not have it. "It suits me," she would say, "and don't you ever do anything with this quilt. It's more than old fabric and thread. These stitches know secrets, the blocks all tell stories, and someday I'll share them." The quilt remained on the bed, fading more and more, tearing until it was nearly beyond repair. Still, Jesse clung to it.

Now, she stood trembling before her only child, and she clung to the quilt and said, "LisBeth, I know you've wanted me to get rid of this thing for years, and I never would. Well now, you're going to hear why. I've told you that the stitches know secrets, and the blocks can tell stories, and now, I think," Jesse paused and took a deep breath, "now, I think, it is time for you to hear the stories."

Jesse spread the quilt on the floor between them, and LisBeth and Augusta leaned forward in their chairs. The firelight cast a warm glow over the room. No one had lighted a lamp, so the three women sat in the half light. Reaching across the quilt to lay her hand on the center panel, Jesse began.

"It starts, here, LisBeth. The Log Cabin blocks are for my home place in Illinois. There was Mama and Papa and my sister Betsy, and me. " Jesse described her home—the trees, the barns, the fields—to LisBeth. She stopped abruptly. "But, LisBeth, your knowing about where I grew up and what it looked like—that doesn't tell you about *me*, does it?" Her voice trembled a little as Jesse went on to tell of her own hope chest, the disappointments of her youth, and how she had married Homer King.

"But Mama," LisBeth interrupted, "all those stories you told me about how much you loved Papa, and how . . . "

"Hush, LisBeth, or I'll never get through it," her mother ordered. "You'll hear it all, but it's hard for me to talk about it. Sometimes it hurts to remember."

Jesse's hand slid across the quilt to the next row of blocks.

"These are still Log Cabins, but they're all cut in half. I made them that way to show that when Homer decided we were leaving Illinois, it seemed to me that my home was all broken up. I felt sort of broken inside too.

"And these," Jesse said, tracing the wheels that had been quilted into the next border of wide, plain strips of cloth, "these are the wheels that took me away from everyone I knew and everything I loved."

Jesse's voice evened out as she recounted the weeks on the trail, the river crossings, the broken axles, and Jacob's death.

LisBeth gasped, "I had a *brother,* Mama?! You never told me! What's the next row mean, Mama? The diamond pieces . . ." Jesse sent a lightning quick plea to heaven for courage. She cleared her throat and then plunged into the next chapter of her life. "Those are about the part of my life it's hardest to tell about. I always knew I should. But every time I tried, I just lost courage."

LisBeth's eyes grew wide with her imaginings of something horrible.

"LisBeth, the diamonds are sewn together to make a triangle, and the triangles make tepees. Indian tepees—tepees I once feared but came to call home . . . after Homer died . . . and I was taken in by the Lakota . . . and met your pa." Jesse looked up at her daughter. LisBeth abruptly sat back in her chair, mouth agape. A furrow appeared between her eyebrows as she tried to grasp what her mother had just said.

Augusta leaned farther forward in her chair, and it creaked as her weight shifted. Jesse jumped at the sudden sound, and rushed forward with the story, telling all she could, trying to tell years in a few moments, trying to tell it before her courage failed her or LisBeth stopped her or Augusta interrupted. But Augusta had no intention of interrupting, and LisBeth was speechless. Exactly what emotion kept her speechless, Jesse could not tell, for she was afraid to look up.

She directed her attention to the quilt, telling its story. She described Rides the Wind and Old One, Two Mothers, who became Soaring Eagle, and Prairie Flower. Finally, she told about Howling Wolf and his dragging her to Pierre Canard's cabin.

"That's the day you were born, LisBeth. That day, in Pierre Canard's cabin."

Jesse continued by telling her daughter about the difficulty she had in naming her. She explained that the W. in her name stood for Wind and that she had almost become Daughter of the Wind. And she shared the depression she had battled, the loss, and finally how finding Suzette Canard's quilt pieces and making the quilt had helped her grief heal. She moved on to the last border.

"And this last border, LisBeth," Jesse said in a hoarse whisper, "this vine is the True Vine, my Lord Jesus Christ, who has wrapped himself around everything that's ever happened to me and made it all beautiful, in his time."

At last she had told every stitch. Jesse was exhausted. Pulling the quilt to herself, she sat on the floor of the kitchen and cuddled it and did not weep.

LisBeth stared in disbelief at the patchwork that spilled from her mother's lap onto the floor. Her eyes followed its pattern upward to the wrinkled hands that held it. They twitched nervously. Finally, LisBeth looked into the solemn gray eyes of the woman who had borne her.

Jesse King was no longer just Mama. With the telling of the quilt she had become a woman who had loved and hurt and kept her faith and grown and triumphed in her own, quiet way.

The silence became too heavy. Jesse broke it. "So, LisBeth, that's how you came to be." As she spoke, Jesse's eyes searched her daughter's face anxiously. LisBeth's expression revealed a storm of questions raging inside. Part of her was angry. She wanted to accuse Jesse of lying. But as she thought back over the memories, she knew that Jesse had never lied. She had always stopped just before the whole truth came out. But she had never lied.

"Why didn't you tell me?"

"I was afraid, LisBeth."

"You were ashamed!" LisBeth retorted.

Jesse stood firm. "I was never ashamed, LisBeth. I've tried

to be true to the Lord and true to your father. But I wanted to protect you from what others might say to hurt you."

A flood of questions began.

"What was he like? What was my father like?" she wanted to know.

The aging face shone with love. "Everything I have ever said to you about your father was true, LisBeth. Everything about his kindness, his character, his love. It's all true. But his name *wasn't* Homer King. His name was Rides the Wind. That's the only thing I didn't tell right." Jesse's voice broke, "And maybe it was the most important thing for you to know."

"The woman at Fort Kearney—that was Prairie Flower?" Jesse nodded and LisBeth began to understand her mother's eager conversation that night.

"What happened to Soaring Eagle?" Jesse told what she knew.

Questions went on and on late into the night until Lis-Beth's mind was too full to grasp any more and Jesse's voice was nearly gone.

At last, LisBeth looked down at the quilt. "Now I understand why you would never let it go."

Jesse looked up. "Are you angry with me, LisBeth?"

"Oh, Mama, I wanted to be angry, but I can't be. You said you didn't tell me because you love me. I know you love me, Mama. How can I be angry with you when all these years you kept the secrets inside? All these years I thought you were just Mama, and there was a whole *world* of things about you I didn't know! I can't be angry, Mama. I have such a *little* lump of troubles to worry over, and you've had such a *mountain* of them." LisBeth impulsively knelt by her mother, encircled her in her arms, and wept her first woman's tears.

Augusta joined in the tears, and when LisBeth and Jesse finally stood up, Jesse smiled sheepishly and said, "Well, Augusta, I told you earlier that I've had my moments, and now you know about all of them. You've been a dear friend, Augusta. I thought you deserved to hear this. I hope it doesn't change things . . . but if it does, I'll understand." Jesse steeled herself and prepared to protect LisBeth from whatever hurtful thing might come their way now that Augusta knew she had taken in a woman of questionable past with a child of questionable heritage.

"Jesse King," Augusta scolded dabbing away her tears and shaking a dimpled hand in her face, "I'm no idiot, and I figured you had a few secrets to tell. And don't think I haven't been able to put two and two together and get four these past few years with all the Indian trouble and seeing your reactions to the news and the talk in the dining room.

"Land sakes, woman! I knew there was more to the Injuns in your story than you let on. I ain't as equality minded as you, Jesse King, but you're a fine Christian woman, and you've raised your daughter to be a fine Christian girl, and what folks don't know won't hurt 'em. And that's that."

So LisBeth and Jesse King and Augusta Hathaway went to their rooms to rest for the hour that remained before dawn. Jesse spread the tattered quilt out on her bed and remembered the things that belonged only to her and Rides the Wind.

Augusta sank onto her down comforter and worried over the future.

But LisBeth lay awake, reviewing it all in her mind, and taking up a heavy burden. *How can I ever marry MacKenzie,* she thought, *now that I know? How can I ever marry any respectable man?* For LisBeth had heard the dining room talk and had read the newspaper articles. They described "fiends in human form" committing "barbarous treachery" with "no regard for human life." Mama had described a man who loved his wife and child. It was all so confusing! *But,* LisBeth reasoned, *we live in the world of whites.* She had seen how half-breeds were treated . . . and now she had become one of them. *My life is all tatters, just like Mama's quilt, but Mama did the best she could.* LisBeth decided to be brave, like her father, Rides the Wind. She would keep the hurt to herself. And in that moment, LisBeth became a woman, just like her mother.

Chapter 29

 . . . but this one thing I do, forgetting those things which are behind, and reaching forth unto those things which are before, I press toward the mark for the prize of the high calling of God in Christ Jesus.

Philippians 3:13–14

"That'll do, Mac . . . you can close 'er up." J. W. barked the order so loud that MacKenzie heard him easily, even though J. W. was in the back storeroom and MacKenzie was sweeping the floor near the display window up front. The order had its desired effect. Two young ladies who had been dallying at the candy counter jumped and scurried out. Mrs. Bond decided she'd take six yards of the double pink and forego the California gold—"although Charity would look *so* lovely in gold at the church social next week." Mrs. Bond made the latter comment as off-handedly as possible. Still, when she spoke Charity's name, she watched young MacKenzie carefully for any reaction to the sound of her daughter's name.

Apparently MacKenzie had something on his mind. Mrs. Bond tried again.

"You *are* going to the church social, *aren't you*, MacKenzie?"

As Mac measured the fabric, J. W. walked to the front of the store, loudly jingling the door keys. Mac cut and folded the fabric, bound it in brown paper, and tied the package with string.

"Shall I put this on your account, Mrs. Bond?"

"Oh, yes, MacKenzie, please," she sighed and rolled her

eyes, "I'm certain Charity will be in for at *least* one more shopping spree before the social. She'll need gloves and . . . oh, I forgot! You're new in town, aren't you MacKenzie? I'm *certain* Charity would be *delighted* to have you join her and her friends at the social. Charity would be *happy* to introduce you to the other young people at the church. You haven't had much chance to meet anyone, have you?"

J. W. rattled the keys again and cleared his throat. "Have a good day, Mrs. Bond. Thank you for coming. My best to the family . . . " He swung the door wide.

Mrs. Bond was not so easily put off. "So, then, MacKenzie, I'll be certain to have Charity stop by tomorrow. You two can make arrangements then."

J. W. raised one eyebrow behind Mrs. Bond's back and shook his head at MacKenzie, frowning.

"Well, thank you just the same, Mrs. Bond. I *will* be attending the social, of course, but I'll probably be late. I have to help close up here, you know, and I wouldn't want Charity to have to wait for me." As he spoke, MacKenzie took Mrs. Bond's arm and politely escorted her toward the front of the store. Agnes Bond suddenly found herself standing on the boardwalk just outside the dry goods store, talking to the closed door.

J. W. had already turned the lock in the door and pulled down the shades. Grasping her package firmly, Agnes launched herself down the boardwalk and across the street. She had not reached the other side before a smile wreathed her dimpled face. *How silly of me,* she thought. *Charity won't want this double pink. I'm sure she'll want me to exchange it, but I'll be much too busy putting up preserves. She'll just have to do it herself!*

When J. W. closed the door to the store, he slapped MacKenzie on the back. "Good work, my boy! Now, let me tell you one thing about the dry goods business. Buy the best merchandise, sell at a reasonable price, and," he winked broadly, "*never,* but *never* let Agnes Bond plan your social life!

A mother in search of a husband for her daughter is not a thing to be trifled with."

MacKenzie grinned back. "Oh, Charity's not so bad, Mr. Miles. She's just a bit spoiled, that's all."

"A *bit* spoiled! Kindness just drips off your tongue, young man."

MacKenzie changed the subject. Pulling a book from under the counter, he said, "Oh! I almost forgot . . . I need to pay for this!"

Miles took it to ring it up and read out loud. "*Memoirs of the Savage West,* by Francis Day." He looked up at MacKenzie. "You interested in the Indian Wars, Mac?"

"I read a review in the paper. It said 'she shows that she understands the great West,' and I thought it might be interesting reading. I was still pretty young when this all started."

J. W. didn't ask any more questions. He took Mac's money, wrapped up the book, and they left the store together—out the *back* door and away from Agnes Bond. Mac jogged briskly around the back of the livery stable and into the hotel's front door. Looking carefully about, he walked quietly through the dining room and into the kitchen where LisBeth was helping her mother prepare supper.

Jesse smiled a welcome. LisBeth didn't look up until Mac called her name.

"LisBeth." It was Mac's turn to feel awkward. Instead of the blushing, trembling girl whom he had seen when he first arrived, here was a calm young woman who seemed—well— downright uninterested in what he might have to say. She'd been acting this way for a couple of weeks now, and he had to admit that it made him feel awkward. It also made LisBeth darned attractive.

Mac held out the package. "This came in over at Miles'. I know you like to read and thought you might enjoy it."

LisBeth took the gift half-heartedly and unwrapped it. Scanning the title she flushed and turned to Jesse. "It's that book by Mrs. Day, Mother. Another tale of bloodthirsty Indians and the helpless white folk they're murdering." Turning to Mac, she added bitterly, "I wonder, Mr. Baird, does Mrs. Day mention at all that the white people in question had just violated another treaty and taken more of the Indians' land? Does Mrs. Day mention the defenseless *Indian* women and children murdered by the infantry?"

"LisBeth!" Jesse snapped. "LisBeth, MacKenzie has shown you a kindness. Where *are* your manners?"

"Thank you, MacKenzie," LisBeth said mechanically.

MacKenzie stared at the book with regret. "I'm sorry, LisBeth . . . I only meant to . . . I didn't mean to . . . " He decided to change the subject. "I really came to ask you to the church social next week. But I guess you won't want to go with me. I'm sorry I . . ."

Jesse interrupted. "MacKenzie, you need not apologize for bringing my daughter a gift. It was a very nice thing to do, and if *she* is too rude to thank you properly, *I* say thank you. Thank you very much for being so kind." Jesse turned to LisBeth, expecting her to pick up with the conversation. Instead, LisBeth carefully removed her apron, folded it across the back of a chair, and left the kitchen.

MacKenzie watched her go. Picking up the wrapping and the book, he turned to leave the kitchen.

"MacKenzie, wait," Jesse said. "Let me go talk to her. I'm sure she'd love to go to the social with you. Just let me go see what on earth has gotten into her!"

MacKenzie grinned. "Thanks, Mrs. King. I sure can't figure her out. I thought she sort of liked me." He became flustered and in front of LisBeth's *mother*, of all people! "Not that she's flirted or anything . . ."

Jesse lowered her voice. "I think LisBeth would be a little fool not to like you, MacKenzie . . . and I didn't raise a fool. If you'll just be patient, I'll try to get to the bottom of this."

MacKenzie settled into the kitchen chair and rolled up his sleeves. "Just put me to work, Mrs. King . . . and I'll be glad to wait." He was suddenly very earnest. "I really *do* want her to go with me to the church social."

Augusta charged in the back door calling, "Jesse, now *here's* a mess of beans if you ever saw one. I just *knew* that garden would be worth the effort!" Augusta had heard Mac's request for work, and setting the basket full of beans in front of him, she slapped him heartily on the back and ordered, "Snap 'em, young man!"

Mac set to work, and Jesse went after LisBeth.

∾

She could hear LisBeth crying before she opened the door to her room. At the sound of the creaking hinges, LisBeth looked up. Seeing Jesse, she said dramatically, "Oh, Mother! I was going to be so brave, so grown up. I just decided I wouldn't *care* that I couldn't marry Mac. I just quit looking at him, and sometimes I don't even think about him. I've decided to go to the university, Mother. I'll study to become a teacher, like Hortense. I'll give my life to teaching, and I won't even *care* that I can't be married. I had it all planned out, and it seemed all right. Besides, MacKenzie never noticed me before."

She added miserably, "Then he had to go and give me that *stupid* book and ask me to the church social. Mother! MacKenzie Baird didn't know I *existed* for all the weeks he's been in Lincoln. How come when I decide I don't *care . . .*"

"But you do care, LisBeth," Jesse interrupted. LisBeth shrugged and made a face.

"You *do* care," Jesse insisted.

"Of course I care," she muttered. "But it doesn't matter. Because no one as nice as MacKenzie Baird would ever marry me."

"Why on earth *not,* LisBeth?"

LisBeth tried not to say it. She didn't want to say it. But the word hung in the air, and at last she grabbed hold of it and flung it at her mother. "Because I'm a half-breed, that's why! I read the papers, Mother. I know what people will think. What they will say. When he finds out the truth, MacKenzie won't want me to walk on the same side of the *street* with him, let alone go to the church social. And heaven forbid that I even *think* the word marriage!"

Jesse grew impatient. "LisBeth, aren't you being just a bit overdramatic? The young man has merely given you a gift and asked you to a church social."

"You don't understand, Mother!" came the angry retort. "I *can't* have a normal life, now, because I'm not a *normal* girl. *My* father ran around the prairie half naked scalping his enemies. How would *that* read on a wedding announcement?!"

LisBeth had flung the words out too hastily to reel them back in. Their effect on her mother was immediate. Jesse clenched both hands around the bedpost until her knuckles grew white. Green flecks appeared in the gray eyes as she said, "For the first time since you were born, LisBeth, I am ashamed of you. Your father wore animal skins instead of wool suits. He spoke a different language. He looked different from the men in our society. But when it comes down to a man's *worth,* LisBeth, those differences don't really make any difference at all. Do *you* think any less of MacKenzie because you know his father was a weak man who committed suicide? Of course not. Will MacKenzie think any less of *you* when he learns that your father was a Lakota brave? I don't know. But I think that MacKenzie deserves something more than suddenly being snubbed by the young woman he likes, without so much as an explanation.

"Perhaps he *will* change his mind when he learns that you are half Indian. But, LisBeth, you have to take that chance. Don't use your parents as an excuse to be miserable. Your future is *your* responsibility, LisBeth. I will *not* be blamed for some imagined happiness that you think I have stolen from you. I wholeheartedly believe that God put me in your father's arms, and you have *no right* to say that there was anything wrong with that.

"Rides the Wind was a wonderful, kind man. I loved him. I *still* love him, and you would have loved him, too, if you'd had the chance to know him." Jesse lowered her voice and said very coldly, "You will *never* speak of him with disrespect again, do you understand?"

Jesse's monologue had been delivered in a tone of anger that LisBeth had never before heard. It made her a little afraid. Now, in the familiar voice of Mama, Jesse added, "Now, there is a very handsome young man out in that kitchen waiting to escort you to a church social. Tell him about your father. I've brought you up to be honest, so tell MacKenzie the truth and take whatever response you get as an answer from the Lord. If MacKenzie accepts you for what you are and still wants to take you to the social, then maybe he *is* the man God has for you. If he doesn't, then you're better off knowing now. There is nothing more challenging, LisBeth, than being married to a man who doesn't approve of you. Don't repeat the mistake I made when I married Homer King. Now, I heartily suggest that you get out to the kitchen and do some apologizing. You may not get a second chance for happiness, LisBeth."

Jesse was trembling with emotion as she finished. Wheeling about, she marched out of LisBeth's room, across the hall, and into her own room. She lay down and pulled her quilt about her, listening to the stillness in the hall outside her door.

A few moments later, she heard LisBeth's door creak and footsteps retreating toward the kitchen. Jesse stayed in her room, waiting, wondering what MacKenzie would do.

MacKenzie and Augusta conversed easily while Augusta

bustled about the kitchen and MacKenzie snapped the green beans. LisBeth stood at the kitchen door watching him work, listening to the tenor of his voice and the easy laughter that he shared with Augusta over an incident at the store that day. His thick black hair had fallen over his forehead as he worked. LisBeth liked the way the veins in the backs of his hands stood out as he worked. When he had finished, he scooted his chair back and stretched easily, both hands behind his head. In the middle of the stretch he saw LisBeth, and immediately both hands dropped to his sides. A smile started across his face.

"MacKenzie," LisBeth asked, "could I talk to you outside for just a minute?"

"Sure, LisBeth," MacKenzie cast a glance at Augusta, who nodded encouragement as the two young people went outside.

In nearly all LisBeth's dealings with him, MacKenzie had been seated at a table while she served him. She had never really realized how tall he was. She liked the way he towered over her. And she liked the way he stayed quiet, waiting for her to sort out her thoughts.

The two meandered across the back lot and into the stable. Jesse's now-ancient mare, Red Star, nickered a greeting and they went down the row of stalls to scratch behind her ears.

"Red Star was all we had on this earth when we first came to Lincoln," LisBeth said. "It had just been renamed from Lancaster then."

"When my folks staked their claim, it was Lancaster."

"You were here then? Why didn't you ever come to town?"

"Pa did all his shopping at Nebraska City. Said Lancaster would never amount to anything."

As they talked, LisBeth began to braid Red Star's mane. LisBeth was silent for a moment. Then, without looking up she whispered, "I know, MacKenzie. I know about your folks, about your pa. I was in the loft the day you told Joseph about it."

MacKenzie looked at her sharply, and she rushed to explain, "The loft is sort of my secret place, where I go to think and to be alone. I was up there that day. I didn't mean to eavesdrop, but there was no way to come down when you were already talking to Joseph."

"It's all right, I guess," MacKenzie said, shrugging his shoulders. Then, an almost desperate plea, "But you won't tell anyone will you? I mean, Pa didn't have many friends here, but I wouldn't want them to think . . ."

LisBeth finished braiding Red Star's mane and looked up at MacKenzie. She promised, "Of *course* I won't tell anyone, MacKenzie. It's nobody's business, anyway."

MacKenzie nodded his thanks, swallowed hard, and stared at Red Star's mane as he asked quietly, "So, LisBeth, will you go to the church social with me? Or maybe you don't want to go with somebody who had a crazy man for a father." His voice was pained.

"Oh, MacKenzie, I don't care about that at all!" LisBeth exclaimed quickly. "You can't blame a person for something his parents did. Goodness, just *think* what this world would be like if we all kept records of past generations." She giggled. "Why, there's not a person in Lincoln who'd have a thing to do with any of the other people in Lincoln!"

MacKenzie smiled. "So, will you go with me or won't you?"

It was getting easier to talk with him. LisBeth looked into his blue eyes earnestly. "First, I have to explain something, MacKenzie. You might not *want* to ask me when you hear it. I hope you won't care." LisBeth blinked hard, "But if you *do* care, if it makes a difference, I'll understand."

She told everything as quickly as she could, stringing sentences together the way she had when she was a little girl. By the end of the tale, she found herself defending her mother, angry at the world that made it necessary for her to explain. Impulsively, she grabbed a curry comb and began to brush Red Star's coat vigorously. She brushed for a long time, and tears began to blur her vision. She tried to resign herself to what seemed to be happening. Then a hand covered hers and squeezed affectionately. Mac took the curry comb away, and bent to kiss the back of her hand.

"So, Miss King, will you do me the honor of accompanying me to the social next Friday evening at the Congregational Church?"

Miss King embarrassed herself by saying *yes!* so loudly that the dozing horse in the stall next to Red Star jumped and kicked the side of his stall in fright. The two young people laughed, and MacKenzie lifted LisBeth into the air and swung her around in his arms.

Sick with apprehension, Jesse had been unable to remain alone for long. She returned to the kitchen to help Augusta with meal preparations, praying earnestly for LisBeth and MacKenzie while she worked. When the two young people burst through the kitchen door together, their happy smiles told the older women all they needed to know.

LisBeth was sobered when she saw her Mother. "Mother, I . . ."

Jesse held up a hand to stop her. "It's all right, LisBeth. I'm glad everything turned out. I've been praying for you both."

"Mother, all four of us know about Papa. Would you tell me a story about him while we make supper?"

The culprit never came forward, but at some time that evening, the first book-burning in the State of Nebraska took place. Francis Day's *Memoirs of the Savage West* found its way into Augusta's cook stove.

Chapter 30

She . . . worketh willingly with her hands."

Proverbs 31:13

It was Saturday evening, the boarders had all been fed and had gone off to bed, and Augusta and Jesse were finishing the day in their usual way. Jesse sat in her rocker by the stove, adding the borders to her latest quilt top. It would be in the fashionable solid greens and reds of the day. Jesse had wanted to try a Baltimore Album style quilt, which one of the ladies at the church quilting group had seen on a trip back east and had described, but Jesse opted for something less complicated, with less intricate appliqué work. *If I work with bigger pieces,* she thought, *then I can spend all the time I want to on the quilting.* Jesse loved quilting, and nothing satisfied her more than covering the top of a quilt with intricate plumes and feathers, then joining them with closely quilted lines and stippling.

While Jesse stitched, Augusta read aloud from the *Commonwealth.* It was no longer the only newspaper in Lincoln, but Augusta remained loyal to the oldest rag and its editor. "They were here when we started Lincoln, and they'll still be here when we've passed on," Augusta explained when a newsboy tried to sell her on the new paper. "I'm proud to call Charles Gere my friend, young man, and he always tells it straight." The aggressive newsboy accepted defeat and went on up the street looking for new territory to conquer.

Augusta squinted at the fine print and read aloud:

"Free from stiffness and vulgarity," August repeated. "Well,
the *entertainment* certainly was—although I can't say the same
for Miss Charity Bond when she caught sight of our LisBeth
on MacKenzie Baird's arm!"

"Augusta!" Jesse chided.

Augusta lowered the paper. "I'm just saying what is, Jesse.
You saw it too. That little snit's been tossin' her curls like a
shameless hussy at every eligible young man that comes to
town. She had her cap set for MacKenzie, and you and I both
know it. I'll never forget the look on her face when MacKenzie and LisBeth walked in together. Her back went ramrod
straight and she just *whirled* across that floor to pull MacKenzie away. Downright rude, I'd say."

Jesse tried to interrupt her.

"Oh, I know, I know . . . she 'just wanted to introduce them
to her friends,' she said. Of course, she had to place herself
between LisBeth and MacKenzie to do it! And she nearly
forgot to introduce LisBeth at all. *'Vulgar,'* I'd say, is the way
to describe that little miss's manners. Her mother should be
ashamed of her!"

"Augusta, what else does the paper say about the event?"
Jesse, ever kind and willing to give "the benefit of the doubt"
to all, tried to change the subject.

Augusta read briefly:

Augusta left off reading again. "*Skillful!* I never saw such skill in making Charity Bond stand out. Agnes made certain that Charity was the centerpiece of every scene, except the one that best suits her. 'The Temptation' would have been the *perfect* part, but then Agnes wouldn't want her darling Charity to appear a temptress. Hmph!"

"Augusta, please . . . just read the news," Jesse pleaded.

"Oh, all right, Jesse! But right is right and LisBeth should have had a part. That's all I say."

"Augusta, you know very well that LisBeth has no interest at all in dramatics. You were in this very room when she begged *not* to be forced to participate."

Augusta pretended not to hear and finished reading the review.

> The scenes were ably accompanied by Mrs. Agnes Bond's fine piano performance

Augusta interjected, "Which gave her every opportunity to loudly introduce the entrances of one Charity Bond,"

> with the assistance of a little fairy played by Birdie Pound, who saluted the audience to announce each next scene. Let it be known that Birdie was a favorite of the audience. The ladies deserve the highest praise for their invention, originality, and artistic skill.

Augusta left off reading to make a final editorial comment, "*Originality*—certainly Charity displayed *that*. I never saw such original schemes to make MacKenzie pay her mind. When she dropped her punch and splattered LisBeth's new dress I wanted to slap her. But MacKenzie saved the day. He took LisBeth's arm and walked back here with her and waited while she changed. Bless that boy's heart."

Even kind-hearted Jesse could not resist commentary on that point. "I must admit, that was unkind of Charity. It *did* look as though she meant to do it. I was proud of LisBeth, though. She doesn't always express such ladylike self-control."

Augusta agreed, "When you first moved in, that child would just blow up for any reason. I remember how she went on and on one day about Warbonnet chasing her favorite kitten. Back then she would talk a person's leg off. I declare, there were times I asked her to just 'practice being quiet' for a while! These past few weeks, though, she's seemed to grow up all at once. We can be proud of her." Augusta was accustomed to taking at least partial credit for any good thing that came out of Lincoln. LisBeth was definitely on that list in her mind.

"You've been a great help to both of us, Augusta. I've thanked the Lord often that he led us to Joseph Freeman that dark night so long ago. And Joseph brought us to you." Jesse brought her sewing close to her face, taking the last few tiny stitches that completed her quilt top as she said, "You are a blessing, Augusta."

Augusta "harrumphed" loudly and returned the subject to LisBeth and MacKenzie. "Think we'll be planning a weddin' soon?"

Jesse spread out the quilt top on the floor before answering. Large plumes cut out of solid reds and greens had been appliquéd around a circular red center on plain muslin to form a pinwheel-shaped flower. Only four of these huge flowers set together were large enough to cover the top of a bed. The sides and bottom edge were bordered with ten-inch wide strips of muslin appliquéd with elaborate vines that intertwined with flowers and leaves.

Jesse answered, "Well, not too soon, I hope. I just got the top finished. I'll need some time to finish the quilting."

Augusta rejoiced, "Jesse King, I *knew* you been thinkin' on it too! Why on earth haven't you said something! I've been nearly bustin', watchin' those two watchin' each other."

Jesse pulled the quilt top back up off the floor. "It's best to let a little time go by. I wouldn't want to rush anything.

Marriage is for life, and I want them to be sure. The longer they wait, the longer I can pray," Jesse stood up and added, in a lighter tone, "and the longer I'll have to create my masterpiece!" She smiled happily. "I'm going to bed, Augusta. The ladies at church have promised to help me get this basted and put in the frame after lunch tomorrow."

"Will they help quilt it too?" Augusta asked. "You might not have as much time as you think!"

"Oh, no, Augusta, this one's not to be touched by any needle but mine."

"Why on earth not?"

Jesse was reluctant to admit it, but she said, "Well . . . Agnes and Ona just don't . . . I don't mean to be unkind, Augusta, but they just don't stitch well enough for this. Besides, I want it to be all mine . . . for LisBeth." Jesse carefully laid the folded quilt top over her arm. "Which reminds me . . . would you mind if I had MacKenzie rig up a quilting frame in here?"

Augusta looked around the crowded kitchen. "I wouldn't mind, Jesse, but there's no room!"

"I thought if I put it on pulleys up at the ceiling, it would be out of the way during the day. Then, at night, when we're visiting, I could lower it onto the backs of the chairs and work on it that way."

Augusta praised her invention and immediately assented. On Monday, MacKenzie and Joseph rigged up the pulleys, and on that evening Jesse began work on what was to be her masterpiece—and her wedding gift to LisBeth and MacKenzie Baird.

❧

Jesse quilted all winter. LisBeth warned, "Mama, you're going to ruin your eyes." But still Jesse quilted.

MacKenzie shook his head at the hours Jesse spent bent over her work. "No disrespect meant, ma'am," he said one evening, "but you've been quiltin' the whole time Mrs.

Hathaway's been reading. She's got the whole paper read to us, and you've got just that one little square the size of my hand filled in. How can you stand it?" He added quickly, "It's gorgeous, Mrs. King—don't misunderstand. It just sure must take a lot of patience!"

Jesse smiled. "That's where you're wrong, MacKenzie. It takes no patience at all to do what you love. Now shelling peas . . . *that* takes patience!" Jesse looked over at LisBeth, who had been doing just that.

"Amen, Mama! I heartily agree. But I'd rather do this than quilt any day."

Jesse bent back over the quilt and returned to stitching. Still, she thought about what MacKenzie had said all that evening and the next day. *Why,* she thought, *do women quilt? Comforters serve the same purpose—and we can tie several of those in one afternoon. Yet, we work and work cutting up scraps, sewing them together, and creating quilts.*

The next evening MacKenzie and LisBeth arrived home early from choir practice. They seemed unusually happy, but Jesse hurried to share her thoughts while they were still organized.

"MacKenzie," she began, "you asked me last night how I can stand to do all this work. I never thought about it. But I've been thinking on it all day today, and I think I have the answer. When a man wants to make his mark in the world, he builds something. It may be a homestead, it may be a newspaper, or a hotel, or a dry goods store. Still, whatever he does, a man can always point to some *thing* and say, 'There—that's what I am. That's what I've done that's important.'

"Now a woman cooks and cleans and dusts, and in just a few hours, it's all gone and has to be done again. When I think about it, MacKenzie, about the only thing that will be left when *I* pass over is my quilts. I think that's why I do it . . . although I never really thought it through until now. There's a great satisfaction in running my hand over a finished quilt and knowing I made it. It must be something like what the Lord felt when he looked and 'saw it was very good' and then rested on the Sabbath."

MacKenzie surveyed the nearly finished quilt. "What's the name of this pattern, Mrs. King?" he asked.

"Princess Feather," Jesse answered.

Taking LisBeth's hand in his own, MacKenzie asked, "Would it be presumptuous of me to ask if you had planned to add this quilt to LisBeth's hope chest?"

Jesse looked up at the couple and grinned. "I could be persuaded to do that. But only if I was assured that her future husband was a man worthy of sharing such a gift."

MacKenzie cleared his throat. "Well, ma'am," he began, "I'm not sure that I'm worthy, but we'd sure be honored if you'd let your masterpiece grace our home. I've asked LisBeth to marry me, Mrs. King, and she said yes . . ." MacKenzie was prevented from finishing the sentence by Augusta, who swept down upon him and LisBeth and caught them both up in a great hug. MacKenzie turned red and finished. "She said yes, if you approve."

Jesse was quiet for so long that both MacKenzie and LisBeth grew nervous. Tears filled her eyes. She fought them back and said quietly, "MacKenzie, in all that you've said and all that you've done, you've proven yourself to be a hard-working young man. Still, there are many hard-working young men about. That alone is not enough to make a suitable husband. Since LisBeth was very little, I have prayed that God would send her a man strong in the faith. I watched you carefully, young man."

Jesse rose from her chair and laid her hands lightly on the top of the quilt. "And it seems to me that you are committed to the Lord. I know that he will enable you to continue in your commitment to my daughter. MacKenzie, I'm proud to give LisBeth to you."

The tears welled up in Jesse's eyes again. "Forgive the tears, children. It's not an easy thing to give your only child away." Jesse looked at LisBeth, whose young face was wreathed in smiles. "God bless you both. You have my blessing."

There was a moment of awkward silence, and then Augusta said loudly, "This calls for a celebration. MacKenzie, would you see if Joseph is still in the livery? I believe he was staying late to attend to that mare of his that's to foal any time. Now everyone wait right here." She hurried out of the room and returned with five crystal goblets on a silver tray. Joseph came in with MacKenzie, smiling his joy and removing his hat. "These were my mother's," Augusta explained. "I keep them in my drawing room, away from the prying eyes of the clientele." As she spoke, she poured the wine.

"To LisBeth and MacKenzie!" she sang out. Clinking crystal brought the evening to a close. Late in the night, Jesse got up, lit the lamp in the kitchen, and bent over the quilt once more. In the morning LisBeth noticed Jesse's latenight addition to the bottom border of the quilt. In her tiniest stitches, Jesse had added:

For L. W. K. B.
by J. K.
1875

Chapter 31

 Entreat me not to leave thee,
or to return from following after thee;
for whither thou goest, I will go;
and where thou lodgest, I will lodge.
Ruth 1:16

The remainder of the winter was spent finishing LisBeth's trousseau and preparing for the wedding. The three women worked long hours. Augusta amazed her friends by picking up a needle and hemming some napkins.

"Well, goodness!" she exclaimed. "Just because I *don't* sew doesn't mean I *can't!* Now, give me that tablecloth!" she ordered.

Augusta thus became the official hemmer. MacKenzie took over the reading of the evening paper on the nights when he was not working late. He was working as much as possible to save for a new home. He had sworn never to return to the homestead that reminded him only of tragedy. It was listed with the land agents for $5 an acre.

LisBeth found it unsettling not to know where she would live after her marriage. Jesse reassured her. "MacKenzie is a responsible man, LisBeth. Once the homestead is sold, he'll have the means to make concrete plans. You'll just have to be patient."

MacKenzie did have plans. The evening he shared them nearly resulted in his losing his fiancée. He announced after supper, "I'm joining the Army."

LisBeth dropped the cup she had been preparing to wash. Jesse paused in midstitch, and Augusta rattled the pile of plates she was stacking.

"MacKenzie!" Lisbeth exclaimed. "What for?"

"To make a life for us, of course," came the defensive reply. "There's need for good men in the west. LisBeth, I can't stand being cooped up in that general store all day. I'll never save enough for a new outfit, and the homestead's not selling. I've got to do something to get on with life and make a future for us!"

MacKenzie had been thinking it through for weeks, and he was not to be deterred. LisBeth was horrified. "But, MacKenzie, the Army, out west . . . it's dangerous! And surely you don't want to *kill Indians* for a living!" LisBeth stressed the words.

"Of course not, LisBeth. I'm not going to be a fighting man. They need all kinds of men. Farriers and sutlers and clerks, and maybe I can do some good." He made his case earnestly, "Look, LisBeth, at some point in all this madness, the white man and the Indian are going to have to make peace. Final, lasting peace. Maybe we can be part of that—do some good—help, somehow."

Jesse interrupted. "MacKenzie, I admire your ideals. But I'm not certain they can be reached by your joining the Army."

MacKenzie was stubborn. "With all due respect, ma'am, LisBeth and me have to work this out on our own."

LisBeth retorted, "I'll thank you not to speak that way to my mother, MacKenzie!"

Jesse quietly responded, "LisBeth, MacKenzie is right. He must do what he thinks is best for you. I should keep my thoughts to myself unless they are solicited. I think you two need privacy."

Jesse gathered up her sewing and retreated to her room. Augusta wiped her hands, made some comment about wanting to read in her own sitting room for a change, and hurried out.

LisBeth and MacKenzie were left alone to settle the issue. What ensued was a typical first quarrel. Neither stayed rational, and neither won. They ended up in their separate corners of Hathaway House, fuming and mentally replaying the event.

Jesse was determined to keep out of LisBeth and MacKenzie's life. She had strong opinions about the Army, and she hated the thought of LisBeth re-entering that hard way of life. Still, she held equally strong beliefs about the role a wife should play in a marriage, and those beliefs guided the advice she gave LisBeth when the young woman came knocking at her door.

"Mother, western Nebraska is a howling wilderness—I *can't* go there!"

"'*Whither thou goest, I will go,*' LisBeth. That's God's plan for marriage."

"But Mother, MacKenzie wasn't fair with me. He never said a word about the Army. I thought he'd grown to like Lincoln, that we would stay here and make a life for ourselves."

"MacKenzie has made it no secret that he hates working in that store, LisBeth. From the first day he arrived in Lincoln, he's told us that as soon as he had saved money for a new outfit, he was headed west."

"But, Mother, I didn't think he meant it!"

Jesse grew stern. "LisBeth, I think you had better seriously reconsider your promise to MacKenzie. Marriage is a lifelong commitment, my dear. Did you think that you promised to love him as long as he made decisions you agree with?"

"No, of course not, but I didn't think . . ."

"Apparently not. You'd better think now, LisBeth. And think hard. Don't try to change MacKenzie. If you're not prepared to be his helpmeet wherever he decides to go, then you'd be doing him a terrible disservice. MacKenzie deserves better."

"Who's side are you *on*, Mother?" LisBeth was appalled that her mother seemed to be against her.

"I'm on the side of what's right for each one of you,

LisBeth. I love you dearly, and because I love you, I'm telling you what you need to hear. Prepare to follow MacKenzie wherever the Lord leads him until death parts the two of you. If you can't make good on that promise, then don't make the promise. Stay here in Lincoln and say good-bye.

"I'm very fond of MacKenzie. If he's intent on a life in the wild west, then he'll need a wife with 'gumption' as Augusta calls it. It you don't have gumption, LisBeth, admit it now. Don't add to a young man's burden by standing between him and what he thinks will make him happy."

"I thought *I* was what made him happy."

"Spoken like a very young and very foolish girl, LisBeth. There's more to marriage than all that romantic nonsense you read about in novels. There's working together for a dream, and nursing through sickness, and losing what you love, and working together to earn it back again. It's the day-to-day that grows a love that lasts, LisBeth. If you're not willing to be by MacKenzie's side day to day, then for heaven's sake don't marry him just because he's handsome and he makes your heart flutter."

"Mother!" LisBeth was embarrassed.

"LisBeth, we've had this conversation before. I *do* remember the 'hearts-a-flutter' stage of my youth. It had very little to do with 'the love that is stronger than death.' The question you have to answer is, which kind of love do you want? The fleeting one or the lasting one?"

"I want both, Mother!"

"And you can have them too. MacKenzie can give you both. But not unless you're willing to put your dreams together with his and go west. So, LisBeth," Jesse took her daughter by the shoulders and said soberly, "either get on the wagon and head west with your man—or get out of his life."

LisBeth pondered the advice. She stood up to go and Jesse added, "You'd better take a long walk and think this over, LisBeth. It's not a decision to be made lightly."

Nature had a part in helping LisBeth make her decision. She followed Jesse's advice and went out for a walk. It had been a lovely early spring evening although clouds had blown in from the west. LisBeth walked only a short way from the hotel when the wind came up and the temperature began to drop. She turned back toward the hotel. Down the street, she could see that someone had hitched up a team and was pulling out of the livery. The wind grew colder and a few flakes of snow began to fall. LisBeth pulled her duster close around her and shivered. She hurried back to the hotel just as the storm began in earnest. Snow was falling harder. Bursting through the kitchen door, she headed upstairs. Augusta peeked around the corner and called up after her. "If you're going up to MacKenzie, dear, he's gone. He just headed out a few minutes ago . . ." LisBeth was down the stairs and out the door in time to see the old wagon disappearing in the distance. The wind was blowing too loud for her voice to be heard as she called after him. Augusta followed her outside. "Come back in, dear. He's just going to the homestead to gather a few things. He said he'd be back first thing in the morning."

But MacKenzie did not return the next morning. The wind howled all night, lashing snow against the hotel and piling it up in huge drifts. Hour after hour LisBeth lay awake, listening to the storm and praying for MacKenzie. When she could not sleep, she made her way to the kitchen where she found Jesse, bent over another quilt, stitching as rapidly as she ever had.

Jesse looked up when LisBeth came in. "He'll be all right, LisBeth. MacKenzie has a lot of common sense. He'll find shelter, and he'll be all right." She managed to sound calm and reassuring, but fear for MacKenzie and her daughter gripped her heart.

It snowed for three days. It took all Jesse's and Augusta's creativity to feed the boarders, who stayed in the hotel dining room by the hour, playing cards, reading old newspapers, smoking, talking politics. The Indian Wars were fought and refought, with Jesse trying her best to close her ears to the discussion.

When the snow finally stopped, the world was a level blaze of white. Everyone in town turned out to help dig out, and soon, people could get about. Carriages moved slowly through the tunnel they had dug down the middle of the main streets.

The snow made wildlife easy to spot, and Joseph trekked on snowshoes for miles, bringing in fresh meat every day. J. W. Miles almost ran out of flour, but Miles was partial to Hathaway House because of MacKenzie, so he kept Augusta at the top of his supply list and secreted his last fifty-pound bag of flour for her. She was smugly satisfied when Cadman House boarders put down their $2 and moved to Hathaway House for a week until the trains came through bringing emergency supplies.

At last, Jesse pulled Joseph aside and whispered, "Joseph, do you think it's possible to ride out to his homestead to check on MacKenzie? I don't know how much more Lisbeth can take . . ."

Joseph shook his head. "I don't give much chance that he made it, ma'am," he said sadly, "but I was just coming in to ask you if you thought I ought to go. What if I find . . ."

"If you find him, bring him back, Joseph. We have to know." Jesse shuddered at the picture that came to mind. "It's cold enough to bring him back, and we'll bury him at *Wyuka*. It'll be a terrible thing, but at least LisBeth will have a grave to visit."

LisBeth came into the kitchen as they finished their conversation. She sensed the topic and called after Joseph, "Thank you, Joseph."

The hours crept by for them all after Joseph left. Emotions ran high and they grew angry with one another over little irritations. At last, Jesse called them all to prayer.

"Dear Lord," she said simply, "you know where MacKenzie is right now. If he needs help, let Joseph find him. If he is well, then bring him to us quickly. And, Lord," Jesse prayed, "if he is with you, please help us to bear it." She added an unspoken postscript, *Lord, LisBeth is so young—if it is your will, don't ask her to face death just yet—please, Lord.*

The women waited all night. Jesse quilted, although her hands shook and she later felt compelled to remove the sloppy stitches. Augusta read aloud to them all until she grew hoarse and had to stop. Both she and LisBeth were nodding in their chairs when the book slipped out of Augusta's hand and hit the floor, waking them with a start. Outside the kitchen door they heard bridles rattling, and horses stomping. LisBeth gave out a little cry as two men stomped into the kitchen, shaking snow all over the floor as they removed their coats and hats.

Joseph was smiling happily, and MacKenzie started to say something but was interrupted by the attentions of a young woman who fairly leaped across the kitchen into his arms, crying happily. Everyone began talking at once, asking questions and laughing irrationally.

"This boy's got some sense, after all," boasted Joseph. "There's but one dugout between here and his homestead. When the storm started, he headed straight for it. Took the horses and all straight inside and sat the four days out."

"And the horses about did me in too," laughed MacKenzie. "They gnawed every piece of furniture in the place and had started on the roof when the snow finally quit. We went on to the homestead, then. Had a terrible time finding the haystacks, but we finally dug one out and then we were fine."

"What did *you* eat, MacKenzie?" Jesse asked.

"Rabbit—plenty of it too. Four days of rabbit!"

LisBeth started to speak, but MacKenzie held his hand up. "LisBeth, I'm sorry I didn't listen better to what you wanted. But the fact is, I just can't live in town. I had to go back to the homestead and think things through. I thought maybe I could start over there." He shivered. "But I can't. Call me a weak man, but there's nothing on that place for me but memories of death and sadness. That's no place to start a new life."

He turned back to LisBeth. "I love you, LisBeth King. I want to marry you. But I'm headed west as soon as the snow melts. Will you come with me?"

LisBeth looked solemnly up at MacKenzie. "MacKenzie Baird, I promised God last night that if I ever got a second chance, there was one thing I was going to say to you. This is it:" LisBeth's voice trembled with emotion as she paraphrased, *"Wherever you go, I will go, wherever you lodge, I will lodge. Your people shall be my people, and your God, my God."*

From the other side of the kitchen, Jesse gave way to an uncharacteristic shout of joy, "Hallelujah!" In a burst of activity, coffee was set to boiling and biscuits were made. Joseph and MacKenzie took the horses to the stable and bedded them down with hot mash and oats, returning to the hotel to enjoy a hearty breakfast.

Only four weeks later, Augusta read her *Commonwealth* with tears in her eyes:

> Miss LisBeth King and Mr. MacKenzie Baird were united in marriage today in a ceremony held at the Congregational Church. Miss King, the daughter of Mrs. Jesse King, a widow employed at The Hathaway House, has been known to us all as a hard-working and God-fearing young woman of high character. Mr. Baird, while known to the citizenry for only a short time, has proven himself to be an honest man and a great asset to the state. The couple left immediately for the West, where Mr. Baird has volunteered to serve our great Army in its efforts to tame the last vestiges of the frontier. We wish them well, and godspeed.

Jesse quilted furiously while Augusta read. Not until the following morning did she realize that her efforts had been in vain, for the tears in her eyes had blurred the fact that she had threaded her needle with the wrong color thread.

Chapter 32

She stretcheth out her hand to the
poor; yea, she reacheth forth her
hands to the needy.

Proverbs 31:20

Both Jesse and Augusta were amazed at how empty life felt without LisBeth. The women remained involved at the Congregational Church and in civic affairs, and Augusta made Jesse a partner in the hotel. Theirs was the first hotel in Lincoln to boast gas lighting, although Jesse did not quite trust it and continued to use her kerosene lamp in her room.

LisBeth's absence introduced her to a new kind of loneliness. Jesse had said many good-byes in her life. Each one had brought its own kind of pain, but all the pain had been dealt with in the same way—renewed fervor in reading God's Word and renewed prayer. This good-bye was no different, except for one wonderful thing: Jesse could continue to pray for LisBeth and MacKenzie. She could continue to share in their lives.

Letters kept them close. LisBeth wrote often—long, detailed letters that described the countryside, the towns, and the people they encountered. Her writing often sounded like the little girl who had talked so quickly, running all her sentences together. Jesse and Augusta read them over and over before Jesse placed them in a pasteboard box in her top dresser drawer.

It took only a few days for them both to realize that they needed to hire help.

"Joseph is a great help, but we're getting older, Jesse. We just can't keep this pace up."

Jesse readily agreed. Doing her share of LisBeth's work wore her out. She found herself too tired to quilt in the evenings and sank onto her bed as early as possible, ever hoping to catch up on her rest and return to her quilting "tomorrow."

Augusta placed an ad in the *Commonwealth* for help. When Jesse went by the office to pay for the ad, she rounded the corner of 10th and K and was nearly knocked over by a young woman running with a child in her arms. After her in hot pursuit was a buxom older woman, holding up her skirts and calling out, "Sarah! Sarah Biddle, you come *back* here this minute!"

Sarah Biddle kept running up 10th Street and out of sight. Her pursuer stopped short and stamped the ground angrily. "Well! I never! Try to help these orphans, and what do I get? Nothing but trouble!" The woman shook her parasol at Jesse, "What did I tell them at the agency? Don't take that Sarah Biddle! She's a bad one; no one will want her if she insists on keeping that cripple with her. Well, now I'm proven right! I'll have the police round her up—I'm done with her. She's going back to New York, that one! I won't be responsible!"

The woman spun around and was off again in the opposite direction, muttering and threatening with every step.

Jesse readjusted her hat, finished her errand, and returned to Hathaway House.

That evening, long after the train for the East had departed without the runaways and the police had been called from their search to settle a disturbance, Joseph Freeman prepared to close up the livery stable when a rustle overhead caught his attention. Pulling the great door closed, Joseph shot quickly up the ladder to the loft. As he reached the top, a flash of color disappeared behind a bale of hay in the corner opposite the ladder.

Joseph brandished his pitchfork. "You might as well come

out, 'cause there's only one way outta this here loft, and I'm not leavin' without whoever that is."

A pair of eyes peered at him from over the bale of hay. A defiant feminine voice retorted, "We'll *starve* to death, then, 'cause we ain't comin' out to be sent back to New York!"

A younger voice echoed, "Yeah, we ain't comin' out!"

Joseph sat down in the hay. "There an echo in here?" Silence.

He tried again. "Well, I was just fixin' to head over to Hathaway House for supper. They fixin' fried chicken tonight. Heaps of it. Mashed potatoes too. And pie. *Ooo-eee* that Miz King, she makes good pie! Too bad you can't come and have some."

Silence. Finally, another defiant comment. "Ain't no Miz King givin' away free meals, is they? We got no money, so we ain't gittin' no fried chicken. 'Sides, 'Granny Grump' is probably waitin' just outside with the police to haul us off anyways."

Joseph used the same voice he had used all his life to calm frightened horses. It was smooth, low, nearly expressionless. "Now, the way I heard tell it was this. Miz Ophelia Granwich left word with the police that if Miss Sarah Biddle and her brother Tom was found, they was to be returned to New York on the next train, unless somebody wanted 'em. Left train fare with the police. 'Course, I don't think they'll be needin' that train fare, 'cause I know Miz King and Miz Hathaway, and they been lookin' for someone to help them in their hotel. Way I figger it, that's a good job for anybody."

Silence. Then, a still-defiant voice tinged with desperation. "Ain't no Miz King gonna want us. My brother's crippled. Can't work hard. Nobody wants us *both*—and *I ain't leavin' 'im! I ain't!*"

Joseph continued to try to calm the terror in the voice. "Let's just have a look. Can't be that bad." He inhaled deeply, "Mmm, think I smell that chicken fryin' now."

Two sets of eyes appeared over the bale of hay. Slowly,

blond-headed Sarah Biddle stood up. Grasping her brother's hand, she pulled him upright, too, then helped him sit on the bale of hay. She swung his legs around so that he faced Joseph, then seated herself beside him and wrapped one arm tightly around his waist.

"You holdin' on mighty tight," Joseph said.

Sarah nodded. "We're together. We're *stayin'* together. Ain't nothin' old Granny Grump can do about it, neither. Maybe I *will* go back to New York. They's a man there already offered me a job. Said I'd get to dress up real pretty too. Said I could keep Tom too—long as he stayed in the back room while I talked to my visitors." She thrust a finely formed chin forward. "Sounds all right to me, I guess. Don't even know why I come on that stupid train, anyhow. Folks proddin' and pokin' and talkin' about us like we was nig—"

Joseph finished the word for her. "Like you was niggers? Guess I know what that feels like. Still, they's worse places to live than Lincoln."

"Guess we'll never find out." Sarah stood up impulsively and hauled her rotund brother up beside her. "We'll be headin' back, I guess. You can show us the police station."

"Not so fast, now, young lady," Joseph replied. "They's plenty of time fer that. Train don't come back till tomorrow anyway. Why don't you two just come and eat with us?"

"Can't, I told ya. We got no money."

"Don't need no money."

Sarah looked at him suspiciously. "How'm I gonna pay if I got no money?" She clutched her brother tighter.

"You ain't gonna pay. Lincoln has this rule. The first night in town, every visitor is entitled to a free meal at Hathaway House. City pays for it. It's a way to get folks to stay on and try us out."

"That the truth?"

"Swear on my freedom papers."

Sarah considered. Tom settled the issue. "Want chitchen! Sarah, want chitchen. I'm hungry!"

"All right, then, Mister. We'll take the free meal."

Joseph stood up. "Just you hand me your brother, and we'll go down."

"No!" She stepped away from Joseph, frightened eyes wide open. "Don't nobody handle Tom but me. You just stay back!"

Joseph held up his hands to calm her. "All right, miss. All right. I'll back down the ladder here. You need any help, you just holler."

Joseph descended the ladder and watched in amazement as the tiny girl wrestled her brother down the ladder, one step at a time. When his left foot hit the first rail, Joseph saw the problem. One leg was at least two inches shorter than the other. A deep scar ran from the ankle up out of sight inside his dress. Joseph decided not to notice. The trio went out and around the back of Hathaway House.

Entering the kitchen, Joseph headed off Augusta's questions. "Miz Hathaway, this here is Sarah Biddle and her brother, Tom. They's just visitin' Lincoln, and I told 'em about the free meal we offer every newcomer. I remembered to tell 'em it's only *one* free meal. They thought they'd come tonight, if that's all right."

Augusta winked at Jesse and entered into the play. "Why, of course, Joseph. That'll be just fine." Turning to Sarah, Augusta said politely, "Would you two like to wash up before supper?" Sarah shook her head, and Jesse took up a role.

"Please come this way, Miss Biddle. We've a room in the back here just for newcomers. It used to be my daughter LisBeth's room, but now we use it for newcomers." Sarah followed Jesse to LisBeth's room. Her eyes widened as she surveyed the comfortable room, the four-poster bed with its clean, crisp pillow covers. A small washstand stood by the bed with linen towels over the bar. Jesse poured fresh water from the pitcher in her hand. She thoughtfully poured two glasses full of water. Sarah plopped Tom on the bed and Jesse left.

"Supper's ready whenever you are, Miss Biddle. Just come out to the kitchen."

After Jesse left, Tom bounced on the bed. "Sarah . . . it's so soft!" he exclaimed. "I *like* it here!"

Sarah scrubbed her face and hands and turned to wash Tom's, careful to remove as much grime as possible. She wet her hands and tried to push his stubborn hair into place. There was a dresser opposite the washstand, and on the top of the dresser lay a lovely dresser set. Sarah inspected it carefully, turning the mirror over to look at herself. She picked up the brush and, looking over her shoulder at the open door, quickly brushed her hair.

"Well," she said at last, "I guess we can go eat now."

"We stayin' *here,* Sarah?" Tom asked.

"Don't think so, Tom. Just eatin' the free meal. Then we'll sleep in the loft 'til the train comes tomorrow."

"But I want to stay here, Sarah!"

"Can't stay here, Tom," she said miserably. Then, she snapped at him to avoid any more questions. "Quit yer' whinin', Tom. We're gettin' a decent meal, ain't we? That's enough! Now let's go eat!"

Sarah and Tom reappeared in the kitchen and ate massive amounts of food. Life had taught them to eat heartily when there was plenty, for tomorrow there might be nothing.

Jesse and Augusta left the children to Joseph's attentions, busying themselves with serving the boarders in the dining room. Sarah and Tom watched them come and go with great interest. Between gargantuan bites of chicken, Tom asked, "Them two ladies own this hotel? Are they nice? How come those people out there don't eat all their food? You folks eat like this every night? When's the train come tomorrow?" Joseph patiently answered each question. Sarah let him talk freely, until he asked his last question. When Tom said, "Can we stay here? You folks eat good!" Sarah elbowed him in the ribs and hissed "Shh!"

The two children sat motionless and drowsy after they had

gorged on supper. When Jesse and Augusta finished their chores, Augusta settled comfortably into her chair and picked up the *Commonwealth*. Jesse said to Sarah, "Miss Biddle, you're welcome to stay in the room you saw—just for tonight, of course."

"Can't stay," came the short reply. "Got no money. Kin we sleep in the loft?" This was directed at Joseph, who nodded yes, imploring Jesse with his eyes.

"Well, now, Miss Biddle, I appreciate the problem of no money. I've been without money lots of times myself. Would you be able to do a little work in return for your use of the room tonight?"

Sarah looked suspicious again. "What kind of work you need done?"

Jesse looked at Joseph. "Well, I'm sure Mr. Freeman could use help feeding the horses tonight. And he usually brings in firewood for the stove. Perhaps you could help him do that."

Sarah hopped down energetically. "Be glad to. I like horses!"

Sarah reached for Tom.

"Oh, it's all right, Miss Biddle. Tom can stay here with us."

Sarah clutched Tom's sleeve. "No! Tom stays with me!"

Tom started awake and rubbed his eyes. "Tired, Sarah. Tom's tired. Wanna go bed."

Jesse laid her hand on the tousled hair and gently stroked. "How about if we put him to bed? Then you can go help Joseph with the chores."

Sarah considered. "You mean in there?" she pointed to LisBeth's room.

"Yes."

"Can *I* put 'im to bed?"

"Of course."

"And you won't take him nowhere while I'm gone?"

"Sarah, I would *never, never* take a brother away from his sister. Families are important. Families should stay together."

She knelt down by Sarah and Tom. "You're a very good sister to care so much for Tom. Come on, let's put him to bed."

Sarah felt something inside let go. Something that was wound tight inside her. It wasn't enough to let her cry all the tears she'd been storing up for the last fourteen years, but it was enough for her to feel that perhaps—just perhaps—there were people in the world you could trust, after all.

She picked Tom up and carried him into LisBeth's bed where he fell instantly asleep, cuddled up to the down pillow. Sighing happily, he didn't even know that Sarah left to do her chores—or that she returned to slip into the nightgown Jesse loaned her and slide in beside him. When Jesse looked in to check on them before turning in, Sarah lay on her side, the hem of Tom's shirt clutched tightly in one hand.

⁓

Sarah sat bolt upright in bed at the sound of the train whistle. Shaking Tom vigorously, she shouted, "Tom! Tom! Wake up! Train's comin'!"

Jesse and Augusta heard the commotion and hurried into the room. "Sarah! Sarah! It's all right. We have several trains come through Lincoln every day. The train to New York won't be back until this afternoon. It's all right—calm down!"

Tom snuggled happily down under the coverlet again. But Sarah pulled the covers back. "Don't matter, Tom. Morning's come. We gotta be outta here. Where's my clothes?" Sarah demanded.

Jesse answered, "Out in the kitchen by the stove. We washed them after you went to sleep. We didn't think you'd mind." As Jesse explained, Augusta handed over the clean clothes she had retrieved from the drying rack by the stove.

Augusta interrupted. "Sarah—Miss Biddle—we'd like to ask you something. Please come out to the kitchen after you're dressed."

Sarah entered the kitchen where Jesse and Augusta sat drinking coffee, looking relaxed. Sarah was wary. "You wanted somethin'?"

Jesse had been elected to speak. "You're gentler than I am, Jesse," Augusta had said. "I'm too prickly. Takes a while to warm up to me. You can say it better—you talk." Augusta dabbed at her eyes. "Those children must never go back to New York! After I heard what Joseph said they were headed for . . ."

"Please, Sarah—if I may call you Sarah—please, sit down."

"I'll stand, thank you." She was not to be easily won over.

"Augusta and I own this hotel together, Sarah. Until recently, my daughter, LisBeth, lived here. She's married now, and we need help. We placed an ad in the paper, but it just appeared today, and we've had no response. Would you take the job?"

Jesse rushed ahead. "You'd be taking on LisBeth's duties. That means helping us cook, clean rooms, garden—whatever's required. We could give you room and board and . . ."

"What about Tom?" Sarah did not let Jesse finish.

"Tom can stay here too."

Sarah stared at them, unbelieving. "Tom's crippled. Can't work much."

"We know, Sarah."

"Why you want him, then?"

The specter of a little mound of stones receding into the distance rose in Jesse's mind. She answered honestly. "When I was very young, Sarah, I lost a little boy almost Tom's age. His name was Jacob. If you stay, and Tom stays, then it'll be just like God giving me my little boy back. I'll get a second chance to have a little boy."

Sarah squinted hard at Jesse's face. "What happened to your little boy?"

"He fell under the wheels of our wagon. It ran over him."

Sarah's eyes grew wide and she whispered, "Tom was

runned over by a wagon too. Only he didn't die. It hurt his leg real bad. He ain't never walked right since."

Jesse blinked back tears. Augusta spoke up. "Sarah, I'm not so gentle talking as Jesse, but I'd like to have you too. You *and* Tom."

Sarah surveyed the kitchen. She drove her bargain hard. "Can we have that room?"

"That's part of the deal."

"Will you leave the bed in it?"

Jesse fought back a smile. "Of course, Sarah. It would be your bed. Yours and Tom's. Although we might want Joseph to build a trundle to slide underneath for Tom. That way you could each have your own bed."

Her own bed represented more wealth than Sarah had ever hoped for. It sealed the deal. "We'll stay," she said matter-of-factly. "What you want me to do first?"

"First," Jesse said softly, "let Tom sleep a little longer. Second, come with me and I'll show you the hotel and teach you some of the things we do as we go through the rooms."

Augusta started up the stove while Jesse walked Sarah through the house, showing her the dining room, the west wing, and Augusta's quarters. "We'd like to add on, but we'd need to hire more help. So we're not sure what to do. For the moment, we're just going to stay small. We're not getting any younger."

"You ain't so old, ma'am," said Sarah. "Yer wrinkled some, but yer hair's not all white yet. You took those stairs real good. You ain't so old." Jesse stifled a laugh, cleared her throat, and thanked Sarah for the compliment.

Back in the kitchen, Augusta found that Sarah knew a lot about kitchens and nothing about dining rooms. "She'll have to help behind the scenes for a while," Augusta advised Jesse later in the day. "Can you handle the dining room alone?"

Jesse assented. "Of course. It'll be better at first if Tom is within sight of Sarah, anyway, until they get used to us."

But Tom became instantly at home in Hathaway House. Limping happily from table to sink, he worked hard every day until his leg began to hurt and he was forced to sit down. Jesse and Augusta asked Doc Patton to stop by and look at the boy's leg.

"A clear case of bumbled medicine," he diagnosed. "No reason on earth why that boy shouldn't have healed just fine. Some doctor just didn't care enough to set it properly. He'll limp for the rest of his life, poor boy."

Jesse smiled. "It's all right, doctor. We'll give Tom a chance in life, anyway. I'm enrolling him with Miss Griswall tomorrow. I think he's a bright boy. Perhaps God has other plans for Tom Biddle."

"Miss Griswall will do her best for him, I'm sure," the doctor agreed. "She's such a *nice* woman."

Chapter 33

For love is strong as death.
Song of Solomon 8:6

"Aunt Jesse! What's wrong?!" Sarah and Jesse were scrubbing bedsheets in the lean-to Joseph had built onto the back of the kitchen. Suddenly Jesse's face went white. She sat down abruptly, holding a clenched fist over her heart.

Sarah was terrified. "I'll get Aunt Augusta!"

"No!" Jesse gasped. "You'll do nothing of the sort. She'll get all flustered and worry over me and drive me crazy. Just let me rest a minute. It'll pass."

Jesse breathed deeply, and as she had predicted, in a few seconds, the pain was gone. She smiled brightly. "Now, see there? I told you it would pass. Now, we'd better get this wash done or Augusta will have our hides!" Jesse returned to the washing. When they had finished, however, a great weariness settled over her.

"Sarah, I'm going in to lie down for just a few minutes. I must have quilted too late last night!"

Sarah worried and wondered what to do. When Tom came in from school, she put her finger over her mouth and pulled him into their room. "Something's wrong with Aunt Jesse, Tom. But she said not to tell Aunt Augusta. I think she needs to see the doctor!"

Tom considered the news, frowning. Then, his face brightened. "I know! I'll pretend my leg's really hurting bad.

Aunt Jesse'll call the doctor for me—then he can see her too!"

The next day when Tom came in from school, he limped badly and sat at the table, rubbing his leg.

"What's wrong, Tom?" Jesse asked.

"Oh, nuthin'." Tom grimaced dramatically.

"Does your leg hurt?"

"Maybe a little."

Augusta interrupted. "I'll have Doc Patton come right over!"

"Aw, I don't need no doctor, Aunt Augusta. He can't do nothin' 'bout it anyhow."

"Nonsense, Tom. If it hurts, then there's something wrong. Doc Patton said it shouldn't hurt much at all." Augusta grabbed her bonnet and was out the door to fetch the doctor. Sarah and Tom looked at each other and smiled furtively. Jesse expressed her concern by ordering Tom to lie down and put his leg up on a pillow.

Sarah complained, "You baby him too much, Aunt Jesse."

Jesse agreed. "I know, Sarah. Guess I'm trying to make it up to him."

Sarah was suddenly serious. "You've done enough already. You and Aunt Augusta. You gave us a home—you've been so nice to us we hardly know how to act. Now we're *glad* about that orphan train we rode on."

Jesse smiled warmly. "We're glad, too, Sarah. The two of you have filled a big empty space in both our hearts. Plus," Jesse winked, "we needed the free labor to keep the place running!"

Sarah had grown secure in her place in the hotel over the months. She kidded back, "Yeah, and you work me like a horse too! I'm gonna be goin' *back* to that orphanage one o' these days, you two don't treat me nicer!"

"You just try it, young lady!" Jesse taunted, shaking her finger at Sarah. "You're not leavin' this place—not ever!" She gathered Sarah up and hugged her. "We love you too much to let you go!"

Sarah had no response to that. She could kid and joke about her new home, but the word *love* was not in her vocabulary—yet. Augusta arrived with the doctor, and he hurried in to see Tom, with Jesse close behind.

"Where does it hurt, Tom?" Doc Patton asked.

"Oh, mostly here," Tom said, pointing to his knee. The doctor worked the joint, checked for swelling, and found nothing. "Well, maybe it's here," Tom said, indicating his ankle. Again, the doctor examined. Again, he found nothing. Looking puzzled, he sat on the edge of the bed. "Now, just when did this pain start, Tom?"

"Yesterday."

"Were you doing something new? Did you try to jump or run?"

"Nope."

"What were you doing when it started to hurt?"

"Talkin.'"

"Talking?"

"Yep. Talkin' to Sarah."

"What were you talking about, Tom?'

"Talkin' about Aunt Jesse."

"And your leg started to hurt?"

"Well, not 'xactly."

"Well, what exactly?" The doctor was growing impatient.

Tom sat up. "We was talkin' 'bout how Aunt Jesse needs to see a doctor and how she won't 'cause she don't think it's anything, and we thought that if you come to see *me,* then you could check Aunt Jesse, too, and figure out why her heart hurts."

Augusta looked accusingly at Jesse. Doctor Patton smiled and patted Tom. "Pretty smart, Tom, pretty smart."

Turning to Jesse he said, "Now, Mrs. King, perhaps *you* would like to clarify this issue?"

Cornered, Jesse was forced to talk. "Well, maybe I have had a few spells lately."

Augusta blustered, "And why haven't *I* heard about this?!"

"Because it's probably nothing, that's why. Just a few times—a little pain—that's all."

"Any other symptoms, Mrs. King?"

"No, not to speak of."

Augusta butted in. "You've been real tired lately, Jesse."

"Oh, that—just working too hard, doctor. I just need to get in a little more rest, that's all."

"Jesse King," Augusta insisted. "When you're too tired to work on a quilt, there's something wrong! Now you've had that quilt in the frame for weeks, and it's hardly started. If you were yourself, you'd have it bound and another one started by now! And don't think I don't know it!"

"All right, all right, Augusta." Jesse turned to the doctor. "I'll come in to see you tomorrow, doctor. These three will never give me a moment's peace if I don't."

Satisfied, the doctor stood up to go. Jesse scolded Sarah and Tom. "And you two! Scandalous behavior—wasting the doctor's time—calling him over here—worrying Aunt Augusta!"

Tom spoke up. "But it worked, didn't it Aunt Jesse?"

Jesse laughed. "I guess so, Tom, I guess it did."

Jesse kept her promise and visited the doctor the next day. He asked her a few questions, listened to her heart, and frowned. He prescribed a few days of bedrest, no lifting, and greater attention to proper diet. Jesse thanked him for his kindness, paid the bill, and ignored his instructions. She convinced herself that she felt much better. Indeed, the pains seemed to have subsided altogether, and she was making progress on her quilt when Sarah came rushing in from an errand in town, the *Evening Star* in hand.

"Aunt Jesse! Aunt Augusta! Look!"

Augusta was not inclined to read the competitor's newspaper. Then the headline caught her eye and she read: "Telegraphic—3:00 A.M.—The Indian War—Bloody news from Stillwater, Montana.—Gen. Custer and a large portion of his command reported massacred.—The red fiends kill the entire Custer family and butcher 300 soldiers." Augusta grabbed the paper and went looking for Jesse, who was setting tables in the dining room.

"Jesse! Whose command did you say MacKenzie had joined last we heard?"

Jesse hesitated. "Goodness, Augusta, can't say that I recall. He's been moved around so much these past few months. Poor LisBeth is so sick of traveling. I surely hope Mac gets some leave soon, if things ever quiet down. I wish Crazy Horse and Sitting Bull would listen to Red Cloud." Jesse paused. "Custer. I think that's it, General George Custer. That's Mac's commanding officer." Jesse had her back to Augusta and continued to make pleasant conversation. "Jesse says he's such a handsome man, and a meticulous dresser. She's met his wife too." Just then Jesse turned and saw Augusta's face.

"What is it, Augusta?" her hand went to her throat. "What's happened?"

"Better sit down, Jesse," came the order.

Jesse sat down, her heart thumping wildly. Augusta struggled to control her shaking voice as she read aloud:

"A battle was fought on the 25th thirty or forty miles below Little Big Horn. Custer attacked a village containing from 2,500 to 4,000 warriors. Custer, fifteen officers and every man belonging to five companies were killed. The battleground looked like a—"

Augusta abruptly stopped reading.

"Go on, Augusta," Jesse demanded. She raised one hand

and pressed the palm to her chest in an unconscious effort to stop the pain that was building there.

Reluctantly, Augusta read on:

"The battleground looked like a slaughter pen, as it really was. The dead were much mutilated . . . A special correspondent of the *Helena Herald* writes . . ."

As Augusta continued to read, Tom and Sarah moved to Jesse's side. Each one put a concerned hand on Jesse's shoulder.

Sarah said, "It'll be all right, Aunt Jesse. MacKenzie probably got moved again. You said he's been moved around a lot lately."

Tom didn't know what to say. He just kept patting Jesse's shoulder.

Jesse put her elbow on the table and rested her forehead on one hand. Her face was hidden from Augusta. Her heart continued to thump wildly. All she could think of was LisBeth. LisBeth married just a year. LisBeth, who was so in love. *Oh, Lord, surely LisBeth doesn't have to go through what I did. There's so much sorrow in the world, Lord, she's not ready. She's just too young to bear it.* Jesse's mind whirled. She looked up.

"LisBeth and MacKenzie may not be affected at all, Jesse," Augusta said hopefully.

"I know that," Jesse croaked. "But then again, LisBeth—my beloved LisBeth—may have just learned that her new husband is dead in the 'howling wilderness' she didn't want to go to."

There it was—that feeling. It didn't hurt; it just felt *odd*. Jesse pushed herself away from the table and went to her room. Sarah and Tom finished setting the tables. Augusta needed to talk. She called out the back door.

"Joseph!" Her faithful friend was never far away. He hurried over from the livery. "Joseph, Jesse and I just learned about the battle on the Little Big Horn. MacKenzie might have been there. Oh, Joseph, how will we bear it?"

Joseph thought for a moment. "We'll bear it just like all the others, ma'am. Just one hour at a time, I expect. Prayin' and wonderin' why, and trustin' the Lord that he knows an' does what's best."

Outside the sound of a coming rainstorm threatened. Joseph murmured, "Good. We need rain." He turned slowly to begin dishing up plates of food for the boarders that were already arriving.

The storm blew in with fury, hurling torrents of rain at the city and turning the dusty streets into a sea of mud. Tom Biddle sat at the kitchen table writing a short essay assigned to him that day by that nice Miss Griswall. As he concentrated, he chewed on his tongue. He wrote with great care, "What I like about Lincoln."

Sarah rushed back and forth between dining room and kitchen, casting concerned glances toward Jesse's room. There was no sound from that direction.

Well, Sarah thought, *at least she ain't cryin'. I guess that's somethin'.*

Augusta threw her concern into her work, filling water glasses, pouring coffee, listening to every comment about the news that had just arrived. She strained her ears, as if by listening to the comments of the citizens of Lincoln she could learn whether or not MacKenzie Baird—young, handsome MacKenzie Baird—was one of those who lay dead on the battlefield so far away.

Only LisBeth knew. LisBeth, the lovely dark-haired young woman who had not long ago learned that she was half Lakota Indian and who longed to know more about her father—and to "help make a difference." Swept up in affairs not of her making, LisBeth had received the news of MacKenzie's fate, and was at that moment writing to her mother in Lincoln to tell her that she would be home soon.

Jesse lay on her back staring out the window. While the thunder roared she had poured her heart out to the Lord. Now the storm was over, and the silence came as abruptly as the thunder had rolled across the plains. She could hear the sounds of the supper hour—voices booming, silverware clanking, chairs scraping the floor as diners settled into their favorite places.

Got to get up now, Jesse thought. With tremendous effort she reached the edge of the mattress to pull herself upright. *Got to get up to help Old One . . . Now why,* she puzzled, *after all these years, why'd I think* that?

The name conjured up memories: an infant in a cradle board, propped up against a tepee pole, watching an old woman crush grain and mix a thin gruel. Her thoughts were confused. Jesse scolded herself, *Addled old woman. I don't need to help Old One do a thing! I* do *need to help Augusta, though. We've got to be ready when LisBeth gets home.*

The sounds of dinner intruded again. Clutching the sides of the mattress she pulled herself halfway up, panting with the effort. *Why am I so tired all the time? Lazy old woman.* But scold as she would, she knew she could not get up. Weariness settled on her, covered her, and swallowed the intent to go out to the kitchen. A dull pain filled her chest and flowed into one arm. Well, for today, anyway, she'd just lie here and rest. Settling under the quilt again, she sighed and turned her attention out the window.

The stormy black sky had faded to dark gray, and in the distance white, billowing clouds blew across the prairie. They began racing one another, tossed by the wind, and the sun shining on them made them appear a brilliant white against the evening sky.

Memories crowded about her: a French trader with laughing eyes; a long ride into Fort Kearney; and somewhere, far back, a little mound of stones receding into the wide plain as a wagon rumbled away. Then *he* came, a Lakota brave, one with his snow white pony. They bounded together across the sky, and with each leap Jesse's heart fluttered. She stood on the prairie, her long red braids decorated with feathers, the part dusted with ochre. She raised a trembling hand in greeting, but he was gone.

Her hand fell back against the quilt, and Jesse saw the clouds again and realized it had only been a memory. She was an old woman, too tired to help with the supper, perhaps even too tired to be of use to LisBeth.

The clouds outside came closer, and the old heart fluttered at the memory of a man who rode on the wind long ago. Now it seemed that he rode again across the sky, into the room. He raised one hand in greeting.

"I will ask the Father," he had said, "and I will come for you."

Jesse sat up in bed, her face alive with a new light. Rides the Wind smiled and reached out to sweep her up behind him.

And the Father said, *"Come home."*

> *The lines are fallen unto me in pleasant places;*
> *yea, I have a goodly heritage.*
>
> Psalm 16:6

About the Author

Stephanie Whitson was born in East St. Louis, Illinois, and received her B.A. in French from Southern Illinois University in Edwardsville, Illinois. A full-time homemaker, Stephanie has been married to her husband, RTW, who shares Rides the Wind's initials, for twenty years. They homeschool their four children and operate a home-based inspirational gift company called Prairie Pieceworks. Stephanie is an avid quilter, and, with a friend, designs quilt pieces marketed nationwide by their company, Mulberry Lane.

For the past five years the Whitsons have lived on ten and a half secluded acres in rural Nebraska. The story of Jesse King was inspired by the lives of pioneers laid to rest in an abandoned cemetery adjacent to the Whitson property.

~

An excerpt from *Soaring Eagle*, the sequel to *Walks the Fire:*

The battlefield was quiet. Only an occasional shot was still being fired somewhere in the woods about a mile down the valley. Here, an eerie silence prevailed, broken only by the occasional low chant of a victory song as the warriors collected souvenirs from the dead.

Soaring Eagle stood surveying the battlefield. At his feet lay the body of one of the soldiers. The stench of death filled the air. Soaring Eagle closed his eyes and inhaled deeply, reminding himself to remember this victory.

Taking up his knife, he crouched down and grasped the soldier's thick, black hair in one hand. The glint of gold stopped the knife in mid-air. It appeared that this soldier would yield up something better than just a scalp.

Soaring Eagle tore the bit of gold from around the soldier's neck, examining the piece carefully. As he turned it over, it fell open, revealing the likeness of a young woman. Soaring Eagle caught his breath and stared in wonder, not at the young woman, but at the other one—the one whose gray eyes stared back at him from opposite the young woman's face.

She was older, but the mouth was set in a serious, straight line. Soaring Eagle remembered. The hair was held back in the way of the whites, but waves and curls that could not be tamed still framed the face. Soaring Eagle remembered. Looking into the eyes, Soaring Eagle knew. Here, looking back at him, was Walks the Fire . . . his mother.